D0674798
www.Tameside.gov.uk
WITHDRAWN FROM
TAMESIDE LIBRARIES

SPECIAL MESSAGE TO READERS

This book is published under the auspices of

THE ULVERSCROFT FOUNDATION

(registered charity No. 264873 UK)

Established in 1972 to provide funds for research, diagnosis and treatment of eye diseases. Examples of contributions made are: —

A Children's Assessment Unit at Moorfield's Hospital, London.

•

Twin operating theatres at the Western Ophthalmic Hospital, London.

•

A Chair of Ophthalmology at the Royal Australian College of Ophthalmologists.

•

The Ulverscroft Children's Eye Unit at the Great Ormond Street Hospital For Sick Children, London.

You can help further the work of the Foundation by making a donation or leaving a legacy. Every contribution, no matter how small, is received with gratitude. Please write for details to:

THE ULVERSCROFT FOUNDATION,
The Green, Bradgate Road, Anstey,
Leicester LE7 7FU, England.
Telephone: (0116) 236 4325

In Australia write to:
THE ULVERSCROFT FOUNDATION,
c/o The Royal Australian and New Zealand College of Ophthalmologists,
94-98 Chalmers Street, Surry Hills,
N.S.W. 2010, Australia

HOLD ME CLOSE

Resting actress Sara Armitage is thrilled to be offered a job, even if it means looking after Lyle Jackson's young daughter Jenny. Sara and Lyle have history and when Carla de Courcy, now Lyle's ex-wife and Jenny's mother, appears back on the scene, Sara is forced to face up to her past. Will Lyle break her heart for a second time or is she strong enough to withstand her love for him?

Books by Margaret Mounsdon
in the Linford Romance Library:

THE MIMOSA SUMMER
THE ITALIAN LAKE
LONG SHADOWS
FOLLOW YOUR HEART
AN ACT OF LOVE

MARGARET MOUNSDON

HOLD ME CLOSE

Complete and Unabridged

LINFORD
Leicester

First published in Great Britain in 2010

First Linford Edition
published 2011

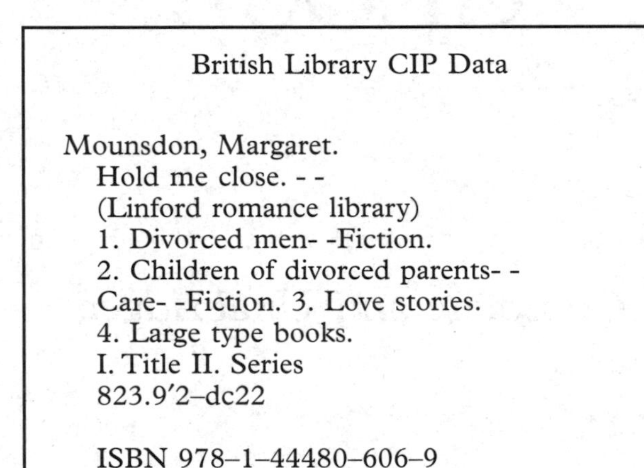
British Library CIP Data

Mounsdon, Margaret.
Hold me close. - -
(Linford romance library)
1. Divorced men- -Fiction.
2. Children of divorced parents- -
Care- -Fiction. 3. Love stories.
4. Large type books.
I. Title II. Series
823.9′2–dc22

ISBN 978–1–44480–606–9

Published by
F. A. Thorpe (Publishing)
Anstey, Leicestershire

Set by Words & Graphics Ltd.
Anstey, Leicestershire
Printed and bound in Great Britain by
T. J. International Ltd., Padstow, Cornwall

This book is printed on acid-free paper

Rekindling An Old Friendship

'Mr Jackson is away in America at the moment,' Mrs Henderson spoke with a soft Scottish burr, 'and in his absence he's charged me with the task of finding a nanny for his daughter.'

'Yes, I understand.' Sara needed to use all her acting skills to keep her smile upbeat. Mrs Henderson must not suspect how desperate she was to get this job.

'Never let them see you bleed,' had been one of her stepfather's maxims and Sara had done her best to live by it ever since.

This job provided somewhere to live and even though the contract was only a temporary one, it would give her time to sort out her life.

'It's most unfortunate that the young

lady Mr Jackson appointed has had an accident and broken her leg. She came with the most excellent references and qualifications. What experience have you had, Miss Armitage?'

Sara could feel Mrs Henderson's eyes working their way up and down her black tights, short red skirt and funky gold lamé top. Most of her clothes were in storage so there hadn't been time to put together anything more suitable for the interview. She also wished she'd toned down her hair colour. Magenta spikes had been fine for the funky musical audition she'd attended last week, but they were not really appropriate for an interview of this calibre.

'I, er, well I used to help out at playschool,' Sara improvised, folding her hands demurely in her lap, anxious to make a good impression, 'and I'm very versatile. Always up for a challenge.'

'Actresses usually are.'

Did she detect a note of censure in

Mrs Henderson's voice? The piercing blue eyes looked the sort of eyes that would stand for no nonsense. Sara bit her lip. It looked like she'd blown it. Why hadn't she thought to borrow one of her mother's cardigans and worn one of her skirts too?

'I understand from the details you've provided that you're resting at the moment?'

Sara nodded, choosing her words carefully.

'Yes, I'm free to start immediately.'

'And how did you hear about this job?'

'From Carla, er, I mean Mrs Jackson. She told me that she and Lyle, Mr Jackson, that is, needed someone at short notice to look after their little girl.'

'We are also looking for someone reliable. Jenny has experienced a lot of upheaval in her life recently.'

The separation and subsequent divorce of one of the nation's best-known actresses and an internationally renowned script-writer had been in all the tabloids. Sara did not usually read the gossip columns, but Carla was one of her oldest friends and the break up had saddened her.

'How do I know you won't be offered an acting part and have to leave us at a moment's notice?' Mrs Henderson asked.

Sara wanted to laugh out loud at the idea, but she didn't think it would be advisable in the circumstances. Her last acting job of any note had been as a pea in an advert for frozen food. It had taken her days to get the green dye out of her hair. Since then telephone calls from her agent had dwindled to nothing.

'I would never do that, Mrs Henderson and Carla, Mrs Jackson, will vouch for me, I'm sure. I'm very reliable and like I said, I'm available immediately.'

'You are a close friend of Mrs Jackson?'

'We were at stage school together and for a while we lived in the same hostel. I knew her when she was Carla de Courcy before she married Lyle, I mean Mr Jackson. We also used to attend auditions together when we were up for the same parts. I bumped into her last week and when I told her my acting work had dried up she thought I might be interested in looking after Jenny.'

'You are aware Mr and Mrs Jackson are now divorced?'

Mrs Henderson was making Sara feel more uncomfortable by the moment. Surely she didn't think Sara was responsible for any of that? She had hardly seen Carla since her marriage. These days they moved in entirely different social circles.

'I read about it in the newspapers,' Sara admitted, 'I'm sorry,' she added.

Mrs Henderson looked down at her checklist and made a few notes. Sara wondered if she should tell the housekeeper about her relationship with Lyle Jackson. It had been over seven years ago and had been no more than a brief romance, when Sara and Carla had been struggling actresses.

Sara was still struggling, but Carla with her ravishing looks, porcelain skin and endless talent, had gone on to bigger and better things. Her name was always featuring in award ceremonies and there was talk about a starring role in a dynamic new film. Her career was going from strength to strength.

Before Sara could say anything Mrs Henderson spoke again.

'The job would entail living in. Would that be convenient for you?'

Sara nodded. Living in was one of the reasons why she so desperately wanted this job.

'Where do you live at the moment?'

'I — er, I'm house sitting. My mother is on holiday. She's due back at the weekend. I did have my own flat but . . . '

Mrs Henderson looked up.

'I don't any more,' Sara finished on a lame note hoping Mrs Henderson wouldn't ask questions. It still hurt to talk about Joe.

'I see.'

'Obviously you would have time off but looking after Jenny could be demanding. Have you the stamina? If you don't mind my saying so, you are very slim.'

'Acting isn't exactly the easiest job in the world either,' Sara pointed out, 'I've had to stand around for hours on end, sometimes in cold and uncomfortable places so yes, I think I have the stamina.'

'Of course,' Mrs Henderson allowed a brief smile to soften her face, 'I know nothing about your profession, but I take your point.'

She looked at her notes again and hesitated leaving Sara with the distinct impression she did not want to offer her the job.

'Do you have any questions you would like to ask me, Miss Armitage?'

Aware she was gripping her fingers so tightly her knuckles protruded, Sara relaxed the pressure on her hands and smiled brightly.

'Mr Jackson has one little girl?'

The change of expression on Mrs Henderson's face was sudden and remarkable. Jenny was obviously the apple of her eye.

'Jenny is five years old and a lively youngster, always into something or other. I can't keep up with her. Seeing to the house takes up most of my time, and what with Mr Jackson being away so much, we are in desperate need of someone to look after Jenny.'

'Does Mr Jackson have sole custody?'

'No. Mrs Jackson has shared custody, but she also has a very busy career so she and Mr Jackson thought it would be better for Jenny to continue to live at Medway Manor with her father. This is a lovely corner of Kent, it's on the blossom route, a very healthy environment for a child, and Jenny is happy at the local school. Neither parent was keen to disrupt Jenny's education or to cause her any more traumas in her personal life.'

Sara nodded. 'Why did the last nanny leave?'

After a short pause Mrs Henderson said, 'She was beginning to form an unwelcome attachment to Mr Jackson.'

Sara suspected there was a lot Mrs Henderson wasn't telling her.

She knew from experience how ruthless Lyle could be when it came to matters of the heart, but it wasn't her business to pry.

'I hope you won't be entertaining any ideas in that direction, Miss Armitage.'

'You have to be joking.'

The words were out before Sara could stop herself, but the very idea of renewing her relationship with Lyle was absolutely the last thing she needed. Her personal life was complicated enough without adding to it.

'I mean,' she sought to soften her words, 'I don't believe in mixing business with pleasure.'

'I'm very pleased to hear it,' Mrs Henderson's voice contained a note of approval.

'Medway Manor is a little remote. You wouldn't find life too quiet?'

'It's exactly what I'm looking for, Mrs Henderson.'

'Do you drive?'

'I have a car,' Sara said. 'It was my mother's. When I moved out of London she let me have it at a friendly price.'

Sara didn't see the need to mention that it wasn't in the first flush of youth and that was why her mother wanted to pass it on.

'There is a daily bus service into town, but a car is an asset.'

Sara felt she had chalked up her first gold star.

'Well, if you have no further questions,' Mrs Henderson capped her pen and stood up, 'Would you like to see over the house? Jenny is due out of school shortly. Perhaps we could have tea together.'

'You mean I've got the job?' Sara's question came out as an over excited squeak.

'I have to be honest with you, Miss Armitage, you would not be my first choice for the position, but as there are no other applicants, I suggest a month's trial basis, if that's convenient for you?'

'Whatever you say.' Sara beamed at Mrs Henderson. 'You won't regret your decision.'

'I sincerely hope not, Miss Armitage. Now if you'll follow me.'

* * *

Medway House was a fine example of early twentieth century architecture. Half-timbered beams, huge brick built fireplaces, stone flagged floors, all added to its charm. Various owners had extended parts of the house, adding on bathrooms and extra bedrooms over the garage and outhouses.

'Mr Jackson had this conservatory built last summer.' Mrs Henderson showed Sara into an airy extension built on to a south facing side wall.

'It's a lovely room.'

Sara looked around at the expensively casual cane style furniture and the brightly coloured throws on the floor. Bookcases lined the walls and several large potted plants created an atmosphere of lived in elegance.

'Mr Jackson spends a lot of time in here working when he's at home and of an evening, he and Jenny like to sit together.'

The coffee tables were covered in a profusion of magazines and board games. Several empty mugs stood on a window ledge and an opened packet of biscuits lay next to them.

'Mr Jackson does not like me clearing up in here,' Mrs Henderson pursed her lips, 'but sometimes I have my own way.'

She picked up a tray and began placing the mugs and biscuits, together with a half eaten bag of sweets, on it.

'Let me.' Sara leapt forward to take the tray out of her hands. 'Just show me where to go.'

'Thank you.' Mrs Henderson looked agreeably surprised. 'Perhaps when Jenny is out during the day, you'd like to give me a hand? The house is in desperate need of a spring clean, but I haven't had time to get around to it.'

Hitting dusty carpets with a beater would be the perfect way to get rid of all her angst, Sara thought, as she put the tray down on the scrubbed pine kitchen table.

The kitchen appeared to be Mrs Henderson's domain. The surfaces were spotless, no biscuit crumb dared show its face on her worktop. A tea tray had been laid out and there was the delicious smell of something cooking in the Aga. Sara's mouth watered. It had been a while since she had enjoyed good home cooking.

They walked out into the corridor.

'There are two main floors to the house, but I thought you might like one of the little attic rooms, Miss Armitage. It would afford you some privacy and because it is so high up the views are spectacular.'

Mrs Henderson showed Sara to a small lavender scented room under the eaves. It was straight out of a fairy tale, all slanted floors and creaking boards.

The wardrobe was a strange contraption that had to live on the landing and the shower was down a small set of steps that would have to be carefully navigated in order not to bang your head on a very low beam. Sara was entranced.

'It's also all we have available at the moment,' Mrs Henderson explained with a half embarrassed smile. 'I wouldn't want you to think we were tucking you away out of sight. Mrs Jackson hasn't yet moved her things out of the house. Her filming schedule has been so busy and downsizing to a flat after living in Medway Manor is quite a problem.'

'I love it,' Sara enthused, hardly listening to what Mrs Henderson was saying. She ran to the diamond-patterned window. 'Look, there's a swing in the garden, and a little pond.'

The sun chose that moment to cut a swathe of light across the lawn. It sparkled on the water and a duck swam into view.

'I'm glad you like it.' Mrs Henderson's voice softened as she watched the gangly girl peer excitedly through the window counting the ducks.

'Jenny's a very lucky little girl to live in such a lovely house.'

Mrs Henderson cleared her throat. 'She is indeed, but for all that the child is not spoilt, although I should perhaps mention one thing.'

Sara swung round, her hazel eyes clouding over.

'Yes?' It would be too cruel if Mrs Henderson decided not to offer her the job after all, she thought.

'It's about Jenny.' Mrs Henderson paused.

'What about her?' From the photograph Mrs Henderson had shown Sara, Jenny looked like any other normal five year old.

'It was remiss of me not to have mentioned it before.'

Sara could feel her heartbeat increase its rate.

'Is there something wrong with

Jenny?' Sara didn't want to ask the question but Mrs Henderson seemed hesitant to divulge what was on her mind.

'She suffers from the occasional asthma attack. That was another reason why her parents thought it would be a good idea for her to remain in the countryside. It's not serious and the doctors feel she will outgrow it given time, but if she gets too excited or stressed, well, it isn't good for her.'

Sara sagged against the wall in a gesture of relief.

'Then the job's still mine?'

'Yes, as we agreed on a month's trial.'

'There's no need to worry, Mrs Henderson. My little cousin suffers from asthma. We always give her plenty of fresh air and a stress free environment and that usually does the trick.'

'My sentiments entirely.' Mrs Henderson's smile was now one of approval. 'If you've finished up here, we'd better go downstairs. I suggest we go and fetch Jenny from school together. It's a lovely walk and we can all get to know each other better.'

Sara closed the bedroom door behind her and followed Mrs Henderson down the narrow steps.

'Be careful when using these stairs,' Mrs Henderson advised her, grabbing the banister. 'They can be uneven in places and do mind your head on the beams. Mr Jackson is always cracking his head.'

She felt a momentary qualm wondering how he would react when he discovered his housekeeper had appointed one of his ex-girlfriends to the job of looking after his daughter.

By the time they reached the ground floor Sara was puffed and when she got her breath back, she realised she didn't mind what he thought about the appointment as long as he let her stay on at Medway Manor. They were both adult enough to realise any romance they had shared was over a long time ago.

Sara's Past Returns

'I have to go into town for some provisions, Sara,' Mrs Henderson called out from the back door of the kitchen. 'Can you manage while I'm out?'

It had taken Sara several days to get the housekeeper to stop calling her Miss Armitage. At first Sara had thought her reserved manner was because she disliked her, but it wasn't so. Mrs Henderson belonged to a generation to whom the use of first names did not come naturally.

Jenny on the other hand had called her Sara from the moment they first met, squealing with excitement when Mrs Henderson had introduced her to her new nanny. She was a sunny natured child and so like her mother that Sara found it easy to bond with the friendly little girl.

'We'll be fine,' Sara called back.

She, Jenny and Daniel the spaniel were all in the garden, playing some sort of complicated game that involved chasing a ball and throwing sticks.

'Will you keep an ear out for the telephone? Mr Jackson may ring. He's due back later today.'

Sara waved an acknowledgement then turned back to keep an eye on Jenny. She did not want to think about Lyle Jackson. The last time they had met had been over seven years ago. He had been a struggling scriptwriter in those days, still looking for his big break. Carla had often made up a threesome when they had all gone out. Sara should have realised she could never compete with Carla — not then and not now.

Carla always had an extra special quality that made her stand out in a crowd. The moment Sara introduced Lyle to Carla, Sara's days with Lyle were numbered. At the time it had hurt badly and the girls' friendship had suffered, but the years passed and Sara now counted the relationship as a part of growing up and had moved on with her life.

She and Carla, while no longer as close as they had once been, were on friendly terms when they bumped into each other, and Carla had assured Sara she would have no difficulty with Sara looking after her daughter and living in what had once been her house, with the man who had once been her husband. She hoped Lyle would accept the arrangement too.

'Sara, look at Daniel,' Jenny squealed, jumping up and down, 'isn't he sweet?'

Sara drew herself back to the present. 'Don't go near the pond,' she called out, watching Daniel leap towards the water. 'I don't want you falling in. You're wearing clean shorts and you know how cross Mrs Henderson will be if you get them dirty.'

It was an empty threat. Jenny was Mrs Henderson's weak point. Nothing the child did could upset her. She quite simply doted on her and Sara saw a new side to the older woman, a soft side she rather liked.

'The pond isn't deep,' Jenny called back.

'Do as you're told, please.' It was difficult to be stern with Jenny. She was such a sweet child, who had inherited her mother's charm for getting her own way.

* * *

Sara had been at Medway Manor ten days now and life had slipped into a pleasant routine. She took Jenny to school every morning, and collected her at half-past three in the afternoon. There were various afterschool activities that Sara helped with and she had acted as chauffeur for Jenny and a car full of giggling classmates on several occasions.

'Sara,' Jenny squealed, 'Daniel's caught a bird.'

Sara looked up from the newspaper she had been reading. A sparrow was in distress and Daniel was barking as it had flapped its wings frantically.

'No.' Sara leapt to her feet and pounded across the grass.

Spooked by all the noise Daniel raced off towards the pond. The bird apparently uninjured flew off and the next moment there was another loud bark followed by a splash.

'Daniel's fallen in,' Jenny shouted, 'he can't swim.'

'Leave him to me,' Sara called out, 'Jenny,' she shrieked as there was another loud splash. She sprinted across the lawn to the scene of the devastation.

Wading into the pond she grabbed hold of Jenny's arm as Daniel scrambled out on to the bank and shook himself dry, showering the girls with droplets of water.

'Ugh, go away, Daniel, you horrid thing,' Jenny shouted. 'You're making me all wet.'

'Look at the mess of you,' Sara said and tried to look cross now she was sure Jenny wasn't hurt.

'You did look scared, Sara,' she giggled, 'but I told you it wasn't deep.' Sara hauled the child out of the water. Jenny wrinkled her nose in disgust at the sight of Sara's white shorts. 'You're covered in pond weed. You'll be ever so smelly and Mrs Henderson will be cross with you as well.'

Jenny didn't look in the least contrite as she executed a little dance of glee on the lawn. In any other circumstances Sara might have seen the funny side of the situation and joined in, but she had been left in sole charge of the child, and the escapade could easily have had a very different outcome.

'And I told you not to go near the pond, Jenny. I'm very disappointed in you.'

Her concern made her words sound much sharper than she had intended.

Jenny's lips puckered at the tone of Sara's voice and her face crumpled.

'S . . . sorry,' she looked a picture of misery now as she struggled to keep her sobs under control. 'Don't be cross with me, Sara. I don't like it when you shout.'

Sara hugged the pathetic little figure who was trying so hard not to cry. 'I'm not cross with you, darling, but you must do as you're told.' She didn't like to scare the child but undue excitement could trigger an asthma attack and that was the last thing she wanted.

Daniel began to bark loudly.

'Oh, be quiet,' Sara bellowed as she untangled herself from Jenny's arms and legs. 'This is all your fault. You are in disgrace.' Daniel took one look at Sara and slunk away to his kennel.

Jenny began to wail again. Sara bit her lip. What had started out as a pleasant afternoon sit in the sun was turning into the afternoon from hell.

'Come on, Jenny,' she coaxed. 'We'd better both go inside and change. Maybe I can put the washing machine on before Mrs Henderson gets back. No harm done.'

Jenny continued sobbing, her breath

coming in short bursts.

'I saw Mrs Henderson making a chocolate cake for tea. Why don't we sneak a slice?' Sara was beginning to grow concerned that Jenny might be working herself up into an attack.

Jenny stiffened and held back from Sara, then her face lightened.

'Daddy,' she emitted an ear splitting squeal and letting go of Sara's hand, raced across the lawn to where her father was standing on the terrace, his face a cold mask of anger as he took in the scene before him.

Sara straightened up and swallowed nervously. Lyle hadn't changed much in the seven years or so since she had last seen him. He had filled out a little and had more of an air of success about him. His chinos were designer cut and the exclusive logo on his polo shirt was one the old Lyle could never have afforded.

The old Lyle wore stonewashed denims and faded T-shirts and had slightly longer hair — but the eyes were the same, deep set and blue, and right now they were about as unfriendly as they could possibly be.

'What exactly is going on?' he demanded.

'I fell in the pond,' Jenny sobbed, 'and Sara is cross with me, but it was her fault. I don't like her any more. Daddy, I'm glad you're home. I missed you.'

Sara raised tolerant eyebrows at Lyle. Jenny was quite the little drama queen when it suited her, exactly like her mother, but from the expression on Lyle's face it was obvious he was not in the mood to share Sara's opinion of his daughter.

'Er — hello, Lyle.' Sara realised it was too late to put her side of the story, but she didn't think there was any need to look at her as though she had been cruel to Jenny. 'Just a bit of a domestic upheaval,' she tried a smile but there was no response from Lyle.

'What are you doing here?' His voice was a whiplash as he looked up and down her damp clothes.

'I'm the new nanny. I'm looking after Jenny.'

'You?'

The one word had Sara feeling about eighteen years old again, and very vulnerable.

'The trained nanny broke her leg. I was available so Mrs Henderson offered me the job at short notice, on a month's trial basis. I bumped into Carla at an audition and she told me you were looking for someone. I've had a bit of experience childminding so it seemed an ideal solution.'

'Not for me it isn't.'

'Why not?' Sara demanded.

What she really wanted to do was to go and put her arms around Lyle and tell him it was good to see him again after such a long time and to ask how he was, but Lyle's body language indicated he did not reciprocate her feelings.

'Mr Jackson, I didn't expect you home so soon. Did you have a good trip?'

Neither of them had noticed Mrs Henderson come out on to the terrace.

'I'm so sorry I wasn't here when you arrived, I wanted to introduce you to the new nanny, Miss Armitage.'

'We've already met, thank you Mrs H.' Lyle's voice was as cold as steel. 'Would you take Jenny inside, please? She's had a bit of an accident in the pond and needs a bath and some fresh clothes.'

'Surely that's Sara's job.'

'Now, please.'

Mrs Henderson went rather pink in the face and Sara felt sorry for her. Whatever issues Lyle had with her, there was no need for him to take them out on the housekeeper. Sara opened her mouth to speak then catching the look on Lyle's face, decided she was in enough trouble without fighting Mrs Henderson's quarter.

'As you wish, sir. Come along,' Mrs Henderson ushered a subdued Jenny into the house.

'Pack your bags,' Lyle said curtly.

Sara tossed back her head. She had been expecting a bit of a battle, not an instant dismissal.

'What did you say?'

'I said,' Lyle repeated slowly, 'pack your bags.'

'Why?'

'I should have thought it was obvious. You're not fit to have control of my daughter. I come home and find her soaking wet and traumatised because she has fallen in the pond due to your inattention.'

'It wasn't like that,' Sara protested.

'She's a delicate child. She doesn't need you shouting at her and kicking her dog. Reasons enough for instant dismissal I'd say, wouldn't you?'

Sara was so angry she was fighting for breath.

'I was not kicking the dog and Jenny was not traumatised as you put it. We were all having fun . . . '

'Obviously we have different ideas of fun,' Lyle exploded.

'That's what Jenny needs in her life

right now, a bit of fun, some rough and tumble on the lawn.'

'What she does not need is a life and death experience.'

'It wasn't. Anyway, you weren't here when Jenny needed you. I was.'

Sara knew she was being cruel but the look on Lyle's face was a reminder of how much he had once meant to her, and how abruptly he had ended their relationship. It was time he took some of his own medicine.

'I don't need you to criticise my way of life.'

'Fair enough, but I stand by what I said.'

'I don't have to listen to this.'

'Well, you're going to.' Sara was growing angrier by the second.

'I think you've said more than enough. Please leave. Now.'

'I haven't said half enough.'

A small muscle flicked under Lyle's right eye as they confronted each other on the terrace.

'I'm sorry,' Sara apologised, instantly

regretting her outburst. 'But can't you see Jenny and I are beginning to build up a special relationship? She needs some stability in her life and I think I can provide it.'

'And I don't,' Lyle snapped back. 'Look at the state of you. You're dripping from head to toe,' he frowned, 'and what on earth have you done to your hair?'

'If you'll just give me a chance . . . '

'You've already had your chance and you've blown it.'

Lyle turned on his heel and almost bumped into Mrs Henderson as she came out on to the terrace.

'Er, Mr Jackson.' She cleared her throat uncomfortably.

'Yes?'

'Would you please lower your voice? Jenny can hear every word you are saying and it's upsetting her.'

For a moment no-one in the garden moved.

'I'm sorry,' Lyle mumbled an apology. 'You're quite right, Mrs H.

Unfortunately Miss Armitage and I . . .'

'He was dismissing me, Mrs Henderson,' Sara butted in. She did not feel the need for diplomacy. 'I didn't mention it at the interview because, to be honest, I thought you might not offer me the job but Mr Jackson is also an old friend of mine. In fact, I was the one who introduced him to his wife.'

'I see,' Mrs Henderson frowned, 'but why should any of that make any difference to the situation? Sara and Jenny get on very well together, Mr Jackson.'

'It wasn't immediately obvious to me.'

'And Sara has been helping me spring clean the house during the day. She's a good worker. Won't you reconsider?'

'I've made my decision. Now, I have a lot of work to do.'

Sara smiled at the housekeeper. 'Thanks for trying Mrs Henderson, but as you can see, Mr Jackson's made up his mind.'

Mrs Henderson pursed her lips. 'As you wish, sir,' she said. 'I must go back to Jenny. Come and see me before you go, Sara, will you?'

Sara blinked hard. She was going to miss Mrs Henderson — and Jenny.

'I'd rather you left without speaking to Jenny,' Lyle said, 'it would only upset her to know you're leaving.'

'But I just can't walk out.'

'All the same, I'd rather you did.'

'What will you tell her?' Sara demanded.

'I'll think of something.'

Sara hesitated then realised there really was nothing else she could think of to say. She straightened her shoulders and drawing on her acting skills said, 'Goodbye, Lyle. Perhaps we'll bump into each other again one day. If we do, I'll try and stay out of your way.'

As exit lines go it wasn't the best, but it was all Sara could think of in the heat of the moment. She removed her wet shoes carefully before she entered the cool of the drawing room, all the while aware of Lyle's eyes burning a hole in her back.

A Worrying Situation

Sara realised she would have to pull into the motorway service station. The needle on her petrol gauge was hovering on empty, besides which she was so angry steam was almost coming out of her ears. It wasn't wise to drive under these conditions. She needed to take a few moments out to compose herself with a coffee and to get some petrol.

The sun was still hot and a quick glance at the dashboard informed Sara it was two o'clock. Her mother would probably be out at work at the health food store, but Sara would need to leave a message to tell her what had happened and to expect her daughter home that evening. Sara bit her lip. She hadn't expected her first meeting with Lyle to be such a disaster.

He hadn't changed. He was still as

stubborn as he had always been. Sara flushed as she remembered some of the things she had said to him in the heat of the moment. She didn't regret saying them, but she wished she had kept her voice down. The last thing she would have wanted was for Jenny to overhear them.

Infuriating as he was, Lyle was still Jenny's father, and she had no wish to damage the relationship. She knew from personal experience what it was like to lose a father to harsh words, but this time Sara couldn't help feeling the whole situation was Lyle's fault. Why had he totally overreacted? No harm had come to his daughter, nothing a clean change of clothes and a slice of chocolate cake wouldn't have put right.

Sara hoped the trauma wouldn't set off one of Jenny's asthma attacks.

Despite Lyle's orders, Sara had crept into the kitchen after she had finished packing, to say goodbye to Mrs Henderson and to tell her to give her love to Jenny.

'She's taking a rest at the moment,' Mrs Henderson had explained. 'I'll tell her in my own words what happened when I get her up for her tea. Now are you sure you're safe to drive back to your mother's house?' she asked with kindly concern. 'I wouldn't want you to do anything silly. Mr Jackson's in his study so I'm sure he wouldn't notice if you stay on a little longer to compose yourself.'

Having assured Mrs Henderson she was fine, which was far from the truth, Sara had flung her bag into the hatchback and without a backward look at the house got into the driving seat and drove off.

Sara ignored the pang of regret in her chest. In the short time she had been at Medway Manor she had grown to love the place, with its higgledy-piggledy staircases and slanting floors. Under Mrs Henderson's guidance they had begun to buff up the woodwork with lavender polish and the surfaces were beginning to gleam again.

'Thank heavens,' Sara muttered under her breath as the service station sign flashed up on the left. It wasn't a moment too soon. She had been clutching the steering wheel so tightly she was just getting cramp in her fingers and the car was beginning to judder. She definitely needed to relax before she continued her journey.

Annoyed with herself for letting Lyle get under her skin, Sara turned off the motorway and headed for the car park. There weren't many people around even though it was lunchtime and with a sigh of relief Sara parked the car carefully and began looking around for her handbag. She was sure she had put it on the back seat, but it wasn't there.

'Don't say I left it behind,' she muttered to herself, unable to face going back for it. If she ever saw Lyle Jackson again it would be too soon. She felt around under her seat. It had fallen on the floor. Sara snatched it up in relief. 'What on earth . . . '

Her jaw dropped as the rug on the

back seat wriggled and a few seconds later Jenny's head popped out of the folds.

'I'm here,' she trilled happily.

'Jenny.' Sara's mouth went dry with shock, 'what on earth are you doing?'

'Hiding from Mrs Henderson.' She giggled. 'It was ever so easy. She thought I was in bed and didn't notice me creep down the back staircase and into your car. Wasn't that clever of me?'

'No it wasn't.' Sara looked over her shoulder, half expecting to see Lyle bearing down on her, accusing her of all sort of felonies. She wasn't entirely sure what the penalty was for kidnap these days and she didn't want to have to find out.

Jenny's smile slipped when she realised Sara wasn't returning her smile.

'I only did it cos I don't want you to leave, Sara. I'm sorry I got you into trouble with Daddy and I didn't mean what I said about not liking you.

Daddy's only grumpy cos he doesn't like flying. Sara?' Jenny finished on an uncertain note.

'Darling,' Sara began, struggling to keep her voice steady. 'I have some important telephone calls to make. Would you like an ice cream?'

Jenny beamed back at her. 'Are you going to telephone Daddy and tell him where we are?'

'I think that would be a good idea, don't you?' Sara opened the back passenger door. 'Come on.'

Jenny scrambled out of the rug.

'It was ever so itchy under there but you never suspected I was hiding, did you?' she asked, her gleeful smile back in place.

'No I didn't,' Sara admitted truthfully. 'Now what flavour of ice cream would you like?' she asked as she locked the car door and took a firm hold of Jenny's hand.

'Strawberry, please.' Jenny skipped along beside her. 'I wanted to bring Daniel along with me too, but I was scared he would bark and give the game away.'

'I'm very pleased you didn't bring him,' Sara said as the automatic doors to the snack bar swept open and she and Jenny went inside.

The queue for ice creams moved slowly and Sara looked anxiously at her watch. It had been over an hour since she had left Medway Manor. Would Jenny's disappearance have been discovered yet? Worse still, would Lyle suspect her of kidnap? The idea was ridiculous but Lyle seemed to think she was capable of absolutely anything when it came to his daughter.

'Sara,' Jenny tugged at her hand, 'the lady's waiting to take our order.'

Several more precious minutes were lost as the girl who was serving, asked Jenny how old she was and why she wasn't at school.

'In service day,' Jenny trilled.

'What ice cream would you like?'

'Strawberry, please. Sara and I are running away,' she confided.

The assistant frowned, ice cream scoop in her hand. She glanced at Sara as her purse chose that moment to drop on the floor, scattering change everywhere. Jenny squealed with delight and chased after the coins. Several customers joined in the hunt.

'Er, thank you,' Sara gasped, aware she had turned beetroot in colour.

Sara guided the child over to an empty table.

Jenny settled down happily and dug her spoon into her strawberry sundae while Sara searched in her bag for her mobile phone. It wasn't where she usually put it.

In all the confusion it must have fallen out of her bag when Jenny had suddenly jumped out from under the blanket and startled her.

Now what was she going to do? Fate really had it in for her today, thought Sara.

She couldn't leave Jenny here alone to go back to the car and fetch it, but that meant losing precious moments while the child ate up her ice cream. She looked around in desperation for a pay phone.

Aware that Jenny's blue eyes were fixed on her as she licked her spoon, Sara forced herself to smile brightly. The child must not pick up on her anxiety and the seriousness of the situation.

'Is that nice?' she asked.

'Mmm,' Jenny swallowed, 'but it's not the best one I've ever had.'

'Isn't it?' Sara asked with a distracted frown.

'Mummy took me to the seaside last week and we had a huge bowl of ice cream. There were three different flavours and lots of nuts and cherries and chocolate and some red sauce. I spilt some on my shirt, but Mummy said it wouldn't matter because she'd buy me another one.'

A sad look flitted over Jenny's face.

'I wish Mummy still lived with us. I know,' she waved her spoon in the air, 'you could marry Daddy then you could live with us, couldn't you? Mummy wouldn't mind. She said you were her best friend and that you were coming to look after me.'

Jenny prattled on but Sara wasn't listening. She had to telephone Lyle urgently but she didn't want to rush Jenny with her ice cream.

Also she needed to get some petrol if she was going to drive all the way back to Medway Manor.

She sneaked another glanced at her watch. Someone must have realised Jenny was missing. What would Lyle do? He hadn't known which way she was heading and Mrs Henderson wouldn't be able to help him either. Visions of helicopters and tracker dogs flashed through Sara's mind.

'Finished?' she breathed a sigh of relief as Jenny took a final lick of her spoon.

Jenny nodded. 'You haven't telephoned Daddy.'

'I need to get my mobile. It's in the car.'

'I'm sticky,' Jenny complained. 'Can I wash my hands?'

'Come on then.' Sara stood up, 'but we have to be quick about it. We don't want to keep Daddy waiting, do we?'

While Jenny had been eating her ice cream two coaches had arrived and the queue to the washroom now snaked round the corner. Sara waited patiently behind what appeared to be a busload of schoolchildren, all of whom, like Jenny, appeared to have been given the day off school.

'Come along,' Sara's patience finally gave out as she chided Jenny who was busy playing with the hand dryer.

Hoping Mrs Henderson would intervene if things got too hairy, Sara held on to Jenny's hand as they fought their way back into the concourse.

'Look, Sara,' Jenny pointed excitedly to the car park. 'Blue lights. It's a police car.'

Sara barely had a chance to register the fact before she saw the ice cream sales assistant talking to two police officers and pointing in their direction. She froze as the woman police constable turned to look in their direction. After a nod to her colleague she began walking towards Sara and Jenny.

‘Her Father Has Reported Her Missing’

‘Would you like to come with me, Jenny, isn’t it?’ The woman police constable smiled and held out a hand to the child.

Jenny shrank into Sara’s side, clutching her fingers so hard it hurt.

‘No.’ She hid her face in Sara’s skirt.

With a sinking heart Sara did her best to explain the situation.

‘I was just about to ring Mr Jackson,’ she began. ‘I didn’t realise . . . ’

‘All in good time, Miss Armitage. We don’t want to upset Jenny more than is absolutely necessary, do we?’ The voice was professionally gentle.

‘You know my name?’

‘Mr Jackson alerted us to his daughter’s disappearance and your car was spotted on the motorway. Now, would you like to come and sit in the patrol car with me, Jenny, while my colleague talks to Miss Armitage?'

'Want to stay with Sara.' Jenny pouted. 'Go 'way.'

'Look, it really doesn't do to get Jenny excited,' Sara began again. 'She's a delicate child.'

'Perhaps you should have thought of that earlier, Miss Armitage, before you abducted her.'

The eyes that confronted Sara's were very official and sent a tingle of apprehension down her spine.'

'You don't understand.'

'You admit that you are Sara Armitage and the child is Jenny Jackson, Lyle Jackson's daughter?'

'Yes.'

'In that case, I understand very well. Her father has reported her missing. It's a very serious matter. Now if you wouldn't mind?'

'The little girl said they were running away,' the sales assistant raised her voice as she rushed over and pointed across at Sara. 'I knew something was not right.'

Jenny giggled and came out from behind Sara's skirt.

'I was hiding,' she confided to the policewoman. 'It was ever so hot and itchy, but it was fun. Daddy didn't know where we were.'

'Shall we go and see if we can find Daddy?' The policewoman had another go at separating Sara and Jenny.

'No. Sara's going to ring him.'

The male police officer had now strolled over to join the little group.

'Hello,' he smiled at Jenny. 'My name's Don. We're rather blocking things here, aren't we?' he said. 'Why don't we all go outside?'

'No.' Jenny dug her toes in. 'Sara, I want another ice-cream.'

'I'm afraid I'm going to have to insist you come outside with us, Madam.' Don put a firm hand under Sara's elbow and began to guide her away from the child.

Jenny was growing redder in the face.

She began to breathe heavily.

'Please, don't excite the child,' Sara insisted, adding in a lowered voice, 'she suffers from asthma.'

'Where's her inhaler?' the woman police officer asked.

'I don't have it with me.'

'Sara,' Jenny wailed sensing the police were trying to separate them. She clung on to Sara's hand. 'Don't leave me.'

By now a crowd of onlookers alerted by the commotion had begun to gather around them.

'Is there somewhere quiet we can go? Please?' Sara demanded. 'Jenny needs air.'

'Everything's under control, ladies and gentleman,' Don said. 'If you wouldn't mind moving on.'

People began to shuffle away murmuring amongst themselves and casting unpleasant looks in Sara's direction.

'You've got to believe me. I didn't know Jenny was in the back of my car, Officer,' Sara said.

'It's my understanding that until this

morning you worked for Mr Jackson?'

'Yes, I was Jenny's nanny. Her father and I had,' Sara knew she needed to choose her next words carefully, 'a rather frank exchange of views and . . .'

'I also understand Mr Jackson dismissed you summarily for mistreating his daughter?'

'Yes, well, no.' Sara ran a hand through her hair.

'I think we would be better off discussing this down at the station. Miss Collins?' Don turned to his colleague.

Sensing they were about to be separated Jenny kicked out at Miss Collins, but her foot missed its target and landed firmly on Don's shin. He jumped back to avoid the impact and fell against a rack of paperback books. It toppled over with a loud smash, spilling books over the floor.

'Jenny,' Sara admonished her, 'stop that.'

Aware she was the centre of attention, Jenny's bad behaviour disappeared and she began to laugh as Miss Collins, in an attempt to right the damage, collided with a tub of fresh flowers. That, too, fell over and water spilled on to the concourse.

Sara grabbed out at Jenny's arm to stop her slipping over on the slippery surface.

'Come on, Sara, let's run,' Jenny said. 'They won't catch us.' Her sturdy legs began pounding their way towards the automatic doors, displaying a remarkable turn of speed for a child who had been on the verge of an asthma attack. Sara raced after her, leaving the police officers to sort out the mess on the floor.

'Stop! Jenny! No!'

The doors swept open. Jenny raced through. Sara raced after her, straight into the arms of Lyle Jackson, who was blocking his daughter's path. The only way for Sara to steady herself and Jenny was to cling on to Lyle who was standing as firm as a rock on the doorway. She could feel his heart beating against hers as she crashed into the wall of his chest.

For a moment she longed to bury her head in his chest and get him to sort everything out but for the second time that day he was looking at her with an expression that conveyed everything he felt about her and it wasn't good.

His fingers felt like vices around her wrist as he held her steady. The blue eyes, so like Jenny's were yet again as cold as an Arctic sea as they looked down at her. Sara gulped as she fought for her breath, gasped and tried to speak.

'Jenny, asthma, didn't want to frighten her.'

She swayed slightly and hoped she wouldn't sink to the floor in an undignified heap. She had only had a glass of orange juice for breakfast and nothing to eat since and lack of food was making her light headed.

'Are you all right?' Lyle's voice wasn't as cold as the expression in his eyes and if she hadn't known better she would have thought he was concerned for her welfare.

'I'm fine. You haven't shaved,' she added as his stubble tickled her ear lobe.

His expression softened a fraction. 'I haven't actually had time to freshen up since I've been home.'

'And I haven't had time to eat anything. Sorry,' Sara drew away from his embrace. The gap between them felt cold and despite the heat of the day, Sara shivered.

'Daddy,' Jenny jumped up and down between them, holding out her arms.

Lyle picked her up and hugged her. 'All right, poppet? I've brought your inhaler with me.'

'Don't need it. We've had such an adventure. Sara and me . . . '

'You can tell me all about it later.'

'Did you really put the police on to us?' Sara hissed, looking over her shoulder.

'What else was I supposed to do?' Lyle's expression was back to being cold again. 'It was lucky Mrs Henderson caught sight of Jenny sneaking into the back of your car.'

'I'm sorry, Lyle, I really didn't know she was there. I would never have dreamt of driving off if I'd had any idea she was under my blanket.'

'Mr Jackson?' Don was still doing his best to tidy up his uniform as he approached.

'Yes, I am. Thank you very much for all your help reuniting me with my daughter, Officer.'

'Do you wish you press charges against Miss Armitage?'

'I keep trying to tell you,' Sara butted in, 'I haven't done anything wrong.'

'That's for the authorities to say, Madam.'

'You can't lock Sara up,' Jenny squealed. 'Daddy.' She began to breathe heavily again, 'I didn't mean what I said about her being horrid. Please let Sara stay. She's ever so good at being a bear.'

'A what?' Lyle looked slightly taken aback.

'School play, last week,' Sara explained. 'The bear went sick and . . . ' Her explanation trailed away, 'I stood in on short notice.'

'To get back to the matter in hand,' Don closed his notebook, 'are you prepared to treat this as a domestic, sir?'

After a few moments' hesitation Lyle nodded. 'I am.'

'Right, we'll be on our way then.'

'Thank you again for all your help.'

Don nodded. 'Miss Collins?' He looked round for his colleague before striding out of the service station.

'Daddy, can I have an ice-cream?' Jenny asked.

'I think we could all do with some refreshment,' Lyle said. 'Coffee?' he looked at Sara.

'I, er, think I should be getting on my way. My mother will be expecting me.' Sara hesitated then added a belated, 'Thank you.'

'What for?' Lyle asked.

'Not having me locked up for abduction.'

'We need to talk,' Lyle put a hand under Sara's elbow. 'Is there anywhere we can go without Jenny overhearing?'

'Would you like me to look after your little girl?' The sales assistant was all smiles as she looked at Lyle. 'My name's Anna. You are the little girl's father?'

Sara smiled wryly as Anna patted her hair into place and gave Lyle the full benefit of her smile. What was it about Lyle that had that effect on women?

He wasn't that good looking. He was quite ordinary, really. She cast a surreptitious glance at him. The years had, she supposed, given him a certain charisma. He was a man who looked as though he knew where he was going.

Jenny gave an excited clap of her hands as she looked up at Anna. 'Please,' she dragged the girl away in the direction of the ice-cream stand. 'I'd like a banana split.'

'Er,' Sara began, 'at the risk of telling tales, Jenny has already had an ice-cream,' she said.

'I don't suppose one more will do her any harm and if she's unwell in the night,' Lyle replied with the hint of a devilish smile, 'you can look after her. I've got jet lag.'

'You mean after all this I still have a job?' Sara demanded.

'Let's have some coffee.'

Sara collapsed on to one of the banquettes and watched Lyle queue up for coffee and sandwiches.

Seven years ago when she had been eighteen years old she thought he had been the love of her life. Sara fiddled with the sugar bowl. The years had treated him well. His career as an international screenwriter had gone from strength to strength and the latest rumour was he was working on a new screenplay adaptation of a best selling novel.

Carla, his ex-wife, Jenny's mother, was after the starring role and if she was successful, a Hollywood career beckoned.

In contrast, Sara's fortunes had

dwindled. She loved acting but she was the first to realise it was hardly a stable profession and competition was fierce. These days she was finding it harder to get out of bed at an unearthly hour to attend an audition, only to learn that the part had already been cast and her agent had forgotten to tell her.

Lyle returned to the table and Sara watched him unwrap a cheese and tomato sandwich for her. It gave Sara an odd feeling in the pit of her stomach to realise that he still remembered cheese and tomato was her favourite sandwich filling. It evoked memories of late suppers in the hostel when Sara, Lyle and Carla had talked long into the night about their plans to change the world.

'Eat,' Lyle instructed Sara and pushed the plate towards her.

'I don't think I can.' For no reason Sara's stomach was now tied up in knots and the thought of food choked her.

'I'm quite prepared to carry my

daughter home,' Lyle replied, 'but slender as you are, I don't think I could carry the pair of you and I don't want you passing out on me.'

'Home?' Sara said carefully as she began nibbling a corner of her sandwich. It was soft and fresh and she soon found her appetite returning. Her cheeks bulged as she took a large bite of cheese and then wished she hadn't. If this was an interview, poor table manners would go nowhere towards getting the job.

'Medway Manor.'

'Then you really meant what you said about keeping me on?'

'Both Mrs Henderson and my daughter seem to have taken a shine to you.'

'I love working there. Every day is different.'

'As long as you don't get too attached to the house.'

'Like your last nanny?' Sara couldn't resist tweaking him. 'And if I understand Mrs Henderson correctly it was not only the house she was attached to.'

'What do you know about that?' Lyle demanded.

'Mrs Henderson mentioned how attached the nanny became to you.' A slow smile moved in Sara's lips. 'You need have no worries on that score, Lyle. I've been there. I've already worn the T-shirt.'

'I'm serious, Sara. You can be a little boisterous and Jenny is a delicate child and — what's so funny?' Lyle broke off from what he was saying with a frown as Sara's slow smile burst into a bout of laughter.

'I'm sorry, Lyle,' she gulped down some coffee to clear her throat. 'But really, to hear you calling me boisterous takes the biscuit. You should have seen your precious little flower of a daughter lamming into those police officers. It was priceless. I wanted to cheer. She's a game little girl, reminds me of myself when I was her age, getting into scrapes, and to hear you describe her as delicate,' Sara wiped her lips with a tissue, 'well, it does take a bit of believing. There was this huge policeman hopping around because she'd kicked him in the shins and Miss Collins covered in flowers and paddling in water.'

A very slow, very reluctant smile moved Lyle's lips.

'Yes, well perhaps delicate was an unfortunate choice of words,' he agreed, 'but there's no getting away from the fact Jenny does suffer the occasional asthma attack.'

'I know and I'm sorry. I didn't mean to over excite her. I think she only acted up because she thought the police were going to separate us.'

'And I've the feeling that if I dismiss you again, Jenny might work herself up to an attack. That is the last thing I want.'

'Does she have them often?'

'Not now. Things have settled down at home and I want to keep them that way.'

'We didn't start off very well, did we?'

Sara dropped her sandwich back on to the plate.

'I must admit I came home expecting to find a trained nanny looking after my daughter. Instead I found a riot going on in a garden that resembled a war zone.'

Sara stretched out her hand to touch his.

'Sorry,' she said then realised she'd covered Lyle's fingers in tomato pips. She dabbed at them with her damp serviette. 'I know I'm not trained, but all Jenny needs is someone to be there, someone who isn't above getting a bit down and dirty with her.'

Lyle carefully removed his hand from under Sara's and wiped his fingers on his own fresh tissue.

'I agree, but,' his expression hardened, 'we have to get one thing straight. If you give me the slightest reason to suspect you have, in any way, caused my daughter untoward distress then I'll have no compunction in dismissing you on the spot again. Do I make myself clear?'

Sara blinked as she felt a shift in their relationship. Until now he had been the ex-boyfriend who had jilted her in favour of her best friend, but now he was her employer, a father who doted on his daughter.

Sara nodded, serious again.

'Yes, and thank you. I was desperate for this job and somewhere to live. I won't let you down.'

As Sara lowered her eyes she missed the softening of the expression on Lyle's face. Had she looked up, she might have questioned the wisdom of her decision to stay.

An Important Meeting

Heads turned at the sight of the blonde woman striding confidently through the restaurant towards the table situated in the bay window. One or two of the more media-aware diners nudged their neighbours and murmured under their breath, 'That's Carla de Courcy.'

Her oatmeal trouser suit worn with a crisp white blouse was elegantly casual. The jacket draped over her shoulders provided a touch of chic that suggested feminine curves in all the right places. As an ex model, Carla knew exactly how to enter a room and today she needed to work her assets to full effect.

Her hair was tied back with a velvet bow in a casual ponytail. A few stray wisps framed her delicate face giving her the appearance of an Edwardian heroine. The look was very together, exactly the right elegant image Carla wanted to project for her lunch date with Monty Daniels.

He was big. He was important. Carla had done her research and realised this was her make or break chance. She desperately wanted to star in his latest production, but it would not do to let Monty know exactly how much.

'Darling.' She air kissed him as he stood up to greet her. 'Am I late?' She batted her smoky grey eyes at him. They were eyes the camera loved. It had been part of Carla's plan to arrive exactly five minutes after Monty, even if it meant hanging around outside the restaurant for over half-an-hour.

'I'm a busy man and I don't like being kept waiting,' he grumbled then smiled, not in the least taken in by her act. He'd been in the business long enough to know every trick in the book and he had spotted Carla lingering in the newsagents, pretending to read a magazine while he dismissed his driver.

Monty was shrewd enough to also recognise that Carla, for all her feminine wiles, was a good actress and she could easily be the next big name in the business. First though, he needed to cast her in one of his smaller budget productions to see how she fared under the pressure and that was what this lunch was all about.

'I've been on to your agent,' Monty began, as the waiter poured out his wine.

'Just water and an undressed green salad for me, please.' Carla turned on her charm for the benefit of the maître d'hôtel who was immediately reduced to the status of a blushing schoolboy.

'Certainly, Miss de Courcy.' He clicked his fingers at an underling who immediately went in search of sparkling well water. 'May I say how much my wife and I enjoyed your last television appearance?'

'You may and thank you.'

'We always try to watch you when you're on.'

Carla could blush prettily and she used the asset now to full effect. No one looking at her would guess that underneath the ingénue image she liked to portray, there lurked an ambition as tough as that of any boardroom businessman.

Monty watched her performance with an indulgent smile. She was a class act and no mistake. If he wasn't a happily married man with the loveliest wife in the world he could almost be tempted to fall in love with Carla himself.

'How very kind of you.'

'I wonder, would you mind?'

A menu was produced for Carla and she autographed it with her flourishing signature.

'Yes.' Monty reverted to the matter in hand as the waiter bustled away to personally see to Carla's salad requirements. 'Your agent tells me you are free to start filming next week?'

'I don't know, am I?' Carla replied casually, desperate not to appear too eager. 'I thought I was in Paris.'

'Of course if you're busy, I could

recast.' This was the sort of game Monty enjoyed.

'No.' Carla recovered herself quickly, biting her lip over her hasty slip. 'I mean, if my agent says I'm free then I'm sure I'm available for whatever you have in mind.'

'It's only a small speaking part, not much more than a walk on, but it's been scheduled for prime time television. It's got a first rate cast and your agent agrees with me that to be seen in this particular production would be a good move. It would also be an excellent stepping-stone to advance your career and to register your presence in the global market. The rights have already been sold overseas.'

The smile that spread across Carla's face almost took Monty's breath away. Some actresses struggled for years to perfect that look. Carla was a natural. It wasn't very often Monty felt so excited by a project. All his professional instincts told him that with Carla de Courcy he was on to a winner.

'In that case, it's a deal.'

They shook hands.

'It's agreed then. The part is yours. I'll firm up contract details with your agent this afternoon.'

Carla's salad arrived and she picked up her fork to toy with a piece of lettuce. Now the business part of the lunch was over, Monty was prepared to indulge in social conversation.

'How's Lyle?' he asked.

'I haven't seen him for a couple of weeks. He's been in talks in America regarding a new screenplay.'

Monty nodded. Lyle and Carla were one of the most fashionable couples in the business. While he didn't normally listen to gossip, he had heard that life in the country did not suit Carla and that had been one of the main reasons for their break up.

Whilst he would not dream of taking sides he could understand how frustrated Carla would have been not to be at the centre of things. Monty himself was an urban man and while he enjoyed occasional lunches in the country like today he was always pleased to return to the town and to feel the pavement under his feet.

'I'm going to call in on Lyle on the way home,' Carla explained. 'Medway Manor isn't far from here and I need to catch up with him and Jenny, my daughter.'

'How old is Jenny now?'

'She's five.' Carla opened her handbag. 'Here.'

She thrust a photograph under Monty's nose. It was impossible not to smile at the happy little picture of the child wearing a butterfly decorated camouflage cap and a pair of huge matching sunglasses. She was holding a jam jar full of tiddlers and beaming at the camera.

'We were on holiday in Devon,' Carla explained, 'and I couldn't resist taking it. Isn't she lovely?'

'She is indeed,' Monty replied. 'She doesn't live with you?'

A shadow passed across Carla's face.

'No.' For a moment she looked very sad. 'I miss her dreadfully, but it's just not possible. When I'm away filming the days are very long and then when I get back I have to learn lines for the next day. Then there are wardrobe fittings and things like make up and hair, the list is endless. It's not a suitable environment for a child. So we decided it would be better if Jenny stayed with Lyle. The arrangement works very well. She's happy at school and has a good circle of friends.'

'Who looks after Jenny when Lyle is in America?'

'We have a housekeeper, and we did have a nanny, but she left. Then we engaged another one but she broke her leg, so I've arranged for a friend of mine to help out. She's a resting actress — Sara Armitage. She . . . '

'Did you say Sara Armitage?' Monty snapped, not looking quite so indulgent.

'Yes. Do you know her?'

'Let's say I know of her,' Monty replied.

Carla blinked, uncertain if she should say any more. Whatever history there was between Monty and Sara she was not aware of it.

'She's my son's ex-girlfriend,' Monty said.

Carla's fine eyebrows rose in surprise.

'Sara and Joe were an item?' In Carla's opinion that was a smart move on Sara's behalf.

'Until she walked out on him.'

Not such a smart move, thought Carla.

'That young woman has a lot to answer for, Joe's been distraught ever since the split.'

'I see.' Carla hesitated before saying, 'well when I bumped into her she said she was looking for somewhere to live at short notice so I suggested she might like to look after Jenny. We go back a long way, but we had lost touch for — er, personal reasons.'

'She walked out on you too, did she?' Monty couldn't resist asking.

This time Carla's blush was a deep red and not quite as becoming as the one she had used on the waiter.

She dismissed Monty's question, saying, 'It was all a long time ago.'

Monty frowned. Stars were entitled to their private lives of course, but he suspected there was more to the history between Carla and Sara, than Carla was letting on.

'So what's Joe doing these days?' Carla asked as the silence between her and Monty lengthened.

'He's on the camera side of things and I'm getting good reports of his work.'

Carla pushed away her half eaten salad. Anyone bold enough to say bad things about Monty Daniels' son was asking for trouble, Carla thought. She wondered briefly what had gone wrong between Sara and Joe then decided it was none of her business.

Sara was her friend and any differences between them were now buried in the past. She was looking forward to seeing her again.

It was a relief also to know that her daughter would be in a safe pair of hands. For all her scattiness, Sara loved children and while Jenny could at times be a handful, she had no doubt Sara would get her measure and that the pair of them would rub along well. She hoped Lyle would see things that way too.

That was one of the reasons why Carla was dropping by this afternoon. She didn't want Lyle doing anything silly.

Mrs Henderson had hinted over the telephone about a little initial difficulty between him and Sara, and Carla wanted any differences ironed out before she began her filming schedule.

She knew from experience that once the production was underway, her free time would be precious and rationed. She wouldn't be able to disappear at the drop of a hat to sort out any domestic problems.

'You haven't eaten very much.'

Monty looked disapprovingly at the remains of Carla's salad. 'I don't want you passing out on set because you've been overdoing the dieting.'

Carla made a face. 'I won't,' she assured him. 'But after Jenny was born I put on a few pounds and it took ages to shift them. Now I like to keep an eye on my figure. I'm as strong as a horse really.'

Monty did not doubt that for one moment. Actresses needed the stamina of a racehorse to cope with filming conditions and the long hours the work often entailed.

He signalled to the waiter for the bill.

'Can I give you a lift anywhere?' he asked as he signed his receipt.

'I've hired a car. It's parked in the multi storey. Living in London I don't drive very often but there's so much catching up to do this week. I've still got loads of stuff at Medway Manor and I have to see Lyle and,' she had been about to say Sara but at the last minute she substituted, 'Jenny.'

'Of course.' Monty stood up.

'Your driver is outside, Mr Daniels,' the receptionist helped him into his coat.

'Thank you.'

Carla paused on the steps outside the restaurant in the afternoon sunshine and watched Monty being driven away in his chauffeured car, a small frown wrinkling her brow.

She would need to talk to Sara about Joe Daniels, Monty's son. It was vitally important that she kept on the good side of Monty Daniels and she didn't want Sara's past love life interfering with her career.

Monty's car purred away into the traffic. With a thoughtful frown Carla began searching in her handbag for her mobile phone.

The Past Revisited

Carla followed the sound of laughter round to the back of the house. The sun slanted on the scene that met her eyes as she turned the corner by the conservatory and she hesitated on the stone steps with a sharp intake of breath. It gave all the appearance of a happy family gathering. She didn't like feeling the outsider. The realisation of what she had given up stabbed her hard in the chest.

Mrs Henderson was sitting in a deckchair contentedly shelling peas with Daniel the spaniel snoozing by her feet. Jenny was capering around the lawn, playing tag with a friend, but what really caused Carla's gasp of surprise was the sight of Lyle and Sara sitting together on a sun lounger, swinging backwards and forwards, laughing as they enjoyed a cold drink.

'Glad to see everyone's hard at it,' she called out as she strolled casually towards the party, ramming a pink straw hat on to her head. 'I've just remembered why the heart of the countryside isn't my thing. This sun is so damaging to the complexion, and as for the grass,' she laughed, 'I dread to think what it's doing to my heels. I've sunk at least six inches.' She picked her way daintily across the lawn.

'Mummy,' Jenny squealed and abandoning her playmate ran towards her with her arms outstretched.

Carla swung her into the air. 'How's my angel?'

'Have you brought me a present?' Jenny demanded.

'Lovely to see you too, Mummy,' Carla replied. 'Only good little girls get presents. Now, have you been behaving for Mrs Henderson?'

'She's not my sole responsibility any more, Mrs Jackson,' Mrs Henderson replied.

At the sound of Carla's voice, Sara

had leapt to her feet. Lyle continued to swing lazily on the sun lounger.

'Carla, we weren't expecting you.' Sara had no reason to feel guilty. She and Lyle had been doing nothing wrong, but all the same she would rather not have been discovered lazing beside him on the lounger.

Carla's smile gave nothing away. 'I can see that.'

Lyle had been working on his new script in the conservatory all morning and had only joined them in the garden a few moments earlier. Sara had been wondering how to extricate herself from his side when Carla had arrived on the scene.

'I'm sorry I haven't been in touch before now to welcome you to the fold,' Carla said, 'but I have been busy filming. Still, it looks like Lyle's taking good care of you.'

'Mummy's a famous actress,' Jenny explained importantly to her friend who had joined the little group by the pond and was busy staring up at Carla.

'Darling,' Carla chided her, 'don't show off. It's bad manners.'

'I've seen you on the telly,' Jenny's friend said.

'Have you, dear?'

Unlike many actresses, Carla never minded being recognised. Sara stood to one side and let Carla bask in her moment of glory. She was pleased her friend was doing so well and didn't envy her all the success she was currently enjoying. She hoped their friendship would not suffer because of Lyle.

'I'll catch up with you later, darling,' she put Jenny down. 'Right now I have to talk to Daddy and Sara.'

'Mummy, Sara and I have been finger painting and, guess what? Sara played the part of the bear in our school play because Kayleigh was sick.'

'She was ever so good,' Jenny's little friend put in.

'I'm sure she was,' Carla agreed. 'Now off you go.'

The two little girls rushed back to

their game, leaving Sara and Carla facing each other.

'I trust playing bears didn't stretch your acting ability too much?' Carla raised an eyebrow.

'It was my first acting job in ages.' Sara admitted with a wry smile. 'I got very good reviews.'

'I'm sure you did.' Carla glanced over to the sun lounger. 'You seem to be getting along well with Lyle. Mrs Henderson mentioned a problem?'

'Nothing we can't handle.' Sara hoped Lyle wouldn't go into details.

'I don't want Jenny unsettled.'

'Carla, you are happy about me being here?' Sara asked.

It was one thing Lyle over-reacting, but Sara didn't want Carla thinking she wasn't up to the job either.

'Darling,' Carla raised her eyes theatrically, 'you have been a lifesaver.'

Sara's lips twitched involuntarily. She could remember when they had been down to their last tin of baked beans and were forced to share one pair of tights because the rest were laddered. To see the new Carla bordering on super stardom was quite an experience.

'Without you I don't know what I would have done.'

'Mrs Henderson has offered me a month's contract . . . '

'Which I would like to extend.' Mrs Henderson tried to extricate herself from her deckchair. 'Daniel, get off my feet. For a guard dog you seem to do an awful lot of sleeping in the sun these days.'

'He's not a puppy any more, Mrs H,' Carla stroked a silky ear. Daniel licked her fingers, 'are you, old boy?'

'Here, let me help, Mrs H.' Lyle offered having got up from the sun lounger. 'Move it, you lazy lump.' He nudged Daniel out of the way and held Mrs Henderson's colander of peas while she sorted herself out.

'Are you staying, Mrs Jackson? Would you like some tea?' Mrs Henderson whipped off her apron. 'If I'd know you were coming, I'd have got in some of that special white tea that you like.'

'Not to worry, Mrs H. China tea will do. Talking to Monty Daniels over lunch has given me such a thirst.'

'Monty Daniels?' Sara's voice was apprehensive.

'Yes,' Carla wagged a playful finger at her, 'and aren't you the dark horse? What's all this I hear about you and his son, Joe?' Before Sara could reply Carla turned to Lyle. 'Hello, darling,' she said softly, 'I have missed you so much.'

They embraced and Sara was forced to look away. Although Carla was no longer married to Lyle there was no doubt he still held a special place in her heart. They looked so right together, this fashionable, talented couple, whose wedding had been a special feature in a glossy magazine. Where had it all gone wrong? Had it been professional pressures? Neither Lyle nor Carla appeared to be involved with anyone else. They also appeared to be in as much love as ever.

Lyle smiled at his ex wife. 'You look

lovely,' he said simply.

Sara picked at some dried paint on her crumpled skirt. In her baggy T-shirt and flip-flops she was no match for the ultra sophisticated Carla de Courcy who managed to look as fresh as a daisy on the hottest day of the year.

At least Carla and Lyle's break up was an amicable one, Sara thought as the pair of them showed no sign of wanting to be released from their embrace.

'Would you like me to stroll down to the local store and see if they've got any white tea?' she offered, feeling very much in the way.

'Darling,' Carla's face lit up, 'would you be an angel? I like the one in the green packet.'

'I shouldn't bother.' Lyle's wink was the undoing of Sara's composure. She grinned as he added, 'they can just about manage to stock workman's tea. Stop playing the superstar, Carla, you're with old friends here.'

'I don't know what you mean.'

Carla's efforts to maintain her composure began to slip as she caught the look on Lyle's face before she dissolved into laughter. 'Sorry,' she apologised, 'it's getting to be a way of life. The stories I could tell you about some of my co-stars, you would not believe.'

Glad to have the old Carla back, Sara joined in the laughter and when Mrs Henderson appeared carrying a loaded tea tray and juice for the children, an impromptu party developed on the lawn.

'I need an injection of real life every now and then,' Carla said from under the canopy of the sun lounger, 'just to keep me sane, otherwise I'll start believing all the hype. How's the screenplay going, Lyle?' she asked.

'I've got the green light, but it's going to be a busy few months. These moguls know how to push a hard bargain and I'm only one of a team. If they don't like what I've written then I'll be out. Don't expect to see much of me in the coming months. I'll be slaving over a hot laptop when I'm not flying across the Atlantic.'

'Poor you,' Carla sympathised. 'Monty's cast me in a small part in a budget production costume drama. He said there might possibly be something for me in — what's the new screenplay called?'

'The working title is *Exchange*.'

'What's it about?'

'Sorry,' Lyle apologised. 'It's under tabs for the moment and the finished product will probably be nothing like the book.'

Do you think you could pull a few strings for me, Lyle?' Carla leaned forward and put a hand on his arm.

'I very much doubt it. I've got no sway with the producers. Besides, if you've got Monty Daniels on your side, you don't need me.'

* * *

The conversation swung backwards and forwards between them. Ousted off the sun lounger, Sara now occupied a dodgy deckchair that had been hauled out of the shed that morning. It was in urgent need of repair, but there hadn't been time to do anything about it yet. Hoping the slats wouldn't give way under her and trying not to make any sudden movements, Sara closed her eyes, glad to have the chance to take forty winks.

Jenny had been up for part of the night, after all the earlier excitement and indulging in too much ice-cream. Sara hadn't had much sleep running up and down the stairs with towels and bowls of water, then reading a bedtime story to Jenny until she finally fell asleep in the small hours.

Sara hadn't liked to disturb Lyle after his comments about suffering from jet lag, and he had not been too pleased when Sara had yawned her way down to breakfast and found him already sitting at the table.

'Why didn't you tell me Jenny was unwell in the night?' he demanded.

'You needed your sleep,' Sara began, wondering if all their meetings were going to result in confrontation. 'Anyway, how did you find out?'

'Mrs H told me. I'm never too tired for my daughter.' He glanced through the pile of mail on the table. 'Remember that in future.'

'Right.' Sara fought to keep her voice steady. The thought of storming into Lyle's bedroom at midnight and dragging him from his bed was unnerving to say the least. 'Jenny's fine now, but if it's all right with you, I think I'll keep her off school today.'

'Good idea.' The sharp eyes were beginning to make Sara squirm. She knew her hair still looked a bit like a hedgehog's but spikes weren't easy to tame when you'd run out of hair gel. She wished the razor cut would hurry up and grow out.

'I'll help Mrs Henderson with a curtain wash, I think.'

'You'll do no such thing.' Lyle looked up from frowning over his post. 'You're exhausted. There are dark circles under your eyes.'

Sara's eyes were watering from the strain of trying not to yawn, but if Lyle Jackson thought she was going to weaken under the strain, he had another think coming.

'I'd promised I'd help her.'

She wished he wouldn't keep looking at her so keenly. She had forgotten the magnetism of his eyes and how they could do things to her system.

'Sara?'

She jerked herself awake. 'Sorry?'

'Asleep on the job?' Carla joked. 'Am I talking to myself?'

'Don't be too harsh on Sara, Carla, Jenny was up in the night.'

'My baby was ill?' She looked across the garden to where Jenny was now running around with her friend.

'She's fine now. She had a minor tummy upset, that's all,' Lyle said.

'Did you call the doctor?'

'There was no need,' Sara assured an anxious Carla. 'She'd eaten too much ice-cream.'

Was Lyle going to tell Carla all that

had happened yesterday? Sara could tell nothing from the expression on his face.

Carla was frowning. 'Too many e-numbers aren't good for her. Do you control her carb intake?'

'I'm not having any of that nonsense,' Lyle said firmly. Sara breached a sigh of relief, glad the question had distracted him. 'Jenny's a normal child and I intend to see she is treated like one.'

'Of course, darling, all the same I can't help feeling anxious. She's my little girl and I'm not always here for her. You've no idea how that feels. I'm scared she'll forget all about me.'

'That's nonsense. Jenny's always talking about you,' Sara said, 'and you heard her boasting about you to her friend.'

Carla's grey eyes softened. 'It's important for a child to know both her parents love her.'

'And Jenny does.'

Sara's thoughts strayed to her parents. She didn't doubt her father had loved her, but he had died when she was a baby. Vernon, her stepfather, had been a wonderful man and she missed him so much. A day didn't pass without her thinking about him.

'Was there something you wanted to ask Sara when you woke her up?' Lyle asked.

'Yes, of course,' Carla turned back to Sara. 'Joe Daniels,' she said.

'What about him?' Sara stiffened.

'Monty says you were his son's girlfriend.'

'But he's not any more,' Lyle butted in.

The quickness of his remark earned him a surprised look from Carla.

Sara took a deep breath. 'If it's all right with both of you, I'd rather not talk about Joe Daniels. He is no longer a part of my life.'

'Fair enough,' Carla replied. She would have liked to know more but there was no way she could press Sara for details, especially not with Lyle by her side.

In the distance the telephone began to ring. 'I suppose one of us should answer it,' Lyle said.

'It could be my agent,' Carla said. 'I left this number with him in case he couldn't get me on my mobile.'

'In that case,' Lyle replied, 'I'll take the call. You never know, it might be for me.'

The two girls smiled at each other as he lumbered across the lawn towards the study.'

'It didn't upset you seeing Lyle again after all these years?' Carla asked as he went inside the house.

'Actually, it was like taking a step backwards in my life,' Sara admitted.

'I know what you mean. This afternoon was like old times, wasn't it, the three of us together, chatting? Are you still cross with me for marrying Lyle?'

Sara shook her head. 'I think we would have broken up even if you hadn't come on the scene. We were all very young.'

'It gave me a few sleepless nights.' Carla smiled from under her huge straw hat. 'I really missed you afterwards and would have liked to explain what happened but I felt so bad about it I kept putting it off and time sort of slipped by and I never plucked up the courage to contact you.'

Before Sara could reply Lyle opened the conservatory window. 'Sara,' he bellowed, 'it's for you.'

'For me?' She raised her eyebrows in surprise. 'Who is it?' she asked.

'Joe Daniels,' Lyle said, before slamming shut the window.

A Disappointing End To The Evening

Sara could hear the swish of the sea through the open window. It was a sound that always had the power to soothe her. The evening breeze fanned her cheeks and brought her a welcome relief from the scorching heat of the day. She rubbed her temples with some cool cologne and took a few deep breaths.

Jenny had been fractious all afternoon and Lyle hadn't eased the tension in the house by demanding a bit of peace and quiet before shutting himself away in the study. Daniel had howled at the sound of his master's raised voice and Sara had been forced to take him and Jenny for a long walk across the fields in an effort to tire them out.

'It's seeing Mrs Jackson last week,'

Mrs Henderson murmured to Sara, 'it always upsets everybody. She was such a focal part of the household. Mr Jackson and wee Jenny are both a bit lost without her.'

Sara could understand. After Carla's whirlwind visit she'd left in a shower of kisses and presents that she had produced from the back of her car. The house had seemed flat after her departure.

Sara couldn't help suspecting that Joe's telephone call in the middle of her visit might have been something to do with Carla. Coming so soon after her lunch with Monty Daniels, it seemed more than a coincidence that Joe should choose that afternoon to contact her when she hadn't heard from him for weeks.

'Don't look so grumpy, darling,' Carla had chided Lyle after Sara had finished talking to Joe on the telephone and rejoined them in the garden, 'Sara and Monty Daniels' son are old friends.'

'You said it was all over,' Lyle said to Sara.

'It is,' Sara had insisted, wishing she now hadn't told Lyle about the relationship and it being the reason for her availability to look after Jenny.

'Then what's he doing telephoning you here?' Lyle demanded.

'There are one or two things of mine he still has and,' Sara shrugged, 'he suggested we meet up again one evening next week.'

'And I think it's a very good idea, Sara,' Carla smiled at her. 'Stuck away down here with only Jenny and Mrs Henderson for company isn't good for you. You need to get out more.'

* * *

Beach View Cottage was the perfect place to unwind after the stresses of the day, and when Mrs Henderson had offered to look after Jenny, Sara decided to take Joe up on his invite for a casual evening at the cottage. She needed a break from Lyle's constant brooding presence and Jenny's hyperactivity.

She loved living and working at Medway Manor, but gradually in Carla's absence everyone was beginning to rely on her more and more and the strain was beginning to get to her.

Sara remembered how she and Joe had spent many happy times at the cottage, down on the beach in the warm weather, jet-skiing and sunbathing, or simply strolling hand in hand along the sand dunes.

'Want me to collect you from Medway Manor and drive you to the cottage?' Joe had offered over the telephone that afternoon.

'No, I'll meet you there,' Sara insisted.

'Scared I won't drive you home again?' Joe joked.

Although it was a joke, Sara preferred to have her own transport and had enjoyed the drive along the coast to St Violet's Bay. Monty, Joe's father had bought Beach View Cottage many years ago as a family bolthole. The area had been fashionable in Victorian times as a water resort, but its popularity had declined over the years, consequently it had escaped all the commercialism of neighbouring seaside resorts.

It was the perfect retreat for stressed out celebrities and Monty made full use of its facilities for business weekends when he wanted to keep the atmosphere informally casual. Joe had full use of the cottage whenever it was free.

Sara watched a van bounce away down the coastal road after delivering their supper. Thai was still Joe's favourite cuisine.

'Who needs to cook when there are takeaways?' was one of his favourite sayings.

He had been born to a mother who, at the age of forty and after twenty years of marriage, had given up all hope of having children. Consequently he had been spoilt senseless from the day he had been born.

To give Joe his due, he was kind

hearted, if a little selfish. Being the son of Monty Daniels had given him an easy start in life, but he never pulled rank on the other members of the camera crew and was always prepared to do his stint of all-nighters when they were under pressure and in conditions that were far from luxurious.

As a result he was beginning to earn his colleagues' grudging respect and gradually people were beginning to refer to him as Joe Daniels in his own right, and not the son of Monty Daniels.

Joe breezed into the conservatory bearing steaming platters of prawns, rice and pineapple, crisps and dips and a bowl of fragrant noodles.

'Tuck in.'

'I don't really know what I'm doing here,' she began.

Two weeks ago the thought of sharing an intimate meal with Joe would have been unthinkable, but after his telephone call, Sara realised there were still one or two issues between them that needed to be put right. They had shared a lot of good times together and Sara hoped now the heat had gone out of the situation that they could remain friends like Carla and Lyle.

'Enjoying a late night supper with your ex, who is hoping you will succumb to his charm and come back to him.'

Joe smiled at her in the old familiar way she remembered so well and began loading up his plate with prawns and rice.

'No,' Sara shook her head firmly, 'that's not what this meal is all about.'

'What do you mean?' Joe demanded with mock severity. 'I didn't go to all this trouble to sweet talk you into a date only to have you say no. And let me tell you getting past Lyle Jackson was no easy feat.'

'Lyle isn't difficult,' Sara protested, not sure why she was leaping to his defence. Nothing had been right since he had returned from America, and if it hadn't been for her loyalty to Carla and the fact that she actually enjoyed her job, she would have been sorely tempted to hand in her notice.

Only that morning Lyle had complained when she and Jenny had danced to some loud music on the radio while they were having breakfast.

'Seems his number's ex-directory. Carla shouldn't have really given it to me.'

Prawns slithered off Sara's fork, back on to her plate.

'Carla gave you Lyle's number?' She had been right to suspect Carla had had a hand in this reconciliation.

'Never mind about her,' Joe gave up on his chopsticks. 'I never could get the hang of those things.' He picked up a fork. 'I'm more interested in us. So where do we stand?' he asked.

Sara cleared her throat. 'I'd like to remain friends,' she began carefully.

'I'd like us to be more than that.'

'We have history, Joe,' Sara reminded him.

'Nothing that we can't talk through.'

'We've done all the talking.'

'There was no need for you to storm out of the flat, you know. You didn't give me a chance to explain . . . '

'Let's not go through all that again.'

Finding yet another acting part had been cast before Sara had a chance to attend the audition she'd arrived back at the flat early and found him ensconced on the sofa with one of the make-up girls. She'd known of his reputation before she'd started going out with him, but he'd promised her those days were over and he wanted to settle down. She'd taken him at his word and to discover he'd been two timing her was more than she could bear. She had no intention of reliving the experience.

Sara had rushed out of the flat slamming the door behind her not bothering to listen to Joe's hurried excuses.

But Sara wasn't a natural creature of confrontation and before their relationship had deepened into something else,

Joe had been a good friend. She hoped that friendship could be rekindled. Joe, it seemed, had other ideas.

'Can't I persuade you to have a rethink?' he wheedled.

'Joe,' Sara said, anxious to avoid any further misunderstanding, 'that part of our life is over. We won't be getting back together.'

'But I told you it wasn't what you think.'

Sara sighed. 'It really doesn't matter now anyway. I've moved on.'

'To Lyle Jackson?' Joe frowned. 'Your ex?'

'There is nothing between Lyle and me,' Sara insisted. She was getting tired of insisting that that relationship too was in the past.

'Fine. I can accept that. You don't see me kicking up a fuss because you're living in his house.'

Sara almost choked on her prawn crisp at the audacity of his remark. 'You don't have the right to object to anything I do in my life, Joe.'

'How about I put on some music to calm things down?' he suggested as he finished his prawns.

'Good idea.' Sara nodded and glanced at her watch. She had told Mrs Henderson she would be home before midnight. She didn't want the housekeeper to wait up for her again as she had done the night Sara had visited her mother.

Her car had played up on the drive back to Medway Manor and it had been two o'clock in the morning before she'd crept into the kitchen, to find Mrs Henderson yawning her head off and an irate Lyle pacing the floor.

She began to sip some water, wondering how soon she could leave. Storms had been forecast for the south coast and she thought she heard a faint rumble of thunder in the distance.

'Why did you really ring me?' Sara asked as Joe sat down again.

'I've told you. I want us to get back together.'

When he wouldn't meet her eyes, Sara asked, 'Can't the make-up girl cook?'

Joe had the grace to blush. He had always been fond of his creature comforts and Sara remembered how she had been foolish enough to iron his shirts and collect his dry cleaning. Having a new girlfriend who didn't do these things must have been an extreme annoyance to him.

'I could offer you a lot more than you get working for Lyle Jackson.'

'Such as?' Sara couldn't resist asking.

'A part in *Exchange*?'

Sara gasped. 'You're not serious?'

'Knew that would get you going.' Joe stretched out his long legs. 'Remember this song?' He hummed along to the tune. 'It was always one of your favourites.' He looked at her, his brown eyes earnest. 'So? What do you think?'

'What about Carla de Courcy?'

'What about her?'

'Hasn't your father promised her the lead role?'

Joe shrugged. 'Nothing's definite, besides you don't owe Carla any favours.'

Sara frowned at the ship's lantern dangling from the wall. Its light cast lengthening shadows across the floor as the light faded from the day. Acting was a precarious profession. Many people left the business because they were unable to make a living at it. Sara had often waited at tables in an effort to make ends meet.

Working for Lyle Jackson had been her first stable employment for a long time. Was she prepared to throw it all in on a whim? She didn't doubt Joe could get her an audition, but deep down she suspected she wasn't a good enough actress for the part. Carla had that extra special quality that could bring the screen alive.

'It's each man for himself in this business.'

Sara shook her head. 'I don't think so. Thanks and all that.'

'Tell you what,' Joe said, 'before you turn me down flat, why don't I sound out a few contacts? Nothing definite, but if things with Lyle don't work out . . . ' He left the sentence trailing.

His mobile interrupted them and while he was answering his call, Sara cleared away the remains of their supper. Whether or not she took Joe up on his offer, she did need to have a serious think about her future.

Looking after Jenny was a job she enjoyed, but she had to be realistic. It wouldn't last forever. Then what was she going to do? Many years ago her mother had insisted she take a course in office skills. She could still touch type but the world of technology had moved on without her and her skills in that direction would be sorely out of touch.

She could perhaps forge a new career for herself as a childminder. Professional couples were always looking for someone reliable to care for their children.

She wiped down the worktops then as Joe was still engaged on his call she opened the back door and stepped out on to the terrace. The sea had turned from blue to inky black. Midges danced in the twilight promising another hot day. Perhaps Jenny would like a trip to St Violet's Bay sometime, she thought. The summer holidays were due to start in a month's time and Sara would need to make up some sort of agenda to keep Jenny occupied.

Carla had half promised to come down during the holidays to help out, but her filming schedule had been brought forward and Sara doubted they would see much of her before September.

'You will do the summer party, won't you?' Carla had asked when she'd last telephoned.

'What party?'

'Jenny always has one when school breaks up. Her birthday's in December and as there's so much else going on that time of year, we have a party for her in the summer. If the weather's nice we hold it in the garden. It's a sort of family tradition. Then in the evening we extend the invitation to the grown ups. Of course I'll help if I can.'

Lost in her thoughts, the rumble of thunder overhead made Sara jump.

'Where are you?' Joe called out.

'On the terrace,' she called back as a fat blob of rain landed on her bare arm.

'Look, sorry and all that,' Joe began, 'but I'm going to have to cut short our evening.'

'That wasn't your make-up girl on the telephone?' Sara teased him with a wry smile.

'Actually, yes it was.'

'I see.' Sara felt annoyed with herself. For a while she had started to believe Joe was turning over a new leaf. 'Well, don't let me keep you.'

'It's not . . . '

'What I think? We've already done that.'

'No. It really isn't. One of her old boyfriends is a cameraman on my crew and he's gone sick, eaten some funny shellfish, she said. There's a bit of a flap on — an all-nighter and they can't reschedule. They've asked if I'll cover for him.' Joe glanced at his watch. 'It'll take me at least two hours to drive to the location. I hate to leave you in the lurch, but you have got your own transport home, haven't you?'

'That's all right. The evening was nearly over anyway and I ought to be getting back to Medway Manor, I think there's a storm brewing.'

'Don't go round the coast road. It floods,' Joe advised her. 'And thanks for tidying up.' He began closing windows and locking up doors. By now the rain was beginning to fall steadily. 'Sure you'll be OK?' He glanced at her car, a look of concern on his face. 'Isn't that your mother's old car?'

'When I get the lead part in *Exchange*,' Sara joked, 'I'll trade it in for a new one.'

'You're on.' After a swift peck on her cheek Joe climbed into his red Italian open top and gunned the engine into life. 'I'll be in touch,' he waved at her as he drove off in a roar of exhaust fumes.

Sprinting through the rain, she wrenched open the driver's door. She would have to drive inland to avoid any flooding. It was a long way round and Sara wasn't too sure of the way. She hoped both of them were up to the journey.

The engine started up, then spluttered and then died. Sara tried again. The car was filled with the overpowering smell of petrol. It caught the back of her throat. She coughed and her eyes filled with tears. Pushing the accelerator to the floor she turned the key again anxious not to flood the engine. The car did not respond. The only sound was that of the rain drumming on the roof.

Old Feelings Return

'Yes?' The telephone was answered abruptly on its second ring. Lyle's voice sounded clipped.

'Lyle?' Sara's heart sank at the sound of his voice. She had hoped Mrs Henderson would take the call.

'Sara? What's happened? Where are you?' he asked in an urgent voice.

'I'm at Beach View Cottage.'

'Where?'

'St Violet's Bay, Monty Daniels' place. My car won't start and Joe's had to go . . . '

'I'll be there as soon as I can.' Lyle didn't wait for her to finish the sentence.

'No, that won't be necessary, I can call out the garage,' Sara began, but she was talking to a disconnected line.

She slammed the steering wheel with the open palms of her hands in frustration — of all the bad luck to have Lyle answer the telephone. If only she had been able to speak to Mrs Henderson, the housekeeper could have covered for her until she managed to get home. Now, she was stranded in the middle of nowhere on a storm driven cliff top until Lyle arrived.

Her car rocked from side to side as the wind buffeted the headland. Sara wasn't normally nervous, she loved the sea and storms didn't scare her, but she knew from experience, in extreme weather Beach View Cottage could be cut off. The water levels had been high on the drive over and she'd noticed several flooded fields. One more violent storm would have the river breaking its banks and this one showed no sign of abating.

Streaks of lightning lit up the night sky as they zigzagged around the bay. The next clap of thunder almost shattered Sara's eardrums. The eye of the storm was now overhead St Violet's.

Sara peered at the luminous dial of

her watch. It would take Lyle at least an hour to drive over from Medway Manor. It wasn't safe to wait that long in the car, but where could she go? Joe had locked up the cottage. The only other shelter was the run down barn that was used as an outhouse to stack logs for the open fire in winter.

Grabbing up an old rug that lived on the back seat of her car, Sara opened the driver's door. She clung on as the wind almost whipped it out of her hold. Careful not to slip on the scrubby grass that was fast turning into a mud bath, Sara raced towards the barn as cold rain sliced into her face.

It was only a distance of a few metres, but by the time she reached it, her hair was plastered to her head and she was soaked to the skin. Her summer top and skirt were scant protection against the violence of the storm.

The wooden door creaked in protest as she pushed it open. The comforting smell of oak wood greeted her as she fumbled her way inside the barn, tripping over her blanket as she pushed the solid door to behind her. It closed with a satisfying solid thump. The latch made a heavy clang as it fell back into place. No storm would get through that thought Sara as she picked her way over the floor to see where she was going.

Clutching her blanket to her chest, she also tried not to shiver. The dry wood gave off some warmth and soon she had arranged a pile of logs into a makeshift bank that she could sit on.

As her eyes grew accustomed to the darkness she spotted a gas lamp under the window ledge. Power cuts were not infrequent during the winter months and there was always a selection of emergency lighting on hand at the cottage.

Sara felt around for some matches and her fingers fumbled on a lighter. A few moments later the lamp hissed into life and emitted a rosy glow. Sara's rug began to steam in the heat. She wrinkled her nose. The odour reminded her of damp dog. It had been years since she and her mother had owned a dog, not since Vernon had lived with them.

Sara bit her lip. She would not think about Vernon. He had let her mother down, just as Lyle and Joe had let her down.

Sara settled down on her makeshift log seat. Her eyelids began to droop and she began to dream of Daniel the spaniel, Jenny's dog. He'd fallen asleep on the back seat of her car, the day she had taken Jenny and her friends swimming and that's what she could smell on the rug. She cuddled it to her and imagined Daniel was there to protect her.

Her lips twitched. As a guard dog he wasn't very good, but what he lacked in security skills he made up for in love. With that thought comforting her she was soon fast asleep.

'Sara?' Someone was shouting her name as her head was rocked to and fro. 'Thank heavens I've found you.'

Sara opened her eyes with a start to find Lyle kneeling in front of her, his hands on her shoulders, a look of concern on his face as he shook her gently awake.

'Lyle?' She croaked, rubbing a hand over her groggy eyes. 'What time is it?'

'Late,' he said grimly, 'it's taken me two hours to get here and I've spent the last ten minutes in a panic looking for you. I thought you'd been swept away to sea.'

'I'm sorry,' she apologised, 'I took shelter in the barn. I didn't mean to fall asleep.'

'Are you all right?' His eyes bore into hers.

'Yes, but my car won't start. It was making a funny noise on the way over and I think I've flooded something. I was going to call out the emergency services but you didn't give me time to explain.'

'They wouldn't have got through, the bottom of the road's flooded. I had to double back. That's what delayed me.'

Lyle still had hold of Sara's shoulders and she was acutely aware of the pressure of his fingers on her flesh through her thin T-shirt.

'H . . . how did you manage to get through?'

'I brought the four-by-four.' He dropped his hands and Sara bit her lip to stop a cry of disappointment escaping them. She steadied herself against the logs.

Aware Lyle was still looking at her so keenly his eyes were as penetrating as the feel of his fingers, she said, 'You're wet.'

Water dripped off Lyle's hair and his eyelashes sparkled with raindrops. He flicked his head like a wet dog.

'What do you expect in this weather?' he snapped. 'I've never seen a storm like it. Joe had no right abandoning you. Did you have another row?'

'No. It wasn't really raining when he left. He got called in to work at short notice and it's not my fault you're wet.

I didn't mean you to come out. I only called Medway Manor because I suspected Mrs Henderson would worry about me.'

'Of course she would worry about you. You know what she's like. Honestly, Sara, at times you can be so thoughtless.'

'I am not thoughtless,' Sara snapped back. 'I told you. My car wouldn't start. That doesn't make me thoughtless.'

'Oh no? You don't think it's thoughtless to drive my daughter around in a car that is barely roadworthy?'

'It passed its MOT.'

'Did it never occur to you that it might need a service?'

'Yes, but . . . ' Sara's breath was coming in short bursts. She was no longer cold, her temperature was soaring.

'Supposing you and Jenny had broken down in the middle of nowhere?'

'All right, I'll arrange a service next week.' There was no point in explaining to Lyle that she had been waiting for her first pay check before she could afford for her car to be serviced. He'd probably forgotten what it was like to count the pennies.

'I'll arrange it,' he said firmly. 'I have an account with the local garage. Here.' In an unexpected movement Lyle thrust a thermos flask at her. 'Mrs H made you some tea.'

Sara wriggled into a more comfortable position. 'Th . . . thank you,' she stammered gratefully.

'We'd better eat the sandwiches, too.' Lyle unwrapped some foil, 'and the fruit cake, otherwise she'll be mortally offended.'

Sara was surprised to realised how hungry she was. The Thai takeaway she'd shared with Joe had been a long time ago. She glanced at her watch and was surprised to see it was gone midnight.

'Mrs Henderson didn't happen to provide you with a couple of inflatables too, did she?' Sara joked, ignoring the tightness of her throat.

Lyle's anger appeared to have died down. His mouth softened into a wry smile.

'I'm sure she would have done if the shops hadn't been closed. Budge up.'

'What?'

'Move over. We're going to have to sit this one out until the storm eases a bit and this floor looks hard.'

'It's not much softer on the logs,' Sara said as she moved as far away from Lyle as it was possible to get, which wasn't easy in the space provided by half a dozen logs. Her legs had gone to sleep and pins and needles stabbed her toes as she tried to work life into them.

'So,' Lyle mumbled through a mouthful of sandwich, 'what exactly happened here tonight?'

In the darkness of the barn and snuggled under the blanket together she could feel the warmth of Lyle's body beside hers. The material of his shirt tickled the sensitive flesh of her arm. She shivered.

The gaslight softened the harsh

planes of his face and made him look younger. There were lines around his eyes that hadn't been there seven years ago and a streak of white in his hair. Sara experienced an absurd urge to stroke it.

'We haven't really talked, have we?' Lyle said. 'There always seems to be a dog, a daughter or a housekeeper in the way.'

'About what?' Sara asked.

'The past. I treated you badly, didn't I? I didn't mean to hurt you.'

'It doesn't matter, Lyle,' Sara said softly. 'I've almost forgotten all about it.'

Sara was glad it was dark in the barn. She wasn't good at fibbing, but she didn't want Lyle thinking she still harboured some sort of schoolgirl crush on him like her predecessor, the one Mrs Henderson had told her about, the one who had been forced to leave Medway Manor for getting too close to her boss.

'I haven't,' he admitted.

'If it's any consolation, I grew used to being ignored when Carla was around.'

She wondered briefly what had gone wrong between Carla and Lyle. Their relationship seemed as close as ever and Mrs Henderson had hinted that Lyle still missed her desperately.

'I know it's far too late to say this, but,' he shrugged, 'sorry. There, will that do?'

'Thank you.'

'I know I've been difficult since I've been home and I apologise for that, too. When you work eighteen hours all day, every day under high pressure, something has to give.'

'Success comes at a price.'

Lyle nodded. 'That about sums it up. I'll be working non-stop on *Exchange* for the next few months. It's groundbreaking intensive stuff and I need to get it right.' Lyle stopped massaging her foot and looked directly at Sara. 'Did you know Carla's pushing for the lead?'

'I — er — had heard a rumour,' Sara admitted.

'I still love her even though we're not married any more.' Lyle's words stabbed Sara in the chest. 'But sometimes she puts me in a difficult position. I have no casting sway with the powers that be on this one. The money men run that side of things. They may want a name or they may go with a new face, no decision's been made, but when it is it'll be nothing to do with me. I'm strictly one of the backroom boys.'

'I understand.'

'I wish Carla did, but she's not above using my name to further her career.'

'I thought your last screenplay, *Lion*, was brilliant.' Lyle's tired brown eyes softened when Sara added, 'you should have won the award. I sat up into the small hours watching the ceremony and I hurled a cushion at the television set when they announced the winner.'

'My work is reward enough,' Lyle said. He relaxed against the bed of logs. 'Can I asked you a personal question?'

Sara stiffened. 'Do I have to answer it?'

'What did you do to your hair?'
'Don't you like it?'
'It's — er, vibrant.'
'I went for an audition, but I didn't get the part — story of my life.'
'Grow it out,' Lyle said softly, 'I don't want Jenny getting ideas.'
Sara tugged at a stray spiky bit. 'Her friends think I look cool.'
Lyle raised his eyes. 'You realise I'll have the head teacher on my back if half her pupils return to school after the summer break sporting spikes of pink hair?'
'I expect the fashion will have moved on by then, so I shouldn't worry about it.'
Sara stifled a yawn.
'We'd better finish the last sandwich,' Lyle picked up the discarded foil package, 'then I'll see about drying out those spark plugs. I don't want to leave your car here, so if you could limp home behind the four-by-four it would save another journey out here tomorrow.'

Sara nodded. While Lyle cleared up their picnic things, she pulled open the shed door and was surprised to hear the rain had stopped. It was too dark to see properly, but rivers of water were draining down the cliff side and the ground was awash. She looked down at her soggy pink sandals. They were ruined.

'Want me to carry you to your car?' Lyle asked.

He was standing behind her. 'No thank you,' she said firmly, 'I'll manage.'

'In that case, once we've got you going, I think we'll try the coast road as far as the pier then turn inland. Is that OK with you?'

'Fine.'

Sara trailed out of the barn behind Lyle, trying hard to ignore the small voice in her head suggesting that she was as in love with Lyle Jackson as she had been seven years ago. The only problem was he was still in love with his ex-wife.

Vernon Decides To Get In Touch

Vernon Pickering sat up straight in shock as the newspaper he was reading shook in his hands. His cup of coffee cooled as he took a closer look at the blurred photograph of a young woman with spiky hair hurrying away from the camera. She was trying to hide her face and it was a bad picture but he would have recognised her anywhere, even though it had been years since he had last seen her.

Sara — his stepdaughter. Vernon took a sip of coffee to ease the dryness in his throat. His head was reeling. To think she had been living so close by and he didn't know anything about it. Their parting had always played on his conscience.

He had wanted to keep in touch with

her after the separation from Sara's mother, but Judy had wisely suggested that they all needed to take time out to come to terms with the situation and as Sara was also going through a tough personal time her mother didn't want her further stressed.

Vernon's life after the separation had passed in a blur and months had gone by and before Vernon quite realised it, they had turned into years.

On a spiral of self-pity Vernon had not even tried to contact either Sara, or her mother, Judy, until it was too late. Now Vernon wasn't even sure where they lived.

He read the brief caption underneath the picture. *Is this Lyle Jackson's latest girlfriend? Caught driving his car yesterday, the young lady in question only offered a crisp, 'No comment,' to our reporter. Lyle Jackson, ex-husband of actress Carla de Courcy, is also one of this country's foremost screenwriters and is currently working on an important new screenplay, details of which are being kept under wraps for the present.*

Vernon folded up his newspaper. He had always enjoyed a close relationship with his stepdaughter, and until the hiccup in his marriage, the three of them, Judy, Sara and himself, had been a close knit family unit. There had been a lot of love and laughter between them.

Then when Vernon had lost his job in a round of cutbacks he had found it difficult to get work. Judy took on extra hours at the bakery but the bills had to be paid and things were desperate.

In the end Vernon had turned to the only other form of employment he knew — the horses. It didn't help their financial situation, but it stopped Vernon hanging around the house all day getting depressed as yet more job application rejections came through the post.

His long afternoons spent at the racetrack which had often stretched into the evening had finally been too much for Judy, who had grown tired of spending her spare time on her own, while her husband tried to work a system that would make them all rich.

It hadn't taken Vernon long to realise after the split with Judy that she had been right. There was no foolproof way to beat the system and he had been a fool to think there was. Too ashamed to admit defeat, he had drifted in and out of casual jobs, until he had finally managed to obtain a temporary gardening position in a country house hotel.

After the head gardener had handed in his notice Vernon had been offered the position on a permanent contract. From that day his fortune had changed.

Always happiest in the open air, Vernon had turned his talents to gardening and now his work was so much admired by visitors to the hotel, he often found himself conducting impromptu tours of the gardens and the huge greenhouses where he grew most of the fresh produce used by the chefs in the kitchens. Pride in his work had afforded him a new respect.

His skin had lost the pallor of his former unhealthy lifestyle and with the loss in weight and improved diet he felt years younger than his former self. Would Judy think so too? Seeing the picture of Sara made him realise how much he had missed them both — Judy, still his wife and Sara, his lovely stepdaughter.

Today was a rare day off. Summer was Vernon's busiest time and he hadn't wanted to leave his deputy in charge, but a chipped front tooth required urgent dental work and while he was recovering from the effects of the injection, he had taken time out in a coffee shop to read the newspaper. His days were so full now it was something he rarely did.

Vernon paid for his coffee then decided to take a stroll to the local garden centre. He was in no hurry to get back to the hotel and he needed to think things through and to clear his head.

He was sure Lyle Jackson had been the name of Sara's boyfriend, but there had been so much going on in his own personal life at the time that he hadn't realised Sara and Lyle were no longer an item until he learned that Sara's best friend, Carla de Courcy, had married Lyle. He would have contacted Sara then, but by the time he heard the news it was well over a year old and yet another opportunity for reconciliation slipped through his fingers.

Vernon frowned. The newspaper had suggested Sara was back with Lyle. Why? And why had she moved out of London? There were chunks of his stepdaughter's life he didn't know anything about. He should have been there for her when things began going wrong, but he'd been so wrapped up in himself . . . Vernon shook his head. It was no good going over old ground. What had passed was past and he had wasted too much time. He needed to think to the future.

Sara, his beautiful stepdaughter was

living less than ten miles away from him. Fate had handed him a chance to get in touch with her and he might never get another one.

He paused by a public telephone box. Perhaps he could make a start by calling Judy's old telephone number. He checked his pockets for change. It was at times like this he wished he carried a mobile phone, but working in the gardens all day, he had no real need of one.

He dialled the number, but there was no connection. The line was discontinued. Vernon hadn't held out much hope but it had been worth a try. He emerged from the phone box.

The sun was warm on his back and he decided to revert to his original plan to catch up with his friend in the local garden centre.

He jingled his coins in his pocket. It was good to feel solvent from a decent day's work. When he was at the hotel there was little outside distraction and he didn't miss his old life. All his meals and accommodation were provided and over the past two years he had built up a reasonable nest egg. He decided it was time to contact Judy again. Perhaps he could treat her to a meal at the hotel, Sara too.

He would need to get himself a proper suit of course. It had been months since Vernon had worn a tie, but it was something The Grange insisted on in their dress code.

In his horse racing days Vernon had possessed no end of suits and ties. He wondered what had become of them. Whatever, he wouldn't like to wear them again. He was a different person these days.

He walked past the rows of hanging baskets at the garden centre and spotted his friend by the water display.

'My wife did your rose garden tour last weekend, Vernon,' the manager greeted him, 'so you owe me one.'

'I do?' Vernon raised his eyebrows, baffled.

'Not satisfied with our little patch

now, is she? I've spent every evening this week digging up the flowerbeds while she's been busy planning a new layout. My hands are a mass of blisters and my back's letting me know about it.'

'Well, if you need any help,' Vernon laughed, 'you know where I am. Want any help today?'

'Aren't you working?' Tony asked.

'I've been to the dentist. Face still feels a bit funny, but you know me, can't sit around doing nothing all day.'

'Well if you're sure you're up to it and as long as you keep it unofficial the barbecue section could do with a tidy up. It's all this hot weather, people are lapping up the stuff, I can't keep up with the demand. If you could clear me some space I'd be grateful, but don't overdo it. I don't want any accidents.'

'I won't,' Vernon assured him.

'By the way,' Tony called out after him, 'I'm expecting a visit from the area manager so if he comes in pretend to be a member of the public.'

'Will do.' Vernon strolled over to the outdoor entertaining display and immediately began tidying up.

Physical work helped Vernon keep his mind off his personal life, but seeing the picture of Sara had jolted his memory. It was time he did something. He had to see his stepdaughter again and let her know this time he would be there for her, should she need him. Perhaps through Sara he could contact Judy too.

His face softened. Judy was still the love of his life. She had been his only girlfriend, and he had counted himself the luckiest man in the world when she had agreed to marry him on their second date. Life had been hard for her, after the death of her first husband and things could have been difficult between him and Sara. But Sara had been too young to remember her real father and she and Vernon had fallen in love with each other from the day they had met.

How could Vernon have been such a fool to throw that love away? It was a mistake he wouldn't make again.

If Judy had moved on then he would wish her luck and not interfere, but if she hadn't . . .

'Time for a rest,' Tony strolled over interrupting his thoughts. 'You've done a good job. I'm expecting a delivery next week and I was wondering where to put it all. Fancy a cup of tea?'

Vernon gave a slightly lopsided smile and prodded his jaw. 'Think I'm getting the feeling back in my face, a cup of tea would be lovely. Moving displays is thirsty work.'

'Would you mind manning the phones in the office while I make it? I won't be long.'

Vernon nodded. He and Tony enjoyed a good working relationship often using the same casual workers during busy periods. It was a system that worked well and ensured they had a bank of reliable staff they could call on at a moment's notice.

Vernon sat down at Tony's desk. The telephone rang and Vernon looked round hurriedly for pencil and paper.

'Mr Jones?'

'He's not here at the moment. May I take a message?'

'We have an order for a new barbecue and I understand they're due to be delivered next week.'

'That's right, Madam,' Vernon replied, 'I've just been rearranging the old stock to make room for the new delivery.'

'That's splendid. If you could tell Mr Jones that I rang. The name's Henderson, do you have our number?'

'If you could perhaps refresh my memory, Madam?' Vernon scribbled down the contact and as he was replacing the receiver Tony came back into the office with two mugs of tea.

'Telephone call?' he asked as he passed one over.

'About a barbecue. A Mrs Henderson? I've got her number here.'

'Don't worry. I've got all the details in a special file for our more important clients. She's ex-directory and we have to keep them separate. I'll ring her back later. They always have a children's party for the little girl about the time school breaks up, then something for the adults in the evening. It's usually quite a big affair. They hold it every year.'

Vernon nodded. 'Saw a picture of my little girl today,' he blurted out.

Tony raised his eyebrows. He had no idea Vernon had been married. He rarely talked about his private life and Tony did not pry.

'Did you?' Tony kept his question casual.

'Actually she's not so little these days. She's twenty-five.'

'Daughters are always little girls to their fathers, I suppose,' Tony replied.

Vernon dragged the newspaper out of his coat pocket. 'There.' He pointed to the picture of Sara.

Tony's jaw dropped in surprise. 'Your daughter works for Lyle Jackson?'

'That's right. She knew him years ago. She used to share a place with Carla de Courcy, his ex-wife.'

'Fancy that.' Tony handed the paper back to Vernon with a smile. 'I had no idea your family moved in such exalted circles. Will you be going to the barbecue?'

'Barbecue?' Vernon asked with a slight frown.

'That was Mrs Henderson on the phone, wasn't it?' Tony asked. Vernon nodded. 'She's the housekeeper at Medway Manor, Lyle Jackson's house. It's his little girl who's having the party.'

'What?' Vernon demanded.

'Look out,' Tony hissed quickly almost spilling his tea over the desk, 'the area manager's walked in. You'd better make yourself scarce. Thanks for your help and all that.'

Before Vernon could say a word he was hustled out of the office. 'Thank you, sir,' Tony said loudly. 'We'll be in touch about the barbecue next week. Ah, Mr Simpkins, didn't see you there.' He turned in feigned surprise to the area manager who was chatting to the check out staff by the tills.

Vernon took the hint and hurried out the back way, his head reeling. In the space of a morning he had discovered his daughter was living less than ten miles away from him, working for Lyle Jackson at Medway Manor and due to another quirk of fate he had the telephone number for Medway Manor burning a hole in his coat pocket.

A Surprising Phone Call

Sara began to wish Carla had never raised the idea of a summer barbecue. So what if it was a family tradition? Circumstances had changed over the past year. Sara had been on the point of confronting Lyle in his conservatory to voice her views on the matter when Jenny had forestalled her by dancing into the kitchen.

'What day are we having my party this year, Sara?' she asked. 'I've done my invitations all on my own. Look.' She thrust a wad of paper under Sara's nose. ''Cos you were so busy. But I don't know the date.'

'There's a good girl,' Mrs Henderson had cooed over the lurid felt pen invitations. 'That's such a help.' She looked at the calendar. 'How about the last Saturday in July, Sara? Would that be convenient? I'm due to visit my sister in August. In fact, I must have a word with Mr Jackson about that.'

Looking at their two hopeful faces and unable to disappoint the excited little girl, Sara found herself agreeing to the last Saturday in July.

The telephone hadn't stopped ringing since. Sara hadn't realised Jenny had quite so many best friends and Mrs Henderson had dug out last year's list and added a few more names for the evening do.

'It's going to be my best party ever,' Jenny capered around the kitchen every time another telephone acceptance came through.

'Doesn't anyone ever refuse an invitation?' Sara demanded.

'Not one of Mr Jackson's,' Mrs Henderson replied. 'The gardens always look lovely at this time of year and he's a very good host.'

Sara bit down the retort hovering on her lips. Lyle may be a good host but he certainly wasn't a good organiser. Ever since the date had been set, she'd hardly seen him. He had decamped to the summerhouse with his laptop and refused to get involved in any of the arrangements.

'Paying the bills will be my contribution,' had been his snappy reply when Sara asked if there were any guests he would like to invite to the evening reception.

'When he's working,' Mrs Henderson had explained, 'it doesn't do to disturb him.'

Although the thunderstorm had cleared the atmosphere for a day or two, temperatures had soared again and Sara was beginning to wonder if they would still need the marquee she had ordered.

'We will if the rain returns,' Mrs Henderson had advised her. 'Best stick with it. One year it was a wash out and everyone poured into the house. Mr Jackson was not best pleased. The carpets were ruined.'

Jenny, thoroughly over excited by the whole affair had started to play up, and

Mrs Henderson was using the occasion as an excuse to embark on a burst of spring-cleaning. There wasn't a surface that didn't gleam, or a carpet that hadn't been beaten to within an inch of its life. Curtains had been taken down and cleaned and the windows were so bright they almost gave Sara a headache every time she looked out of them.

True to his word, Lyle had arranged for Sara's car to have a thorough overhaul and like the house, every part was now in pristine working order.

There had been a brief tussle between them when Lyle had insisted on meeting the costs.

'I don't want you breaking down again, so think of it as insurance.'

'But it's my car.'

'And it's my daughter you drive around in it to her after school activities, not to mention half the rest of her class. We are responsible for those children when they are in our care. How do you think their parents would feel if, due to your stubbornness, everyone was stranded in a storm like the other night because your car wouldn't start?'

Sara had fumed. She couldn't fault Lyle's logic, but she hated to be indebted to him. She also hated to admit that her car had never run better in her life. Her little engine purred along the Kent lanes now and with all her dents and bumps knocked out of the bodywork, she was like a new car.

The drive home from Beach View Cottage after the storm had taken well over two hours due to all the flood diversions and by the time they had finally driven into the forecourt of Medway Manor, the first streaks of dawn were visible in the sky. Lyle had informed Sara in very curt language that there was no way either of them were going through that experience again.

Mrs Henderson had been beside herself with worry and had clucked around Sara like an anxious mother hen.

All of which made Sara feel intensely guilty and realised she was being foolish in not accepting Lyle's offer to pay for the maintenance to her car.

Sara stopped polishing to pick up the telephone as it rang yet again. It was Carla.

'Hi. How're things?' she asked.

'Busy. How about you?' Sara asked.

'Up to my eyes in it. You would not believe the hours I am working. The director is an absolute slave driver. I was only supposed to be on call for two weeks, but the schedule's slipped badly and as another actor's dropped out, my part's been built up.'

'That's good news, isn't it?' Sara asked, 'think of the extra exposure.'

'It's also a lot of extra work.' Carla sounded tired. 'I don't know when I'll get a day off and I'm not sure I'll be able to come to the barbecue. I know I said to Jenny I'd be there and I'll do my best, but I can't promise anything.'

Sara bit her lip. That was so like Carla. The wretched barbecue had been her idea in the first place.

'That's all right,' Sara said, appreciating it wasn't really fair to sound off at Carla, and it wasn't her fault her workload had increased. 'I understand and I'm sure Jenny will too. With a bit of luck she'll tire herself out with her friends in the afternoon and won't miss you.'

'I know you mean well, Sara, but it doesn't make my day to know my daughter won't even miss me at her party,' Carla sighed.

'Sorry,' Sara apologised. 'I do tell her all the exciting things you're doing and we talk about you every night before she goes to sleep.'

'Bless you for that,' Carla said.

'Did you want to talk to Lyle?' Sara asked.

'Is he there?'

'He's taken himself off to the summerhouse, says there are too many interruptions in the main house.'

'Same old Lyle.' Carla laughed, back in a good humour. 'Don't disturb him.

Is he working on *Exchange*?'

'I think so.'

'I bumped into Monty Daniels yesterday. He said the talks with the backers are going well. It's all very exciting,' Carla paused. 'How are things between you and Joe?'

Sara had not heard from Joe since the night at thc cottage. 'Did you give him this number and tell him I was here?' she demanded.

'I have to admit I did, darling. Nothing wrong in that, is there?'

'No, but I was trying to move on.'

'Why? He's a good career contact.'

'For who?' Sara demanded, well used to Carla's ways. She knew Carla wouldn't be above using Sara's connection with Joe if it put her in Monty Daniels' good books.

'You, of course.'

'My acting career is never going to match yours. In fact, I've put it on hold.'

'Don't do anything hasty,' Carla sounded anxious. 'Ditching Monty

Daniels' son is not a good move.'

'I already have.'

'That's not what I heard. In fact, there's a rumour doing the rounds that you're up for a part in *Exchange* and Joe is helping you. Is it true?'

'It's only gossip, Carla. You don't want to believe everything you hear. You know what people are like. What they don't know they make up. Joe was probably showing off. *Exchange* is going to be a big vehicle for you. I'm not going to cramp your style. Anyway, I don't expect to hear from Joe again.'

This wasn't entirely true, but Sara wanted to squash any stories about the pair of them still being an item. Media attention was not something she enjoyed. Being pursued by photographers on her day's shopping trip had been a nasty shock. Sara did not like having her privacy invaded and she didn't like to think what would happen if the press got a sniff of a further story about her.

Lyle hadn't been best pleased her

cover had been blown either.

'They didn't hurt you, did they?' he demanded when she told him how she had been pursued by the press.

'Of course not. It was a bit of a shock, that's all. I mean, how did they find out I was working for you?'

'That's what I would like to know,' Lyle replied grimly, 'and if I ever find out who tipped them off they'd better stay out of my way.'

He'd flung Mrs Henderson's newspaper into the rubbish bin and stormed off back to work on his script.

Sara overheard someone call Carla's name.

'Sorry, darling, I've got to go. Needed on set. Give Jenny a kiss for me and tell her I'll make it up to her once filming is over.'

'Mrs Jackson's career seems to be going from strength to strength, doesn't it?' Mrs Henderson remarked as she and Sara put the final touches to yet more party food. The freezer was bulging and by Sara's reckoning they had laid up enough food for a siege, but Mrs Henderson still insisted on a daily bake. 'It'll mean a lot of extra work for you if she gets this new role.'

'For me?' Sara looked up from the tray of sausage rolls she was taking out of the oven.

'She'll be away filming most of the time, and what with Mr Jackson flying backwards and forwards to America, someone's got to look after young Jenny.'

'Why does everyone rely on me?' Sara demanded.

'Because, my dear,' Mrs Henderson smiled at her, 'Medway Manor could not function without you.'

* * *

Sara hadn't realised until then quite how reliant everyone seemed to be on her. Mrs Henderson had been talking about extending her holiday visit to her sister in the summer and Sara's temporary contract of a month's work had been extended with Lyle assuming she would stay on indefinitely.

The telephone began ringing again.

'What now?' Sara muttered, but before she could pick up the receiver, she heard Lyle taking the call in the drawing room.

'It's for you,' Lyle strolled into the kitchen. 'Joe Daniels.'

Sara's heart sank as she took in the grim expression on Lyle's face. Further confrontation with him she did not need.

'I can't imagine why he's ringing me,' she began in an effort to placate him.

'Don't you think you'd better take the call and see? Any coffee on the go, Mrs H?' Lyle asked, picking up a newly baked biscuit from the cooling tray.

'Yes, of course. I could have brought it out to you in the summerhouse, Mr Jackson.'

Lyle shook his head. 'I needed a break to stretch my legs.'

Mrs Henderson bustled away to see to the coffee and Sara crept into the drawing room and picked up the receiver. 'Joe?'

'Sorry I haven't been in touch sooner,' he began.

'You shouldn't be ringing me here at all.'

'Why not?' Joe sounded surprised. 'Lyle doesn't mind, does he?'

'I mind.'

'That's a pity because I've got some good news for you. I've managed to get you an informal audition for *Exchange*.'

'Joe, thanks and all that, but I'm not interested.'

'You can't be serious,' Joe sounded annoyed. 'I went to a lot of trouble to fix things up. There are actors out there who would give their right arm for an audition.'

'Then offer it to them.'

'You don't seem to understand what I've done for you, Sara.'

She began to grow annoyed. 'Look, Joe, you were the one who telephoned me. This interview was your idea, not mine. I'm sorry if you feel let down, but

I never wanted the audition in the first place.'

'That's not what you led me to believe, but if that's the way you feel,' he snapped, 'there's nothing I can do about it.'

'It is.'

'You might have told me earlier,' he grumbled.

'I tried to that night at Beach View Cottage, but you drove off.' Sara had been about to add: when you left me stranded in the storm, then decided she didn't have the energy for another argument with Joe.

'If you really mean what you're saying, then this is goodbye,' Joe said.

'I thought we had already said goodbye,' Sara replied and then winced as Joe slammed down the receiver.

'Another tiff?'

She had been unaware that Lyle had come into the room.

'That was a private call,' she turned on him, 'you had no right to listen in.'

'I didn't need to. From the way you

were yelling at each other, I should think half the village heard you.'

'You may as well know now, before you hear it from another source. The other night at the cottage Joe promised me a part in *Exchange*.'

'Did he indeed? Since when has Joe Daniels been appointed casting director?'

'I tried to explain I wasn't interested but he rushed off before I could tell him.'

'Leaving you to call me up to rescue you?'

'I did no such thing,' Sara flashed at him. 'I didn't need rescuing. I was calling Mrs Henderson.'

'Because your car wouldn't start and without me you wouldn't have got it going again.'

The look on Lyle's face was infuriating Sara.

'I would have managed — somehow,' she insisted.

Lyle's slow smile told Sara he didn't believe her. Sara didn't know why she was reacting so strongly to Lyle's goading.

'Have a biscuit?' he held up the plate he was still carrying. 'Mrs H's finest.'

'No thank you.' Sara would have swept out of the room if the telephone hadn't started ringing again.

'Aren't you going to answer it?' he asked. 'It's probably another of your boyfriends.'

'For your information I don't have a string of boyfriends. I don't have a boyfriend at all.'

'In that case,' Lyle picked up the receiver. 'Hello? Medway Manor? Yes. Yes, she is. You'd better speak to her yourself. Who's calling please?'

Something in Lyle's voice caused Sara to turn round in the doorway.

'It's for you,' he said in a voice as hard as stone.

'Who is it?' she asked.

'It seems you do have a boyfriend you've forgotten about. Someone called Vernon?'

Sara was glad she was holding on to

the door as the room began to sway.

'Do you know a Vernon Pickering?' Lyle asked.

'Yes.'

'He says he would like to invite you out to dinner at The Grange.'

'What?'

'I suppose you'll be free now you've ditched Joe.' Lyle handed over the receiver and walked out of the room, carefully closing the door behind him.

An Unforgettable Meeting

The restaurant was bustling with lunchtime diners. Lyle sat opposite Monty Daniels at one of the tables that overlooked the terrace leading down to the landscaped gardens.

'I've heard good reports of the cuisine here,' Monty said as Lyle settled down. 'They've got an excellent chef who uses only their own fresh garden produce.'

The raised dais offered the two men a degree of privacy away from the other tables for which Lyle was grateful. Monty rather enjoyed fine dining and being the centre of attention, but leisurely lunches weren't really Lyle's thing, although he had to accept a certain amount of networking was important in his line of business and an update meeting with Monty was overdue.

Unaware of the interest his presence was attracting from the other diners, most of them female, Lyle sipped his mineral water.

'I can't tempt you to a glass of Cabernet Sauvignon?' Monty asked.

'I tend to avoid alcohol in the middle of the day if I'm working in the afternoon.'

'Very wise,' Monty replied and took another sip of his wine.

Monty was in an expansive mood and he was all smiles. Lyle was the most important writer on the team and he was anxious to know how things were progressing.

'So, how are you?' Monty asked, 'You're looking well. It must be all the Kentish fresh air.'

'Thank you.' Lyle was glad Sara had reminded him to shave before he had left home that morning. When he was on a roll his work took preference over everything else. Between them, Sara and Mrs Henderson made sure he had a presentable shirt to wear and that his jacket was crease free. Lyle wished he could loosen his tie. It was warm in the restaurant and he was finding the atmosphere slightly claustrophobic.

'And how is your lovely ex-wife?' Monty asked.

'Carla? As far as I know she's well, too. We haven't seen much of her lately.'

'I'm getting good feedback on her latest performance,' Monty informed him. 'I understand she's not difficult on set, she's always on time and knows her lines.'

Lyle acknowledged his words with a smile.

'I know little about Carla's side of the camera, but she was always very professional. I'm pleased for her, she works hard and deserves her success.'

'I must say it's refreshing to deal with a high profile couple who are still on speaking terms with each other, even though they are no longer together,' Monty said.

Lyle fiddled with his tie. He rarely gave interviews and felt uneasy talking about his personal life, although he appreciated Monty had a vested interest in Carla's personal circumstances he couldn't shake off the feeling that Monty was probing.

'As you know we have a daughter and neither of us wants her to be disturbed by our change of circumstances. As far as Jenny is concerned we are still a loving family and that is what matters most to Carla and myself, besides which I have tremendous respect for my ex-wife. She is an extremely talented woman and a loving mother.'

'Very commendable.' Monty nodded his approval. He cut a delicate square of toast, spread some paté on it and chewed thoughtfully before he spoke again.

'You do realise that if Carla is offered a lead role in *Exchange* it may mean a move to America and she would probably want to take Jenny with her?'

Lyle was too experienced to betray

any emotion in front of Monty. The thought had crossed his mind and it was one that bothered him. His home was here with Jenny, but he realised the child needed her mother, and if Carla chose to live in America it could mean a significant change in everyone's lives.

'Nothing's certain yet, is it?' Lyle asked carefully.

'Another wise answer,' a slow smile spread across Monty's face, 'and you're right. In this business nothing is certain. However, I should like to know how you feel about things?'

'Like I say, Carla is a very talented actress. If she gets the part then she will of course have my full support and we may have to have a rethink on our domestic arrangements, but as the project is only in its early stages any comment from me might be a little premature.'

'You know how to deliver your public relations,' Monty conceded with an understanding smile.

'I was under the impression this

lunch was to discuss my progress with the working script,' Lyle reminded him, 'not my wife's career.'

'Indeed, yes.' Monty was all expansive smiles again and signalled to the wine waiter to refill his glass. 'May I know how your work is going?'

'To schedule, but it's tough.'

'Are there any problems?'

Lyle on his own ground was now happy to fill Monty in.

'Working on a groundbreaking piece like this is challenging. It's contemporary and I'm enjoying it. It's one I want to get absolutely right.'

'I would expect nothing else from a writer of your calibre,' Monty agreed. 'Will you need to go to America again?'

'Possibly, but not in the immediate future. I can work from home and I like to be there when Carla is away filming, especially as we have Jenny's summer holidays coming up. My housekeeper always takes a break with her sister in August and then there's the barbecue, so things are quite busy at the moment.'

'Ah yes. I have received my usual invite for your summer party. Thank you. I will send a reply via my secretary. I hope to be able to attend. All these plans do not interfere with your work schedule?'

'Sara is seeing to all the arrangements for the barbecue. I haven't been involved very much. Things are a bit hectic, but I can manage. I'm in constant internet touch with the rest of the scripting team and we conference call daily.'

Monty's smile had thinned at the mention of Sara's name.

'Sara Armitage, she has recently taken over as your daughter's nanny, I believe?'

Lyle nodded as the waiters replaced their starters with two rare steaks.

'I wasn't aware she was trained in childcare.' Monty cut into his steak and nodded his approval to the hovering waiter.

'She isn't, but we needed someone at short notice and she and Jenny seem to get along fine.' Lyle hesitated before adding, 'Sara, too, needed to rearrange her personal life.'

They were treading on delicate ground now. Lyle fully realised how important Monty was to both his own and Carla's careers and had no wish to antagonise him, but there was no escaping from the issues he had with Monty's son, Joe, over the way he had driven off leaving Sara alone at the cottage in the middle of the worst storm the country had experienced in years.

'Sara is also a friend of your ex-wife's?'

'They shared a hostel in their student days, yes. In view of the family connection it seemed an ideal solution to our problem. Jenny is very happy with the arrangement and that's important too.'

'Of course.'

If Monty was aware of Lyle's past relationship with Sara he made no reference to it.

'You know about my son's relationship with Miss Armitage?'

'Yes.'

'I can't say I'm too disappointed that it's over. She's a very independent, self-willed young woman. My son is an altogether different sort of person. At first I was very annoyed when she walked out on him. It upset his mother who dotes on him.'

'She'll get over it,' Lyle said briskly.

'I'm sure you can understand Joe is as precious to his mother and I as your daughter is to you. I want the best for him.'

'With due respect, Monty,' Lyle felt obliged to point out, 'your son is twenty-nine years old. He's a grown man and quite capable of running his own life. My daughter is only five.'

'That's as maybe.' Monty shrugged off Lyle's comments. 'But when I learned of Sara's friendship with Carla I almost did not want to consider Carla for the lead in *Exchange*, then I realised that was very short sighted of me.'

Lyle bit his lip. It was only deference and respect for Monty's senior years that prevented him from saying that in his opinion Monty was acting like a fool. Carla had absolutely nothing to do with Joe's personal life, or Sara's come to that, and anyway if the rumours were to be believed, Joe hadn't exactly been the innocent party in the break up.

'I'm glad you changed your mind,' Lyle chose his words carefully, wondering how soon he could make his excuses to leave. They'd dealt with the business of the day and it was growing uncomfortably warm in the restaurant. Someone had opened the large double doors that lead on to the terrace but it seemed to make no difference to the temperature inside. Lyle looked longingly at the party outside doing the garden tour.

Accepting Monty's lunch invitation had not been the welcome break he had been expecting from the chaos that was currently Medway Manor, and he found himself wishing he'd chosen to share one of Mrs Henderson's modest soup and sandwich lunches in the kitchen.

Lately lunch had become something of a ritual. When Sara joined them the atmosphere was always relaxed and full of laughter. She knew exactly how far to go when teasing Mrs Henderson and the older woman displayed a rare talent for mimicry that had both Lyle and Sara often helpless with laughter.

Sara's hair had grown and was looking much more feminine.

He'd noticed a change in Mrs Henderson, too, ever since Sara's arrival. She had been beginning to crack under the strain of Carla's departure and the extra workload it entailed, but Sara's cheerful nature and willingness to help with any of the chores had made a big difference. These days the house was no longer the cold shell it had been after Carla's departure. Now it was a home full of warmth and laughter.

The family atmosphere didn't stop

his heated exchange of views with Sara, but he didn't mind that either. No family was perfect and the occasional difference of opinion only served to spice things up between them.

Lyle's lips curled into a reluctant smile as he remembered how only that morning Sara had given him as good as she got when he voiced his opinion on what he thought of the noise being made by the gang of workmen erecting the marquee in the middle of the lawn.

'Of course,' Monty was speaking again, 'I suppose I should be grateful to Miss Armitage. She actually turned down Joe's offer of an audition for a part in *Exchange*.'

Monty finished his wine and dabbed his mouth with his serviette. 'As I understand it from my son he very foolishly made professional promises he had no right to. He placed me in a rather delicate situation. Miss Armitage's refusal to be considered for an audition was, I am forced to say, a great relief.'

'I'm pleased she solved your problem for you, Monty.'

'Yes,' Monty appeared not to notice the stiffness in Lyle's voice. 'I think we can safely assume any feelings between them are now over.'

'I should think they were over the night Joe abandoned Sara at Beach View cottage.'

'He told me all about that. He was called in to work at short notice. He had to go. Sara understood this.'

'And I'm sure you'll understand how I felt when she rang to say her car wouldn't start and she was stranded.'

'You can hardly blame Joe for that, and to a girl of Sara's resourcefulness I'm sure that didn't present a challenge.'

'I had to drive out there to rescue her.'

Monty shrugged. 'That rather proves my point, doesn't it? In the long run things work out. Now, cheese?' Monty indicated the dessert trolley.

Lyle shook his head. 'Just a black

coffee for me please.'

As Monty chose a portion of a creamy fruit and meringue concoction with extra strawberries, Lyle's attention wandered back to the tour party in the garden outside.

The stragglers were bringing up the rear. A lone couple strolled along laughing together, hand in hand as they shared a joke.

The man was a lot older than his partner and as they walked the sunlight caught the woman's face.

Lyle blinked unable to believe his eyes as the man cupped Sara's face in the palm of his hand and kissed her tenderly on the top of the head. Lyle felt as though someone had punched him in the stomach. In the early afternoon sunlight Sara had never looked lovelier in her sundress and he wanted to race outside and drag the man away from her.

Monty finished pouring cream over his dessert.

'You could be right, Lyle, about Joe's

behaviour at Beach View cottage. Perhaps I should apologise to Miss Armitage on his behalf. What do you think? Will I see her at the barbecue?'

It was a moment before Lyle felt able to reply.

'I shouldn't worry about Sara, Monty,' he said in a voice he barely recognised as his own. 'As you said, she's a resourceful girl and I think you'll find she's already found a replacement for Joe.'

'Have You Told Her About Us?'

It felt so natural to slip her hand into her stepfather's Sara thought, as they strolled through the rose garden together. He squeezed her fingers in acknowledgement of the gesture.

'I've missed you so much,' he said gently. 'Am I forgiven?'

'There's nothing to forgive,' Sara assured him. Dressed in his smart casual uniform of open necked shirt and grey flannel trousers, he looked a different man from the last time she had seen him when he had tried to explain to her that he would be moving out of the family home for a while as he and her mother both needed some personal space. Sara had been confused and angry and upset and hadn't listened to anything he wanted to say.

'I think there is. I should never have lost contact with you and I am ashamed that I did, but your mother was unhappy and I could see we needed time apart. I hadn't thought our separation would last as long as it did.'

'Me neither.'

Sara had been so distraught over losing Lyle to Carla that she hadn't given much thought to contacting Vernon later to see how he was getting on. When her life had settled down again he had moved on from the temporary address he had given her mother and any further attempts to contact him had resulted in a dead end, but she never stopped hoping that one day he would contact her and now that day was here, she could hardly believe he was standing beside her and looking so well.

'I can't tell you how happy I was when I saw your picture in that newspaper. I felt as though I had been given a second chance.'

'And to think,' Sara admitted with a

reluctant smile, 'I actually ran away from that cameraman. If he hadn't been so persistent and followed me he never would have got that picture. I'm surprised you recognised me. It wasn't a very good shot. I was about to lash out at him with my handbag.'

'Well, you looked so scary it did almost put me off,' Vernon teased her, 'but you know me. I'm made of strong stuff although my heart was in my mouth when I dialled your number. It took me ages to pluck up the courage. In the end the lads threatened to lock me in the staff room and not let me out until I'd made that call.'

'I'm glad they did.'

'Was that Lyle Jackson who answered the call?'

'Yes,' Sara did her best to keep her voice steady.

'I hope he didn't mind. I shouldn't really have dialled his number. Tony told me it was ex-directory and it only came into my hands by accident. But I couldn't think what else to do and in the end the temptation was too much. If Tony hadn't hustled me out of his office that day and shoved my note in my coat pocket I would never have gone back for it. I mean it was a breach of confidence, wasn't it?'

'I won't tell anyone what you did. Anyway, you're entitled to use Lyle's telephone number,' Sara protested. 'You're family.'

'Quite right.' Vernon's face broke into its battered smile. Many years ago he'd been involved in a motorbike accident, after which he'd required extensive plastic surgery.

Now, no one, not even Sara who loved him dearly, could say he was a handsome man, but that didn't alter how she felt about him.

She was prouder of him than she had ever been in her life. He had his fair share of faults, but he'd pulled himself back from the brink and made a success of his new life, and now she'd found him again she had no intention of losing him.

'I can't believe you're responsible for all this.' She gestured to the crowning glory of the rose garden and the delicate trelliswork surrounding the water feature.

'Neither can I,' Vernon admitted. 'I've been so lucky. If this job hadn't have come up when it did I don't know what I would have done. I was drifting around not really doing anything much.

'Now my days aren't long enough to achieve all I want to. I've got plans to extend the kitchen garden and I've been given an increased budget for next year's season.

'The management was overwhelmed by the success of my garden tours and the extra business it brought in. We always do a roaring trade in cream teas afterwards and Ricardo, the head chef, is in line for an extra rosette and they don't dish those out lightly. He says if he gets it it'll be because of the quality of the vegetables we grow in the kitchen garden.' Vernon's face was alight with excitement as he recounted his successes.

'That's absolutely terrific, Vernon.'

'And,' he added as an afterthought, 'I haven't been near a racecourse for years. I don't even miss the horses any more. Would you believe on my days off I now read gardening catalogues? When I'm not catching up with my beautiful daughter, that is.'

They smiled into each other's eyes. Vernon tucked a stray strand of hair behind Sara's ear.

'How is Judy?' he asked.

It was the first time he had mentioned Sara's mother. Sara could have given Vernon her new telephone number and told him to contact Judy himself, but she suspected the reconciliation with her mother might not run so smoothly.

She'd been forced to move after Vernon's departure and there'd been a lot of upheaval in her life.

'Working as hard as ever running the health food store in town,' Sara replied.

'I'm always trying to get her to take a holiday, but you know what she's like.'

'Does she enjoy the work?'

'Some days are harder than others, but you'll never hear her admit she's tired.'

'She always was as stubborn as a mule that one.' Vernon's voice was almost a growl of disapproval. 'I used to have to force her to take a day off.' He paused. 'Have you told her about us? About me?'

'Not yet.' Sara shook her head. 'I'll need to pick my moment.'

'Understood.' He nodded, 'but don't wait too long. I've let enough time slip through my fingers. I don't want her to forget me completely.'

'She would never do that, Vernon. There's been no one else since you left. She'd probably kill me for telling you this, but I happen to know she keeps a picture of you in her bedside table.'

'She does?'

'Do you remember the year we spent your birthday by the sea?'

Vernon threw back his head and laughed. 'I've always tried my best to forget it. It poured with rain the whole time and whose idea was it to take a picnic to enjoy on the beach?'

'Mum's probably. She'd even made you a cake and she was determined we'd eat it even though the wind was howling round us and rain was falling out of the sky like there was no tomorrow.'

'She didn't keep that dreadful photo of me shouting at her as that seagull pinched my sandwiches, did she?'

'I'm afraid she did. Actually it always makes us laugh.'

'Does it?' Vernon asked wistfully. 'That's good, because I was absolutely at my worst that day, wasn't I?'

'Yes,' Sara admitted. 'You were so grumpy we had to warm you up on the pier.'

'Didn't I win a brooch in one of those silly machines?'

'Mum's still got that too.'

'Has she?' Vernon's voice was a bit hoarse now.

'I'll ring her as soon as I can,' Sara promised, 'but things are a bit hectic at Medway Manor at the moment, what with Jenny's party and the summer barbecue.'

'Tell me about yourself and this job of yours. I want all the details. This Lyle Jackson you're now working for, is he the same Lyle Jackson I remember from your past?'

Sara could feel a faint flush staining the delicate skin around the base of her neck. 'Yes,' she admitted.

'I thought so. What happened between you?' Vernon asked softly, hating to see the distress in her eyes. 'I wish I'd been there for you when it all blew up.'

'I introduced him to Carla.'

Vernon nodded. 'You don't need to say any more.'

'Did you ever meet her?'

'Only once. She's a famous actress now, isn't she?'

'Yes.'

'And Lyle Jackson's a scriptwriter?'

'A very successful one.'

'But they're no longer married?'

Vernon raised a querying eyebrow.

'That's why I'm looking after Jenny, their daughter. Carla's in the middle of moving into a flat, but her filming commitments mean it's taking much longer than she would like.'

'It sounds a very modern situation. Mrs Jackson doesn't live at Medway Manor any more, but you do?'

'I know it sounds strange, Vernon, but it's working well. I take Jenny to school in the morning then the day is my own until she comes home. I help out around the house. Mrs Henderson, that's the housekeeper, she also lives in, but she finds the house a bit too much to handle on her own.'

'I'm glad you're chaperoned,' Vernon said rather primly. 'I don't want Lyle Jackson worming his way into your affections again.'

'You need have no worries on that score, Vernon,' Sara assured him. 'Lyle and I, well, let's just say the chemistry's not there any more.'

'I wish I could believe you,' he said,

his eyes boring into hers.

Sara bit her lip. She had forgotten how Vernon could tune into her every mood. He wasn't convinced by her words and if she was totally honest neither was Sara herself. She knew how Lyle felt about her, he had made his feelings perfectly clear, when he accused her of all sorts of things at the time of Vernon's telephone call, but none of that stopped Sara from feeling about him as she did.

She knew it was illogical, but the night in the barn at Beach View Cottage had resurrected all the old feelings she had for him and she knew she was as hopelessly in love with him as ever.

'I haven't mentioned anything yet to Lyle,' Sara changed the subject, 'but Mrs Henderson told me in confidence last week she is actually thinking of leaving and going to live permanently with her sister. They've been talking about it for a while. Her sister is also a widow and has recently retired from her job, and Mrs Henderson says although she loves her job,, ever since Carla left she's been finding things are getting on top of her.'

'What will you do if she does leave?'

'I don't know. I'm at a bit of a crossroads myself. I have been thinking about giving up acting and training as a childminder. It's something that has always interested me.'

'Good idea. I'll support you while you're training,' Vernon said. 'So you needn't worry about finance. I dare say we could even fit you up with a room here somewhere. Childminding would be a much more steady job than acting and with so many couples working you'd never be out of a job.'

'Mr Pickering?' A middle-aged lady approached them. 'I'm sorry to disturb you, but I was wondering if you could let me have a few details about the type of soil here and how you work it?'

'Go ahead,' Sara nodded at Vernon and the pleasant faced visitor, 'I'll rest up here for a few moments and enjoy the sun.'

She glanced at her watch as she sat down on one of the benches placed around the water feature. Time was getting on. She would need to leave soon, to pick up Jenny from school.

* * *

It had been a good opportunity to meet up with Vernon today, especially as Lyle was meeting Monty for lunch and Mrs Henderson wanted to change her library books.

After dropping her off at the bus stop, Sara had driven on to The Grange. It would have been too complicated to accept Vernon's initial invitation to dinner in the restaurant as that would have meant taking the evening off and Sara felt disinclined to advise Lyle of the true nature of her relationship with Vernon.

Sara wondered briefly what her mother would say when she told her about Vernon. She was a hard working, proud woman and although Sara did not want to feel disloyal she couldn't help suspecting that some of the blame for the break up was her mother's. She didn't doubt Vernon when he said all he had been trying to do was to provide a better life for her and Sara. With a little more understanding on both sides, things might have been resolved a lot sooner.

She sighed and closing her eyes raised her face to get the full benefit of the sunshine. Today was a little cooler than it had been recently and it was pleasant to enjoy the gentler heat.

In the distance she could hear the murmur of voices as the last of the visitors made their way through the gardens. It gave her a thrill of pride to hear them discussing Vernon's work in glowing terms.

'That was quick,' she said opening her eyes as a shadow blotted out the sunshine and someone sat down on the bench next to her.

Only it wasn't Vernon. It was Lyle Jackson.

'What are you doing here?' Sara asked in astonishment as she opened her eyes.

'I could ask you the same thing,' he said as he loosened his tie and opened his collar. He slung his jacket over the back of the seat and rolled up his sleeves. Sara tried not to notice the fine down of hairs on his arms.

She turned away and looked around for Vernon. She hoped he wouldn't come back and find her with Lyle. He was quite capable of making a scene if Lyle began to get difficult.

'If you must know,' he said, 'I was having lunch with Monty in the restaurant, when I looked out of the window and saw you and,' he paused, 'your new boyfriend enjoying a very cosy walk across the grass hand in hand. That is Vernon, I suppose?'

'So what if it is?' Sara responded, a challenge in her eyes.

It had not entered her head that Monty would choose to come here for lunch, but it made sense. The Grange had been generating a lot of publicity recently and Monty always had his finger on the pulse when it came to current fashion.

'I never thought I'd say this but I almost feel sorry for Joe Daniels. It didn't take you long to find a replacement, did it? Isn't that Vernon rather old for you?' There was scorn in Lyle's voice as he posed his question.

'That's my business, isn't it?' Sara was outraged by the personal nature of his remarks. If they hadn't been in such a public place and the fact she didn't want to embarrass Vernon, she would have told Lyle exactly what she thought of his suspicions about her.

'And to think I was beginning to believe there might be an innocent explanation behind his telephone call the other evening.'

'Believe what you like, it makes very little difference to me. Now I must be going.' Sara stood up and straightened her dress. 'It's nearly time to collect Jenny from school.'

Lyle also stood up, slinging his jacket over his shoulder.

'I think your boyfriend is trying to attract your attention.'

Speechless with a mixture of anger and confusion, Sara watched Lyle stroll back to the hotel, ignoring Vernon as he walked straight past him.

Vernon rejoined Sara. 'Who was that?' he asked.

Sara shook her head. 'It doesn't matter.' She kissed Vernon on the cheek. 'I'll be in touch again soon. I have to go.'

An Emotional Day For Everyone

'I don't know what's wrong with everyone today,' Mrs Henderson complained. 'It must be the heat.'

Sara looked up from trying to get Jenny to finish her cereal.

'Mr Jackson snapped at me because his tea was cold. I pointed out it was hot when I poured it out. Carrying it across the lawn to the summerhouse does it no good.'

'You should have let me do it,' Sara reproached her.

'I couldn't,' Mrs Henderson looked scandalised. 'It wouldn't be proper. He was in his pyjamas and dressing-gown.'

'Don't want it.' Jenny pushed away her bowl so violently, milk slopped over the table.

Mrs Henderson pursed her lips.

'Jenny,' Sara chided the child. 'Say sorry to Mrs Henderson at once.'

She crossed her arms and glanced at Sara. 'Tastes funny.'

Sara took a deep breath.

'Then what about some toast?' she asked. 'You must have some breakfast and you're not leaving the house on an empty stomach.'

'In my day,' Mrs Henderson began.

'Yes, all right,' Sara snapped, then added, 'sorry.'

'We're none of us ourselves,' Mrs Henderson accepted her apology with good grace. 'Is the wee mite sickening for anything?'

Sara felt Jenny's forehead. It was hot, but not alarmingly so.

'Perhaps we'll let you off breakfast today,' she said then catching the child's gleeful smile added, 'but just this once. If I hear bad reports from your teacher you'll eat double porridge tomorrow.'

'Yuk.' Jenny made a face.

Sara grinned. Porridge was one of

Jenny's big hates and threats of double portions of the stuff normally quelled any rebellion at the breakfast table.

'Come on then.' Sara glanced at the wall clock. 'We're still a bit early as you didn't eat your breakfast, so we'll walk to school today. We can take the long way round by the meadow and look at the horses. We could both do with some fresh air to clear our heads.'

'Good idea. Fresh air never did anyone any harm.' Mrs Henderson opened the kitchen window wider. 'I shall be glad when that thing's gone.' She nodded at the marquee. 'Goodness knows what it's doing to the lawn.'

'Yay, party day's only two days away,' Jenny executed a little dance as Sara sorted out her school bag and slipped two of Mrs Henderson's shortbreads into a pocket. The housekeeper did not approve of snacks if meals were not finished, but Sara didn't want the child going hungry all morning.

'Is Mrs Jackson coming to the barbecue?' Mrs Henderson asked in a lowered voice so that Jenny wouldn't overhear them.

'She wasn't sure,' Sara replied.

'That's a shame.'

'She's doing a lot of extra filming and can't get a break.'

'I hope she doesn't take Jenny to America with her,' Mrs Henderson said. 'She's so happy here.'

'Me too. I mean,' Sara added hastily, 'I hope Jenny stays here.'

'You'll stay with me, Sara, won't you if Mummy goes to America?'

Mrs Henderson raised her eyebrows at Sara.

'And who's got elephant ears?' she asked.

Jenny giggled, saving Sara from thinking up a reply.

'Someone called Mac The Magician has just rung up.' Lyle strolled into the kitchen, his hair damp from the shower. 'Says everything's fine for Saturday afternoon.'

Sara, who could smell the scent of aqua shower gel on his skin, carried on sorting out Jenny's school bag.

'Any more of your excellent tea, Mrs H?'

Recognising the olive branch for the apology it was, Mrs Henderson immediately began reheating the pot.

'Daddy,' Jenny ran across the room and into his arms. 'Sara says she's going to force me to eat two breakfasts tomorrow.'

Lyle's eyes met Sara's across his daughter's head. 'Did she indeed?'

'Indeed she did not.' Mrs Henderson leapt to Sara's defence. 'And you're a young minx, telling tales,' she said to Jenny. 'She wouldn't eat her breakfast, Mr Jackson.'

Lyle frowned. 'You know I don't like her missing meals,' he said to Sara. 'The doctors say it's important to steady her metabolism and that means regular meals.'

'Sara's put some shortbread for break in her school bag.' Again Mrs Henderson leapt to Sara's defence.

Sara flushed. She had been silly to

think her little subterfuge with the shortbread would have got past Mrs Henderson's sharp eyes.

'Can I have it now, please?' Jenny demanded. 'I could eat it on the way to school.'

'You'd better take some extra,' Mrs Henderson produced another bag. 'Although I don't approve of eating in public.'

'Come on, Jenny,' Sara urged, 'if you want to see the horses, we're going to be late.'

Lyle gulped down his tea. 'I'll come with you,' he said unexpectedly.

'What?' Sara jolted away from him in surprise.

'I was working late last night. Think I need to clear my head too and I want to call in at the bank.'

* * *

The trio shuffled out of the kitchen, Sara careful to ensure she placed Jenny between Lyle and herself.

'Would you like some quality time alone with Jenny?' Sara asked Lyle as they reached the gate. 'You could take her to school on your own.'

'No.' Both Lyle and Jenny spoke together.

'Want you both to take me to school, like a proper Mummy and Daddy.'

Sara flushed bright red.

'Come along then.' Lyle grabbed Jenny's hand and with a sardonic look at Sara said, 'Let's play mummies and daddies.'

Sara thought she would scream in frustration by the time they reached the school gates. Jenny had used every trick in the book to delay them, showing Lyle the horses and naming every one before sitting down on the stile to eat all the shortbread, very, very slowly.

'I must apologise for my remarks the other day,' Lyle said quietly as Jenny was stroking one of the piebald ponies. 'What you get up to in your spare time is none of my concern.'

'Even though you think Vernon is old

enough to be my father?' Sara couldn't resist retaliating. She saw no reason to let him off lightly.

It gave her a thrill of satisfaction to notice a muscle tighten in Lyle's jaw.

'I understand he's the head gardener at the hotel?'

'And you don't approve of that either?' she taunted.

'That wasn't what I meant and you know it.' Lyle turned away from Sara and looked at his daughter. 'A child needs a mother,' he said unexpectedly.

Sara blinked in surprise. 'Er, yes, well, I'm sure Carla will be down to visit as soon as there's a gap in her filming schedule. She's promised to come on Saturday if she's free.'

'Yes. Of course.' The smile when it came was unexpected and almost blinded Sara. 'Jenny's very fond of you, isn't she?'

'I'm,' Sara chose her words carefully, 'very fond of her too, although she's a scamp at times and you don't want to believe everything she says.'

'She says she loves you.'

Sara was beginning to feel dizzy. She'd had far too much emotion than was good for her this morning.

In the distance Sara heard the church clock chime the hour. 'Come on, Jenny, hurry up,' she called over, 'or we'll be late.'

'Daddy made us late,' Jenny crowed letting go of Lyle's hand as she scooted into the playground.

The teacher was all smiles and hardly noticed Sara was there as she listened to Lyle's apologies, charmingly delivered.

'That's quite all right, Mr Jackson. I wish more fathers took time out to walk their daughters to school, especially ones as busy as you.'

Without a backward glance at Sara she led Jenny and her schoolmates into class.

'I'd best be getting back,' Sara said. 'I can't leave Mrs Henderson to do everything.'

'Have you heard from Joe Daniels

again?' Lyle asked showing no inclination to move on.

'He's coming to the evening barbecue on Saturday with his new girlfriend,' Sara replied, 'and in case you're wondering I haven't invited Vernon. Now if you'll excuse me.'

* * *

By the time Sara had walked back to Medway Manor her T-shirt was sticking to her back and she began to wish she had never suggested the morning walk to school.

'Sara, is that you?' Mrs Henderson called out anxiously as she pushed open the kitchen door.

'What's wrong?' Sara asked taking in the housekeeper's pale face.

'It's Daniel.' Her voice was agitated and full of concern.

The dog looked up at them from his basket, wagging a feeble tail.

'I nudged at him to get up.' Mrs Henderson was almost fighting back the tears, 'but when he tried, he couldn't. He's dragging his back legs.'

Sara knelt down and stroked the soft head. Daniel whined into her hand.

'Can we get him to the vet do you think?' she asked.

'The details are here somewhere,' Mrs Henderson inspected the notice board then unpinned a card. 'Here they are.'

'I'll get the car out,' Sara raced outside and bumped into Lyle coming through the back door.

'What's the matter?' he grabbed her by the shoulders to steady her.

'It's Daniel,' Sara was unaware she was crying until she felt tears trickling down her cheeks.

'Calm down and tell me exactly what's happened.' Lyle wiped her cheek gently with his thumb.

'He's lost the use of his back legs.' It was difficult to speak without sobbing. 'I'm taking him to the vet.'

'We'll use the four-by-four,' Lyle said immediately. 'It'll be less bumpy. Where is he?'

'Inside. Mrs Henderson is making him comfortable.'

'You go and get him. I'll warm up the car. Best let me drive,' Lyle headed for the garage.

* * *

Never had a five-minute journey seemed so long to Sara. Daniel looked up at her with a pleading look in his milky eyes as Lyle drove carefully down the rutted lane and into the village. There was a parking place right outside the vet's and by the time Lyle had turned off the engine Sara had already opened the passenger door.

The touch of Lyle's hand against hers was firm as he gently relieved her of the basket and carried Daniel into the vet's.

'He was a rescue dog, so we don't know exactly how old he is,' Lyle explained to the vet.

The vet nodded. 'Some of them are badly treated as puppies.' Making soothing noises to Daniel, he gently ran his hands over him. 'There's a growth in his abdomen.' He paused. 'I'm afraid the pain will get much worse. I could put him out of his misery now. It's only a matter of time . . . '

'No,' Sara put out a hand and stroked a silky ear. 'We can't do it. Jenny will be distraught.'

'It would be the kindest thing,' Lyle's voice was very gentle, 'and you wouldn't want the poor old boy to suffer more than is absolutely necessary would you?'

Tears were now openly streaming down Sara's face. She couldn't remember the last time she had cried but the pent up emotion of the past few weeks was getting to her and she was reduced to a sobbing wreck. Lyle's arms round her were firm but gentle as he guided her into the waiting room.

'I can't leave him,' Sara's voice was muffled by Lyle's shirt.

'We'll wait,' he said after a quick nod to the vet.

Sara couldn't speak on the drive back to Medway Manor. Lyle had taken charge of things at the vet's and the basket was in the back of the four track.

'Look after Sara, would you Mrs H?' Lyle asked as he quickly explained to the older woman what had happened.

'Come along, Sara.' Mrs Henderson was all motherly concern and more stoical about what had happened. 'It's for the best. We'll leave Mr Jackson to take care of things.'

'W . . . what about Jenny?' Sara found herself sitting at the table and being made to drink a cup of hot sweet tea.

'We'll have a little ceremony when she gets home from school. There's no need to distress the child more than is absolutely necessary. Perhaps in time we'll have another dog.'

'Jenny won't want one,' Sara insisted, 'no one could replace Daniel.'

Mrs Henderson put out a careworn hand and stroked one of Sara's. 'First things first I'd say, wouldn't you?

Children are very resilient, you know. Jenny will take it in her stride. Now finish that tea. There's Mr Jackson now.'

Mrs Henderson stood up and had a murmured conversation with him in the doorway before leaving them alone. Lyle sat down beside Sara.

'You look about six years old,' he said in an attempt to lighten the atmosphere, 'with your face all streaky with tears.'

'How can you make jokes at a time like this?' Sara demanded. 'Daniel's dead.'

'I'm not joking,' he said quietly. 'And I'm sure you made his last days very happy, you know, you and Jenny, even if you did half drown him in the pond. He was a good old boy and never complained about you.'

Sara tried to smile through her tears.

'You weren't so nice about him when he fell asleep on your script and you couldn't find it in the middle of that conference call.'

'Yes, well,' Lyle tried to justify himself, 'that was different.'

'Only because it happened to you,' Sara hiccupped.

The atmosphere in the kitchen went very still as they took time out to look at each other.

'Sara,' Lyle cleared his throat.

'No,' she backed away from him.

'No what?' he demanded.

'Whatever it is you're going to say.'

Tears clogged her eyelashes as she tried to blink. Why did he have to look so wonderful after all they had been through? This wasn't the time or place to be thinking such thoughts.

'I only said what I did about your friend, Vernon, because I'm jealous,' he said slowly.

'What was that?' Sara gasped through a mouthful of hot tea.

'I know I've got absolutely no right to be, jealous that is, after what's gone on between us, but there it is.'

'How can you be jealous?' Sara echoed in a soft voice.

'Ridiculous, isn't it? When I came home that first day and found you on the lawn in the middle of a riot with Jenny I couldn't believe my eyes. You looked exactly how I remembered you and I realised what a fool I'd been all those years ago, letting you slip through my fingers.'

'I didn't harbour such feelings about you. To be honest, Lyle, after the way you ditched me for Carla I never wanted to see you again.'

Sara's heart was beating so fast, she could hardly breathe.

'Of course, I'll always love Carla,' Lyle admitted.

'So will I,' Sara said then attempted a smile. 'Looks like we've got ourselves a very sophisticated eternal triangle.'

'There are several different kinds of love, you know. I suppose the first intensive feelings I had for Carla sort of ran out. I'll always love her, because without her I wouldn't have Jenny, but . . . '

'Lyle, where is this all leading?' Sara asked.

'Nowhere,' he said, 'but I wanted you to know.' He stood up. 'I'll collect Jenny from school this afternoon and explain what's happened if you like.'

'Where,' Sara swallowed, 'where is Daniel?'

'I buried him under the trees round the back of the pond. I thought that was appropriate. He always loved it there.' Lyle looked at his watch. 'I'm late for my conference call. Will you be all right?'

Sara nodded, but she was far from all right. She continued to sit at the table and finish her tea. In the distance she could hear the telephone ringing and Mrs Henderson's voice as she took the call. It was her sister and she began discussing their plans.

After today Sara suspected things at Medway Manor would never be the same again.

Sara Can't Fight Her Feelings

Music floated up from the lawn. The party was in full swing. Although the day had been warm, the evening air was rapidly cooling and the marquee was bulging at the seams as guests congregated around the buffet, gossiping and catching up on news.

Jenny's friends had been collected by their parents hours ago, but she had been too excited to settle properly after all the excitement of the day and Sara had allowed her to stay up late, but now she was struggling to keep her eyes open and had at last been persuaded to clean her teeth and change into her nightie.

'Doesn't Mummy look beautiful?' she asked, her eyes shining as she crouched on the window seat in her bedroom next to Sara and looked down at the partygoers in the garden.

'Yes, she does,' Sara admitted with a lump in her throat.

How could anyone compete in the beauty stakes with Carla de Courcy? Sara thought. She made a plain white blouse and stonewashed denims look stunning. She wasn't even wearing make up and her hair was freshly shampooed and hanging loose down her back.

'After weeks of struggling into corsets, wigs and thick pan make up, darling,' she told Sara, 'I couldn't face the works for your party. I couldn't even face dressing up either. Hope you're not cross? I threw on the first things I could find and hared down here as soon as filming was over. I wasn't sure I'd make it until the last minute. You would not believe how tired I am, but I had to see my baby again. I didn't even have time to buy her a present but I'll make it up to her next week.'

'I'm sure Jenny will understand. The best thing is that you're here,' Sara hugged her. 'I'm so pleased you made it. I hope you enjoy the party.'

'You've done wonders with the garden,' Carla enthused. 'I love the Chinese lanterns and the tree lights and it's lovely to see so many old faces. I haven't had time to catch up with anyone in ages.' Carla waved to an acquaintance and blew kisses to an elderly man who was eating sausages from the barbecue. 'I'm so glad you were able to keep up the tradition. Somehow the summer wouldn't be the same without our barbecue.'

As Sara looked down from the bedroom window she saw Carla dancing with Lyle and whispering something into his ear, a smile of pure happiness on her face. He nodded, then laughed with her and drew her closer into his arms.

'I like Mummy and Daddy being happy together, don't you?' Jenny persisted with her questions.

'Yes, darling I do. Now time for bed,' Sara said as she pulled back the sheets, 'jump in.'

Jenny gave another enormous yawn and scrambled under her duvet. 'Do you think Mummy will come and kiss me goodnight?'

'I expect she will later, but we don't want to disturb her and Daddy right now do we?'

'P'raps they'll get married again,' Jenny said as she enveloped Sara in an enormous hug. 'I'd like that, wouldn't you?'

'Very much,' Sara lied, 'now are you going to settle down?'

'You won't leave me like Mummy did, will you?' Jenny's voice was getting sleepier. Sara was saved from replying as Jenny added, 'Thank you for a lovely day.'

'My pleasure, darling.' The words almost choked Sara.

* * *

Seeing Carla and Lyle together made Sara finally realise any foolish ideas she had about Lyle, were exactly that — foolish ideas. Despite what he had said that day in the kitchen, he was as in love with Carla as he had ever been. It was no surprise to Sara. Tonight Carla had never looked lovelier.

And now Carla's filming schedule was over she would have more time to visit Medway Manor, more time to be with Lyle.

'Do you think Daniel enjoyed the party too?' The question was a sleepy murmur from the bed.

'I'm sure he did,' Sara smiled and tucked Jenny in.

Mrs Henderson and Lyle had been right. After a few tears and a little ceremony under the trees, Jenny had accepted the loss of her dog, with the calm philosophy of a child.

'Shall I leave your light on?'

'Please. Love you.' Jenny was now almost speaking in her sleep.

Sara crept out the room and bumped

into Mrs Henderson patrolling the corridor.

'There you are.' The housekeeper pounced on her. 'I've been looking for you all over the place.'

'I was putting Jenny to bed.'

Mrs Henderson nodded. 'She'll sleep like a top. Are you going back to the party?'

'I was going to freshen up.' Sara looked down at her T-shirt. It was stained with barbecue sauce and her hair was in desperate need of attention.

'It's going well, isn't it?' Mrs Henderson said. 'Tell you what, we could both do with a bit of a break. Why don't I snaffle us two glasses of wine? I wanted to have a quiet word with you and there's no chance of that downstairs.'

'I'll be up in my room,' Sara said as Mrs Henderson disappeared in the direction of the kitchen.

Sara negotiated the narrow staircase, remembering to duck her head under the beams. In the short time she had been at Medway Manor, she had personalised the little room under the eaves with a few touches from home — her own duvet and some cushions and a scarlet rug to provide a splash of colour on the floor.

She loved the comforting noise of the pipes first thing in the morning as hot water gurgled through the system while she lay in her bed listening to the birds chattering around the chimneys.

Ripping off her shirt, she threw it in the bin before dragging a clean one out of her drawer. She dragged a brush through her hair extricating some brambles.

'Here we are.' Mrs Henderson was back and holding a tray. 'I loaded up with a few nibbles too. I thought some sandwiches and savouries would be in order. I don't know about you, but I haven't had time to eat a thing.'

'Mmm, lovely.' Sara took the tray from Mrs Henderson and cleared a space on her dressing table stool. She sat down and scooped up a handful of crisps. Mrs Henderson perched on the bed.

'It's very cosy up here, isn't it?'

'I love it,' Sara's cheeks now bulged with smoked salmon. Like Mrs Henderson, she'd hardly had a bite of food all day. There hadn't been time.

'Was that your Joe Daniels with a new girlfriend?' Mrs Henderson asked as she filled a savoury pancake with a tomato relish.

'Yes.'

He'd turned up with a girl Sara didn't recognise and virtually ignored Sara all evening. Sara didn't mind. It was easier not to speak to him when all they did was argue.

'I thought it was him I saw talking to his father. Glad you're not together any more. I know I shouldn't say this, but I don't think much of his father either.' Mrs Henderson frowned. 'Careful of that dip, Sara, it's a bit messy.'

Sara could not help laughing at the sight of the normally prim housekeeper waving a sausage on a stick at her as she made short work of her wine.

'I could tell from the start, he wasn't right for you,' Mrs Henderson insisted.

Sara had given Mrs Henderson an edited version of her relationship with Joe Daniels over coffee one morning after the incident at Beach View Cottage. She felt she owed her some explanation especially as Mrs Henderson had waited up for her.

'Mrs Henderson . . . ' she began.

'Morag, dear,' she insisted. 'My name's Morag. I'd like you to use it.'

'Are you sure?' Sara raised her eyebrows in surprise. Not even Lyle was allowed to call her Morag.

'I should know my own first name, dear.'

'I mean are you sure you want me to use it? You may regret the invitation in the morning.'

Morag shook her head. 'I'm Scottish dear, and a glass of wine is not going to turn my head.'

'Very well then, Morag it is.'

Mrs Henderson beamed at her. 'I

wanted to have a word with you away from all the hullabaloo downstairs.'

Sara stopped nibbling as she waited for Morag to continue. 'Apparently Mr Jackson's off to America next week so I intend to tell him and Mrs Jackson tonight.'

'About your plans to leave?' Sara felt a qualm of concern.

'Yes. My sister's pressing for a date and I thought, well, my holiday seemed as good a time as any. With you nicely settled I don't think there'll be a problem.'

Sara's heart sank.

'Is it quite the right moment?' she asked, hoping to persuade the housekeeper to stay on a little longer.

'I think so. I don't know when Mrs Jackson will be down again and the party will be beginning to break up soon. Like I say, my sister's got us a nice little flat down where she lives in Dorset. Apparently they are like gold dust. She has already moved in and I'd like to join her as soon as I can.'

Sara put down her sandwich. She no longer felt hungry. 'And you've really made up your mind to leave?'

'I have.'

'I'm going to miss you.'

'You must come and visit, dear. You'll always be most welcome.'

'Thank you.'

'You know, when I first saw you with that dreadful hair,' Morag shuddered, 'I wasn't at all sure you'd be suitable for Jenny and if it hadn't been for your friendship with Mrs Jackson, I don't know that I would have taken you on, but there was no one else and I don't mind admitting I was wrong.

'After her parents' split Jenny was a very nervous little girl, but under your care she has blossomed. Even the loss of her dog didn't upset her too much and that would have been unthinkable a couple of months ago.'

Sara hesitated. 'If Carla should get the lead in *Exchange* and move to America, I may have to leave as well.'

'That's a great pity. What will you do?'

'I've been thinking about taking a course in childminding.'

'You know you can always come to me for a reference, don't you, dear?'

'That's very kind of you, Morag.' Sara leaned forward and squeezed her hand. 'Thank you.'

Morag was now rather pink in the face. 'Goodness, have we drunk all the wine?' She held up her empty glass.

'Hello. Am I interrupting anything?'

A voice in the doorway made them both jump.

'Mrs Jackson,' Morag turned.

'Having a midnight feast, girls?'

'I hope you don't mind, Madam. Sara and I were taking a few moments out for some refreshment. It's been rather a long day.'

Sara couldn't help noticing how dewy-eyed Carla looked, like a woman newly in love.

'Good idea. I hate to break things up but can I have a quick word with you, Sara? It's about Jenny.'

'I'll make myself scarce.' Morag

stood up and began clearing up the glasses and plates.

'Leave that,' Sara insisted, 'I'll bring it all down later.'

'Thank you, dear. Do you know where Mr Jackson is, Madam?' Morag asked Carla.

'You'll find him in the summerhouse, Mrs H, having a word with Monty. Sure you can negotiate the stairs?' she asked.

'Do my best,' Morag called back as she bent her head under the beam.

'She's a love, isn't she?' Carla laughed. 'So,' she settled down on the bed, in the space vacated by Morag. 'I haven't had a proper chance to talk to you. How're things?'

'You heard about Daniel?'

'I did.' A shadow crossed Carla's face. 'Poor old boy. Thank you for looking after him — and Jenny. I miss doing things like that.' She paused, 'Still, it's all going to change from now on.'

Before Sara could say anything Carla

went on, 'The thing is I'd rather like to take Jenny out of school for the day next week. We've had so little time together recently. I was lucky to get away tonight as it was. I've just been in to kiss her goodnight. I can't believe how quickly she's growing up. Soon she won't even be a little girl anymore. She seems so happy now and I suspect a lot of it is down to you. I suppose I should feel jealous.'

'There's no need to be,' Sara assured her quickly.

'What about you and Lyle?' The question trailed.

'Anything between us is all in the past,' Sara said firmly.

'Not according to the newspapers,' Carla said.

'Carla,' Sara protested, 'Surely you didn't believe that story they printed about us?'

'I'd rather hoped it was true actually,' Carla admitted.

'Well it wasn't,' Sara replied firmly.

'Anything you say.' Carla held up her

hands in a gesture of peace.

The two friends sat together in silence for a moment.

'Anyway,' Carla was the first to break it, 'Lyle said I was to ask you if it would be all right — the school thing? Apparently you've got to request official permission for a day out from the teacher? If it's against the rules, I'm sure you can sweet talk them round. I would ask myself but I have to go back to London. Use the famous Armitage charm.'

'What day were you thinking of?' Sara asked.

'Wednesday. I know for sure I'm not needed for any callbacks that day. I'll ring down on Tuesday evening to firm up.'

'Fine.' Sara nodded. 'There shouldn't be a problem. The children break up on Thursday so rules are relaxed a bit this coming week.'

'That's all arranged then.' Carla sprang to her feet. 'Better go and chat up Monty Daniels. See if there's any news on my audition for *Exchange*. Thanks for inviting him by the way.'

'Are you still in line for the lead?' Sara asked.

'It's hush hush at the moment, but fingers crossed.' Carla brushed her lips against Sara's cheeks. 'You look better than I've seen you for ages, Sara. Must be love.'

'Carla,' Sara protested.

'Joe wasn't right for you, you know,' Carla ignored her protest.

'That's what Morag said.'

'Morag?' Carla gasped in surprise. 'Are you referring to Mrs H?'

'I am and if you must know,' Sara did her best to keep a straight face, 'she invited me to use her first name tonight.'

'She didn't!'

'She did.'

* * *

Lyle found the two of them doubled up with laughter a few moments later. He hesitated on the threshold of Sara's room reluctant to break into the scene.

Carla was the first to notice him.

'Darling,' she held out a hand, 'you'll never guess what, Mrs H said Sara can call her Morag. Isn't it a scream?'

'I'll say,' he replied slowly, 'it's an honour and a tribute to Sara's charm and you shouldn't laugh about it.'

Sara flushed to the roots of her hair and pretended to load the tray with the remains of the impromptu party.

'I can see I'm in the way here,' Carla's eyes were twinkling as she took in Sara's discomfort. 'I'll leave you two alone.'

'No need,' Lyle replied. 'I need to talk to you, Carla, about Mrs H actually and Sara, there's a telephone call for you downstairs.'

'For me?'

'It's your mother.'

* * *

Sara snatched up the receiver. 'Hello?' she asked, breathless from rushing down the stairs.

'Is that you, Sara? Have I interrupted a party? There's a lot of background noise.'

'What is it? What's wrong?'

'Nothing's wrong, dear.' Her voice sounded lighter than it had done in ages. 'I've had a telephone call from Vernon. He said you gave him my number.'

'I was going to ring you myself, Mum, but there wasn't time. We met up the other day. I can't go into all the details now . . . '

'I'm so glad you did, darling. I didn't quite understand everything he said, something about a photograph in the newspaper and some gossip about you and Lyle Jackson?'

'No, there isn't any,' Sara tried interrupting but she was wasting her breath. Her mother was clearly too excited to listen to any explanation.

'Anyway, we're having lunch next week at The Grange. That's the hotel where Vernon works, isn't it?'

'Mum, that's wonderful news. I couldn't be more pleased.'

'And it's all down to you,' her voice was very soft. 'I know I haven't been the easiest person in the world to live with since he left us, but I never stopped loving him. Thank you, darling for bringing us back together again. I really do owe you one.'

'Tell me all about it later, won't you, Mum? And good luck.'

'Not bad news I hope?' Lyle's voice behind Sara made her jump as she put the receiver down.

'No, the best news in the world actually.'

'In that case,' Lyle held up some champagne, 'what say we celebrate?'

He poured out two chilled glasses.

'Here you are and here's to your best news in the world.'

'I shouldn't really be mixing my drinks. I've just had some wine with Morag,' Sara protested after a small sip.

Lyle put down the glasses. 'In that case, we'll dance. Perhaps you hadn't noticed but they're playing our tune.'

The next moment she was in his arms as he led her gently around the furniture in a rather unsuccessful attempt at a waltz. Chairs kept getting in their way and Sara was forced to cling on to Lyle in an attempt not to trip over coffee tables.

'We don't have a tune,' she protested, the third time she came into contact with a desk. Dancing wasn't easy with Lyle's arm round her waist and the firm wall of his chest against hers.

'I lied,' he admitted with his slow smile, 'I felt like dancing with you. Nice, isn't it?'

'I saw you dancing with Carla in the garden.'

'A man is allowed to dance with is ex-wife in the garden, isn't he?'

'Yes, but . . . '

'Stop talking,' Lyle chided her, 'and dance.'

Sara closed her eyes as she swayed against Lyle. This could probably be the last dance she would ever have with him and she wanted to savour every moment.

'Thought I'd find you in here,' Carla's low laugh behind her had the effect of a cold bucket of water on Sara. She jumped away from Lyle as if she had been stung. Carla smiled at her. 'Why don't I turn down the lights? After all you don't want an audience do you? And that lot in the garden are looking mightily interested in your performance.'

In one fluid movement she lowered the lighting, whispered, 'Enjoy,' and left the room. Only the smell of her exotic perfume lingered on the air.

A Situation Arises

'Have you got everything, darling?' Carla asked as Jenny ran down the stairs, ready for her day out with her mother.

'Carla,' Sara grabbed her sleeve, 'we need to talk,' she lowered her voice, anxious not to be overheard but wanting also to clear up any misunderstanding between them.

'If it's about last Saturday,' she began.

'Come on, Mummy,' Jenny squealed. 'Want to go.' She tugged at Carla's other arm.

'Yes, be off with you.' Morag Henderson interrupted and began shooing them out of the kitchen. 'You can talk to Mrs Jackson later, Sara.'

'But . . . ' her protests fell on deaf ears.

'Have a lovely day.' Morag Henderson waved Carla and Jenny off down the drive. Sara stood by her side trying to control her frustration as they drove off.

'Alone at last,' Morag said as the car turned out of the drive and into the rutted lane, 'what a relief. I don't mind telling you, Sara, it'll be a pleasant change to have the place to ourselves for the whole day.'

Outside, the workmen had finished taking down the last of the marquee and the contract caterers had tidied up the grounds.

'Thank goodness the garden's returning to normal and they didn't make too much mess. The grass is recovering nicely too. I'm so glad it didn't rain on us. In fact I'd say it was a very successful barbecue, wouldn't you?'

Sara nodded. Lyle had been generous in his praise for all her hard work, but now the party was over everything seemed rather flat.

'How about some elevenses before we get on with the day?' Morag suggested. 'I've made a fresh batch of shortbread.'

Wishing she had had a chance to clear the air between herself and Carla, Sara sat down at the pine kitchen table. Carla had breezed in half an hour earlier and kissed Sara on the cheek as if nothing was wrong.

All the same, she had caught Sara dancing intimately with her ex-husband and that did take some explaining, especially as only moments earlier Sara had been protesting that there was nothing between herself and Lyle.

'What with some guests staying over for Sunday lunch and the contractors not dismantling the marquee until this morning, this is the first chance I've had, Sara, to update you on my news.'

Sara drew her thoughts away from Lyle and back to what Morag was saying.

'Did you manage to tell Lyle you were leaving?' she asked.

'He said he had suspected something of the sort was afoot,' Morag admitted, 'but we didn't really have much of a chance to discuss things, what with all the visitors and interruptions. Anyway he was fine about it and understood my reasons. I have promised to stay until things are sorted out with Mrs Jackson. Hopefully we'll know something later this week.'

Sara nodded. Once Morag had spoken to her sister and settled on a leaving date, Sara would need to give some thought to her own plans.

'What about you?' Morag asked. 'Have you decided on your future?'

Sara blushed. It was impossible to talk about Lyle without remembering their dance on the night of the party. Carla's driver had come to collect her soon after she had discovered them together in the conservatory. Sara had quite expected a scene from Carla before she'd said goodbye.

Instead she had looked genuinely happy and although she was a good actress, Sara didn't think she would have been able to hide her true feelings so well, if she really had been angry with the pair of them. All of which left

Sara feeling very confused.

'I haven't really had time to talk to Lyle either.'

Which wasn't strictly true, but after the party Sara had made it her business to stay out of his way. Dancing with him had been a moment's madness, which she must never let happen again and the best way to ensure it didn't was to keep as busy as possible.

'Do you know what time Mr Jackson will be back from London?' Morag asked.

Lyle had left early that morning, telling Mrs Henderson he would probably be away all day and not to wait up for him if he was late back.

Sara shook her head. 'He didn't say. I think it depends on whether or not he can reschedule the American trip.'

'I can't keep up with all the comings and goings,' Morag admitted. 'Life with my sister is going to be a lot calmer, I hope. Er, don't think I'm prying, Sara, but I understand your mother telephoned on Saturday night?

Is everything all right at home?'

In all the confusion of her emotions, Sara had almost forgotten the call.

'She and my stepfather are thinking of getting back together again. They've been separated for a little while and,' Sara hesitated, not wanting to go into details, 'they're going to meet up at The Grange for a meal to see how things go between them.'

'That's grand news,' Morag's face was wreathed in smiles. 'If only Mr and Mrs Jackson would follow their example, then we'd all be free to get on with our lives.'

'Yes,' Sara admitted quietly, 'we would.'

* * *

Any thoughts Sara had about returning home to live temporarily with her mother had gone out of the window with the news that she and Vernon were going to give their marriage another try. Of course with Vernon living in-house at The Grange, and her mother's job at the health food store, certain adjustments would have to be made, but nothing that couldn't be overcome with a bit of give and take.

'Well, I suppose we'd better get on.' Sara washed up her cup and saucer and put it on the draining board.

'Oh, would you look at that.' Morag tutted behind her.

'What is it?' Sara turned round.

'Jenny's left her inhaler behind.'

'But I put it out on the side for her to take with her.'

'She was so excited she must have overlooked it.'

'She should be all right without it,' Sara said. 'She hasn't had an attack since I've been here and being with Carla won't stress her.'

'All the same,' Morag frowned, 'her father likes her to have it on her at all times.'

'Doesn't Carla have a spare?' Sara asked.

'I'm not sure. Oh well, no good

worrying about it now.' Morag placed it on the shelf above the Aga. As she did so she looked down at Daniel's empty basket. 'I suppose we should get rid of his things. It'll be easier with Jenny out of the way. Why don't we do it today?'

* * *

When Jenny hadn't returned by late afternoon, Sara began to grow concerned. She looked at the clock in the hall. It was after five-thirty and Carla hadn't rung in either to say they would be delayed.

'I hope nothing's happened to them,' she said as Morag washed up the tea things.

'Did Carla leave a contact number?' she asked.

'Her mobile's switched off. I've left messages on her voicemail, but she hasn't come back to me.'

'What about Mr Jackson? Do you think we should try to contact him?'

'There's nothing he can do and I'd

rather not worry him just yet.' Sara could imagine his reaction if she told him Jenny was still out for the day, and without her inhaler. Whatever the reason, it would be bound to be Sara's fault Jenny had forgotten it.

'I'm sure Jenny will be all right. She is with her mother,' Morag tried to reassure her.

'All the same,' Sara bit her lip glancing at the wall clock for the tenth time in as many minutes, 'they are late.'

'They've probably been held up somewhere. Goodness knows there are enough roadworks round here, and Jenny was that excited about having her mother to herself for the whole day they've lost track of the time, I expect.'

'I'm sure that's it,' Sara agreed, wishing she didn't feel quite so worried. She wasn't given to intuition, but she couldn't shake off the feeling that something wasn't right.

The call came two hours later when Sara was beginning to get seriously worried. She had been on her own in the kitchen watching the clock go round, jumping at every sound. Morag had retired to her room to watch television after speaking to her sister on the telephone and Lyle had not returned from London, leaving Sara pacing the floor in anxiety.

'Where are you?' she demanded as Carla's faint voice came down the line.

'I'm not too sure. I've been immensely stupid. I forgot to check the gauge before we left Medway Manor and we've run out of petrol. We're OK, but I think I've tired Jenny out. She's sleeping on the back seat. If I give you a rough map reference could you fetch us? Have you got sat nav?'

'I'll find you.' Sara grabbed up her coat. Lyle had used the four-by-four to get to the station that morning. She would have to take her own car. Glad that Lyle had had it serviced she snatched the keys off the hook.

'By the way,' Carla said before she hung up, 'Jenny's left her inhaler behind.'

'I know,' Sara said. 'I'll bring it with me.' She rang off and after a quick look round the kitchen went in search of Morag to update her on the news.

* * *

'Mrs Henderson?' Lyle's telephone call woke the housekeeper up from her snooze. The television set blared in front of her. 'Is everything all right? Sorry I didn't ring you sooner. The meetings went on for longer than scheduled. I will be home later.'

'Mr Jackson?' Morag muted her television set as she tried to gather her wits. 'Er, everything's fine.'

'Did Jenny have a good day out with Carla?'

'She isn't back yet.'

'Sorry, missed that, the taxi went under a bridge. What did you say?'

'Sara's gone to fetch Jenny.'

'Sara's gone with Jenny? Where?'

'I don't know,' Morag admitted, wishing she had paid more attention to

Sara's hurried update of the situation. Her favourite quiz show had been on and she had only been half listening to what Sara had said before she rushed out.

'I thought Jenny was with Carla.'

'The car broke down, I think.'

'I had it serviced,' Lyle's voice was thick with anger now. 'Sara had no right to take Jenny out in it if it was still playing up.'

'I'm a wee bit concerned, Jenny went out without her inhaler.'

'What's going on? Where's Carla?' Lyle's voice was now whiplash sharp.

'Have you tried her London flat?' Morag began to grow concerned at the tone of Lyle's voice. 'Mr Jackson,' she began, anxious to make the situation clear. 'You're not thinking Sara has kidnapped Jenny again, are you?'

As Morag was speaking the line went dead.

'Hello? Mr Jackson? Are you there?'

There was no answer. Morag replaced the receiver with a frown. She was now fully awake and rather worried that she had given Lyle the impression that Sara had kidnapped his daughter. The situation was utterly ridiculous, but she knew from past experience that Mr Jackson was quite capable of alerting the police if his suspicions were aroused, and would the police believe in Sara's innocence for the second time?

But surely Lyle now realised how much Sara loved the child? She would never harm Jenny. Besides, why would she want to kidnap her? Morag tried to convince herself that she was worrying unnecessarily. With a worried frown she turned off her television set and went down to the kitchen to see if she could find Carla's mobile telephone number on the notice board.

As she searched for it she saw Jenny's inhaler was still on the shelf where she'd placed it earlier that morning.

A Huge Misunderstanding

'He's so sweet, isn't he, Sara? Look, he's licking my fingers.' Jenny stroked the puppy's soft fur. 'It was a surprise, that's why Mummy couldn't tell us where we were going and why she was in such a hurry this morning. There were only three left. I picked this one because he's got white feet like Daniel and brown spots and silky ears.'

Sara sat on the carpet next to Jenny who was looking unusually flushed.

'He's lovely, darling, but I think he's actually a she.'

'I don't mind,' Jenny gave a little cough and a sneeze. 'This carpet's all dusty.'

Sara was unable to shake off a feeling of unease. The flat could do with a clean. Obviously Carla hadn't had time to do anything much, all the same, dust wasn't good for Jenny's asthma.

If only they hadn't forgotten to bring the inhaler. Sara had looked for it in the kitchen before she left, but it wasn't in its usual place on the side where she always put it and where she'd left it that morning. She hadn't wanted to waste more precious moments looking for it so she'd taken a chance and left without it. Now she was beginning to regret that decision.

'In that case, I'm going to call her Trixiebell, Trixie for short. Do you like the name?'

'It's lovely.'

The puppy made snuffling noises as it burrowed into Sara's skirt. Sara wondered how much longer Carla was going to be.

After a mad dash along the motorway and when she was halfway to London, Sara had finally found her and Jenny stranded in a lay-by, eating hot dogs from a mobile catering van.

'Am I pleased to see you, I feel such a fool.' Carla had jumped out of her hire car and thrown her arms around Sara.

'I should sue that car hire company. They're not supposed to let out their vehicles without a full tank of petrol.'

'How's Jenny?' Sara peered through the back window. The child was curled up on the rear seat and nestled in her arms was a puppy.

'I'll explain everything later. Sara, do you think you could drive us back to London? I know it's a lot to ask but if you haven't got enough petrol we can stop at the service station. I've got my credit card on me. I would have walked down there myself and got some petrol myself but I couldn't leave Jenny and the puppy in the car on their own and they were too tired to walk with me.'

Carla ran a hand through her hair. 'It has been such a day. Why did I ever think eighteen hours on location was a hard slog? It's nothing compared to being a mother and taking your daughter out for the day to get her a puppy.'

'Tonight? You want to go to London tonight?' Sara demanded.

'Yes.'

'Wouldn't it be easier to go back to Medway Manor, have a good night's sleep then go back to London in the morning?'

'There isn't time. While I was waiting for you I had a call on my mobile, Monty Daniels wants to see me this evening at a West End hotel. It's about *Exchange*. He's been holding big meetings all day. The producers are only over here for twenty-four hours and they want to cram in as much as possible. That's why my auditions's been scheduled so late and at short notice. We should just about make it if you put your foot down. What do you think?'

'I don't know,' Sara hesitated.

'There's no need to worry about Jenny. She'll be fine with you. Sara,' Carla grabbed her arm. 'This is all I've ever worked for. You don't understand what this means to me. It's my whole future. I'll never get another chance like this.'

Sara bit her lip. She had forgotten just how selfish Carla could be at times.

'Jenny hasn't got her inhaler with her and with a new puppy, I really don't think it would be a good idea.'

A sly look came into Carla's eyes. 'Lyle will be very grateful.'

'Why should that matter to me?' Sara demanded.

'Come on, Sara, you can't fool me, I'm your oldest friend. You're as potty about him as you ever were. Last Saturday's performance in the conservatory didn't leave much to the imagination.'

'That's not true.'

'And I am absolutely fine with it. Don't worry. You two were made for each other. If you must know Lyle was doing nothing but talk about you while I was dancing with him in the garden. Honestly, boring or what?'

'What did he say?' Sara demanded.

'I haven't got time to go into all that now,' Carla dismissed her question with a wave of her hands. 'But, if you drive me to London and I get this part?' she raised an eyebrow, 'it might be very convenient for you.'

'I don't understand.'

'I'll be dividing my time between here and America.'

'But if Lyle and Jenny go with you . . . '

'Lyle will never leave Medway Manor and I'm not sure I would want him to. Neither would I want to uproot Jenny. Anyway let's not worry about all that now. Come on.' Carla glanced at her watch. 'We've got just over an hour. Think you can do it? Please? Pretty please?'

Sara found herself agreeing reluctantly to the drive, and once she had assured herself that Jenny wasn't overtired she had pulled out into the traffic again.

'I'll have to leave you in my flat with Jenny while I go for my audition. There's not much room, but if you could look after her and the puppy? I'll be forever in your debt. I promise to be as quick as I can, but to be honest I don't know how long it's going to take.'

* * *

Sara glanced at her watch. Carla had been gone for over two hours. Not long by producers' standards, but when you were alone in a half furnished pied à terre with a young child and a puppy for company, it seemed like a lifetime.

Sara hoped Morag would tell Lyle what was happening if he should telephone Medway Manor. Carla had not had time to arrange a landline in the flat. Sara would have liked to use her mobile to update Morag on developments, but Carla had asked her to keep her line free for urgent calls.

'I feel sleepy,' Jenny murmured.

Her eyelids were drooping. Sara turned out the light and hauled Jenny on to her lap, covering her with a blanket. 'If Mummy isn't back within the next half hour we'll go to sleep in her bed. It's been a long day hasn't it?

Are you hungry?'

Jenny shook her head. 'You won't leave me will you?' she asked again clinging on to Sara's jumper.

'Of course not.'

'Promise,' Jenny insisted.

Sara frowned. It was unlike Jenny to be clingy, but this wasn't the first time Jenny had tried to extract a promise from her. Had Carla said something about the move to America? Was that what was unsettling the child? Jenny began to whimper. Sara stroked her hair and Jenny drifted into a restless sleep. Alone with her thoughts Sara watched the light fade from the day. Lights began to twinkle on the river. It was a peaceful sight and Sara's head fell forward too.

Trixie snuffled down next to them as Sara began to doze off. The rattling of a key in the lock awoke her. Jenny was a deadweight on Sara's legs, which had gone to sleep under the strain. She tried to struggle to her feet without disturbing the sleeping bundle. Trixie sensing movement under the blanket began to stir and bark. Jenny whimpered in discomfort, as the room was flooded with electric light.

'What on earth . . . '

It was Lyle's voice. He was across the room in two strides.

'What is going on?' he demanded.

'Lyle? I wasn't expecting you.'

'I bet you weren't.' He prised his daughter out of Sara's arms.

'Daddy?' Jenny nuzzled up to him. 'Tired.'

'Have you got no sense of responsibility?' Without giving Sara a chance to explain he shouted at her, 'Not content with failing the first time I suppose you wanted to have another go at kidnapping my daughter.'

'What on earth are you talking about?' Sara's voice was also dangerously close to anger.

'Well you tripped up this time.'

'And so did you. Would I be holed up in Carla's flat if I was thinking of running away with Jenny?'

'I don't know what you're thinking half the time.'

A pulse was hammering hard at the side of Lyle's temple as he glared at her. Sara began fighting for breath. She was almost too angry to speak.

Jenny let out a wail of distress. Her face grew red.

'Daddy, don't argue with Sara.'

'We're not arguing, darling,' Sara tried to reassure the child. 'Daddy's tired and . . . '

'Sara,' Jenny began wheezing, 'I can't breathe.'

'Where's her inhaler?' Lyle demanded.

'We left it behind,' Sara's voice was equally panic stricken. 'Doesn't Carla keep a spare one here?'

The puppy was now running around in circles at their feet. Lyle almost tripped over it as he hunted for Jenny's medication. 'Yes, but I've no idea where it would be.'

'Daddy,' Jenny wailed again, 'I don't feel well.'

Lyle looked at Sara over his daughter's head.

'I'm taking Jenny to A & E. You'd better wait here for Carla and pray nothing happens to Jenny.'

Lyle raced out of the flat leaving Sara alone with Trixie.

* * *

'You said what?' Carla faced her ex-husband in the cramped confines of her flat. 'And keep your voice down, Jenny's sleeping soundly now, no thanks to you.' Carla glared at Lyle. 'Now run it past me again.'

'Mrs Henderson said you weren't back. Then there was something about kidnapping. The line kept breaking up. I didn't know what was going on.'

'Whatever you thought Mrs Henderson said did you seriously believe Sara would kidnap your daughter? And if so why?'

'She didn't want the child to go to America with you.'

'That's rubbish and you know it.'

'I heard her and Mrs H talking about

it in the kitchen one day.'

'You know what they say about listeners not hearing any good of themselves.'

'They weren't talking about me.'

Carla flapped her hands in dismissal.

'It doesn't matter what they were talking about. Honestly, Lyle, I know you've been under a lot of pressure lately but not to put too fine a point on it I think you've gone bananas.'

Lyle shook his head. 'I . . . ' he licked his lips. 'Perhaps I have. I don't seem able to think straight when it comes to Sara, but it was the last straw when Jenny had her attack.'

'For your information, Sara was here looking after Jenny and her new puppy because I had to go for my audition. I had to think on my feet and I agree perhaps Sara shouldn't have been here, but that again was my fault. My hire car ran out of petrol. Sara came to the rescue then drove us all up to London, at great personal inconvenience I may add. She was against the idea, but I persuaded her otherwise.

'It was my fault Jenny didn't have her inhaler with her, not Sara's. I had so much on my mind I forgot about it. Sara had placed it in its usual place on the kitchen worktop. Mrs Henderson, who is in no way to blame either, moved it and Sara couldn't find it. Rather than delay things she drove out to rescue us. Now,' Carla held up a hand as Lyle tried to intervene, 'I think she deserves your heartfelt thanks, don't you? Rather than an accusation of kidnap?'

'What was I supposed to think? Jenny had disappeared. You weren't answering your mobile. Mrs Henderson wasn't making sense.'

'And neither are you. You nearly caused Jenny to have her first asthma attack in months and all because you're in love with Sara Armitage.'

'What did you say?' Lyle asked slowly.

'You heard me. I've known about it for ages, even if you haven't. It's probably why things between us didn't work out. Deep down I have always known she was your first love. You just got your timing wrong. Well don't muck it up for a second time.'

'Carla,' Lyle began.

'Lyle,' Carla passed a hand over her forehead. 'My head is splitting. It's been a long day. I haven't the strength to argue with you. If the situation with Sara is troubling your conscience, then don't worry about it. I've already told Sara it's fine with me and as for Jenny,' Carla looked to where their child was breathing normally and sleeping soundly, 'I think I can honestly say it's all right with her too.'

'Since you seem to know so much about this friend of yours, did you also know she's already replaced Joe Daniels with a new boyfriend?' Lyle asked.

'She has?' Carla asked in amazement. 'Who?'

'With a man old enough to be her father.'

'She never said anything to me.'

'His name is Vernon Pickering. He works as the head gardener at The Grange. I saw them together when I had lunch there one day with Monty.'

'Vernon Pickering?' Carla raised her eyebrows.

'Have you met him?'

'I haven't actually, but I know all about him.'

'Sara told you?'

'At times you can be so exasperating. I bet you didn't ask her who he was. You jumped to the wrong conclusion again, didn't you? Of course Vernon Pickering is old enough to be Sara's father because that's exactly who he is.'

'That's nonsense, her surname is Armitage and she calls him Vernon.'

'He's married to her mother and has been for years, ever since Sara was a baby. He's the only father she has ever known. Her mother and Vernon, well you don't need to know all the details, but they lost touch. Sara was trying to get them back together again. Vernon saw that paparazzi picture of Sara in the newspaper and contacted her. That's also why her mother telephoned Medway Manor the night of the party and probably why Sara was so happy dancing with you in the conservatory afterwards.'

'She never said anything about it to me.'

'She didn't have to. It was none of your business, besides which,' Carla added, 'I expect you accused her of all sorts of behaviour with this man old enough to be her father.' Carla's face was beginning to crumple with amusement. 'I'm right, aren't I?'

'What's so funny?' Lyle demanded. 'What was I supposed to think? They were holding hands in the rose garden.'

'And you were jealous.'

'No I wasn't.'

'If that doesn't beat all.' Carla looked at him with affection. 'Don't bother to deny it, Lyle. You've always been a hopeless fibber. Your face gives you away every time.'

'Where is Sara now?' he asked.

'She left hours ago after I got back

here and telephoned the hospital and the doctor assured us Jenny was fine. After all the things you said to her, she was very upset.'

Lyle's shoulders sagged. 'I seem to have made a mess of things, haven't I?'

'Frankly, yes. I was going to suggest you stay the night on the sofa, but now I think the best thing is for you to get back to Medway Manor as soon as possible and make your apologies to Sara on bended knees. You'll be a lucky man if she accepts them, but knowing her generosity of spirit, I think she will. Now off you go. I'll look after Jenny and the puppy. And for heaven's sake try not to accuse the poor girl of any further felonies.'

'Carla,' Lyle gave a tired smile. 'I love you.'

'And I love you too,' she said, 'but not enough to be married to you. Now off you go.'

Lyle Accepts His Feelings

Streaks of dawn were painting the sky purple as Lyle drove the four-by-four into the forecourt of Medway Manor. The gravel spurted under his tyres as he circled the flowerbed and came to a halt by the kitchen. His eyes were gritty from lack of sleep and his neck was tight with tension from the strain of concentrating on the drive from the station home.

He had managed to catch an early train down from London, but hadn't been able to sleep during the journey. His mind was reliving his final scene with Sara and whichever way he played it, it did not look good.

The back door opened a crack casting a sliver of light on the grass as he jumped from the vehicle.

'Who's that?' a voice called out. 'Who's there?'

'Only me, Mrs H,' Lyle replied as he strode towards the housekeeper. 'Have you been up all night?'

'Of course I have.'

'You should have got some sleep.'

'I couldn't sleep knowing Jenny was ill. How is she?'

'She's absolutely fine. The hospital said it was nothing more than an anxiety attack caused by all the excitement. They would have kept her in but she wanted to stay over in the flat with Carla because of the new puppy.'

'I have been that worried about her,' Mrs Henderson breathed a sigh of relief. 'Another dog, did you say?' she asked.

Lyle ducked his head under the beam by the back door and entered the kitchen.

'I did. It was a surprise present from Carla. That's where they went yesterday, to pick it up.'

'Such a fuss,' Morag Henderson tutted. 'I shall be having words with Mrs Jackson when I next see her. Why she couldn't have told us in advance, I don't know. Well I'm glad everything turned out fine. You know Sara and I have only just got rid of Daniel's basket yesterday? Wouldn't you believe it? I'll have to go shopping in the morning for some new things. A puppy makes a lot of work.' Mrs Henderson gathered herself together and began bustling round the kitchen. 'It's not as if we haven't got enough to do already.'

'Where is Sara?' Lyle demanded. 'Is she back? I didn't see her car parked outside.'

Mrs Henderson began filling the jug kettle. 'I'll make you some tea. You look in need of refreshment, Mr Jackson. Would you like some toast too?'

Lyle sat down at the table. 'Thank you. Is Sara asleep?' he asked when Mrs Henderson didn't reply to his question.

'She's gone,' she said in a quiet voice.

Lyle's head shot up. 'Gone? Where?'

Mrs Henderson's mouth was set in a prime line of disapproval.

'She was that upset when she got

back, I had a job to calm her down, I can tell you. I understand you accused her of kidnapping Jenny?'

'I need to speak to her,' Lyle said.

'Any misunderstanding which arose was my fault and I apologise.'

'How could it be your fault, Mrs H?'

'The telephone line was not very good when you called. It kept breaking up. I have to admit I was tired and I'd fallen asleep in front of the television set. Your call woke me up and I missed some of what you were saying.'

'Your apology really isn't necessary,' Lyle said.

'All the same, you'll also do me the courtesy of listening to my explanation,' Morag said firmly.

'Very well.' Lyle crossed his arms and prepared to be patient. 'What is it you have to say?'

'Sara's been the glue that's held us all together these past few weeks.'

'I agree with you.'

'Jenny has never been happier. Sara has driven her and her friends all over the place without complaint. She's sewed costumes for the school play. She's helped me spring clean the house from top to bottom. She's coped with the loss of Daniel and she single-handedly organised the summer party — and Mrs Jackson was a difficult act to follow on that one. When I told her of my plans to leave, she never once thought of herself and how it might affect her. The girl has been an absolute treasure. To have you hurl spurious accusations at her must have been the final straw.'

'Mrs Henderson,' Lyle took a deep breath and unclenched his fists. 'You're not telling me anything I don't know. Now where is Sara?'

'All in good time. I haven't finished yet. I was very wrong about the girl and I'm the first to admit it. When she came here I had my doubts about her ability to look after Jenny, but I soon changed my mind. I saw beyond the funny coloured hair and the strange dress sense. She's a lovely girl and it's about time you realised that fact. I don't know what went on between the two of you in the past, again it's none of my business, but at the risk of sounding rude I expect if it went wrong it was your fault, Mr Jackson. You can be very foolish at times.'

The housekeeper groped in her apron pocket for a tissue. 'I know I shouldn't be speaking to you like this . . . '

'Mrs H,' Lyle's voice was gentle, 'you know me well enough to say whatever you like.'

'Sorry, sir. It's the lack of sleep getting to me, I think. But what you said about Sara, it wasn't fair.' She sniffed loudly. 'It's time someone told you.'

'Told me what?' Lyle asked, careful not to raise his voice.

'Vernon Pickering is her stepfather.'

'I know that now. Carla also told me.'

'I understand you thought the pair of them were . . . ' Mrs Henderson paused, 'in a relationship.'

It had been years since Lyle had

blushed, but he coloured up as Mrs Henderson continued to lecture him like an errant schoolboy.

'I won't have you thinking things like that about Sara. They're not true.'

'I know. I don't know what got into me. I apologise. There,' he smiled at Morag, 'does that satisfy you? If you tell me where Sara is I'll apologise to her as well.'

'It seems to me it's time you did more than apologise to her.' Mrs Henderson put away her tissue and began buttering burnt toast and pouring out tea. 'Breakfast.' She all but banged the plate down on the kitchen table.

'I will do whatever you wish, Mrs H, but I need to know where Sara is.'

'I'm sure you do, but the girl needs some rest. There's no way I'm going to let you go knocking on doors and waking everybody up this time of the morning. We all need to calm down a bit. You've upset Sara more than enough for one day.'

Lyle knew when he was beaten. Admitting defeat he picked up his mug of tea. It was hot and scalded the back of his throat. He took a bite of toast and swallowed it quickly, realising he was very hungry.

'That's better,' Mrs Henderson watched him finish his third slice of toast.

She removed his plate then turned to the kitchen shelf and picked up an envelope. Before she could give it to Lyle the wall telephone rang. He leapt up to answer it.

'Sara?'

'Sorry to disappoint you, darling,' Carla laughed down the line. 'It's only your ex-wife.'

'Jenny's all right, isn't she?'

'She's still fast asleep. I wanted to check you got back in one piece. You roared off into the night as if a dragon was on your tail.'

'I've been back about half-an-hour. Mrs H was waiting up for me.'

'That poor woman. The hours she spends waiting up for you don't bear thinking about. No wonder she's leaving.'

'You can forget the lecture, I've already had one from Mrs H.' The housekeeper had moved discreetly out of earshot. Lyle lowered his voice. 'If she hadn't already handed in her notice, I'd be almost tempted to give her the sack. You should have heard some of the things she said to me.'

Carla laughed. 'That bad, was it?'

'And some.'

'Listen, darling, two things. I'll get the studio car to drive Jenny and Trixie home after lunch if that's all right with you. I know the driver well and he's perfectly reliable. Can you make sure someone will be in for her?'

'Of course. Carla?' Lyle began.

'Hang on. I haven't finished yet. I won't be able to drive her back myself, firstly because that ghastly little hire car's still parked in the lay-by. I'm all set to do battle with the hire company in the morning. But that's not my big news. I also won't be able to drive

Jenny back because,' Carla took a deep breath, 'I'm going to be very busy.'

'You got the part?' Lyle finished what she had been going to say.

'Yes.' Carla's voice was an excited squeak. 'Isn't it wonderful news? Monty called me on my mobile a few moments ago.'

'It is. I'm so pleased for you.' Lyle did his best to sound surprised. Monty had told him at their meeting the day before that the part was virtually in the bag for Carla, but that he wasn't to mention it to a soul. 'Congratulations.'

'Will you tell Sara for me?'

'I can't.' Lyle was brought back to reality with a jolt.

'Why not?'

'She's left, walked out on me and I don't know where she's gone.'

'Good for her,' Carla said.

'She hasn't been in touch with you, has she?'

'No. 'Fraid not.'

'I need to talk to her. I said some things that need un-saying.'

'In that case, my darling,' Carla trilled down the line, 'if you've lost her, you'd better go out and find her, hadn't you? That way we may all get some peace round here and don't forget you both have my blessing. Get off,' Carla shouted making Lyle jump. 'Sorry, got to go, the puppy's waking up and scratching the chair. Good luck with the Sara hunt. Give her my love when you do find her and tell her she has my permission to be as rude as she likes to you because you deserve it.'

* * *

Lyle poured himself another cup of tea. He was going to have to exert all his charm on Mrs Henderson if he wanted to find out Sara's whereabouts.

'Finished your call?' Mrs Henderson emerged from the cold room, where she'd been putting a wash load in the machine.

'It was Carla. She's been cast in the lead for *Exchange*.'

'Good news indeed.' Mrs Henderson's face was now wreathed in smiles. 'Will you all be moving to America?'

'I don't think so. I'm hopeful Carla will let Jenny stay here, with me and . . .'

Mrs Henderson picked up the discarded envelope.

'She left this for you,' she said, handing it over. 'I'll leave you to read it in peace.'

Lyle ripped it open before Mrs Henderson had left the kitchen.

Lyle, he read,

I can't stay on at Medway Manor any longer now I know what you really think of me. I can understand you being upset over Jenny's disappearance, but it was a shock to realise you thought I had kidnapped her to stop you taking her to America. I thought your opinion of me was higher than that. I'm sure Morag will look after Jenny until she leaves for America, that's assuming Carla gets the part. If not, well, I expect the trained nanny's broken leg will be healed by now and you can re-employ her.

I'm sure she will be a much more suitable individual for the post. She would never be so unprofessional as to go haring through the Kent countryside looking for a lost ex-wife, a child and a dog, all stranded in a lay-by in a car that's run out of petrol.

Thank you — for everything. You probably won't believe me but the last few weeks have been the happiest of my life.

Break a leg!

Sara.

Lyle screwed up the letter and threw it in the bin.

'Mrs H,' he roared and yanked open the kitchen door. The housekeeper almost fell in on top of him.

'There's no need to shout, Mr Jackson.' She straightened her apron. 'What is it now?'

'Do you know where Sara's gone?'

'I do.'

'Will you tell me?' Lyle asked with

exaggerated patience.

'She made me promise not to.' The housekeeper's eyes twinkled. 'So I won't.'

'Mrs H, please,' Lyle begged. 'I have to know.'

'I'm saying nothing.' She relented with a smile. 'But you might like to freshen up. They operate a smart dress code at The Grange.'

Lyle's brow cleared as the full meaning of her words sunk in. 'She's at The Grange?'

'You didn't hear it from me. And Mr Jackson,' Morag called after him as he dashed up the stairs, 'if you should bump into Vernon Pickering don't, for heaven's sake don't start accusing him of being Sara's new partner. Remember he's her stepfather and treat him with respect because one day he may be your stepfather-in-law.'

Lyle Approaches Vernon

'Mr Jackson.' The manager of The Grange greeted him as he mounted the steps to the entrance hall. 'Good to see you — and congratulations. It's just been on the early morning news — about Miss de Courcy.'

'Thank you.' Lyle nodded his acknowledgement to the manager.

'And I understand you're part of the team writing the screenplay. Quite a family affair.'

'Er — yes.'

The manager looked at his watch and said with a smile, 'you are a little early for lunch. We can do you some breakfast, or coffee?' He was far too discreet to enquire the reason for Lyle's unscheduled visit. In his years of fronting hotels he'd learned to see everything but say nothing, and this looked a classic example of an occasion when it was best to say nothing.

Lyle hesitated. 'I wonder, Mr Barrie, if it would be possible to have a word with one of your employees?'

'Certainly. Which one did you have in mind?'

'Your head gardener.'

'Vernon Pickering? He's our best man. You're not intending to steal him away from us, are you? Because if that was the case, I would have to refuse your request.' Mr Barrie smiled.

'No, it's nothing like that.'

'Good. Actually I'm not sure where he is at the moment. At this time of the day he could be in any number of places. He may be in the kitchen discussing the day's menu with Ricardo. Would you like me to have him paged? You could talk over coffee in the lounge? You won't be disturbed there.'

'Is that allowed?' Lyle asked carefully. He had no wish to make further trouble for Vernon or Sara.

'Leave it to me.' Mr Barrie bustled

away. 'Why don't you go through?'

Lyle strolled across reception and into the large airy lounge. His heart was beating like a trip hammer. He had no idea what he was going to say to Vernon Pickering or what Sara's stepfather might say to him.

In the corner of the room Carla's face flashed up on a wide television screen. He watched her interview knowing only too well the pressure she would now be under. Her intense ambition had been one of the reasons their marriage had broken up.

Carla's career was her life. It always came first. She loved Jenny of course, but being a stay at home mother was not for her. To her credit she was a wonderful actress and Lyle knew she was the perfect choice for the lead in *Exchange*, which promised to be the most challenging, powerful film of the decade.

'Will this role mean a move to America, Miss de Courcy?' the interviewer was asking her.

'Mr Jackson?' Lyle spun round before he could hear Carla's reply.

Vernon Pickering was standing in the doorway. He was wearing his indoor uniform of grey flannel slacks and casual shirt open at the neck. There was no welcoming smile in his eyes as the two men shook hands.

'Thank you, Tracey,' Vernon said to the waitress who came in with a tray of coffee.

'I'll put it down here, Mr Pickering, shall I?' she asked with a friendly smile. 'Then you can help yourselves. Congratulations, Mr Jackson,' she added going a little pink, 'ever so pleased to read about your wife.'

'Thank you.' Lyle hadn't quite realised how much media attention the news would attract or that he was quite so well known.

'Shall we?' Vernon indicated two seats by the coffee table. The two men settled themselves down. 'I presume,' Vernon began, 'this is about Sara?'

Lyle nodded. 'I would like to see her.'

'I'm sure you would, but there are one or two things we need to clear up first.'

Lyle's lips moved into a rueful smile. 'If you're about to tell me what you think of me and my behaviour towards Sara, I can save you the time. I've already been told twice in fact — once from Carla and once from Mrs Henderson, my housekeeper.'

'And you're about to hear it from me.' There was no softening response in Vernon's eyes. 'By the way, before I start I hope young Tracey was wrong just now?'

'About what?'

'She referred to Carla de Courcy as your wife. I was under the impression this was no longer the case.'

'Carla is my ex-wife.'

'I thought that was so, but I wanted to be sure. I'm not having my Sara involved with a married man.'

'I can find the papers if you like,' Lyle offered.

'That won't be necessary. Now,' he

began, 'I understand you also have a daughter?'

'Jenny. Yes. She's five years old.'

Vernon paused. 'I inherited my daughter when I married Judy, Sara's mother. Sara was very young and I have been the only father she has ever known.'

'I want to explain . . . '

Vernon held up a hand. 'You'll have plenty of time to talk in a minute. For the moment it's my turn. My marriage was a very happy one, until I was foolish enough to neglect my wife. I won't go into details, but with Sara's help I hope we will be reconciled. I know how painful a separation can be and I intend to see that from now onwards my wife always comes first. The separation strengthened our marriage, but it was a painful time for us all and I wouldn't want to go through it again. Neither would I want Sara to be involved in any marital unpleasantness.'

'I understand. I am on good terms with my ex-wife,' Lyle explained, 'we are no longer married, but there is mutual respect between us, for ourselves and for the sake of our daughter. Carla is also a best friend of Sara's. There is no animosity between them.'

'Even though it was your ex-wife who split you and Sara up?'

Lyle hesitated. His next words were of vital importance and he didn't want to get them wrong.

'Carla said something interesting the other day about Sara and I getting our timing wrong. I think she was right. Mr Pickering, I know I treated Sara badly in the past and I'm determined to try and make things up to her. I can't say I wish I'd never married Carla because to be frank that would be untrue, but the only feelings I have for her now are deep respect and warm affection. She knows that too and I think she feels the same way about me.'

'I appreciate your honesty.' Vernon nodded. 'However, Sara came to me in a bad way earlier this morning and to be equally frank with you, I think if you had walked in behind her, I might have been in danger of punching you on the jaw.

'My daughter is a wonderful, hard working girl. She is not a successful actress like your wife, but that doesn't make her a lesser person in my eyes, and to hear what you said about her, well, even if only one half of it was true, it makes me question your real feelings for her.'

'Mr Pickering,' Lyle took a deep breath, 'Carla, my ex-wife told me that you and your wife, Sara's mother, had lost touch with each other.'

'Yes. That was why when I saw that picture of Sara in the newspaper I had to contact her.'

'With the greatest respect may I suggest that at the time of your separation you may have said things you later regretted?'

'Hmm,' Vernon nodded thoughtfully. 'I did and I take your point.'

'I'm not for a moment criticising your behaviour, but my reasons for behaving as I did may possibly have been the same. Sara walked back into my life when I was at a low ebb. I was getting over my break up with Carla. I didn't want to be reminded of how badly I had behaved towards Sara in the past. I wanted to find fault with her, to ease my own guilt.

'Then later, I began to realise that all the old feelings I had harboured for her had never died, they'd merely gone to sleep and seeing her again had awoken them. Does that make sense?'

'It does.'

'I thought first of all that she and Joe Daniels were still an item, then when I realised they weren't I allowed myself to begin to fall in love with her again. When you appeared on the scene . . . '

'With spectacularly bad timing,' Vernon smiled in sympathy.

'Exactly. I was having lunch in the restaurant when I saw the pair of you walking together in the garden. You were so happy and at ease in each other's company. I jumped to the only conclusion that I could think of.'

'I suppose I should be flattered that you could possibly think a man of my age would hold any attraction of that nature to a girl like Sara.'

'Well,' Lyle smiled ruefully. 'I did. I'm sorry I was so rude to you that day when I walked straight past you, but I didn't trust myself to speak to you.'

'Just as well really. Judging by Sara's account of your recent outburst, when you're angry, you don't hold back.'

'Do you think Sara wants to see me again?' Lyle asked.

'It depends what your intentions are.'

'I want to ask her to marry me.'

'I see. You don't think it's too soon to take the plunge again after your last marriage?'

'I've known Sara a long time, longer than I've known Carla.'

'True.'

'And?' Lyle prompted after they had lapsed into a few moments of silence.

'If you've come to officially request my permission to ask for her hand in marriage, then I won't object, but as for Sara,' Vernon smiled, 'she's a modern independent young woman. She may turn you down.'

'I'm prepared for that eventuality.'

'Then good luck.' Vernon leaned over and shook Lyle's hand. 'By the way, I don't envy you your task one little bit. To say she was angry when she crash landed on me in the small hours is putting it mildly.'

'I said some harsh things. She had every right to be angry. Is she here?'

'No. She stayed for an hour or two to rest up but the hotel is fully booked and they didn't have a spare room for her. She'll be back later. She's gone over to her mother's to fetch her here for lunch. If things go well you'll be very welcome to join us.'

'But it'll be a family occasion.'

'If Sara accepted your proposal then you will be part of the family.' Vernon stood up. 'I have to get back to work.'

'Of course.'

Vernon looked at his watch. 'Shall we

say quarter to one?'

'I'll be here,' Lyle replied.

'For heaven's sake don't turn up clutching a bunch of flowers,' Vernon advised. 'If Sara's still mad at you it would be a waste of money.'

'And if she's not?' Lyle asked with a wry smile.

'I'll give you a bunch of my best roses from the garden. See you later.'

Lyle watched Vernon walk out into the garden and breathed a sigh of relief. He hadn't been looking forward to his interview with Sara's stepfather, but now it was over. He glanced at his watch. In a few hours' time he had to face Sara. Still not sure where that relationship would go, he walked back to the car.

'Do You Accept My Proposal?'

Lyle stared out of the conservatory window. Now the marquee had been dismantled the lawn looked bare and unloved. The workmen had removed the lights from the trees and everything was back to normal. After the hustle and bustle of the past week the house was uncannily quiet.

He ran a hand through his hair. Why was the time taking so long to reach a quarter to one?

There were several emails in his inbox to be dealt with and he tried to occupy his mind by replying to them. He made one or two telephone calls before eventually the hall clock struck midday. He closed his laptop. He still had three-quarters of an hour before he was due to meet up with Sara.

He showered and changed into a fresh shirt and tie, feeling like a teenager on a first date. Would Sara agree to speak to him or would she storm out of the hotel? He wouldn't blame her if she did.

Lyle was at the bottom of the stairs when the telephone rang. He snatched up the receiver before the answerphone could cut in.

'Lyle? Monty Daniels here.'

Lyle's heart sank. 'I'm on my way out, Monty. Can it wait?'

'Just a couple of things.'

It was gone half-past twelve before Lyle was able to put the telephone down. High on the adrenalin of Carla's publicity, Monty had not been in the mood to be rushed.

Lyle eased the four-by-four out of the drive, hoping he wouldn't meet anything coming the other way as there wasn't much room to pass oncoming vehicles. Monty's call had seriously delayed him and now he only had a quarter of an hour to get to The Grange.

He reached the end of the lane safely but had to stab his foot quickly on the brake when Mrs Henderson lurched out in front of him. She was weighed down with several large parcels and began waving frantically at the sight of the four-by-four.

'The taxi driver wouldn't come any further,' she gasped. 'Said he couldn't turn round at the top and the ruts in the lane ruin his suspension.'

'Why didn't you ring me to come and fetch you?' Lyle demanded.

'I thought you were going out to lunch.'

'You'd better jump in.'

'Won't you be late for your date?'

'You can't struggle back with all that shopping. Besides, most of it looks like it's for Jenny's new dog.'

'It is,' Morag Henderson agreed, clambering into the passenger seat and taking several moments out to fumble with her seatbelt as she did it up. 'Don't want to bang my head,' she explained, 'if we go down a pothole.'

'Ready?' Lyle asked, resisting the temptation to sneak a look at his watch.

He reversed into a passing place and turning round began driving back up the lane, careful to avoid anything that would jolt his passenger or her shopping.

'Is there something wrong with the steering?' Morag gasped, clutching on to the dashboard as the car swerved violently as they reached the gates of Medway Manor.

Lyle swore under his breath. 'I think we've got a puncture,' he said through gritted teeth as he brought the car to a steady halt before jumping out of the driver's seat. 'It's the front nearside tyre,' he confirmed his worse suspicions.

'You can't drive with it like that,' Morag said. 'What are you going to do?'

'Change it.' Lyle ripped off his jacket and undid his tie.

'Can I do anything to help?' Morag asked.

Lyle handed her his jacket and tie.

'Take these inside for me,' he said adding, 'please.'

None of this was her fault, but Lyle couldn't resist feeling fate wasn't on his side this morning.

The wheel nuts were stiff and it took Lyle several attempts to loosen them. By now he was perspiring freely and his shirt was smeared in dirt and sticking to his back.

Eventually he slotted the spare in place, finished the job and rinsed his hands in the utility room. He realised he was far too late for lunch now. He would have to call The Grange and try to speak to Vernon to apologise.

Upstairs he threw his soiled shirt into the laundry basket and pulled on T-shirt and jeans and ran a comb through his hair.

Loud barking drew him downstairs. Jenny had arrived back and was out in the garden with Trixie yapping at her heels.

'Daddy,' she called over.

He blew her a kiss. 'Be with you in a

moment, poppet.'

He could hear voices in the kitchen. The studio driver was with Morag, drinking a cup of tea.

'Will you be going out to lunch now, Mr Jackson?' she asked.

Lyle shook his head. 'I don't think so. I've a conference call booked this afternoon and Monty Daniels asked me to be on hand later should the publicity people be in touch.'

'Want me to move my car, sir?' the studio driver offered. 'I think I'm blocking you in.'

'No. That's all right. Finish your tea.'

'Would you like a sandwich, Mr Jackson?' Morag asked.

'Thanks, Mrs H. I'll be outside with Jenny.'

'I'm doing her a glass of juice. I'll bring you a tray.'

Lyle sauntered on to the terrace. Trixie raced towards him, falling over her paws. He bent down to stroke the soft ears. The garden looked so lovely in the afternoon sun and Jenny couldn't be happier. Had he thrown everything away by his stupid behaviour? He supposed with Sara gone and Mrs Henderson under notice, they would have to leave Medway Manor and move to America with Carla.

'Mummy says Trixie will remind us of her while she's away.' Jenny was breathless with excitement as she caught up with the puppy.

'We may be going with Mummy,' Lyle broke the news as gently as he could.

'Don't be silly, Daddy, we can't go to America now. That would mean leaving Trixie behind.'

'So it would.' Lyle looked thoughtfully at his daughter. If only Sara was still here everything would have been perfect.

'Where's Sara?' Jenny demanded, tuning in to his thoughts. 'I want to show her a new trick I'm teaching Trixie.'

Lyle straightened up slowly. He didn't know how he was going to tell

Jenny that Sara had left. He hoped the stress wouldn't bring on an asthma attack.

'There's something I . . . ' he began.

'She's here,' a voice behind him spoke.

'Whoopee.' Jenny raced towards Sara.

She was standing between the doors of the conservatory holding a tray of sandwiches and soft drinks.

'Morag says you haven't had any lunch. I haven't either. Would you mind if I join in?' she asked.

'Sara, Sara,' Jenny jumped up and down with excitement. 'I've got so much to tell you. Mummy's got a part in a film and she's going to America.'

'And I can't wait to hear all about it.'

'Jenny?' Morag Henderson called from the kitchen. 'Where are you?'

'Here,' she trilled, 'with Daddy and Sara.'

'You've got a visitor come to tea.'

'Yay.' Jenny raced away. Trixie raced after her leaving Lyle and Sara facing each other on the terrace.

Lyle took the tray from Sara and put it down on the table. 'Would you like to sit down?' he asked, ignoring the rushing feeling inside his head.

'Thank you,' she replied.

He noticed she was wearing a pinky coloured top and a summer skirt.

'You look very smart,' Lyle complimented her, not daring to ask why she had come back.

'Do you realise we are actually being polite to each other?' Sara asked with a wry look on her face.

'So we are. It's amazing what I can do with a bit of practice,' Lyle admitted, sitting down opposite her.

There were dark circles under Sara's eyes and Lyle suspected that like him she hadn't slept a wink last night.

He took a deep breath. 'Did your stepfather tell you I went to see him early this morning at the hotel?'

Sara raised her eyebrows. 'He didn't, no.'

'He invited me to join you all for lunch.'

'You didn't take him up on his invitation?'

'I couldn't.'

'I see.'

'No, you don't.'

'You don't have to make excuses, Lyle,' Sara insisted.

'Because,' Lyle battled on with his explanation before he ran out of nerve, 'Monty delayed me on the telephone. Then I bumped into Mrs H at the bottom of the lane. She'd been buying stuff for Trixie and I had to drive her back to the house. We went over a nail or something and I had a puncture, so I had to change the tyre. Then Jenny arrived back and her driver blocked me in.' Lyle frowned. 'Is that funny?' he demanded as a dimple of laughter dented Sara's cheek.

'I believe you,' she said, 'no one could invent such a complicated story.'

'Well, I just wanted you to know that I would have been there.' Lyle couldn't fight off the suspicion that things weren't going well between them. 'I had hoped to have a quiet word with you at The Grange. Medway Manor is far too full of interruptions for private conversations.'

'So, what did you and Vernon talk about?' Sara asked.

'Can't you guess?' Lyle lowered his voice, anxious not to be overheard.

'I'd rather you told me.'

'He's a very special man your stepfather, isn't he?'

Sara nodded. 'Yes. He is.'

'I'm sorry I was so rude about him.'

'You should apologise to him.'

'I have and I need to apologise to you too, Sara. I totally lost it in Carla's flat. I'm sorry.'

'There's no need to go over old ground.' Sara's smile was on the shaky side now.

'I don't know what got into me, rushing in like that. I was so relieved to find you both safe and sound then when I thought Jenny was having an asthma attack I said the first stupid thing that came into my head.'

'It was pretty stupid,' Sara agreed, 'thinking I would kidnap Jenny. Did you read my letter?' she asked.

'Yes.' Lyle nodded. 'Mrs H gave it to me and before you think she betrayed your trust she didn't tell me where you were. I sort of worked it out for myself.'

'I'm glad you did.'

'Have you changed your mind about leaving?' Lyle leaned forward eagerly.

'No one likes to be accused of kidnapping a child — twice.'

'Is that yes or no?'

Sara hesitated, but before she could speak, Lyle added, 'Your mother and Vernon are prepared to give things another try. Couldn't we follow their example?'

'That's why I'm here actually,' Sara admitted. 'I felt very much in the way over pre-lunch drinks. They were holding hands and looking into each other's eyes. They didn't need me there, so I made my excuses and left. As I've still got some stuff here I decided to come back and collect it.'

'Is that the only reason?' Lyle asked.
'Should there be another one?'
'You're still intent on leaving then?'
Sara's face gave nothing away as she looked at Lyle.
'Would it help you to know I've had three lectures on the error of my ways, from Mrs H, then Carla and then Vernon? They all told me what a fool I've been and if I didn't shape up I'd probably lose you forever.'
'So I'd be wasting my time telling you I agree with them too?' A soft smile curved the corners of Sara's mouth.
'You could try but I think I've got the message.' Lyle picked up Jenny's orange juice and drank some to ease the dryness in his mouth. 'Do you really have to leave?' he asked.
'Do you want me to?'
'I never want to be parted from you again,' Lyle admitted.
'Even though I'm a totally unsuitable nanny for your daughter? One who drowns dogs and gets stranded in remote places when her car won't start?'

'I wasn't talking about you as a nanny, Sara. I want you to be my wife. Your father gave me permission to ask for your hand.'

'For once you seem to have done the right thing,' Sara's voice was gentle now.

Loud music from the house made them both jump as Jenny and her friend began dancing to a new routine. Trixie joined in barking loudly.

'For heaven's sake.' Lyle leapt to his feet as the studio driver began tooting his horn.

'Sorry, am I blocking you in?' Jenny's school friend's mother dashed out of the kitchen and ran towards her car. 'Won't be a moment. Oh, there's another car in the way.'

'Think it's mine.' Sara stood up. 'I'd better go and move it.'

In the distance the telephone began to ring.

'Mr Jackson?' Morag called out, 'it's for you.'

'Why did you have to come back now?' Lyle demanded with a gesture of irritation, 'I had the place to myself this morning. It was perfect for a quiet conversation. Look at it now. It's a mad house.'

'Is that what you want?' Sara asked, 'because if I do play a significant part in your life I don't think you're going to get it.'

'You mean,' Lyle had difficulty getting his words out anxious to avoid any further misunderstandings, 'you aren't going to go off and train to be a childminder?'

'I might do that anyway if I give up acting.'

'Yes, of course. But what about us?'

'Us?'

'You and me. Do you accept my proposal?'

'Of marriage?'

'Yes.'

'You haven't asked me.'

'I just did.'

Morag Henderson walked on to the terrace holding the telephone. Lyle ignored her.

'But I'll do it again if you insist. Sara, will you do me the very great honour of agreeing to be my wife?'

She looked hard at him for a long moment. 'Sara?' Lyle prompted, 'you haven't replied.'

'My answer's yes,' she said softly.

'It's Mrs Jackson,' Morag Henderson interrupted then with a knowing smile said, 'I mean Miss de Courcy on the telephone, sir.'

'Tell her Sara and I are busy getting engaged and that I'll call her back,' Lyle shouted over.

'Don't bother, Mrs H,' Carla laughed down the line. 'I heard him. Tell him I'll expect an invitation to the wedding.'

'Daddy, are you going to marry Sara? Can I be your bridesmaid?' Jenny raced on to the terrace with her little friend in hot pursuit.

Her mother poked her head round the side gate.

'Excuse me,' she called over to Sara. 'Is that your car? Only I can't get out.'

Laughter bubbled up in Sara's

throat. 'Be with you in a minute.'

'This must be the most public proposal of marriage ever,' Lyle complained and tried to look annoyed with his daughter, but failed. Instead he drew Sara into his arms. 'Promise you'll never walk out on me again?'

'Only if you promise not to put the police on to me the next time Jenny and I go out for the day.'

'It's a deal,' Lyle said and kissed her. 'Now hadn't you better go and move your car?'

THE END

Other titles in the
Linford Romance Library:

LADY CHARLOTTE'S SECRET

Fenella Miller

Determined to fulfil her promise to a friend, Charlotte defies her brother and sets out on a journey in secret. But the person most at risk is herself, as circumstances conspire to leave her helpless in the care of a stranger. Dr James Hunter is a modern man, dedicating his life to aristocracy. When he discovers Charlotte's secret will it destroy their love?

SNOWBOUND

Fay Cunningham

When Amy agrees to help famous cosmetic surgeon Ethan Stopes write his memoirs, she is expecting a few quiet days in the country. Instead she spends an eventful Christmas trapped in a lonely manor with Ethan, his ex-wife, and his two children — and falls in love . . . Amy discovers Ethan's secret, and passions flare as the snow deepens. Somehow, she must help the enigmatic surgeon finish his book before it is too late . . .

THE BLACKSMITH'S DAUGHTER

Roberta Grieve

Tilly Masters hopes to follow in her father's footsteps as the village blacksmith and is upset when he takes on an assistant. But she falls in love with Nathan and is devastated when he enlists and is sent to France. She vows to wait for him but her aunt has other ambitions for her — marriage to the local squire's son. Will Tilly succumb to his advances or cling to the hope that Nathan will return from the war?

Sully looked over his shoulder at the woman standing there in front of his cell – an exotic island nymph with the face of an angel.

No way. He was either drunker than he thought, or he was still asleep and in the middle of the same dream from last night. Oh, yeah, this was the little honey from his dream. His hands had tangled in all that black hair. She had the same sexy dark eyes. The same pouty lips, too.

Grinning, he muttered, "Come on, baby, climb on in here and we'll start the party all over again."

He was two steps from the bed when his sexy dream-lover spoke and stopped him in his tracks.

"If I were you, I would be thinking about a way out of here instead of having a party. The men who visit this cell don't usually live very long."

Sully turned slowly. "You're real?"

Dear Reader,

In *Sleeping with Danger*, you're about to meet the most menacing of all Merrick's elite agents – the Irish gun-runner dubbed Mad Dog Paxton long before he left Dublin to become Onyxx's deadly weapons expert. It's been eighteen months since Sully Paxton was left for dead in an Onyxx incursion that went sour in Greece. Where has Sully been all this time? What has he survived?

As many of you know, I'm a huge fan of bad boys. I hope you enjoy spending time with him and with the woman who is about to steal his heart.

For updates on future releases, my backlist or if you missed one of the previous books, log on to www.wendyrosnau.com.

Wendy Rosnau

Sleeping with Danger

WENDY ROSNAU

All the characters in this book have no existence outside the imagination of the author, and have no relation whatsoever to anyone bearing the same name or names. They are not even distantly inspired by any individual known or unknown to the author, and all the incidents are pure invention.

First published in Great Britain 2008
by Harlequin Mills & Boon Limited,
Eton House, 18-24 Paradise Road, Richmond, Surrey TW9 1SR

ISBN: 978 0 263 86001 6

46-1008

Harlequin Mills & Boon policy is to use papers that are natural, renewable and recyclable products and made from wood grown in sustainable forests. The logging and manufacturing processes conform to the legal environmental regulations of the country of origin.

Printed and bound in Spain
by Litografia Rosés S.A., Barcelona

ABOUT THE AUTHOR

Wendy Rosnau resides on sixty secluded acres in Minnesota with her husband. She divides her time between her family-owned bookshop and writing romantic suspense. She is the 2004 recipient of the Midwest Fiction Writers' Writer of the Year Award.

Wendy loves to hear from her readers. Visit her website at www.wendyrosnau.com.

For Jerry

Chapter 1

They had stopped beating the hell out of him five days ago and started feeding him regularly. The thick gray mush and a cup of water now came every day instead of three times a week.

No longer numb, he slowly became aware of his wretched existence, as well as the pain that raped his body with every breath he took. He was given two weeks to contemplate the change in the routine—to consider whether it was a blessing or a dark omen—before they came for him.

Even though the sun was low on the horizon, he squinted against the brightness as the heavy iron grate overhead was unlocked and he was pulled from the pit and dropped like a sack of garbage on the rocky ground.

In the beginning the hole in the earth where they kept him had been a tight fit, but that was months ago. These days they could have flushed him down a sewer pipe, he was so damn thin.

"On your feet. *Greegorah!*"

The old instincts that had kept him alive for a year and a half were still a part of his memory. Those memories urged him to get up and fight back, but he was physically broken. Even the guards' orders didn't rally him to his feet.

"Get up. Now!" Pedro gave him a vicious kick. The guard's steel-toed boot connected with his ribs. He grunted, bit back a pitiful moan, then flattened his dirty hands out on the hard ground and pushed his body upward. After three tries he managed to get to his knee, and there he remained, too weak to stand.

Again Pedro used his foot, and like a rotten stump in a windstorm it toppled him easily. His head struck a jagged rock and split open his forehead.

"That's enough."

It was Argo who had spoken. A man twice as brutal as Pedro. He waited to feel more pain from the commander of the guards, but for some reason the short-legged Greek with a passion for sadistic torture wasn't interested in making him scream today.

He forced himself back to his knees, and as soon as he did, the two men grabbed him under his arms and began dragging him toward the old Greek monastery. A few yards from the back entrance he managed to get his feet under him. When the guards let go of him, he leaned heavily against the stone wall while Argo retrieved a key from his pocket. When the door swung open a blast of sour air stole his breath. Whatever was down there was dead, or close to it.

Pedro pulled him away from the wall and that's when he saw the steep stairwell that led down into the bowels of the sanctuary. There was no way in hell he was going down those narrow steps on his own power.

"Move. I don't have all day to babysit your ass."

Pedro gave him a shove and he reached out and saved himself from eating another rock by grabbing on to the door.

Argo took a pack of cigarettes from his shirt pocket, shook one out and pinched it between his lips. Firing it up, he said, "A smoke takes me four and a half minutes. See you at the bottom."

With the clock ticking, he shuffled forward and flattened out one hand against the cool stone wall. Then, like an old man, one step at a time, he started down the narrow steps as the faint smell of tobacco was swallowed up by the stench below.

With each painful step he imagined Argo's cigarette between his own lips. Imagined inhaling the nicotine—what he wouldn't give for a little buzz right now.

You can make it, he told himself. Slow and easy. One step at a time.

A smoke takes me four and a half minutes. See you at the bottom.

In the old days he would have taken the steps four at a time. Hell, in the old days he would have turned on the two guards and snapped both their necks in less than...*four and a half minutes.*

He never let go of the wall, and like an infant who had just learned to walk, he tested out his balance with each step he took.

He heard Argo and Pedro start down.

Three more steps.

Two.

One.

He came off the last step just as Pedro came up behind him. The guard looked disappointed that he'd managed to make it without falling on his face.

Out of breath, he sagged against the wall as Pedro pulled a wooden stick from the belt loop on his pants. One quick jab to his ribs and he was on his hands and knees.

The stick came at him again, this time it made contact with his bare ass and the hard whack drove him forward and he sprawled spread-eagle on his belly.

The caustic odor in the air burned his nostrils, and it reminded him that this hellhole was definitely a death trap. So this is it then, he decided. This was where he would die.

"We have our orders, Pedro?" Argo grumbled. "Get him on his feet."

"Stupid orders, if you ask me."

"Do you want to tell *him* that?" Argo asked. "Every man here is expendable. Even you and me. Now get him up."

Pedro reached down and hauled him to his feet, then gestured down the corridor. "Move."

He shuffled forward, heard voices in the distance. After he'd gone twenty yards he realized that what he was hearing was a chorus of moaning.

He continued on toward the noise, each step twice as painful as the one before it. The corridor took a hard left, and when it straightened out he was standing in a large circular dungeon—a dungeon of horrors.

In his wildest dreams he hadn't expected anything like this. His eyes followed the iron cage around as it wrapped the outer wall—a cage eight feet wide and ten feet high. At least two dozen men stared back at him. Men just like him, naked and broken, starved beyond recognition. Some were huddled in corners. Others, those who could still stand, were clinging to the bars of the cage, their eyes ghostlike and too big for their bony faces.

Did he look like that?

It was obvious that food and water had been as scarce in here as they had been in the pit. No, maybe he had fared better. He'd been able to eat the rats and bugs that fell between the grates that had imprisoned him in the hole.

His eyes shifted to a slab of concrete ten feet square and two feet thick in the middle of the room. On it stood a small wooden table, a toilet, sink and a cot—the mattress covered with a sheet.

He stared at the simple, bare-bones amenities. To a man who had been living in hell for over a year they looked like the Ritz. It reminded him of the stripped-down apartment in Dublin where he'd lived for a short time with Paddy, with one big difference—the room at the rundown Dunroy Hotel had walls, even though they were paper-thin and he'd been able to hear old man Murphy beat his wife late at night and, on his days off, screw the neighborhood whore.

He didn't see the leg shackle and chain cemented into the center of the floor until Pedro prodded him up on the slab and manacled one of his ankles.

Since he'd been imprisoned his senses had been heightened. His sight was as crystal-clear as an owl's in the dark of night, and his nose was as razor-sharp as a hound dog on the scent of a rabbit.

He immediately picked up the aroma of food though it was faint—the air was fetid with human waste—and turned slowly to search out the source. On the table was a covered tray, and beneath it was something edible.

He forced the food and the gnawing hunger in his belly from his mind and focused on the clothes folded on the foot of the bed—a pair of green fatigues, a black T-shirt and white boxers.

"Wash up, and use the soap." Argo motioned to the bar at the sink. "You smell like the butt of a dead carcass. Then eat and get some rest."

Wash up.

Eat.

He glanced at the sink, envisioned the water flowing out of the tap. Fresh water, not some contaminated swill the color of piss.

He didn't understand why he was being given these things after all this time. Instead of questioning the gift, he should be kissing his enemy's feet. But as he looked around the room at the naked starving men, the idea of accepting his good fortune in front of these poor bastards ripped his heart out.

"Why me?" he asked.

"Guess you drew the long straw, pretty boy."

"What about them?" he asked, his eyes drifting to the dying menagerie in the cage.

Argo grinned. "Today they all wish they were you. By tomorrow they will want to cut your heart out and eat it. And that's no lie. Before we can get the dead out those boys are licking their chops."

The guard's words prompted him to turn his attention back on the cage. He scanned the individual faces, his eyes drawn to one man who was leaning against the back wall. When he saw the scar that traveled from his right hipbone to his knee, he whispered, "Roth Erwin."

"Recognize someone?" Argo's grin spread. "That one's about ready for the bone pile. He no longer fights for food. But like the others, he will hate you by morning. And when he dies, he will haunt you from his cold grave. They all will."

After the two guards left, he stood there like a monkey at center stage of a circus. He was so damn dirty and hungry, and still he didn't move. He glanced at the covered food tray on the table. The urge was there, the need, but he couldn't do it.

He walked to the sink and turned on the faucet. It was a pretty sight, the water spilling from the tap. He tucked his head under and let the water flow into his mouth and over his dry lips, then scrubbed his hands until they stung.

He found a clean washcloth and towel on the floor next to the sink and he went to work shedding the layers of dirt from his face, working his way down his body. And all the while the smell of the food continued to torture his belly.

It was a slow process, removing the crusty layers of dirt, but he kept at it until he began to feel human again. But he wasn't clean when he finished—it would take days to scrub the imbedded filth from his body, maybe weeks.

How long was he going to be here?

Still avoiding the food, he dressed in the issued clothes. Finally he pulled out the chair at the table and sat down. With a room full of eyes glued to him, he lifted the cover off the tray and stared at two fat slices of meat, potatoes swimming in butter, a chunk of bread and a clean cup that he could take to the sink anytime he felt like it.

He glanced at the silverware, but he didn't pick up the fork. He should be celebrating right now—water, a bed, food.

He should eat it quickly before it was taken away from him like some cruel joke.

In the past year he'd been flogged, tortured and starved, but none of it compared to the mental anguish ripping him apart at that moment.

How could he do it?

How could he betray these dying men by eating the enemy's food while they watched?

Because you want to live, the voice inside his head whispered. *You can't help them if you don't help yourself first.*

The truth staring him in the face from all sides, Sully Paxton did what he was trained to do—survive. He picked up the fork, speared a piece of meat, then closed his eyes and opened his mouth.

Adolf Merrick, commander of the Onyxx Agency, tossed two sleeping pills into his mouth and chased them down with a glass of water. He'd started taking the pills a few weeks ago after he'd broken it off with Sarah Finny.

Guilt was a bitch. For two years he'd convinced himself, and Sarah, that he wanted a new life, but what he wanted was his old life back. Since that wasn't possible, the alternative was to walk away from Sarah and live with his memories and pray it was enough.

The pills knocked him out so he could sleep, but the downside was they prevented him from dreaming. Dreaming was what had kept him sane for twenty years. It's where he lived with Johanna, where he kept her memory alive and the loneliness at bay.

He'd told Sarah he couldn't see her any longer. He blamed it on obstacles at work. What he should have told her was that even with Johanna gone, he couldn't forget their life together—didn't want to—and that the Agency was the only thing that made him feel remotely alive.

Merrick climbed into bed and closed his eyes. He needed to find an apartment of his own. He'd been living out of a suitcase in a hotel on the Potomac in Arlington for three weeks—ever since a fire had destroyed his apartment in Washington. A fire that had blown up the entire building.

Gas leak my ass.

Like a well-aimed hammer the pills sent Merrick into a dead sleep just after ten o'clock. He never moved again or made a sound. Not even a soft snore drifted into the stuffy hotel room until predawn, when he came out of his drug-induced sleep as if a bell had gone off inside his head.

The room was still dark, and he wondered what had wakened him. Then he heard his cell phone ring.

He looked at the clock on the nightstand. It read 5:30 a.m.

He reached for his phone, read the unrecognizable number, then flipped it open and put it to his ear. "Merrick here."

"Did I wake you? Or are you having another sleepless night imagining your hands around my neck? Do you ever sleep these days, old buddy?"

The voice from the past jackknifed Merrick straight up in bed. "Cyrus."

"Back from the dead. Oh, that's right, I never died."

"How did you get my number?"

"The same way I survived Prague. I never give up. You lit a fire inside me that day you left me in that minefield drowning in my own blood. Betrayal can be powerful motivation."

A few weeks ago Merrick had learned the identity of the Chameleon. Cyrus Krizova was alive. One of their own agents had become a terrorist, and for the past twenty years—while everyone thought he was dead—Cyrus had been targeting the Onyxx Agency, and Merrick.

There had been no betrayal in Prague. Only pure agony when he'd been forced to leave a comrade behind, but now Cyrus was the enemy.

Merrick snapped, "You son of a bitch, I'm going to kill you."

"You should have done it twenty years ago. If you had, you wouldn't be sleeping alone tonight. You are sleeping alone, right? Of course you are. If you want a man dead, there's only one way to make sure. Put a bullet through his heart, and two in his head. That shouldn't have been too hard. I wasn't going to run off. An animal caught in a trap is treated better than I was. And let's face it, you were the best exterminator in our outfit."

"We're trained to kill the enemy, not our own."

"You were chickenshit, is that it?"

"I had a job to do, and I did it the best way I knew how. It was a damn hard decision to make."

"As I recall you had help making it. Paavo Creon swayed you to leave me, but it was your choice. You were in command. I think it went something like, we can carry out only one man. Cyrus will die before nightfall. He's six-four. Weighs two-twenty. Briggs is forty pounds lighter."

Merrick was transported back twenty years, his memory as clear as if it were yesterday—the carnage, the blood, the smell of death all around him. His team had been on their feet one minute and the next they were scattered like broken toys in a playground.

Leave him, Adolf. You have to think about the men who can survive.

Every man in the outfit had been hit. The skin on his own back had been peeled like an onion, and he could see his guts coming through a hole in his side the size of his fist. One man had died on impact. Peter Briggs had shrapnel in both legs—later he would lose them—but he was still lucid, his eyes wide and his voice full of fear, begging not to be left behind.

But Cyrus…he hadn't made a sound. No, he wasn't dead, but he was headed for the grave. There was no doubt.

Hell, his face was almost gone.

Yes, he should have ended Cyrus's suffering with a bullet. He'd tried. He'd pulled his gun, aimed, but he couldn't pull the trigger. Not on his comrade. Not his best friend. So he'd saved the others, and filed a false report about who had died on impact.

"Reminiscing?"

"If you wanted revenge, why not just come after me?"

"That was the plan. But first I had to put myself back together. Starting with a new face."

"So you cloned Paavo Creon."

"An ingenious idea, don't you think? Of course I wanted revenge on him for his part in leaving me in Prague, but that would come later. It took a number of plastic surgeries, but eventually I became his twin. You should have seen the look on his face when he realized he had a double and it was me."

"What happened the night of the fire at Paavo's home?" Merrick asked.

"Paavo arrived home unexpected. I'll never forget the look on Muriel's face when she saw both of us. That's when she realized she'd betrayed her husband with me. The fire wasn't planned but it was the perfect way to get rid of her and take Paavo prisoner. I never intended to take the little girl, but Evka had her father's instincts for survival. I rewarded her for that by making her my daughter. She never knew I was the double until your agent interfered a few years ago. By the way, how is she doing?"

"She's waiting for the day I call her and tell her I've killed you and avenged her parents. And for myself. Why did you have to kill Johanna?"

"She was your most cherished possession. What you loved most. You destroyed my life, so I destroyed yours."

"You had Fiora."

"She remarried a year after the Prague incident. I couldn't allow someone with so many flaws to raise my children."

"You killed her?"

"She was the past and I needed to concentrate on the future. I needed more surgeries, money to make that possible. While I was in the hospital I began to think about your flawless, beautiful wife. Remember that picture you used to carry with you? Her image became my lifeline, and that's when I realized she was the perfect revenge between us."

"You're dead, Cyrus. I'm going to kill you."

"You're going to have to find me first. So far you've failed miserably, just like you failed to protect your wife."

"You're insane."

"What I am is somewhere out of your reach, and right now you're wondering where that is."

"I'm coming, Cyrus. It doesn't matter whose face you stole, or what island in Greece you're hiding on, I'll find you, and when I do I'll put a bullet in your heart and two in your head."

"That's the spirit. I was hoping you'd still feel that way. I have unmeasurable patience, and it seems you've acquired a lengthy amount yourself. I wouldn't want you to give up too soon."

"I'll never give up."

"Good. The game is far from over. That's why I called."

"What have you done now?"

"I've been in touch with a friend of ours."

"No friend of yours is a friend of mine."

"I suppose he would agree with you. Nonetheless, Holic Reznik sends you his regards."

"The assassin is behind bars at Clume. Your sidekick is never going to see the light of day."

"Behind bars the last time you checked. When was that?"

No, Merrick thought, it wasn't possible. Holic was in solitary confinement in the highest security prison in the U.S., surrounded by a twenty-four-hour guard.

"Semtex makes a helluva hole in brick and steel if you know how to pack the load. As you know, I'm an expert when it comes to blowing things up. Still living out of a suitcase?"

Merrick was on his feet now, but before he could say anything more the phone went dead. Quickly he punched in his superior's phone number. "Harry?"

"Merrick. Hell, I was just about to call you. There's been an explosion at Clume."

Merrick closed his eyes, listened to Harry's account of what they believed happened. It was the perfect time to set Harry straight—he was talking terrorist attack. The perfect time to tell him about the phone call he'd had with Cyrus. What would he say if he told him Cyrus Krizova was alive, and that one of their own Onyxx agents was the Chameleon?

But if he revealed everything to Harry now, he'd never get the chance to avenge Johanna.

He asked, "What about the prisoners?"

"It's too early for a body count. It'll take days to sort through the rubble."

Merrick didn't need to wait days to know they wouldn't find Holic Reznik among the dead. Cyrus had him. The question was, why? The assassin's mangled hands made him as useless as a one-legged frog in a jumping contest.

Merrick hung up the phone and dressed in jeans and a black sweater. As he walked past the window he saw it was still snowing. The Potomac was as gray as the sky, as gray as the day he'd left Cyrus in that minefield in Prague.

Chapter 2

For fifteen months Melita had been confined on the barren islet Despotiko. Some days it felt as if she would die there. She felt that way tonight as she hurried along the goat trail back to the monastery. For weeks she had been slipping out after dark in search of someone to help her escape the island.

The village was three miles away, the harbor lined with boats. She could stow away so easily. The problem was convincing one of the fisherman in the village to risk it.

What she needed was a gorilla with brass balls and a death wish. That's what one of the fisherman had told her tonight. But there was no gorilla on the island, and that meant outside of growing wings, she was not getting off the island.

It was almost dawn and she couldn't get caught outside the periphery. Melita picked up her pace and crested the rocky knoll. She heard the sea rushing the rugged shoreline, and up ahead she could see Minare. The monastery's tall tower in the moonlight.

The first guard she slipped past was dozing against a rock. The second, too busy taking a leak off the rampart to notice her. Number three had left his post altogether.

She moved through the flower garden, almost home free. Ten feet from the back door she saw a shadowy figure step onto the stone path. At first she thought it was Hector, but her bodyguard—and more importantly, her friend—was supposed to be inside keeping watch over the long corridor that she had to slip past to reach the stairs that would take her back to her bedroom in the tower.

She was about to softly speak his name into the darkness when the shadow revealed himself. "Restless again tonight, Melita?"

The heavily accented voice stopped her dead in her tracks. It was her father's houseguest, Holic Reznik.

He sauntered toward her with the grace of a stalking panther. He was smoking a cigarette, and he held it awkwardly in his disfigured hand a few inches from his lips. Both hands had been damaged in a shoot-out he'd been engaged in months ago. Holic was an assassin, and the maiming had been the result of a scrimmage with two government agents. It had cost him two fingers on his right hand, and the thumb on the left, as well as extensive nerve damage.

For a number of weeks she had watched him from afar, wondering why the assassin had arrived and decided to stay. At the moment that question didn't seem as important as the one affecting her breathing right now. Did he know where she'd been tonight? If so, did he know that her trips to the village were forbidden?

"I asked you a question, Melita. Restless?"

"I like taking walks before dawn," she said. "It's the quietest time of day."

His lips curled around the cigarette, sucked hard, then sent a cloud of smoke into the warm island air. "I rise early myself, but for a different reason. My hands pain me. They keep me up at all hours."

His Russian accent was colored with a sharp German influence. Sharp like his unnatural eyes, set deep into his sockets. Even though his dark complexion and masculine features would easily attract women, when Melita looked at him all she saw were his eyes—black soulless eyes…the eyes of a killer.

On the other hand, when he looked at her, she got the feeling he was stripping her naked one piece of clothing at a time.

Holic was in his early forties, not overly tall, with short, thick black hair in its early stages of growing out.

Hector had warned her that Holic was a randy womanizer, and that she should avoid him. That was just what she intended to do.

Melita forced herself to take two more steps. "I need to get inside."

"Before a guard spots you and reports it to your father?"

That wasn't going to happen if she could get inside in the next five minutes. She'd learned the guards' routine. Names, schedules and who took their job seriously. She knew which guard drank too much, who snuck off to the kitchen for a late-night snack and who couldn't keep his eyes open past midnight.

She'd planned her trips accordingly, and for several weeks she'd been able to slip away and return without anyone the wiser.

Until tonight.

"I'm not forbidden to take walks," she challenged.

"An extremely long walk tonight," he offered.

"Have you been following me?"

"Of course. A man seeking an advantage does what he must. You are persistent. A commendable quality. But the villagers will not help you escape your life here."

"I have no life here."

"Perhaps I can make it more meaningful."

Spoken like a man who thought he had the miracle cure for what ailed every woman.

"Do you know why I'm here?" she asked, wondering just how close a friend he was to her father, or if it was strictly business.

"You're being punished for bad judgment. I'm in agreement. Taking a common guard as your lover was in poor taste."

He relaxed his stance, his confidence overflowing. His open white shirt revealed that he shaved his chest, and the painfully tight fit of his jeans confirmed that his miracle cure for what ailed a woman, ailed him more. She was surprised that he could walk in such a state.

"The villagers are too frightened of what will happen to them if they show you any mercy. As they should be. There would be no leniency for the fool who helped the Chameleon's daughter escape him. But perhaps I know of a way you could regain your freedom."

He smiled, then reached out and stroked her cheek with the back of one of his disfigured hands.

Even though his hands were an obvious handicap to him, she'd seen him out on the target range every day. He was still a superb marksman. Speed was perhaps the only flaw in his execution.

When he began to trail his fingers down her neck she pulled away. "I believe your…*way* of helping me would only serve you. I suspect that's why you haven't told my father about my late-night walks?"

"I see no reason to alarm him about something that isn't going to happen. Well, at least not without my help."

"So if I share your bed, you're prepared to forget you saw me this morning, is that it?"

"I'm prepared to forget it, and give you a future elsewhere."

"My father would kill you if he knew what you're suggesting."

"No doubt, he would. Your lover suffered an agonizing death. Did he scream much? I was told your father made you watch."

Melita refused to let his cruel words rattle her. She was used to her father using Nemo's violent death as a tool to control her.

"You're wasting your time if you think you can blackmail me into your room after midnight."

"One night would never be enough." He glanced at her bare feet. "I'm curious if this rebellious spirit follows you into the bedroom, or if last year you were the victim of a silver-tongued playboy when you surrendered and lifted your skirt for Nemo."

He was a bold bastard, and Melita met his boldness with a bit of her own. "Which are you hoping for? Do you like victims or rebellious bitches?"

He laughed. "You are delightful, sweet Melita. What I hope for is a chance to find out. Do me a favor, and I will do you one."

"I think I'll stay in my prison." She tried to walk past him but he blocked her exit.

"Don't dismiss my offer too quickly. Your lover is dead. Your father owns every breath you take. Have you forgotten what freedom feels like?"

"The question is would I be free?"

"If I decide to talk to Cyrus, it won't go well for you. You've been slipping out at night for weeks, trying to persuade a fisherman at the village to sail you off the island."

"Go to my father and tell him your tale. But before you do know that my story will be quite different. I didn't go to the village tonight, nor have I ever."

She tried to go around him again, but this time he grabbed her arm, his grip so tight it would surely leave a bruise. He tossed his cigarette to the ground, pushed her against the stone face of the monastery and trapped her there.

"Taming you will be my pleasure, and it will happen soon. I will have you. A little preview of what it will be like, hmm..."

He smelled of tobacco and whiskey, and she thought perhaps it was the whiskey that had prompted such crazy talk. But it wasn't just talk. Suddenly he tangled his fingers in her long black hair and jerked her head back. His free hand flattened out on her belly and he moved it slowly upward over her left breast. Squeezed.

"Very nice. More than I expected." A second later his hand was around her neck, squeezing until she couldn't swallow. "Hear me, Melita, you and I will party soon, and I promise you that you will enjoy yourself. I know I will."

Melita closed her eyes as his lips crushed hers in a cruel kiss, and then he was grinding his body against her.

He forced his tongue down her throat and he raped her mouth with a promise of what was to come later. He was disgusting and vile, and the taste of him made her want to gag, then it made her want to scream.

Where was Hector? She was off schedule now. He should be checking his watch and starting to worry about her.

Desperate, Melita slipped her hand into her pocket and closed her fingers around the little bell she carried with her to call the goats that roamed the island, and to signal Hector in case she ran into trouble. Pulling it from the folds of her skirt, she rang it.

It was a gentle bell that could be missed in a windstorm, but tonight the breeze was but a whisper, the night as quiet as a graveyard. If Hector was nearby he would hear.

Holic's mouth slackened and he pulled back as the bell registered somewhere inside his lust-crazed head.

When he let go of her neck, Melita sucked air into her lungs, the rush making her almost dizzy. She whispered this time when she spoke, her throat raw and bruised from his abuse. "Hector will be here within seconds. How do you want to die?"

He stepped back from her. "You have him trained well. I wonder if your father knows that your bodyguard's loyalty is in question. I think it's time your watchdog learned who pays his salary."

He left her then, slipping into the darkness just as Hector appeared. Angry and scared, Melita rubbed her neck as she took her frustrations out on him. "Where have you been?"

"Following your instructions."

"But I'm late."

"Does that mean you had some luck tonight?"

Six feet, six inches, Hector dwarfed her, but he would never be as frightening as Holic Reznik. He was a gentle giant with none of the qualities it took to be a ruthless guard in her father's camp, or an assassin for hire.

"No, I had no luck. No one in the village will help me. It's a lost cause."

"Why did you ring the bell?"

"Holic Reznik saw me. He knows I've been to the village. And he knows why. He..." She stopped before she spilled the rest of what had transpired between them. Hector wasn't violent, but he was protective of her. She didn't want him doing something stupid.

"I'm afraid he intends to tell my father," she confessed.

"I'll deny it. I'll say your early-morning walk was to pick flowers and visit the goats. That I was with you the entire time."

She slipped the bell back into her pocket. "The question is, who will my father believe?"

"You picked flowers and played with the goats. That is our story. Stick to it. Now go inside, and get that frightened look off your face or he'll read the truth the minute he sees you."

Melita looked up into Hector's kind face. How he had come to be in her father's employment she didn't know, but he didn't belong here any more than she did.

She glanced around, spied the lavender growing in the garden and plucked a handful, then hurried inside.

Sully scratched another mark into the leg of the wooden table with his fingernail. He'd been on the platform thirty-six days. Still shackled like an animal, he'd put on weight and started to regain his strength. It was due to three meals a day, and Argo's determination to return him to the man he used to be. The question was why.

Physically he was winning the fight, but emotionally he was raw and heartsick. He was surrounded by pain and misery, his dying audience a constant reminder that he had become their enemy.

Argo was right, they hated him now. If he was tossed into the cage with them they would rip him apart and feast on his remains.

Like he did each evening after supper, he washed at the sink, then went to bed early. Lying on his back staring at the dark ceiling, he was constantly aware of the men ten feet away. Eyes closed, he could still see their skeleton faces and misshapen bodies—bodies that continued to grow weaker as his grew stronger.

He'd planned to share his food with them. How would

anyone know? But they would know, Argo told him, pointing to a camera on the wall. If he tried to toss food to anyone, they would be taken out and killed.

The men haunted him day and night. His nightmares were his reality—and sometimes he would startle and realize his own cries had awakened him.

He jerked awake now, but this time it wasn't due to the men moaning, or a nightmare. He angled his head and listened, picked up the sound of heavy footsteps moving down the corridor.

When the light came on, he swung his legs off the bed, the chain around his ankle rattling on the concrete.

Argo entered the dungeon. He pulled a key from his pocket and stepped up on the platform. "It's time," he said, then unlocked the manacles on Sully's ankle.

"Time for what?"

"Your taxi just arrived."

Sully didn't get up.

"Don't tell me you're going to miss us here?"

That would depend on where Argo was taking him, Sully thought. For the past month he'd felt like a cow being fattened for slaughter. He was no longer hungry every hour of the day, or crawling with parasites. But there was no comfort in it.

Argo slid his gun off his shoulder and aimed it at his chest. "Get up."

Sully eyed the weapon as he stood. He recognized the make. It was a Czech Skorpion M-84. The design had been deferred, then later buried altogether. At least that was the story.

Now who could be manufacturing bad-boy Skorpions?

It didn't take a genius to figure that out. The Chameleon was involved in everything from contraband to global anarchy.

"Let's go. Take it nice and careful, pretty boy. You wouldn't want my finger to slip on this trigger."

Sully stepped off the concrete platform, then stopped to glance one last time at the circle of men huddled naked and hungry in their iron death trap.

Three men had died last week.

He searched out Roth Erwin and found him lying on his side with his knees curled up into his chest. He hadn't moved from that spot in two days. Sully looked for some sign of life. Suddenly, as if Roth could feel his eyes on him, he opened his, then Argo nudged Sully in the ribs with the M-84.

"Move out."

Sully left the dungeon and walked down the corridor. Weeks ago he'd been worried about his legs collapsing beneath him, but tonight there was no fear of that.

He hadn't been outside in a month, so when he stepped into the moonlight he embraced the warm night breeze on his face. He took a long, deep breath—the clean air better than the best sex he could remember.

Again Argo nudged him with the gun barrel. "Head for the dock."

Barefoot, Sully followed the uneven path that went up a rocky knoll. When he reached the craggy summit, he spotted a cruiser riding the water a hundred yards offshore. The sleek cigar boat was a badass smoker that no doubt had enough horsepower to outrun anything on the water. Its lines were similar to the Halmatic VSV used by the British for seaborne covert insertions, and the American Rigid Raider interceptor. It also resembled his own cigar boat that he'd used when he was a gunrunner in Ireland.

A small fishing boat was waiting at the end of the dock, Pedro seated in the stern. He climbed in and sat down on the middle seat. Argo covered the bench across from him in the bow.

The M-84 still pointed at him, Argo said, "The boss man wants you alive, but accidents happen. Stupidity could get you killed tonight, pretty boy."

Sully had no intentions of making a stupid move. Not with a gun aimed at his chest and nowhere to run. He was a good swimmer, but his endurance was questionable. He'd survived too long in hell to throw it away on a futile escape attempt.

Argo would pick him out of the water like a rubber duck floating in a carnival pond.

Pedro sent the boat out to sea and headed for the cigar boat. Once Sully was handed over to the crew, his wrists were cuffed and his ankles were shackled. In irons once again, he was shoved into a seat and locked down, and then the cruiser took off, skimming fast and furious over the water.

The four-man crew were armed with Czech Skorpions, and yet they were dressed like fishermen.

Sully kept his ears open, and his eyes out to sea. He had traveled the Greek Isles over the years, and although he couldn't speak the language fluently, he could speak some and had no trouble understanding the men's conversation on the boat.

Before long one of the rebels had unwittingly provided him with their destination. Despotiko was a small island that sat southwest of Paros and east of Sifnos. That meant they were headed north.

Sully glanced back at the fading image of the rocky island where he'd spent most of his incarceration. There were over two thousand islands in the Greek Isles, many of them nameless. The odds of finding this place again would be slim, but not impossible.

He could no longer see the monastery. With the new day dawning, he put to memory passing landmarks—anything that would help him find his way back to *hell island*.

There...he'd named the island, and he promised himself that if he escaped whatever fate he was headed for, he would be back. He only hoped that some of the men would still be alive.

It had been five hundred and twenty-two days since his capture at Castle Rock when the Chameleon's men had ambushed his Onyxx team, and he'd been left for dead. By now Sully was sure Merrick had replaced him.

He pushed the memory of his old life out of his mind. Argo said he'd been given the gift of life. He didn't know why that was, or what he would find on the island of Despotiko, but for some reason he was feeling optimistic. It must be something in the air he was breathing, he decided.

Sully suddenly smiled, knowing what it was. It was the scent of freedom, and it smelled as sweet as a field full of Irish lavender.

The vase of lavender sat in the middle of the table on the balcony outside Melita's bedroom, high in the tower. She stared down at the wooden post beyond the garden, at the blood on the ground, and the guilt nearly brought her to her knees.

It always happened there, and she knew why. Her father loved to make her watch.

She wiped the tears off her cheeks as she heard him speaking to the guard posted outside her door. Moments later her father appeared on the balcony sipping a cup of coffee.

"Nothing like a little morning excitement to get the blood pumping."

"Hector did nothing wrong. How could you beat him?"

"Every man at Minare has a purpose. A specific job. You were Hector's job. I've told you before when you disobey me, your actions have consequences."

"Then punish me," she railed. "Beat me, not him!"

"The punishment fit the crime. I've learned the best way to teach you a lesson is through your misguided attachments to the hired help. Your loyalty to Hector is touching, but you should be more concerned with your loyalty to me."

"Loyalty to a father who keeps his daughter locked away like a prisoner."

"You made the choice. A bad choice, but a conscious one. For months I've been waiting to hear you confess regret. Today I see that you've learned nothing from your hiatus away from those you love. Reckless mistakes are costly. Today Hector paid the price." He took a sip of his coffee. "It's a good thing I'm a patient man, and I value my children. I rarely give second chances. But I've had to make countless concessions where you're concerned."

"Lucky me."

"Yes, you are. As your father it's my job to keep you safe from my enemies, and of course, yourself. You do seem to enjoy tempting fate."

"And who will keep me safe from you?"

"No one. I am the center of your life, Melita. Get used to it."

"I hate you!"

"Now if I could just channel that anger into something productive we would be making progress. Your latest escapade has proven what I already know. You're cunning and smart. A survivor, like me. My blood is your blood. That is a fact you can't deny and I intend to never let you forget."

"If your blood runs through my veins it's because I've had a transfusion. I'm nothing like you."

"What you are is a fool if you think rebelling against me will enact your freedom. I control your life as I do Hector's, and every man who works for me. Hector looked me in the eye and lied to me this morning. He made an error in judgment. His loyalty should be to me, not my daughter. You know how I detest flaws in my men as well as my children." That said, he made himself comfortable in one of the heavy iron chairs at the balcony table.

He was dressed in his business clothes today, his crisp white shirt stark against his sun-baked face and neck. His black pants were creased, and his shoes as shiny as his short silver hair.

Was he leaving the island again? He'd stayed longer than usual, most likely because of Holic Reznik's arrival. But he would be growing anxious to see Callia. He never stayed away from Melita's stepmother for very long.

She pitied Callia as much as she loved her. She must have patience of steel to put up with her father. Or perhaps she was blinded by love. No, her father was unlovable. Callia was just as much a prisoner as she was. The only difference was her island home wasn't a monastery with a view of a whipping post from her bedroom balcony.

He cleared his throat, and Melita refocused her thoughts. "Where is Hector?" she asked.

"He's been confined to his quarters."

"I want to see him."

"No. At the moment he's not feeling well enough to have a visitor. Your time would be better spent here in your room thinking about how you want to spend the rest of your life—locked in a room, or enjoying the freedom I can give you."

"How could you believe a stranger over Hector? Holic Reznik is—"

"A trustworthy associate of mine. I've known him for years. If he says you've been sneaking off to the village in an attempt to escape the island, then I believe him. By the way, I'll be leaving in two days for a few weeks. While I'm away

Holic will be in charge. Make trouble in any way and he has my permission to string Hector up on the firing range for target practice."

Melita's knees went weak. "You can't leave Holic in charge! He wants—"

"He wants what?"

"He lied to you because I rejected him this morning when I was coming back from…picking flowers. He was in the garden and he attacked me. He shoved me against the wall and…touched me. He told me if I would spend time in his bed he would get me off the island. When I rejected his offer, he told me he was going to make trouble for me."

"And where was Hector while this was happening?"

"He… He was close by."

"Hector didn't mention Holic had attacked you. The truth is Hector would have snapped Holic's neck if that was true, and I would have rewarded him for it. Any man fool enough to touch you without my permission is a dead man."

"Holic did touch me, and he made it clear he will do it again. You can't leave him in charge while you're gone."

She waited for her father to digest every word, waited for him to rethink giving Holic the keys to everything at Minare, including the one to her bedroom.

"Holic is not an idiot. He knows what my plans are for you, and he also knows I would kill him if he laid a hand on you. I've done it before, remember?"

Yes, she remembered. She would live with her part in Nemo's death forever. She motioned to the flowers. "This lavender is fresh this morning, and—" she raised her chin and pointed to the bruises on her neck "—so are these. Holic choked me when I tried to get away."

He studied the marks on her throat, then pulled a silver case from his pocket and opened it. Taking one of his favorite cigars from it, he pinched it between his lips. Setting the case on the table next to his coffee cup, he lit the cigar with a lighter he took from his pocket. "As I said, you're a cunning little fox. You probably put those bruises there to aid your story. It's something I would do." He grinned. "Like father, like daughter."

Melita glanced at the lighter on the table. He'd had it a long time, and she'd watched him finger it and stroke it like it was something special. He did it many times a day. "What do the initials P.C. stand for?"

He slipped the lighter back into his pocket. "It's the name of an old friend. Before he died, Paavo Creon gave it to me. He was generous, that way. He shared everything he owned with me before he died."

"And how did he die?"

"Tragically."

"Was he also in the business of torturing and killing?"

"Be careful, Melita."

"I don't believe he was a friend. The devil has no friends. All he has is enemies, and you must have more than your share. More enemies than rocks on this island. If your own children hate you, then—"

"Enough!"

It would never be enough. The vision of Nemo tied to a wooden stake on her father's yacht flashed in Melita's mind. She would have given her own life to save him, but nothing she had said had made any difference.

"Reminiscing, Melita? Are you seeing Nemo screaming for his life, or is it all the blood you can't forget? You were the cause of that, just as you were the cause of Hector's suffering this morning. We've had this conversation a dozen times. As

I told you, your betrayal killed your lover, just like your foolish trip to the village this morning has scarred Hector for life."

"Stop it." Melita covered her ears.

Her father stood quickly and jerked her hands away from her ears. "It's time to grow up and embrace the life I'm prepared to offer you, Melita. Agree to surrender to me and we'll begin again."

What he offered she wanted no part of. To live a life controlled by him would be worse than death. The only thing she wanted was to forget she was Cyrus Krizova's daughter.

"Punishing Hector today served a dual purpose. It was a warning to my men that I don't tolerate failure, and it was also a reminder to you that your selfish actions hurt other people. We both know how much you hate being the catalyst to a disaster. Next time you slip out of your bedroom before dawn think about Hector dangling from a rope in Holic's iron sights."

"I'll never surrender."

"I can wait you out, Melita. Your life here does not alter mine. Surrendering to me might seem like a prison cell itself, but it can also be the key that unlocks the door. Your brother learned that. As imperfect and weak as Simon was, eventually he learned that fighting me hurt him more than accepting his birthright."

"Simon's sick. He can't fight back or choose for himself."

"You're not listening. I choose for all my children."

"Then choose for me to go back to Mykonos. I'll live there quietly with Simon and take care of him. You can forget us and we'll forget you."

"That's not an option."

"Why? I loved living at Lesvago. I wouldn't leave. I wouldn't ever leave. And Simon needs—"

"Peace and quiet."

"What does that mean? Has he contracted another blood infection?"

"No, that's not what ails him these days, but it's nothing for you to concern yourself with. Enough about Simon. I've decided that starting tomorrow you will spend every afternoon with Barinski in the lab. His lack of organization is affecting his productivity. You like to organize things." He touched the flowers on the table. "While I'm gone you can keep his records orderly."

"Take me along with you. I miss Callia and Erik."

"No. That would be rewarding you for going to the village against my orders." He bent and sniffed the lavender in the vase. "Remember you have the power to keep Hector and the villagers healthy. You don't need another death on your conscience to send you off the balcony, or slitting your wrists again." He angled his head and blew smoke into the air, then he sent his eyes slowly over her from head to toe. "There's something else. I've ignored this ridiculous costume far too long. You will start wearing the clothes in your closet, and shoes on your feet."

Melita raised her chin. "If you want me to dress like your daughter, I will…for your promise to stop killing the goats."

He sighed heavily. "So we're back to that, are we? The goats on this island are raised for food, Melita."

She turned and gazed out over the balcony, the wind lifting the hem of her peasant-style red cotton skirt. The air was fresh and balmy, and she could smell the wildflowers that grew randomly along the rocky path. The goat herd was there munching on the foliage in the sunlight.

She turned and faced her father. "Make this place a refuge for the goats. You could demand it. Do it father, and I will…consider surrendering my life and my soul to you."

"And what would the villagers eat for meat?"

"The villagers are fishermen. They can eat fish."

"Despotiko, a refuge for those shaggy beasts?" He laughed. "It's unfortunate that your pets are weekly turned into steak, but that is the life of a goat. Perhaps it would be wise to refrain from naming them."

"My loyalty in exchange for the lives of a herd of goats," she promised, sure she had lost her mind.

He stepped forward and brushed the back of his hand along her cheek, then just as quickly he sent his hand into her hair and grabbed on. Melita cried out in pain and dropped to her knees at his feet.

He said, "You have never been, and never will be, in a position to make a deal with me." He let go of her and she slumped forward. "Ask me for your forgiveness. Say it, damn you, or I will slaughter that herd of hairy beasts within the hour."

She knew he would do it. Would make her watch.

Tears began to fall and she couldn't stop them. She gulped air, whispered, "Forgive me, father?"

"I didn't hear that."

Melita cleared her throat. "I said, forgive me, father."

He reached down as if he were going to touch her head, the act of a caring father who was sorry he'd lost his temper. Instead he grabbed her arm and hauled her back to her feet.

"Pick flowers. Play with your goats. Name every damn one of them. But if you want to save Hector a bloody ending, you will keep yourself within the boundaries of Minare. And when I return to the island, I will expect you to greet me wearing shoes and looking like my daughter, not some island waif."

When he let go of her, Melita stumbled back into the balcony railing. Righting herself, she heard voices in the distance. She scanned the trail that lead to the sea, and saw one of her father's guard patrol cruisers had docked.

"Are you expecting company?" she asked, drying her eyes with the back of her hand. She prayed it was Simon. She needed to see him. Needed to make sure he was all right, and to tell him she forgave him for his part in Nemo's death.

"Inside, Melita. You are to stay up here the rest of the day." When she didn't move, he pulled her away from the balcony. "Inside."

Melita obeyed her father, but the minute he left the tower, she was back out on the balcony straining her neck to see who had arrived.

There had been no visitors to Minare for months except for Holic Reznik. Please, God, she prayed, let it be Simon.

To her disappointment, the man who came ashore looked nothing like Simon. But then no one looked like her white-haired, albino brother.

The stranger wore his black hair to his shoulders, and he was being escorted by two guards. He walked ahead of them shuffling forward like an old man. Or maybe he was crippled.

As she continued to watch from the tower, Melita realized that the man was neither old, crippled, or a friend of her father's.

What hindered his normal stride was a pair of iron manacles around his ankles.

Chapter 3

The double-agent scenario wasn't a new idea. Regeneration, better known as brainwashing, had been around in the spy world for decades. But a year ago Cyrus had decided to take the theory a step further. He'd spared no expense on the latest technology—the bowels of Minare now looked like a space-age conspiracy.

Every genius plan had problems to iron out. A week ago those problems had allowed his guinea pig to slip through his fingers. But it wouldn't happen again. He knew what had allowed Jazmin Grant to escape him.

Human nature, or what he referred to as the lust factor, could be a secret weapon or could short-circuit a double-agent's brainwashing at a crucial moment. But not this time. With Sully Paxton, he planned to take the problem out of the equation.

Cyrus stepped into the lab and stopped in the doorway. He had come to tell Barinski that Sully Paxton had arrived and that they would begin the regeneration procedure again. The idea of snatching up Merrick's elite agents and regenerating them one by one put a smile on his face.

"Barinski?"

When the doctor didn't answer, Cyrus walked into the animal room where all the research and theories were tested out on lab rats. He found Barinski coddling one of the rats, talking to it like the damn thing understood every word he said.

"Perhaps you need to invest in a hearing aid, or I should install a bell on your door," Cyrus said by way of introduction.

Unaware that anyone had entered his sanctum, Barinski jumped and let out a startled cry. His squawk of surprise frightened the rat. The rodent clamped down on Barinski's finger. The doctor squealed again and dropped the rat, allowing it to scurry out the door.

Cyrus swore. He hated rats. Hated everything about them. He'd existed on a steady diet of rodents in Prague for months after Merrick left him to die. Since then he hadn't been able to look at a rat without remembering his desperation.

"I want that *thing* found. You know what I'll do to it if I find it first."

Barinski winced at Cyrus's words, then at the blood dripping from his finger. He pulled a handkerchief from the pocket of his baggy pants and wrapped it around the injury.

"Is there something you came to discuss with me?"

"Paxton's here." Cyrus tossed a file on Barinski's work-table. "Everything you need is there."

"What kind of shape is he in?"

"Better than I expected. There's a picture in the file of him when he was pulled from the pit. It's not the same man who came off the boat today. But I'm not surprised. Adolf Merrick scoured the countryside to find Paxton and five others just like him. They are the toughest bastards alive. Adolf Merrick's pride and joy. And because they are, I want them. All of them, starting with Paxton."

His latest plan was perhaps one of his most ingenious. The concept of Sully Paxton's allegiance being stripped from Onyxx was perfect revenge. It would also aid him—a man in his line of work could always use an elite private army ready to serve his cause. They would kill whomever he needed silenced, and his shipments would always be delivered on time, whether it was guns, drugs, or the blueprints of the latest, most indestructible submarine.

Yes, Paxton would be the first. After he'd seized control of Merrick's elite fighters, he would poach both government and private agencies all over the country.

"I've gone over your notes concerning the emotional malfunction of Jazmin Grant. Our success in converting these agents is contingent on complete surrender, both body and mind. Physically it won't be hard to bring Paxton back to the iron man he once was. He's halfway there."

Cyrus had instructed his men at Vouno to put Paxton through hell. From the day he'd captured Sully Paxton at Castle Rock he'd had him beaten and tortured, and anything else he could do to him to make him scream.

From personal experience he knew that what didn't kill a man always made him stronger. And now Paxton was even more indestructible than ever before.

"Your job will be stripping his memory and reprogramming him. But before you get started I want to ensure that he doesn't end up like Grant."

"Grant's problem was—"

"I know what the problem was. The lust factor made her vulnerable. It got in the way of her loyalty to me."

"Lust factor?" Barinski was staring at him like an idiot.

"She surrendered to her sexual attraction for Ash Kelly if you remember," Cyrus reminded him. "I don't want the same thing happening again. That's why I've decided my army of stallions are going to be gelded. Starting with Paxton."

Barinski was hesitant in his response. "I've never performed a surgery like that."

"I'm sure you'll be able to figure it out."

"Yes, of course, but—"

"You have two months to turn Paxton into a human robot."

"Two months. If I worked day and night it would take me twice that long."

"You're selling Paxton short. He'll be ready in two months."

Barinski found his glasses on his forehead and slid them onto his bulbous nose. It helped his squinting, but magnified his fish eyes to the size of a giant sea monster's. "Where is he now?"

"He's in a cell down the hall. Remember, your future is dangling by a thread, Barinski. I usually don't reward failure with a second chance. And I do see Jazmin Grant as your failure. Not mine."

"I'll do my best."

"Let's hope your best will keep you alive at the end of two months. To help you, I've instructed Melita to be your second pair of hands." Cyrus's eyes drifted to the open door of Barinski's office. It looked like he'd turned his rats loose in there. "She can keep your files in order to help speed things up, but I don't want her anywhere near Paxton."

"It would be a pleasure to work with the angel."

Cyrus rolled his eyes and grunted. "I have no use for angels, Barinski. Melita has more of the devil in her than anyone knows. That's why she is so important to me. Remember, two months. Disappoint me and I'll have you digging your own grave before I plant you in it."

That said, he left the lab and headed down the corridor to the holding cells. He saw Barinski's rat as he rounded the second turn in the hall. It was wedged into a corner trying to be as invisible as possible. He pulled a switchblade from his pocket and flicked it open. Then, before the rat had a chance to take its next breath, the blade was in the air moving toward its target.

The rat never knew what hit him. As he lay on his side twitching and dying, Cyrus put his foot on the rodent's narrow head and crushed it beneath his foot. Then he reached down, picked up his knife with the dead rat still impaled on it and continued down the corridor to welcome Sully Paxton to Minare.

Sully was dozing on the cot in his cell when he heard heavy footsteps. The cell where he was incarcerated was dry, and it didn't stink like the dungeon on Hell Island. There was fresh air coming from somewhere, and that told him that the tunnel was open-ended. If he managed to get free, there would be a way out of the monastery other than through the front door he'd entered.

He sat up, but before he could get to his feet, the Chameleon was standing on the other side of the iron bars grinning at him.

"You're not surprised to see me?"

"I don't surprise easy."

"But you must be curious why you're still alive, and why I've decided to change your address."

"I figured you'd tell me when you were ready. No sense losing sleep over what I can't change."

"That's what I like about you, Paxton. You're a man who

says what he thinks, and believes what he says. That's why I've taken such a special interest in you. I hate to admit it but Merrick has a talent for picking winners. Normally when recruiting a team of special agents, you would look for sterling military jarheads. But Merrick being Merrick went looking for the wildest vigilantes alive. Truly the name *rat fighters* fits the M.O. of his most elite."

Sully glanced at the rat impaled on the Chameleon's knife and wondered if the rodent was a visual aid. "Am I supposed to conclude that I'm going to end up like that rat?"

The Chameleon laughed. "Not if you're smart. And we both know how smart you are. A street-smart Irish gunrunner."

"Is that it? Need a gunrunner?"

"Perhaps. You know, Paxton, I find it fascinating that you're still alive. That your mind is still processing rational thoughts and you're on your feet. It's a testimony to your endurance. My screening process is a bit barbaric, and more often than not the result is disappointing, but you haven't disappointed me at all. That's why I've decided to reward you."

"And this is my reward, more iron bars? I vote for a room with a view and a beautiful woman for a few hours."

"The cell is only temporary. A few tests to ensure you haven't contracted any contagious diseases, and you'll be moved. However there will be no view in your new quarters, and I promise you that very soon women will be the furthest thing from your mind once you begin working for me."

"You can't believe I would ever agree to work for you."

"Not willingly, no."

"I could kill myself in here. Snap my own neck. That would flush your plans down the toilet."

"If that was your intention you would have done it at Vouno."

Vouno.... Was that the real name of Hell Island? Sully wondered.

"No, already you're in survival mode...again. Death at your own hands would mean you had failed Merrick, and more importantly, make you a coward. What I've observed over the years about the Onyxx six is that each of you have a private code of ethics that demands survival at any cost. That's what Merrick saw in each of you. Why I knew no matter what I ordered done to you at Vouno you would survive."

The Cameleon spoke of Merrick as if he knew him personally. Sully sized up his jailer. At Onyxx the Chameleon's identity was unknown. But that hadn't altered the fact that he'd topped the list as the most wanted international criminal for over a decade.

"Who are you?" he asked, never expecting to get a straight answer.

"You don't recognize me? That's right, you wouldn't. Not unless you knew my history, or you'd talked to Merrick recently. Which we both know you haven't."

Was he saying that since his capture Merrick had uncovered his identity?

"Your boss and I go way back. We were friends before he betrayed me."

"Before Onyxx?"

"No. We were both recruited by the NSA. We were the first team of Onyxx operatives at its conception."

There had been talk at the Agency that the Chameleon could be a rogue agent. Sully said, "Long time to hold a grudge."

"I assure you it's more than a grudge. I believe my file at Onyxx states that I died just outside of Prague in a minefield. As you can see, Mr. Paxton, Cyrus Krizova is very much alive."

So the Chameleon finally had a name. Cyrus Krizova.

"You and I have a lot in common. We were both left for dead by our comrades, and we have both survived."

"You're saying Merrick deserted you? Not a chance."

"You find that hard to believe?"

"I know Merrick. That's not his M.O."

"Like your team, there were six of us. Merrick was the field commander, Briggs was point man, Paavo Creon was the typographer and, like you, I was the weapons expert. The others…well they're not important. Like you, Paavo was a regular pretty boy. That's why, when I needed some repairs done on my face after I stepped on that mine, I decided to take his. He wasn't going to need it anyway."

The smug look on Krizova's face told Sully that Paavo was probably dead.

"You killed Merrick's wife?"

"What I did was save her from wasting her life with a man with no honor. He didn't deserve a woman that flawless."

"Johanna Merrick wasn't a part of your war with Merrick."

"As you know there are always casualties in wartime. Like me, your Onyxx team left you for dead at Castle Rock. Are you telling me you don't harbor any resentment?"

"I was caught behind enemy lines. Fallen comrades are left for dead. It's standard policy at Onyxx."

"That's noble of you, Paxton, but while you were left for dead, Sly McEwen was carrying out Jacy Maddox. A fallen comrade at death's door. He should have been left behind, too, but he wasn't. They didn't even try to look for you."

So they had all made it out alive. It was the first Sully had heard. But instead of resenting Sly for getting Jacy out, all Sully felt was relief. His teammates had survived Castle Rock. That was good news.

"You'll be in good hands with Dr. Barinski." Cyrus looked

at his watch. "Before I say goodbye, do you have a meal request for dinner? I have an excellent chef. Whatever you're craving, I'm sure Cosmo can accommodate you. And of course as much as you want. You're still underweight."

"In that case, how about your heart on a silver platter," Sully replied, "and a six-pack of Killian's Irish Red."

Cyrus chuckled, then stepped forward and slid the rat off his knife and tossed it between the iron bars to land at Sully's feet. "An appetizer while you wait for your meal to arrive. I ate rats in Prague to stay alive. I know in the pit you did, too. You see, Paxton, you and I have even that in common. And I'm sure there is much more."

An hour later a guard delivered Sully his supper. To his surprise it was served on a silver platter, and beneath the domed cover was an animal's heart and a six-pack of beer. It wasn't Killian's, but the brand could have been from Tasmania and two-thirds dog piss and Sully would have drank it.

It was the first time in days that he had passed on a meal. He picked up the dead rat, tossed it next to the heart and covered the tray. Then he carried the six-pack to the cot and fell asleep nursing his thoughts with a liquid meal that went straight to his head.

In the morning Sully woke up with a screamer of a headache. The beer had tasted good going down, but he was paying for it now. His tolerance to the booze wasn't what it used to be.

The urge to relieve himself forced him to his feet, and he staggered to the toilet. Normally he could handle drinking all night, but being out of practice had given him a helluva buzz.

He moaned as he put one foot in front of the other. The toilet was five feet away but it felt like five miles. He unzipped his pants, took a stance and let it flow.

He was in the middle of a heavy sigh when he heard a noise behind him. He looked over his shoulder as he continued to perform his normal morning bodily function and stared at the woman standing in front of his cell—an exotic island nymph with the face of an angel.

No way. He was either more drunk than he thought, or he was still asleep and in the middle of the same dream he'd conjured up after midnight. Oh, yeah, this was the little honey he'd been sucking on in the dream, his hands tangled in all that black hair. She had the same sexy dark eyes. The same pouty lips.

Sully felt his body jerk to attention. Wanting to continue down that horny road he'd traveled all night, he left his fly open, flushed the toilet and staggered to the cot.

He looked back, saw she was still peering at him through the bars. Grinning, he muttered, "Come on, baby, climb on in here and we'll start the party all over again."

He was two steps from the cot when his sexy dream-lover spoke and stopped him in his tracks.

"If I were you, I would be thinking about a way out of here instead of having a party. The men who visit this cell don't usually live very long."

Sully turned slowly. "You're real?"

"If I'm not, why are you talking to me?"

Sully rubbed his unshaven jaw, studied the woman as she studied him. He decided she was real—his dream-lover had been naked. The only thing naked on this little beauty was her feet. She wore a white peasant blouse and a bright blue skirt.

"Are you the nun who drops by to pray for the lost souls, or the monastery whore who guarantees the condemned die happy?"

He saw her chin jack upward. It was obvious she wasn't amused by his prison humor, and didn't find him as appealing to look at as he did her. She was taking him apart a piece at a time, as if he was some side show at a carnival.

For a month he'd been eating and sleeping and pissing center stage. It had given new meaning to the words *caged monkey*.

"Buy a ticket to the circus, did you, honey?"

"What?"

Sully took a few steps toward her. "I don't do tricks. If you're expecting to see me pull a rabbit out of my ass, it's going to be a long wait. No rabbits in here."

He thought his comment would chase her off. It didn't. Instead it put a smile on her face.

"You think that's funny?"

"If you could perform such a trick, I pity the rabbit."

So she could give as good as she got. He liked that in a woman. She was a gutsy little nymph, and the most beautiful creature he'd ever seen in his entire life. The cruel joke was she was on the outside looking in.

"Ever done it through a pair of iron bars?" he asked.

"Is that what an imprisoned man misses most?"

"When you've been locked up as long as I have, it's close to the top of the list."

"It's been one day. I saw you arrive yesterday."

"Relocated."

"From where?"

"Vouno."

She frowned. "Never heard of it. What's your name?"

"What's yours?"

"I asked you first."

She had barely gotten the words out when a male voice sounded in the corridor. By the surprised look on her face it was clear she recognized the voice and didn't want whoever it was to find her there. She quickly glanced around, then said, "He can't find me in here."

"Who?"

"Holic." She swung open the door to the empty cell next to him and slipped inside, then hurried to the cot and dropped to her knees. Flashing him her small sexy ass, she wiggled under the cot and disappeared.

From her hiding place, she said, "Don't tell him I'm here."

"I won't tell if you give me your name."

Sully heard her swear, two very nasty words in Greek. Smiling, he said, "A generous offer. You can try it through the bars as soon as I get rid of my visitor. For now, I'll have your name."

She swore again, then told him. "It's Melita."

On her belly, feeling the damp stone floor seeping into her clothes, Melita peered out from beneath the cot. She wrinkled up her nose as the sour smell suddenly gave her the urge to sneeze.

Oh, God.

She reached up and pinched her nose, concentrated on slowing her breathing until the urge passed. If Holic found her there she would be in worse trouble than she already was. The slimy bastard would like nothing better than to put her against the wall with another ultimatum.

She saw two pairs of feet stop outside of the prisoner's cell. One was Holic's. He always kept his black boots as shiny as a mirror. The other pair were easy to identify as well—green tennis shoes.

What was Nigel Barinski doing here with Holic?

Melita pressed her cheek against the dirty floor to get a

better look. The prisoner had taken a seat on his cot. He was dressed in green fatigues and a black muscle shirt. He'd zipped up his pants, and she found herself looking long and hard at him again. Over six feet, his black hair grazed his broad shoulders—shoulders that looked rock hard even though he was extremely lean.

She was curious as to who he was, and what her father meant to do with him. So curious it had caused her to use bad judgment and search him out.

"On your feet, Paxton," Holic ordered.

"Unlock the door," Nigel insisted. "I can't examine him from out here."

Holic dug a key from his pocket and inserted it in the lock. The cell door swung open, and Nigel stepped inside. Holic returned the key to his pocket and followed, pulling a handgun from the holster on his belt. He aimed the weapon at the prisoner they had just addressed as Paxton.

"I said on your feet, back against the wall," Holic ordered.

There were a few minutes of silence, then Paxton stood and Nigel set his medical bag down on the cot. "I need a blood sample to test for any diseases or infections. I have him scheduled for the decontamination chamber after lunch. I want him bug-free before I bring him to the infirmary."

Melita listened to every word Nigel said. She had no idea what his purpose was here at Despotiko, but she knew he wasn't simply a doctor who kept her father's guards healthy.

"Remove your shirt, Mr. Paxton."

Melita saw the prisoner's shirt fall to the floor at Nigel's order, but before she could see much else, Nigel blocked her view.

"I read your file. It was impressive. Surviving what must have been a living hell has made you quite valuable."

"I imagine you know all about survival living with that face," Paxton said.

Melita heard Holic laugh. "That's probably the only thing we'll ever agree on, Paxton."

Nigel lived with constant ridicule over the way he looked. Melita felt bad for him, although, she had to admit his appearance was unusual.

The blood sample taken, Nigel kicked an empty beer can. "There will be no more alcohol. From now on you'll be on a strict diet to get your weight back up. My orders are to have you at one hundred percent in two months. That'll take work on both our ends. Now your pants, Mr. Paxton. Drop them, please. I need to examine your phallus and scrotum for the surgery."

Surgery? Melita wondered what kind of surgery Nigel would be performing on that part of Paxton's anatomy?

A few seconds later she had her answer when Nigel said, "I have orders to castrate you."

When the prisoner didn't move, Holic stepped forward and shoved the barrel of his handgun underneath his chin. "Drop you pants, Paxton."

Melita saw Holic take a step back. Saw the prisoner's pants drop to his ankles. Nigel moved forward, blocking her view once more, then suddenly he moved left.

Buy a ticket to the circus?

Paxton's words popped into her head, but she wasn't witnessing any freak show. What she was viewing was more like a peep show, and worth every penny.

She heard Barinski mumble something to himself. Finally, he said out loud, "I've never done this kind of operation before. But it can't be too hard."

Paxton was in the process of pulling up his pants when out

of nowhere the smell of mold on the floor climbed up Melita's nose. Unprepared for it, she sneezed.

"What was that?" Holic turned to stare through the bars into the empty cell where Melita hid. She squeezed her eyes shut, sure she would be discovered any second.

She heard something that resembled her sneeze, and her eyes popped open just as Paxton said, "I've been sneezing all day. There must be something down here that I'm allergic to."

Holic laughed. "I'd be more worried about Barinski tickling my crotch with a knife than allergies, Paxton." To Nigel, he asked, "What's the reason behind castrating him?"

"After he's been reprogrammed we don't want him thinking about anything but the job he's going to be trained to do. Our last attempt at reprogramming an agent misfired because her lust factor got in the way." Nigel scratched his head. "I suppose a practice run on one of my rats is in order. I can't afford to screw up again." Nigel picked up his medical bag. "See that he's brought to the infirmary after he's been disinfected."

Sully jerked the zipper up on his pants and damn near neutered himself without Barinski's help. He winced, then gave an empty beer can a hard kick, sending it into the wall.

He heard Melita dragging herself out from under the cot in the next cell, and turned to see her getting to her feet.

When she came out of the cell, he said, "Get me out of here."

"Me?"

"Who else would I be talking to?"

"Why would I help you? I don't even know you."

"Because I just saved your ass, and it's time to return the favor."

"By the sound of it your ass isn't what's in jeopardy. What did he mean reprogrammed?"

"How the hell should I know? What I do know is that sticking around here to find out is going to—"

"End your partying days."

She looked away, but Sully saw a glimpse of a smile. It pissed him off, and he said, "You wouldn't think it was so funny if you were in here and I was on the outside looking in."

"I suppose not. Lucky me. If you're thinking of breaking out of here, it won't happen. Minare is heavily guarded, and there's no easy way off the island."

"That guard with the crazy doctor has the key to this cell. Get me the key, and I'll worry about the rest."

"He's not a guard. That's Holic Reznik and there's no way I'm going near him."

"What do you want for helping me out of here? Name it, and it's yours."

She thought a minute, then asked, "Do you have a boat?"

"Stashed under the cot?"

"That's what I thought." She shrugged. "No boat, no escape. Goodbye."

"Wait!"

She didn't stop. She was gone, and with her, Sully's last hope.

Starve him. Strip him naked. Beat him until he couldn't move. He'd survived all of it and more. But turning his brain into mush, and—

"What's your first name?"

Sully spun around to see that Melita had come back. "Why?"

"You know mine."

"Why does it matter? I plan to hang myself before Reznik comes back."

She gave him a frown. "Suicide is overrated."

"What would you know about it?"

She turned to leave.

To stop her, he said, "My name's Sully."

She turned back. "No one is named Sully."

"It's short for Sullivan."

"You have an accent."

"I'm Irish."

"Paxton isn't Irish."

"It's a long story," he said, trying not to scare her off again. "Maybe if you got me out of here, we could discuss it over a beer and dinner a few thousand miles away."

"Were you serious about giving me whatever I wanted if I helped you, Sully Paxton, even though you don't have a boat?"

"Dead serious."

She took a step closer and lowered her voice. "What if what I want is for you to take me with you? What if we left the island together? Would you agree to that?"

"Done."

"Just like that?"

"I'm a man with few options, honey. Be my angel of mercy and I'll not only get you off the island, I'll take you wherever you want to go."

"Without a boat?"

"I'll swim you out of here on my back if I have to."

"Some men would promise anything to get what they want. Especially a man in your position. How good is your memory?"

"My what?"

"Do you remember what you say? More importantly, do you follow through? You see, I can't just take your word for it."

"My promise is solid."

"*Promise.* That's a word I haven't heard in a while."

"If you knew me, you wouldn't have to doubt it."

"That's my point. I don't know you."

"If you're serious about wanting out of here, I'm the man who can make it happen. Anywhere you want to go. Barinski said he read my file. Find it and read it. Once you do, you'll know I'm your man."

She was taking in everything he said, and he could see she was definitely considering his offer. It didn't matter why she wanted off the island, only that she did—as badly as he did.

"I have to go," she said.

"When will I see you again?"

"When I decide whether I can trust you or not. If I do decide to help you, we'll need a boat. Do you have any money?"

Sully patted his pants pockets. "Used my last quarter to call home."

"There are boats at the village. I've already tried to get someone there to help me get off the island, but they're all too afraid."

"Why?"

"That's a stupid question. Why do you think?"

"They're afraid of Krizova."

"He owns everyone on this island."

"Including you?"

"I'm not the one behind bars."

"And still you're here, where you don't want to be."

She started to walk away again. He made one more plea. "Read my file."

She never answered him.

Sully put all his energy into believing that if Melita read his files, she'd be back. But by afternoon when she hadn't returned, he started to pray for a miracle. What arrived on the heels of that prayer was Holic Reznik, and minutes later he was headed for the disinfection chamber.

Chapter 4

For weeks Melita had been searching for a savior on the outside of Minare, when she should have been searching for an accomplice on the inside who was motivated.

Sully Paxton certainly had gotten a lot of motivation this morning. Perhaps she'd found her gorilla with brass balls.

Read my file. Once you do you'll know I can get you out of here. That I'm your man.

Insurance was always a good thing. It wouldn't do her any good to let the gorilla out of his cage if he was all talk and no show.

Melita entered the lab and found Nigel in the animal room feeding the rats, and chatting with them about how his day was going. Asking them about theirs.

"So I'm not the only one who thinks animals understand."

Nigel turned slowly. "Hello, Melita."

"Hello, Nigel. Don't tell anyone but I talk to the baby goat all the time. I've named her Kit and I think she likes it."

Nigel's smile slid. "Don't get too attached to her. You know what always happens to them eventually."

She glanced around the room, saw an empty cage. "Where's Brando?"

"He got loose. I'm hoping I can still find him, but so far it's not going so good."

"I'm sorry."

"It was my fault. I frightened him and he got away. Have you come to work? Your father told me you were going to start today." He smiled, and it made his lower lip sag like a badly hinged trap door. "He mentioned organizing the files in my office."

Perfect, Melita thought. That was exactly where she wanted to be.

"I heard what happened yesterday."

"I should have been more careful when I went out for my walk."

He eyed her. "Are you saying Holic Reznik lied? The rumor that's circulating is that you went to the village to find a way to escape from the island."

She had never told anyone but Hector about her plan to leave the island. She could talk to Nigel about the goats, his rats and the garden, but she'd never shared anything more. She suspected he knew the story behind Nemo's death, though.

"You've always avoided talking about what you do here for my father. I think this is one of those times when I should keep my private affairs to myself as well."

"Which means you did go to the village."

"It's best if I don't involve you. I don't want you hurt."

"Like Hector was yesterday."

"I was the one who should have been beaten, not him. Hector isn't to blame."

"He's your bodyguard. He's responsible for keeping you safe."

Melita followed Nigel back into the lab and headed for the office. "You just do whatever you need to and don't mind me. I'll have your office in order in no time."

The minute Nigel disappeared Melita rounded the desk littered with stacks of papers. She shuffled through a handful, turned over one pile and suddenly she saw it. Sullivan Paxton's file.

She sat down and opened the file and nearly threw up. The man in the picture that stared back at her couldn't be *him.*

Melita closed her eyes, then opened them again. He was standing naked against a wall, his face was skeletal, and his eyes were sunken into his sockets. She could count every rib. He was filthy, and his hair matted to his head.

She turned the picture over, unable to look at him any longer. Her father had done that to him. She didn't need any proof. She knew it was true. Knew what he was capable of.

She started to read the file. Sullivan O'Neill, aka, Sully Paxton. Born in Dublin, Ireland. Orphaned at age three. Thief. Gunrunner. Smuggler. Recruited as a government special agent for the NSA—the Onyxx division. Weapons expert for seven years. Nicknamed Mad Dog. Killed at age thirty in insurgency at Castle Rock. She read the date. That was a year and a half ago.

It took her another ten minutes to finish reading the file. When she closed it, she sat back and turned over the picture and stared into his eyes, studied his body. He had a horrible scar on his thigh. She remembered the scar from yesterday when she'd hid under the cot and Nigel had made him drop his pants.

It seemed impossible that the man in the picture was the same hard, virile man in the cell down the hall, but they were one and the same.

Melita organized Nigel's office and when she left the lab every file was back in its place. But one file remained in her thoughts, along with a picture of a man who had defied death even when all hope and dignity had been stripped from him. And with that truth came the answer she'd been looking for.

She had found her gorilla.

There wasn't a parasite alive that could survive Barinski's disinfection chamber. In fact Sully hadn't been so sure he was going to survive it, either.

He'd been stripped and shoved into a cement closet that was three feet square. He'd endured the chamber twenty minutes with a sophisticated overhead spray system drubbing his naked body with the force of a hurricane.

For sure he'd lost two layers of his hide, and he'd left the chamber gasping for air, his eyes watering and his lungs on fire.

Afterward he'd been ordered to put on a white hospital smock, then marched down the corridor to Barinski's infirmary.

Cyrus was right, the room had no windows. What it did have was padded walls, a bed on wheels and the sterility of a hospital ward.

It went without saying that he would fight going under the knife. But he was afraid that Cyrus Krizova had already anticipated that. He would find a way to restrain him, and knowing Krizova's M.O. he wouldn't see it coming until it was too late.

Supper arrived hours later. He wasn't so sure that the food hadn't been drugged, and so he didn't eat it.

Where the hell was Melita? Had she forgotten about him? Or was she at that moment arranging the great escape?

He hadn't been able to get her off his mind since he'd laid eyes on her. Besides wanting her to come through for him, he kept wondering why she was there. He supposed he should be grateful for whatever reason she had ended up on the island. He wasn't much of a gambler, and she was bad odds. But so far she was it…maybe his only chance for escape.

Again he wondered how she'd gotten mixed up with Krizova. If she was a prisoner she wouldn't be allowed to roam free. But if she wasn't why couldn't she leave the island whenever she wanted to?

Suddenly a thought occurred to him. The best way to keep an army of guards as loyal and happy as well-fed puppies was to provide a little merriment. Was Melita the island's entertainment?

The idea didn't sit well with him, but it could explain her reason for wanting to leave, and her freedom within the walls of Minare.

Sully heard the door open and he turned to see Barinski enter with a smile on his freakish face.

"I'm happy to report that you're disease-free, Mr. Paxton. Good news for both of us. Now we can proceed." Barinski glanced at Sully's supper tray. "Was there something wrong with your meal?"

"I don't eat as much as I used to."

"Come now, Mr. Paxton, you don't want to be force-fed through a tube, do you? You're still thirty pounds away from your ideal weight. We're not pouting, are we?"

Sully stared at the little man. He really was goofy-looking. His Bozo-red hair was the real thing, and he had the longest arms of any man he had ever seen.

"I guess we are pouting. Well, I'm not looking forward to this surgery, either. But I have my orders. I hope you won't hold this against me."

Sully continued to stare at him, and the look clearly told the doctor he wasn't going under the knife without one helluva fight.

"You should rest. The surgery is scheduled for tomorrow morning. So far there's no reason for a delay. Toby's doing fine."

"Toby?"

"One of my rats. The biggest one I've ever bred. I clipped him an hour ago and he's doing fine." Barinski headed for the door. "I suppose you've noticed the camera." He pointed to the small electronic device high on the wall. "You're never alone, Mr. Paxton. So if you need anything just speak your mind. I'll hear you. These days I rarely leave the lab to eat or sleep."

Melita tossed and turned the entire night. She had decided that she couldn't leave without seeing Hector first, but she had tried and the guard stationed outside his room had denied her entrance on her father's orders.

She climbed out of bed and pulled on a pair of jeans and an off-the-shoulder red peasant blouse, then left her room before the sun was up. She saw the goats eating on the path close by, as well as a number of guards at their posts. Confident there wouldn't be any repercussions for getting a little air, she headed for the big rock where she liked to sit and watch the sunrise.

Already the day was warm and she had pulled her hair back from her face in a fat braid. The goats raised their heads when they spotted her and they trotted toward her. Leading the herd was the most recently orphaned kid.

Melita's heart ached for the little goat. Her mother had been slaughtered a week ago. She understood the goat herd's value on the island—the animals were raised for food—but still she couldn't be rational about killing something so innocent.

She hadn't expected to care about them when she had been brought here, and for several months she had hardly noticed them. But over time they had become a part of her self-healing. Against her better judgment she'd attached herself to them.

"I can't help it," she said, scooping up Kit and holding her close. "I love you, little one."

She settled on a rock and watched the sun come up as she held the goat in her lap. She could see her father's yacht in the distance. He would leave today for two weeks. She was anxious to see him sail, and once he had, she would get busy making plans to leave the island. She'd decided that Sully Paxton deserved his freedom as much as she did—perhaps even more—and so she would tell him today that their deal was on.

She was so wrapped up in petting Kit and musing about freedom, that she didn't notice Holic heading her way until it was too late. Before she could get off the rock and get away, he was blocking the path back to the monastery.

"Good morning, Melita." Holic's eyes slowly drifted over her, then locked on the small goat.

Like a protective mother, Melita pulled Kit closer. "I have nothing to say to you."

"What I have to say to you won't require any talking on your part, only listening. I've been put in charge while your father is away. I thought you should know that as soon as possible so you could start planning how you're going to make up for your rude behavior the other day."

Melita worked on keeping her composure. She was getting off the island soon, so she let him talk.

"I hated telling your father about your trips to the village but you left me no choice."

Melita said nothing.

"I warn you, should you make another attempt to leave Minare your father has given me orders to kill that oversized bodyguard who has attached himself to you. As your father pointed out, your reckless actions are, yet again, responsible for another poor slob's misery. I can see how it could happen. What man wouldn't want to please you? But for the next two weeks it's you who should be concerned with pleasing me."

Melita refused to listen to anything more he had to say. She pushed herself up from the rock and walked past him, carrying Kit.

"If you're thinking about speaking to your father, you better hurry."

She stopped, turned and saw Holic pointing to the small boat that was headed away from the dock. It was her father, and he was leaving. She looked back at the man who had just become her jailer for the next two weeks. Smiling, he came toward her and reached out one of his scarred hands to pet Kit's head.

"Did you know that when danger is afoot a goat herd will form a circle, their heads to the center, and wait to be picked off one by one by their predator. I've watched dogs massacre an entire herd that way. Of course a gun is quicker, but after you drop three or four there is no sport in it and it becomes monotonous."

Melita pulled Kit closer, the gruesome picture he'd painted making her sick.

"Have you ever begged for anything, Melita? The old

adage, 'when you give you get,' applies here. It's a simple concept. Keep me happy and you will get to keep what makes you happy."

His gaze drifted to Kit and she understood clearly what he was saying. "Don't hurt her, Holic, she's an innocent animal."

"Of course not, Melita. I'm not a monster. Just a man who knows what he wants and how to get it. See you tonight. Dinner is at seven."

Holic's words haunted Melita all the way back to the monastery. She knew exactly what he wanted, and a dinner companion was simply the overture to getting her on her back.

She looked down at Kit. "I don't know what to do, but one thing is certain, I won't let him hurt you. And he won't be able to if he can't find you."

She headed for the monastery with Kit in her arms. Inside, she hurried down the corridor and up the stairs to her bedroom.

If Holic's pattern held, he would be cloistered in his room for several hours this afternoon. Hector said Holic had a drug habit. How her father could trust a man who functioned on a daily high was beyond understanding, but then she was past trying to figure out anything her father did.

In her room she made a bed for Kit in her closet and tucked the small goat inside. "You have to stay here for a while," she instructed, "and you have to be quiet."

Once she left her room, she headed for the tunnel, ready to settle her deal with Sully Paxton, but when she got there his cell was empty. That's when she remembered what Nigel had planned for him.

Minutes later, Melita bolted into the lab. "Nigel, we have to talk."

He was straddling a stool, bent over a microscope. "Good

morning, Melita." He raised up, glanced at her, then quickly reached over and turned off a monitor tucked back into a corner on the counter. "Could we talk later? I don't feel very well at the moment."

"That makes two of us. That's why I need to talk to you."

She saw a rat in a small cage on the counter. Recognizing the cubby rodent, she wondered if he was sick—he looked lethargic. On closer inspection she realized he wasn't just sick—Toby was dead.

"What happened to Toby?"

"He hemorrhaged last night."

"How could that happen?"

Nigel came off his stool. "I don't want to discuss it. What do you need?"

She glanced around the lab, noted the three closed doors. She had never been in any of the other rooms except the office and the animal room. She remembered that yesterday Nigel had told Holic to bring Sully to the infirmary after he'd been disinfected. So which room was the infirmary?

She moved around the lab, contemplating the question. "Did you know that my father left Holic Reznik in charge while he's away?"

"Yes. He told me."

"Holic has asked me to dinner tonight." She hesitated, faced him and came out with her dilemma. "The other day he made it known to me that he's determined to sleep with me."

"What?"

"I had the same reaction, and when I rejected him he told my father about…"

"About your visit to the village."

"Yes. It's been a terrible few days, but today is turning out to be a nightmare," she confessed. "I haven't been able to see

Hector. Holic has threatened to kill Kit if I don't have dinner with him, and—"

"I tended Hector's wounds. Six nasty cuts on his back, and one on his cheek, but he'll be fine. Don't worry about him. He's as strong as an ox. About Holic—"

"I've hidden Kit, but there's no guarantee that Holic won't find her if I don't show up at seven. So I intend to go."

Nigel glanced at the clock, then began searching the counter as if he'd lost something.

"What are you looking for?"

"My glasses."

"They're on your forehead."

"Oh, yes." He pulled his glasses down and settled them on his nose. Mumbling under his breath, he started out the door.

"Where are you going?"

"To talk to Holic."

"You can't, Nigel. If Holic finds out you know what he's up to, he could hurt you."

"No, he won't. At the moment I'm too valuable to your father. For how long, I'm not sure. When your father finds out who I've killed… Well, I'll have to deal with that later. Your predicament is far more important."

When your father finds out who I've killed…

Melita felt physically sick. No, Sully couldn't be dead.

"Don't look at me like that. Like you, I didn't come here of my own free will. I do what I'm told to stay alive, and sometimes accidents happen." He glanced at Toby, lying lifeless in his cage. "I'd like to bury him in your garden. Would that be all right?"

Melita nodded woodenly.

"Where did you hide Kit?"

"In my room, in the closet."

"Don't leave the lab."

When Nigel was gone, Melita studied the three closed doors. Sully was behind one of them and he was…dead. She wanted to see him. She couldn't explain why, but she had to. She thought about what she'd read in his file. What he'd survived.

The doors were all triggered by electronic locks. She searched the lab, suddenly spied the monitor Nigel had turned off when she'd entered the room. Curious, she pushed the first red button. Slowly the screen lit up and a picture materialized.

For a moment she just stood there and stared at Sully Paxton in the hospital bed. He looked peaceful in death, and she felt warm tears collect at the corner of her eyes.

She pushed the green button next to the red one. She heard a click, and turned around to see a light flashing above the far left door.

It was a slight rush of cool air that woke Sully. He was a light sleeper, and his keen hearing picked up footsteps as someone entered the room.

He kept his eyes closed, sensed Barinski had stopped at the foot of his bed. He opened one eye a slit, but it wasn't the freak that was staring at him. It was Melita.

He didn't move a muscle, unsure if Barinski had his pop-eyes glued to the monitor in the other room. "Is he watching?" Sully whispered, keeping his eyes still closed.

"Sully? Oh, thank God you're alive. I thought—"

"Is he watching?"

"Who?"

"Barinski?"

"No. He left the lab. I've been looking for you. I thought… never mind what I thought."

Sully opened his eyes and sat up. She looked like she'd been crying.

You're alive… He wondered what she meant by that?

He swung his legs off the bed and stood.

"Should you get out of bed?"

Sully dismissed the question, his attention focused on the open door. "How many guards in the hall?"

"Two."

"Outside?"

"A bunch."

He turned to look at her. "A bunch? Now there's a number I can work with. A bunch as in six, eight or two dozen?"

"Never mind about the guards. I went to your cell, but you weren't there."

"They moved me yesterday. You knew they were going to." Sully walked to the open door and peered out.

"I guess I forgot. Are you on painkillers? You're moving like nothing happened."

He turned and scowled at her. "Something happened all right. I damn near got my hide torn off in that disinfection chamber."

"I think you should get back in bed. How long has it been since you came out of the anesthesia?"

"Anesthesia?" Sully suddenly realized why she was talking about painkillers and staying in bed. She thought Barinski had snipped his *jack*.

"I'm sorry. I didn't realize Nigel intended to do the surgery so soon."

I'm sorry… If he had lost his good ol' boy, a simple "I'm sorry" wouldn't have come close to easing his pain.

She was chewing on her lip, as if she had a piece of bad news to tell him. What could be worse than what she was already thinking?

"Please lie down."

"Why?"

More chewing on her lips. "Toby's dead. Nigel said he hemorrhaged." Her pretty brown eyes drifted to that area of his body in question. "That's why you shouldn't be up." She winced. "I'm sorry. I suppose that's going to be a sensitive word from now on. The important thing is bed rest, and keeping the swelling down."

As angry as Sully was at her, she was damn entertaining just now. Her cheeks had turned red, and if she didn't get off that lip soon there would be nothing left of it.

"So the rat's dead. He puffed up like a balloon and then…bang."

"Toby was Nigel's pet. He loved that rat. I feel just terrible for him."

She felt sorry for him, but terrible for Barinski.

In that moment Sully made a decision. It was probably bad timing, but she deserved it for standing there whining about a dead rat and poor Barinski, when she should have been consoling him. Okay, he hadn't been clipped, but her "I'm sorry" wasn't enough.

He said, "I've been incarcerated for over a year. What kept me alive was imagining my life normal again. Part of that included rising to the challenge, if you get my meaning."

"I know. I'm upset with Nigel."

"Upset with him. Is that mildly upset, or really upset?"

"You're angry. I understand that, but Nigel didn't have a choice."

Sully wanted to wring her neck, instead he offered her a pitiful look. "So if Toby's dead, that gives me how long before I puff up like a balloon and go bang?"

"Don't talk like that. Just get back in bed."

Sully worked the pitiful look a little harder, then threw in an ugly look, as if a sudden pain had just struck his groin. He faked his knees giving way. He didn't want to think about what kind of an idiot he must look like in the hospital smock acting like a weak puppy. It was definitely not Mad Dog Paxton's M.O.

She raced toward him, grabbed him around the waist and used her small size to keep him on his feet. She was stronger than she looked, and she felt even better than he had imagined she would up against him.

He slipped his arms around her shoulders and pulled her closer. They were standing toe-to-toe, and he angled his head and rested his chin on the top of her head, giving her just enough of his weight to convince her that she was the reason he was still on his feet.

"I read your file like you told me to," she said against his chest. "It said you're really tough. You're going to have to be tough now. And you're smart, too. You know there's more to a man than what's…down there, right? I mean, that doesn't change how smart you are, or how good you are at your job. And if there's an upside… Sorry for using that word again. Anyway, if there is, now you don't have to worry about whether you were any good at it or not."

Sully had the urge to toss her on the bed and show her just how good he was. Instead he pretended to soak up her revival speech. And when she raised her head to look at him, he offered her a dumb-ass fool smile of hope. If he could have squeezed out a tear, the moment would have been perfect.

"You're getting kind of heavy."

"Right." He walked her backward until he had her against the wall. He let go of her and put his hands on the wall on either side of her. Then he lowered his head and sniffed her silky hair. "You smell good. It makes me remember things. At least I still have my memories."

Her eyes drifted, as if she were remembering a private time of her own. "Yes, there's that. Memories are all we have sometimes."

Sully slid his hand to her shoulder, then moved it slowly down her slender arms, dragging her blouse farther off her shoulder. She didn't even notice.

She had beautiful skin, soft and smooth, and it took Sully off his game for a moment. He closed his eyes, her sweet scent sucking him in like a stiff wind. He swayed forward and leaned his forehead against the wall.

"Are you all right?"

"A little dizzy."

"You need to be in bed."

Only if you agree to join me, Sully thought. Instead, his lips touched her ear and whispered, "Do me a favor?"

"What do you need?"

He straightened, hesitated as if he were wrestling with what he *needed*. Finally, he said, "Can I kiss you?"

"Kiss me?"

"I haven't kissed a woman in over two years." Sully fed her another woeful look. "I'm asking too much. Forget it."

"No. It's just that…" Her eyes focused on his mouth. "I suppose I owe you that much."

She sure as hell did, Sully thought. He reached up, slid his hand behind her neck and tipped her head back, saying, "One kiss. After all, I'm harmless, right?"

The moment had come and she closed her eyes in silent surrender. Sully stifled a groan as he lowered his head and brushed his lips against hers.

One kiss, he thought. He deserved it. He'd earned it. One kiss, and he'd be out that door and on his way.

Melita had been expecting a chaste quick kiss of the generic variety. But this kiss was the kind that sparked a dying flame to life. The kind of kiss you can't plan for. The kind of kiss that memories are built on.

The image of Nemo surfaced, and she made a starved little noise in the back of her throat and clung to the kiss. She responded like a lover who had been lost in a storm…lost and rescued.

She raised her arms and threaded her fingers through Sully's hair, pulled him closer. Felt his body settle, then melt into her. She pressed herself to him with more urgency, and he responded in kind—the evidence hard as steel against her belly.

Hard as steel…

Melita came out of her kiss-induced memory of Nemo with a start. Gave Sully a shove back. "Wait a minute. It can't… If you're… Then Nigel didn't…" She glanced down and that's when she saw the proof flagging his smock. "You bastard!"

She bolted away from him, then wiped his kiss from her lips.

"I thought you deserved some solid proof that I'm still in one piece." He started for the door. "The clock's ticking, honey. Come on, let's get out of here."

"That's it? You sucker me, and that's all you have to say?"

"I'm sorry. How's that?"

He didn't sound sorry in the least. "You're—"

"Getting out of here. Now stop whining and let's go."

"Not if I was being shot at sunrise. Go. You deserve whatever you get if you walk out that door."

He turned back. "Freedom is what I'm going to get."

"A second of freedom before the guards in the hall shoot you." She jammed her hands on her hips. "And to think I was worried about you."

"If you're staying behind it's no skin off my ass."

Melita's only chance for freedom was about to walk out that door and get himself shot.

Fine.

Good.

No, not good. She might survive Holic tonight, maybe, but he would certainly have her on her back before her father returned. "Wait! What about our deal?"

"You just said you're not coming. Make up your mind. If you're going, shake your ass."

Melita thought about Kit and Hector. She couldn't just leave them. "Have you forgotten we need a boat?"

"How could I? You keep harping on it."

"I'm not going without a boat. And those guards out there aren't going to just let you walk out of here. We need a plan."

"I already have a plan. I'm getting out of here. That's the plan."

"I should have realized that you never intended to take me with you from the very beginning. You're a liar and a coward."

Of everything she had read in Sully Paxton's file there was nothing that hinted he was a coward, but it was the one word that seemed to register in that one-track mind of his. The look he nailed her with a second later was pure venom—as if she'd just spit on his mother's grave.

He came at her so quickly she didn't have time to get out of his way. She was back up against the wall, his fingers gripping her shoulders.

"I thought you said you read my file."

"Every word."

"Then you know I'm no coward."

"Prove it. Give me until dawn."

"You're asking me to trust you?"

"Yes?"

He snorted. "Yesterday you knew what was going to happen to me, but instead of doing something about it you went to bed last night and never gave me a second thought. Suppose tonight you do the same. By tomorrow I might damn well be sharing a grave with Toby."

"I had a lot on my mind yesterday."

"And I didn't? The truth is, honey, if it had been you in that cell and I knew your identity was about to face a knife in the morning I wouldn't have waited around for the axe to drop, then show up after the fact with a lame 'I'm sorry.'"

"Okay, I screwed up. I won't do it again." Melita sucked in a ragged breath. "I can't leave this minute. Dawn, Sully. Wait until dawn." When he looked as if he was about to say no, she pleaded. "*Parakalo*. Please wait for me and I promise Nigel won't come near you with a knife."

"The door's open now. I would be a fool to hang around here and trust that you'll be back. I'm no fool, honey."

"What you can trust is that I want off this island as bad as you do, and you're my only hope."

"I must be crazy."

"Is that a yes?"

"Damn it!" He released her and turned his back on her. Swore twice more.

"You won't be sorry."

He spun around. "I already am. How about we seal this new deal?"

He was staring at her lips. Suddenly Melita knew what he expected. "We already sealed it."

"One more. You enjoyed it. Admit it."

"I enjoyed it because I was kissing someone else."

He laughed. "That's a good one."

"It's true. It might have been your lips, but it wasn't you I was kissing."

"If that's your excuse for wanting to kiss me, then—"

"I didn't want to kiss you. It was all your idea."

"You kissed me back."

"I was kissing Nemo."

"What's a Nemo?"

Melita gave him a look that clearly told him that he was trespassing on sacred ground. She was about to enforce it with a warning when Holic's voice in the hall jerked them both to attention.

For the second time, she bolted away from the wall. "Get back in bed. Hurry. I'll be here before dawn."

She hadn't reached the door before he snagged her arm, pulled her up against him and planted a kiss on her lips that took her completely by surprise.

When he released her, he said, "If you're confused about who just kissed you, the name's Sully. I'll be here waiting at dawn. Don't get lost."

Chapter 5

It was just like Holic to use her father's study for his private dinner, complete with lit candles on the table and soft music.

Evening had come too quickly, but Melita was on time as she stepped into the room wearing a yellow silk shift and a pair of Greek sandals that drew attention to her shapely ankles and beautiful legs. Her long black hair hung smooth and straight to her waist, and she had gold hoops in her ears.

Holic turned from the window on hearing her enter the study, his snake eyes taking her in all at once. "The goddess is punctual, and dressed to kill. I knew you wouldn't disappointment me. You know I admire loyalty above all else. Even if yours is to a mindless goat."

"At least you understand why I'm here."

"It doesn't matter what brought you to me, only that you came."

"My father told me you two have been friends a long time. I'm being polite." Polite, as in she had no choice if she wanted to keep those she loved from being harmed.

"He used the word *friend?*"

"Yes." Melita's only plan tonight was to keep Holic talking. She was holding on to faith, and praying for a little luck. She asked, "If you are friends, does that mean you also share my father's enemies?"

"I didn't realize you were so interested in Cyrus's business affairs."

"That's what he wants."

"Yes, I know. Do you have a head for business?"

"My father calls me a cunning little fox. I know I have instincts that could prove useful."

"For instance?"

"I hate snakes. But you can't avoid them altogether, so you must learn how to live among them. The tricky part is surviving the enemy unscathed."

"You see a snake as an enemy?"

"If he bites, and his venom is deadly, then he is the enemy. Take Onyxx. They have been biting—"

"Too long. It's time your father ended it."

"Yes, I agree with you. He should." She knew she was taking a risk by mentioning the government agency, but after reading Sully's file, she was curious about how he'd become her father's prisoner and why.

"I wasn't aware your father had discussed Onyxx with you."

"He hasn't said anything specific, but he has hinted that he's working on something important. You know, of course, how much my father loves a good challenge."

"Onyxx is more than a challenge. More like an obsession." He studied her a moment, then said, "Cyrus will destroy

Onyxx. I only hope he gets to it soon. This cat-and-mouse game he's been playing with Merrick is becoming a bore."

"Is that why you're on the target range every day? Do you plan to be part of Onyxx's demise?"

"I've gone a few rounds with the men of Onyxx already. Have no doubt that I will be very beneficial to your father when he decides to finish them off."

Melita looked at his hands, still wondering how much help he could really be.

"Speed never transcends accuracy, Melita. I'm still the most accurate assassin alive."

She jerked her head up and saw that he had caught her staring at his hand with the missing thumb. Then his eyes shifted to the low V-neck of the silk shift that exposed an inch of cleavage.

She had rummaged in her closet for something to wear—something befitting Cyrus Krizova's daughter. Her wardrobe was limited; most of her things were still at Lesvago in Mykonos City. But she had found the yellow silk tucked in the back of the closet and decided this was the sort of dress a snake would enjoy. The dress clung to her like a second skin.

It was risky wearing such a revealing dress, but she'd hoped that by being polite and engaging, Holic would be interested in a little game of cat and mouse himself. Some men enjoyed the chase as much as they did catching their prey. She believed Holic could be one of those men. She just needed to stay calm and avoid agitating him. He went on the attack when he felt as if he were losing control.

If she could survive tonight, by dawn she would be gone with Sully.

She glanced at the clock. 7:20.

"Are you hungry?"

"Yes. It's been a busy day, and I forgot to eat."

"First a toast to you, Melita. A cunning little fox. Soon to be my fox."

He handed her a glass of white wine and she accepted it. She brought the glass to her glossy lips and sipped slowly as she looked him over. Not in the same way he had her, of course. He was the enemy, the snake.

Tonight he wore brown pants and another white shirt that contoured his lean torso. He had narrow hips and slight shoulders. He wasn't well built, but his strength had surprised her yesterday in the garden. He was more dangerous than he looked.

She wondered if he was high tonight. If he was, it didn't affect his speech or his thought process. It had, however, enlarged his pupils. They were huge.

"I checked with the cook to see what your favorite dishes are. He told me *psito* sole, and *tyropita*."

He walked to the table and lifted the covers off the entrees. To Melita's relief there was grilled sole surrounded by roasted vegetables, and cheese pie.

She had almost expected to see goat. That was her father's trick—insist she dine with him, then serve her one of her pets. And all the while she was being forced to eat the meat, she was wondering who had died.

Might I suggest refraining from naming the goats, Melita, if you're going to feel sick every time we sit down to a meal?

She reminded herself how slippery snakes were. Holic's kindness in serving the sole wasn't without motivation. He was trying to buy his way into her bed tonight.

The idea repulsed her, but she never let him see how much. Instead, when he pulled her chair out for her, she thanked him and sat.

Once she was settled on the chair, he lowered his head,

lingered. "You smell as good as you look. Sweet and exotic like the lavender in your garden."

He brushed her ear with his lips. He had been drinking more than just wine, but again, he was very much in control.

He took his seat across from her, and then the evening was off and running.

Running... Yes, she felt like knocking the table over on him and running as fast as she could out that door. But that wasn't part of the plan.

Don't get anxious.

And don't let your anger make you reckless.

Stay in control.

Don't agitate.

Remember you're gone tomorrow at dawn.

"Melita, did you hear me?"

Holic's voice broke into her thoughts. She saw he had his glass raised. She hadn't heard his second toast. It didn't matter. Whatever it was, she was sure it would curdle milk.

She raised her glass, smiled. "To you, Holic. May you get everything you—"

"Desire?"

She was going to say deserve. As in a bed of nails with a guillotine overhead. "Yes, to the end of the evening."

"You are no longer angry with me?"

Careful. Don't make it too easy for him. It will make him suspicious. "Would it do me any good?"

His smile spread. "You are a beautiful fox, Melita. You know when there is no escape. Acceptance can be liberating."

"I haven't accepted anything," she promised.

"You're just like your father. Perhaps he's right. You would do well in the business."

The idea that she was in any way like her father made her

ill, but she had to admit there was one thing that they had in common. Her father lived for revenge, and Melita didn't deny that for the past year she had been, too. Only she preferred the word *justice.* And if the God she prayed to each night was listening, then someday soon she would have her justice for Nemo's senseless death. And likewise, if Holic harmed one hair on Kit's head, she would extract her justice on him as well.

He served her the fish and vegetables, passed her the cheese pie. She ate slowly, rested between bites and watched the clock. And hoped that her luck would hold, and that she would be in one piece at the end of the evening.

But her hope died when Holic chose that moment to blow luck out the window.

"I want you to know I'll be gentle with you tonight. I know you're not a virgin, but I expect your experience is limited. I don't mind that. I enjoy tutoring." He set down his wineglass, and studied her, with his elbow resting on the table and his chin propped against his closed fist. "Was Nemo your first?"

It was obvious her father had discussed more with Holic than just business, but she wasn't going to share more than this meal with Holic.

"I'm twenty-five years old," Melita pointed out. "My personal experience is my private business."

"That's an idealistic thought. You're Cyrus Krizova's daughter. You have no private business. Your father's enemies are constantly looking for a device to use against him. What better device than children. Why do you think you're here?"

That offhanded question set Melita to thinking. She wondered if there was more than one reason why she had been dropped in the middle of nowhere with an army of guards to watch over her.

She said, "Nemo wasn't my father's enemy."

"Not until he touched you."

"Does that mean you will go from friend to enemy after tonight?" That gave him pause, but not for long. She was shocked to hear what he said next.

"I mean to convince your father that we are a perfect match. Of course, it will take time. He's very protective of his possessions."

Then why did he leave me here with you? Melita wanted to ask.

He dropped his hand and leaned back in his chair. "You didn't answer the question. Was Nemo your first? Was he the only one?"

She said nothing.

"By not answering, you realize that you have answered me. He was your first and only. Good."

Melita set her fork down. She couldn't play this game any longer. Forgetting about the plan to keep him talking, she shoved her chair back and stood. "I thought you were married."

"I was. Mady is no longer my wife." He came out of his chair quickly and walked toward her.

Melita wished she could sit back down, but there was no going back now. He was standing in front of her, reaching for her and pulling her into his arms. Dinner was over, and she'd agitated him. His breathing had gone from even to erratic in a heartbeat.

His hands moved around her back and he jerked her against him. "Was it the food, or are you eager to be tutored?"

"Let me go."

"I think not, Melita. Remember the goat. Remember Hector. Your performance tonight can save them. You want to save them, don't you? Put your arms around my neck."

Melita slowly brought her arms up and settled them around

his neck. She could feel his heart racing, feel his erection growing as he slid his hands lower to fondle her backside and push her hips into him.

She closed her eyes, tried not to do anything foolish. She knew what would keep Kit and Hector safe, but maybe there was another way. She jerked free from him and shook her head. "I don't want another man to die, Holic. Not even you. If you touch me, my father will kill you."

"He will never know." Before she could get out of his reach, he had her back in his arms. "Don't be a little bitch, Melita. The dress. The way you smell. The way your eyes tease a man's soul."

He was very strong, and even with his injured hands he secured her to him and crushed his lips against hers. The taste of wine on his lips, the way his hands were pawing at her dress…

She tried to twist free again, but he had only one focus, and that was to have her right there in her father's study.

Desperate to make him stop, Melita opened her mouth and when his tongue slipped inside she bit down hard. He shoved her away from him with a surge of super energy, howling in pain.

Melita stumbled backward, lost her balance. She cried out, saw Holic reach for her. She crashed into the glass coffee table and it shattered on impact. Glass flew as she hit the floor hard, sending broken shards into her flesh. She lay there, unable to get up, moaning in pain.

She heard Holic swear, then he was bending over her. "You stupid bitch!"

In that moment the door swung open and Melita looked up to see Hector hurry inside. He wore a bandage on his cheek, and he was wide-eyed as he stared at her on the floor.

Hector wasn't part of the plan, but she was glad to see him anyway.

"What happened?" he asked, his voice laced with venom and worry.

"She fell," Holic explained. "Get out. I'll take care of her."

"There is something more pressing you should take care of, Mr. Reznik," Hector said. "I know you were left in charge, and I was just informed that your yacht in the cove is on fire. The men are working to bring it under control, but—"

"A fire? How the hell did that start?"

"I don't know."

"Son of a bitch!" Holic glanced at Melita, then back to Hector. "Clean her up, and take her to her room. I'll be there shortly." Then he was bolting out the door past Hector.

The minute he was gone Hector hurried toward her. "Melita, how bad have you been hurt? Can you get up?"

"Help me, Hector."

He lifted her into his arms and set her on her feet. A sharp pain in her side stole Melita's breath and she bent over. The pain sliced deeper, and she sucked in her breath and cradled her side.

"There's a lot of blood. I'll take you to Nigel. He'll know what to do."

"I'm all right. We have to leave, Hector."

"What are you talking about?"

"We're leaving Minare. Right now. Tonight."

"We?"

Melita headed for the door, still holding her side. "Where's Nigel?"

"I'm here, Melita." Nigel appeared in the doorway. "Oh, God, what did that bastard do to you?"

"What do you think happened?" Hector snapped. "We were too late."

Melita stepped around Nigel and started down the hall, unaware she was leaving a trail of blood behind. She had more important matters on her mind. Halfway down the hall she realized that Hector and Nigel weren't following. She turned around. "I'm leaving Despotiko tonight, and I want you both to come with me."

"We can't take off," Hector protested, "without—"

"A gorilla. Yes, I know."

"A what?" Both men spoke in unison, then looked at each other as if she'd lost her mind.

"He's in the lab." Melita looked at Nigel. "Sully Paxton is going with us."

Sully had just taken a piss and was heading out of the bathroom when the door swung open and Barinski hurried inside. His face was pale, and his glasses were askew, magnifying one eye and making him look twice the freak that he already was.

"I warn you, if you harm her in any way, I'll kill you. I've never done anything of the sort before, not on purpose anyway, but I promise you, I'll do it."

Sully arched an eyebrow. "Is this supposed to mean something to me?"

"It will eventually." Nigel tossed Sully a pair of pants and T-shirt. "Get dressed, Mr. Paxton, and be quick about it. We're leaving."

Sully grabbed the clothes out of midair. He didn't know why Barinski had suddenly switched sides, or why Melita hadn't waited until dawn, but that didn't matter. The words *we're leaving* had him jerking on the pants. He noticed that Barinski looked more than a little frazzled. He asked, "What's happened?"

"He damn near killed her, that's what happened. Hurry up, man. The guards will return soon."

Sully ripped the smock off and dove into the T-shirt. Pulling it over his head, he asked, "Are you talking about Melita? Who tried to kill her?"

"That bastard Holic."

"Is she all right?"

"I don't know yet, Paxton, but I'm worried. She's leaving a blood trail everywhere she goes, and she won't stop long enough for me to assess the damage." Barinski dropped a pair of boots on the floor, then headed back out the door. He never closed it.

Sully jammed his feet into the boots and then stepped through the door to find the crazy-looking scientist tossing files into a wastebasket. Once it was full, he torched them. As the flames shot toward the ceiling, he continued to fuel the fire with more files.

Sully heard a noise in the hall, and when he turned around he saw a guard enter the lab. He'd never seen a man so damn big in his life. He looked liked a professional wrestler who crushed bones for a living. He glanced around the room looking for a weapon, but before he could get something in his hand, the big guy said, "She's upstairs packing. Where's her goat, Nigel?"

She's upstairs packing.

Barinski looked up. "In the animal room with the rats. Hurry, Hector."

The big guy nodded, and within seconds he was back through the door with a long-eared black-and-white goat tucked under his arm.

"We've got to go, Nigel. Forget the files. Take whatever you can't live without."

The sound of her voice had Sully turning to see Melita in the doorway. She had a small bag on her shoulder, and a gun in her hand. Her hair was wild around her face, and she was wearing a low-cut sexy yellow dress covered in blood.

He damn near killed her.

"What the hell happened to you?"

"I had an argument with a glass table. Neither one of us won. Come on."

"Where are the guards?"

"They're out at the yacht in the cove. It's on fire." She glanced at Hector and smiled. "Your idea?"

"It was the best I could do on such short notice. When Barinski told me about Holic's dinner plans I knew you were in trouble." He gave the doctor a narrow-eyed look. "If I had been let in on the plan a little earlier in the day, I could have done better."

Barinski muttered something back at Hector as he tossed a handful of papers into a briefcase and slung it at Hector. "I'll just be one more minute," he said, then disappeared into the animal room.

Sully could smell freedom. It was going to happen, maybe not the way he'd imagined it, but there was no time to consider how and why these men had suddenly come to Melita's aid. If the guards were out, then they needed to move now.

He stepped forward and slipped the gun off Melita's shoulder. "I'll take that."

She didn't fight him for the gun, although she did nail him with a warning look, followed by, "Don't make me sorry."

"There's a way out through the tunnel." Hector took Melita's bag from her, then headed out the door.

Barinski started past Sully, and that's when he saw the cage the little man was carrying. He blinked, unable to believe his eyes. "What the hell do you think you're doing with that?"

"I can't leave them."

"There's no way in hell we're taking a cage of rats along."

Melita gave him a dirty look, then she said to Barinski, "Nigel, you can take them. Get going." To Sully, she said, "The rats are his family. Would you leave yours behind?"

"I didn't agree to take a gypsy caravan with us."

"You said if I helped you, you would help me."

"*You.* That's the key word here."

"Hector, Nigel and the animals go where I go. We can argue about this until the guards come back, or we can go."

"Have it your way, but they keep up, or get left behind."

He went out the door with the Czech Skorpion anchored to his hip. It felt good to be in control again. The gun felt good. He felt strong. Maybe not one hundred percent, but he would get there. It was only a matter of time.

He passed the crazy doctor, who was waddling like a penguin carrying his family of rats. He caught up to Hector, who had tucked the goat inside his shirt. He would address the animal issue later, he decided. Or maybe he would just take it upon himself to do what needed to be done. Or maybe he would do nothing and not look back.

But he did look back, and that's when he saw Melita holding her side as she struggled to keep up with the pace he'd set. Even the rat lover was doing better than she was.

He told Hector to keep moving, then turned back. When she saw him head toward her, her chin hiked up. He slowed his pace and matched her step, tried to put his arm around her to help.

She pushed him away. "If I need your help, I'll ask for it."

"I doubt that."

Sully stayed beside her, and soon Barinski and Hector were out of sight. He felt a gentle breeze on his face. They were deep in the tunnel now, the promise of freedom minutes away.

He had Melita to thank for that, and he would thank her by getting her off the island. But it was never going to happen at this pace. Without warning, Sully scooped her up in his arms.

"Put me down!"

"You're in no shape to argue. How bad is it?"

She kept her hand pressed to her side, and wrapped one arm around his neck. "It feels like something is cutting me in two."

Sully didn't like the sound of that. *I had an argument with a glass table. Neither one of us won.*

Within minutes they reached the end of the tunnel. The night was full of stars and there was too much moon. Sully saw Barinski perched on a rock breathing like he'd run a marathon. Hector was standing beside him with the goat's head peeking out of his shirt, Melita's pack on his shoulder, and Barinski's briefcase in his hand.

Hell, he wasn't going to make it. Not with this circus dragging his ass down. He said to Hector, "I suppose there isn't a pair of wheels around here we can steal."

"No. But there's a goat cart out front."

"A goat cart?" Sully grimaced…now there was a helluva good idea. Maybe they could harness up the rats. He set Melita on her feet, and she leaned into him.

Hector said, "The cart is used for—"

"I don't give a damn what it's used for. Get it."

Hector nodded, stepped forward and handed Sully the goat, then set Melita's pack and Barinski's briefcase on the ground.

Sully urged Melita down on a rock next to Barinski, and tucked the goat under his arm.

"I don't think I can make it," she said suddenly. "You're

right. I'm going to slow you and the others down, and probably get everyone killed. Take Hector and Nigel and—" she reached up and touched the goat's head "—and Kit, too. Holic will kill her if she's left behind with me."

Sully hunkered down beside her. Brushing a strand of hair out of her eyes, he asked, "What happened tonight?"

"Holic forced her into…you know. That's what happened."

"Nigel, that's enough."

"It's my fault. I shouldn't have let you go near him. I'm sorry, angel."

"What's he talking about?" Sully asked.

"Holic threatened to kill Kit and Hector if she didn't have dinner with him tonight."

"Nigel, I said be quiet."

"Where's Krizova?" Sully asked.

"He left the island this morning."

Nigel said, "We were too late, weren't we, Melita?"

"Nigel, no more!"

"Too late for what?" Sully's eyes drifted over her body. Hell no, had Holic raped her?

She locked eyes with Sully. "I know what you're thinking, but it didn't happen. We argued, and I stumbled."

"Into a glass table? Somehow I don't think that's how this happened."

It feels like something is cutting me in two.

Sully swore, suddenly realizing the seriousness of her injury. She had glass imbedded in her side. "Do you have a knife?"

"Why?"

"Come on, honey. Do you?"

"In my bag."

Sully passed off the goat to Barinski then reached for the bag and unzipped it. Rummaging through a few clothes, he found the knife, then turned to her, grabbed her dress and stuck the end of the knife into the side seam and cut through the silk in one quick upward motion.

"What are you doing?" Nigel insisted.

"It's glass," Sully said before he even examined the wound. "You've got glass in you, Melita. It's going to keep working in deeper and deeper unless I get it out."

"You? No! Why not Nigel?"

"I'm sorry, angel, but I lost my glasses. I can't see a thing without them."

Sully whispered for Melita's ears only, "Remember Toby? Put your money on a sure bet, honey. That would be me."

He heard a noise, swung around and aimed the Skorpion into the night. But there was no need. It was Hector dragging the goat cart over the rocky terrain. "We must hurry. The yacht is still burning, but not for long."

"We're not going anywhere until I get that piece of glass out of her," Sully said.

"Glass?" Hector knelt down beside Melita. "You should have told me."

"Hector. Go keep watch." Sully picked up Melita and laid her in the goat cart. Climbing in beside her, he lifted the bloody silk from the open wound. She had a sweet little body and a nasty gash. Those were the first two things he noticed. The third was that the amount of blood she was losing warned him that something was aggravating the problem.

"Do you know about things like this?" she asked.

He glanced up and looked into her worried face. "I'll fix you up, honey. You just close your eyes and be ready to count."

"Count?"

Sully probed the area and felt the piece of jagged glass. He wondered how long it was, how badly it had already ripped her up inside. He glanced at her. Her eyes were closed and her face was moist with perspiration.

He hadn't been happy to see the full moon when he'd stepped out of the tunnel, but now he was glad for it—he would need all the light possible to see what he was doing.

He said, "Start to count, honey."

She opened her eyes. "Wait. After you get it out, I want you to take Hector and Nigel and go. Promise me you'll take the animals, too."

"My deal was with you. One deal at a time." Sully reached for her hand and laid it on his thigh. "You squeeze my leg, and hold on. Now close your eyes and start counting."

She did as he told her.

"One… Two… Three…"

Sully slid two fingers into the gash.

"Four… Five…"

She moaned pitifully, squeezed his thigh. "Six."

He wanted the glass out of her on the first try. That meant he had to get a good grip.

More moaning. "Seven."

He took a chance. Held on and pulled.

"Eight!" She squeezed his thigh, dug in and held on.

"Got it." He didn't take time to pat himself on the back. He tossed the jagged inch-long piece of glass out of the cart and probed the wound again, not wanting to hurt her further, but he needed to make sure he hadn't missed anything more.

She moaned.

"All done," he muttered. "There's nothing else inside."

The wound was bleeding heavily now. He grabbed the hem of her dress and cut off a wide, three-inch strip and quickly wrapped it around her waist and pulled it tight, then leapt out of the cart. "Hector."

"I'm here. Should we take her to the village?"

"No. They'll search there first."

"You need a boat," Melita reminded him.

Sully looked over his shoulder. "One thing at a time. Is there a cave close to the water?"

"There are a few, but the men know about them," Hector said.

"You sure? Maybe one less memorable. The last place they'd look."

Hector thought a minute. "There's a grotto on the south side of the island. They might overlook it."

"Let's hope they do. Barinski, get that damn cage in the cart." Sully slid the Skorpion off his shoulder and handed it to Hector, then tossed the doctor's briefcase and Melita's bag in alongside the cage.

"Are we going to the grotto?" Hector asked.

"You're going," Sully corrected.

"You're not going with them?"

It was Melita who had asked the question. Sully turned to see her trying to sit up. "Don't move."

"They can't make it without you," she said.

"Take it easy. I said I'd get you off the island and that's what I intend to do. I'm going to stay behind and be a diversion, then I'll catch up." To Hector, he said, "Give me a landmark so I can find you."

Hector thought a minute. "Head straight south. When you reach the sea you'll see two large rocks thirty feet offshore. They sit side by side and rise up out of the water twenty feet high. The grotto is left of the rocks. It's fed by the sea, and you must go in on your knees, but it opens up quickly. We will be there."

"How far away?"

"Two hours on foot at a good clip. Three, maybe a little longer with the cart."

"The cart? I'm not going," Melita argued.

Sully knew that Hector was reading his mind. He was a soldier, after all, and they had a lot in common.

He grabbed Barinski by the shirt. "Your job is to make sure she stays alive. That wound will need cleaning when you get to the grotto, and a fresh bandage so she doesn't get infection."

"I'm a doctor. I know what to do."

"Tell Toby that."

Barinski lowered his head. "How did you know about that?"

Sully ignored the question. "If Melita doesn't make it, I'm going to feed those rats to you one by one, then slit your throat. Understand?"

He moved back to the cart. "You're going to the grotto. I'll meet you there."

She stared at him a moment, shook her head. "No, you won't."

"Yes I will. If we're lucky that fire will last another thirty minutes, but I'm not betting on it. Holic is going to need something to keep him busy for a couple more hours. That'll be my job. When you get to the grotto, stay put."

Hector motioned for Sully to take a short walk. "If they catch her—"

"They won't."

"If you don't come, what will we do?"

"I'll come."

"You seem sure."

"I'm sure."

"I've heard the guards talking. They say you've killed a lot of men…true?"

"All men are killers, Hector. I'm just better at it than most."

Hector nodded. "It's true. A man doesn't always choose it. Sometimes it just comes to him."

"How many guards?"

"Ten. They're all out at the yacht."

Sully turned to Melita. She was avoiding looking at him. He wanted to convince her that he wasn't going to run out on her, but he didn't know what he could say that would change what she was thinking. The best thing he could do was to get this circus on the road.

His eyes still on Melita, Sully rapped on the side of the goat cart with his knuckles. "Hector, get this wooden beast moving."

Chapter 6

Sully had three objectives, and he went to work with the tenacity of a bulldog who had just chewed his way out of an iron trap.

It took him longer than he would have liked to find Krizova's office in the tower. From the window, Sully could see flames shooting skyward offshore. But soon the fire on the yacht would be under control and the guards would return to their posts. He had work to do before then.

He quickly ransacked the office, then broke in to a locked storage room which contained an arsenal of weapons. He found a duffel bag and started filling it. He found a map of the islands and pocketed it along with a SIG Sauer. Put on the leather shoulder holster, then slid a state-of-the-art MP-5 submachine gun into the holster, complete with ammo. He bagged extra ammo, then discovered the motherlode—a small box of Astrolite, a roll of packing tape and a pile of cash.

"She must be my lucky charm," Sully muttered, thinking

about Melita with a smile—the explosives would be the perfect diversion, and the cash was going to haul their asses off to freedom.

Armed and feeling better about the odds, he sat at Cyrus Krizova's desk and picked up the phone. He dialed the number that he'd recited a dozen times a day since he'd been captured, then sat back and waited.

It would be early morning back home. Home… He'd never really considered D.C. home, but right now he was feeling a closeness to the city and the men there that had become his family.

He supposed home was wherever you felt wanted and needed. Where you felt an attachment. Where you were valued and respected. He'd gotten all that in Washington, and Adolf Merrick had made it possible.

The phone rang six times. He didn't want to leave a message. Merrick was a man who dealt in hard facts. He needed to—

"This is Merrick. I recognize the number. What do you want now, you son of a bitch?"

"A six-pack of Killian's Irish Red," Sully said.

"Who the hell is this?"

Sully cleared his throat, then he said, "*Madoo Miri* reporting in, sir."

He used the nickname he'd earned as a gunrunner in Ireland, the one Merrick and the boys had continued to use at Onyxx. He'd certainly been a *mad dog* when he'd been railroaded into the agency.

"Paxton…Paxton! You're alive?"

"Still breathing."

"Where the hell have you been?"

"To hell and back, compliments of the Chameleon. Or should I say, Cyrus Krizova."

"If you're calling from this number then I assume he's with you now?"

"No, he's not. He told me you discovered his identity."

"A few weeks ago. Are you healthy?"

"A few pounds lighter. You know how it goes in a prison cell. You lose your appetite when the chow tastes like vomit. But I'm alive."

"Damn, it's good to hear your voice." There was a moment of silence, then Merrick asked, "Where are you?"

"I'm on the island of Despotiko. It's a Greek island—"

"I know where it is. How long can you hold out?"

"I can't stay here. I've got to move now. I have a favor to ask."

"Anything."

"Four hours south of here there are two dozen men dying in the sinkhole I just got sprung from. I was moved yesterday. Cyrus called it Vouno, but that could be his own point of reference. A lot of islands don't have names. I've got landmarks to help you find it." Sully relayed the information, then said, "I want those men rescued. If you can't do it—"

"I'll do it. You have my word."

"You're going to need medics and a rescue team. It's heavily guarded. Pick up all of them, Merrick. The dead, too. Hell, they might all be dead by now. One more thing. I think the island is the base for Cyrus's contraband. I believe he's selling Czech Skorpions. If I'm right, the cache is there."

"What about you? Where will you be?"

"To get out of here I made a deal with someone. I need to see that through." Sully heard footsteps on the stone stairway. "I've got to go. I'll be in touch."

He hung up the phone and quickly stood. He'd purposely lit a lamp and set it near the window where he knew it would be spotted. He'd left the door ajar.

He rounded the desk and took his position as his visitor's footsteps slowed in the hall.

"Hector? Is that you? What are you doing in Cyrus's office?"

The door swung open and Sully stepped out from around the corner and elbowed Holic Reznik in the face, then drove his knee into the man's groin. Holic's legs buckled and he went down hard, blood spraying from his nose and mouth, as his crippled hands clutched his crotch.

As Holic lay moaning and trying to figure out what the hell just happened, Sully kicked him in the ribs hard enough to break more than one. "That's for touching her and thinking you had the right," he said.

While Holic was trying to force air into his lungs, Sully hunkered down and bound his hands together, then ripped a four-inch piece off the roll and slapped it across the bastard's bloody mouth. He returned to the desk, took out one of Krizova's Cuban cigars from a wooden box lined in velvet and lit it, then added the cigar box to his cache in the duffel bag.

Smoking the flavorful cigar, Sully said, "Get on your feet."

Reznik rolled to his side, struggled to his knees. It took him four tries to get up. When he was finally standing, Sully aimed the SIG at his chest. "Out the door, slow and careful."

They made their way down to the lower level. In the hall, they encountered a guard who had returned to his post. Sully shot him before the man could draw his weapon. He shot two more guards on the way to the holding cells. There, he ripped the tape off Reznik's mouth and shoved him inside one of the cells and locked it.

"You're a dead man, Paxton," Reznik threatened, holding his ribs.

Sully grinned. "I've been hearing that for years. It's old news. I figure Cyrus checks in daily. If you're lucky he'll find you before you start gnawing off your own fingers to stay alive. What few you have left. If not—" Sully shrugged "—then I guess you're the dead man."

"Where's Melita?"

"You talking about my lucky charm?"

"What have you done with her?"

Sully pulled a pocket watch from his pants and looked at it. He had lifted it from Cyrus's desk drawer. He nodded to Holic Reznik. "Time to go."

He stopped on his way out of the tunnel to set an explosive charge of Astrolite. The guards were on to him by now and he came face to face with two. Sully didn't blink or hesitate—he shot them both before they could raise their guns. A hundred yards from the tunnel he took cover behind a rock and fired a round of ammo from the MP-5 submachine gun into the tunnel. The earth shook and fire lit up the sky.

Melita heard the second explosion and squeezed her eyes shut. "Hector, stop. We have to go back. Sully's in trouble."

Hector kept pulling the cart. "We stick to the plan. He'll catch up."

"Catch up, my ass," Barinski snorted. "He's a free man now. The minute he left us he was running for the village to steal a boat. He suckered you, Melita. That explosion is probably the yacht's fuel supply. Paxton is long gone. He's a—"

"He's an Onyxx agent. I know who and what he is, Nigel. I read his file in your office. I also know what you were about to do to him on the orders of my father." She motioned to the rats in the cage. "I know what happened to Toby, too. How could you even think about doing that to a human being?"

"And if I didn't follow orders what do you think would

have happened to me? I told you before. I didn't apply for this job. I was impressed into service."

"Sully didn't run out on us," Hector insisted, "and he's not dead. He'll catch up. If we make it to the grotto before he does, we wait for him."

Barinski let out another rude snort. "You're an idiot, Hector."

"And you're a stubby freak," Hector countered, never slowing his pace as he doggedly pulled the cart over the rough terrain.

"Stop fighting." Melita glanced back in the direction of the monastery, unable to forget Sully jogging back into the tunnel as Hector had jerked the goat cart into motion. She didn't care what Nigel said. That explosion was bigger than a gas tank going off on a yacht.

Because they had to move quickly, Merrick wasn't able to rally his entire crew. Jacy Maddox was in Montana, and Bjorn Odell in the Azores. But he had been able to enlist the help of Sly McEwen, Pierce Fortier and Ash Kelly.

They were in the air within an hour, on their way to Fort Campbell, Kentucky. There they would enlist the help of the 160th Aviation Battalion—their specialty, armed attack, insertion and extraction.

"When are you going to tell us what our mission is?" Sly asked as the Night Stalker rolled down the runway.

"Now works," Merrick said as the plane took flight. "We're headed to Kentucky, then on to Greece. This morning I learned the location of one of Krizova's hideouts."

"Is he there?" Pierce asked.

Every agent at Onyxx had been on more than one mission in pursuit of Cyrus Krizova.

Merrick shook his head. "No, he's not, but my source tells me there's a prison camp set up there," Merrick explained.

"Is the source realiable?" Sly asked.

"Did you confirm it?" Ash injected.

"I didn't need to. The source was reliable."

"How do you know that?"

"Let me finish, Ash." Merrick took a deep breath, then said, "This is going to be hard to believe but I got the information from Sully Paxton. He called me this morning."

Ash shook his head. "That's not funny, Merrick. I saw him go down at Castle Rock. He's—"

"Alive. Cyrus captured him and Sully's been rotting in Krizova's prison since our failed mission at Castle Rock."

Everyone knew what that meant. If Sully had been Cyrus's prisoner for over a year, he couldn't be in very good shape.

"How bad is he?" Sly asked.

"Honestly, he sounded good."

"If Sully's in that prison, how did he contact you?" Pierce asked.

"He's not there any longer. I don't have all the details. He was moved recently to another island. Somehow he was able to escape."

"When do we pick him up?"

The question came from Ash. Merrick heard the anxiousness in his voice. Ash had always blamed himself when Sully went down at Castle Rock, presumed dead.

"Merrick? Where's Sully now?"

Ash's second question told Merrick that he wasn't going to rest easy until he laid eyes on his comrade.

"He was on an island called Despotiko, but he's not there now. He said he'd be in touch."

"Did he mention Krizova, and where we can find him?" Sly asked.

"No. But he did say that his escape would be a good diversion for us. I have to agree with him on that. Once Cyrus learns Sully has escaped, his attention will be on him, not our raid on Vouno."

"So he's playing decoy for us?" Pierce grinned, then elbowed Ash. "He's all right. He's thinking like the old Sully. That's a good sign. He can't be too bad off."

Ash arched an eyebrow. "Either that, or he's decided he can't make it out alive and he's playing choir boy."

Merrick cleared his throat. "Our mission is a complete takeover of the monastery. I promised Sully that every man, dead or alive, will be recovered from the prison. Questions?"

It was a typical coastal village—close-knit whitewash stone structures aligning a harbor crowned with boats.

Sully arrived a few hours after midnight and moved quickly through the narrow sleepy streets. If the villagers had heard the explosions from the other side of the island they knew better than to let curiosity drag them out into the night.

Sully crept through the maze of houses and headed for the harbor. He had made good time, pushing himself, knowing that the fishermen would be up before dawn to prepare their boats for a day at sea.

He was tired and it reminded him that his strength wasn't what it used to be. He missed his iron body, missed his endless stamina.

He spooked a few goats, woke up a rooster and hurried through the dark alleys. The harbor was still quiet, the sea calm, and the stars were dancing on the glassy sea.

Sully looked out over the water, the fresh air feeding his lungs. That's what he'd missed most in prison. The wind in his face and his lungs dragging on all that clean air.

He assessed the boats in the harbor, knowing what he

wanted. But finding it in this harbor was going to take a bit of luck. "Come on, Melita, spin me some more good fortune."

He ignored the sailboats and small fishing skiffs, and chose a large launch most likely used for catching octopi, and diving for sponges. Nothing here was meant for speed, and that was what he'd been hoping to find.

He'd have to take the launch, he decided. He hopped aboard the *Artemis.* She was forty feet long, crafted from wood, with an enclosed pilothouse. He checked her out quickly. Engine. Fuel. Then went below deck. Two bare-bones staterooms, a toilet and sink. Galley.

Accommodations for royalty.

The boat was well cared for. That meant her owner was as dedicated to the *Artemis* as he was to his family. That pretty much guaranteed a dependable engine, and the galley would be well stocked.

Sully didn't think twice about stealing the launch. He waited thirty minutes before turning over the engine, that way the villagers would think one of their own had woken up early to get a jump on a normal day.

A quarter mile from shore he asked the boat for more speed, and sent the launch south, knowing that as soon as the fishermen saw one of their prize boats gone they would rally and be smoking his ass.

He only hoped that he could outrun them. And then there were Krizova's men to think about. The guards who had survived the second explosion would already be searching the island and the coast.

But he was in his element now. He knew boats, and he knew the sea. And he knew something else, too. He knew he wanted to see Melita again.

She didn't believe he intended to catch up with her. Hell, she probably thought he had already forgotten about her.

"Not a chance, lucky charm. Not a chance."

The news came to Cyrus Krizova during breakfast. He was seated on the terrace of his extravagant mansion on a private island south of Naxos when he got the call. He was wearing a white robe, not yet dressed because he'd spent the morning making love to his wife. They were in the middle of a champagne breakfast to celebrate his return home after weeks of being away.

The bit of *loukanika* and *tyri omeleta* he'd just swallowed, however, turned into a ball of acid as he considered the disaster being relayed to him over the phone, killing the perfect moment with Callia, and the memory of her on her back moaning as he drove into her with the stamina of a raging bull.

The urge to strangle the messenger at that moment shoved Cyrus to his feet and he left Callia at the table on the sun-drenched terrace. He glanced back. His lovely wife was watching him with those beautiful curious eyes of hers. Eyes that he dreamt about when he was away from her.

If he had a weakness—or a mild debility—it was Callia. She had truly become the love of his life, but he was careful with that fact. He detested vulnerable men. Weakness was the road to destruction.

Just look at Adolf Merrick.

"I need to take this call," he said in a voice that belied his anger, then he left her and began walking down the stone steps to the sandy beach.

He owned many islands—some of them peaceful havens to escape the demands of his business, many of them shelters and warehouses for his black-market goods, and some like

Vouno, where he kept a growing number of his enemies caged like animals.

"I can talk now. You said Paxton escaped. What the hell happened, Holic?" Cyrus barked into the phone.

"I'm not sure. Somehow he was able to set my yacht on fire, cause a diversion, and then..."

"Then what?"

"I was out at the yacht trying to put out the fire. When I was returning, I noticed a light on in your office. I went up and found Paxton. He was armed. After he broke three of my ribs, he locked me in one of the cells."

"And where were the guards?"

"They were fighting the fire. After that was under control, I had instructed them to return to their posts. Paxton shot four and we lost three in the explosion."

"Explosion? What explosion?"

"Paxton set off the Astrolite. The monastery is in ruins."

"Melita? Is she all right?"

"I...don't know."

"What do you mean, you don't know?"

"She's gone. I think Paxton took her hostage."

Cyrus was livid. "Have you sent the men after him?"

"Yes, but—I've only been able to recover three guards. They're out looking now."

"If Paxton gets off the island, you're dead, Holic. Find my daughter."

"And when I find them, I will kill Paxton, right?"

"No, Holic, you can't kill him. I'll deal with Paxton. What about Barinski?"

"I haven't found him yet. My guess is that he's beneath the rubble in the laboratory, but I can't confirm that."

"Confirm it soon." Cyrus's eyes glazed over as he stared

out over thc azure water. His anger still raging, he calmly said, “I left you in charge, Holic. You will find Paxton and Melita.” He looked at his watch. “You have six hours. You know me, Holic. I never make idle thrcats. Don’t fail me in this or you will wish Paxton had killed you.”

Chapter 7

"How long have I been sleeping?" Melita woke up with a start. They had made it to the grotto—it had taken four and a half hours. She glanced down and for a moment she wondered why she was wearing Hector's shirt, then she remembered. Her dress had been in shreds and the clothes in her pack had gotten soaked on their hike through the grotto.

Nigel was sitting next to her, talking to his rats. "Hours now. There was no reason to wake you. He didn't come. Not that I thought he would."

She sat up slowly. Her side felt like it was on fire, but she wasn't going to mention it. "What time is it?"

"I don't know. Don't move around too much. You lost a lot of blood."

Melita peeked under the shirt to see that Nigel had put a fresh bandage on her side. "How long did I sleep, Nigel?"

"Do you remember me cleaning the wound?"

"Yes. It stung awful, and—"

"You passed out. I've been keeping a close watch on you. You've been out for hours."

"Hours?"

Nigel hesitated. "It's not daylight yet, but soon."

Nigel was probably right, Sully Paxton had skipped out on them. Melita leaned forward and put her head in her hands. "He's not coming," she whispered, perhaps needing to say it out loud to resign herself to the fact.

"No. Like I said, he ran the minute he left us."

"You don't have to keep saying that, Nigel. I get it. He's not coming, and I was a fool to trust him. There, are you happy?"

"You weren't foolish. You were filled with hope. I'm sure it seemed like a good idea at the time. You were desperate, and he knew it."

"He was desperate, too."

"And could move faster on his own."

That was certainly true enough. Melita settled her hand on Kit's sweet head where the little goat was curled up next to her. "How are you doing, baby? You must be getting hungry." She glanced around the wet cave. "Where's Hector?"

"He's outside. He's keeping watch. He refuses to believe that Paxton has left us for dead. I think we should go back, Melita. We could say that Paxton overpowered us and forced us to go with him. We could say we escaped him. If we go back—"

"I can't go back, Nigel. I have to try to get off the island, and you and Hector need to disappear. If my father learns you aided my escape, he'll have you and Hector shot."

"She's right. We can't go back." The words came from the entrance of the cave. Shirtless, Hector stood hunched over in the doorway, his pants wet to his knees. "We wait for Paxton."

"He's not coming, you idiot." Nigel scrambled to his feet.

"He went straight to the village when he left us, and is probably on a boat halfway to Turkey by now."

"Why Turkey?" Hector asked. "I thought he lived in the U.S."

Nigel rolled his eyes. "I was just using Turkey as an example, you idiot. He could have gone anywhere. Turkey. Russia. Africa. It makes no difference where he went. He's gone."

"Stop it, you two. Arguing isn't going to change anything. We have no food, no boat, and if Sully has deserted us—"

Nigel threw up his hands. "You don't see him anywhere, do you?"

Melita glared at him. "Since," she interjected, "Sully has deserted us, we need to come up with a new plan."

"Without a boat we're stuck here," Hector reminded her.

"Then we go to the village and steal one."

"Not the village," Hector protested. "By now the guards are there."

"Do you have a better idea, Hector?"

Suddenly there was a noise outside the cave. Melita shoved herself up to her feet. "Hector?"

"Could be the guards." Hector motioned for Melita and Nigel to crawl deeper into the cave, then he took the gun from his shoulder and disappeared outside.

"Take Kit and do as he says," Nigel instructed, then picked up his cage of rats.

Melita took Kit, moved ten feet farther into the cave and settled behind a rock. She heard Nigel struggling with his cage. Heard him curse. She raised up and looked over the rock and saw him fall hard to his knees. He let out a howl that probably echoed straight out of the cave.

"Be quiet," she scolded. "And hurry up."

"I shouldn't have agreed to come," he muttered.

"You're here now." And because it was her idea, Melita said, "Hand me the cage."

"You're not in Turkey?"

"Turkey?"

"I can't wait to see Barinski's face when he sees you. He said you would be in Turkey by now."

Hector had lost the bandage off his face and the exposed cut was going to be a permanent scar—a distinct C-shaped cut, deep into his cheek. He also had whip marks on his back. Sully wondered about both, but he decided now was not the time.

He asked, "Why Turkey?"

"That's what I said. Why would you go to Turkey when you made a promise to Melita to come back for her?"

"How is she?" Sully asked.

"She'll be doing better when she sees you. Did you find us a boat?"

Sully slapped Hector on the arm, then slipped into his old Irish brogue. "And a fine boat she is, mate."

Hector returned Sully's grin. "I knew you were a man of your word."

Sully handed him a bottle of water from the pack on his back. "I hid the *Artemis* in a cove west of here about a half mile down the coast. The villagers are out combing the area looking for the thief who poached her."

The cove where Sully had left the boat wasn't all that hard to spot, but the fishermen wouldn't bother to look for a forty-foot launch in a channel so narrow that it defied logic—the *Artemis* had fit that bottleneck tighter than a G-string on a stripper.

Hector drained the bottle of water in three gulps, tossed the bottle, then led Sully inside the grotto, first on their knees, then in a bent-over crouch.

There was a fissure overhead and the early morning sky was casting a glow inside to help them see. To their left, the rocks had eroded away where the sea rushed in. Over time it had cut a water channel eight feet below them that looked about three feet deep. They stayed on the ledge and continued to move deeper into the cave. For another thirty yards the hole in the earth grew narrower, and it forced them to climb down the ledge and drop into the water.

Sully wondered how Melita had managed, and it again made him anxious to get to her.

They could walk upright now, climbed back up an even sharper ledge. Another twenty yards and Hector called out. "Melita."

"We're here."

Her voice was strong. Sully felt relieved, but still eager to see for himself. One look at her and he'd know her condition.

He spotted her at the same time she spotted him. She came from around a rock like a fire was chasing her straight into his arms.

"Sully! Oh, God, you came."

It was a helluva greeting, and he put his arms around her, inhaled her sweet scent, as relieved to see her as she was to see him. He had always avoided women who smelled too good. He'd joked that they smelled like a ball and chain. But Melita smelled like fresh air, and he'd been without that a long time.

He lowered his head and whispered in her ear. "You didn't give up on me, did you?"

She pulled back and looked up at him. "You did promise."

"That's the thing about Irish boys. Get one to make a promise and he's fu— As faithful as a pagan mercenary."

She let go of him then, stepped back and gave him a quick shakedown. "You're in one piece."

He noticed she was favoring her side. "It appears to be true. How about you?"

"I'm good."

"She's lying. She needs a pint of blood."

Sully paid Nigel a dirty look for the medical opinion, then faced Melita again.

Melita said, "We heard an explosion. I thought—"

"A little diversion. So I take it you're happy to see me."

"Yes." She smiled, and what followed was an awkward silence as they looked at each other. Sully glanced past her to see both Barinski and Hector watching them with curious eyes. To lighten the moment, he dug in his pack, tossed Nigel a bottle of water, then handed one to Melita. "If I had known this was the welcome I was going to get, I wouldn't have sailed to Turkey first." He locked eyes with Barinski.

Hector laughed. It was followed by Barinski giving the big guy a nasty look, then a piece of his mind. "Do you have to repeat everything you hear, you idiot?"

"That's what you said."

"Idiot. A big dumb idiot."

"I'd rather be big than a stubby freak."

"Stop it, you two." Melita scolded the men like a mother reprimanding her rebellious children.

Sully enjoyed watching her in action. "Hector, take the goat and head for the *Artemis*. You know where you'll find her."

"You found us a boat?"

He was expecting another hug for that, but she held back. Sully grinned. "I was tired of hearing you harping about it.

She's not fast, but she's sound." He looked at Hector again. "Stay away from the shoreline. Keep undercover. Barinski, if you're bent on dragging those damn rats with you, I suggest you shag your ass, or I'll be climbing over it on my way out."

When neither man made a move, Sully said, "Get going."

When they still didn't budge, Melita said. "Do as he says. We'll be right behind you."

Satisfied, Hector nodded, then scooped up the goat. As he walked past Barinski, he grinned. "Come on, stubby, shag your ass?"

"I don't like boats. I don't like any of this. But boats... I think I'm allergic to water. It makes me nauseous."

Hector glanced at Sully and they shared a grin. "I'm sorry to hear that, stubby," Hector sympathized with his grin still in place. "Maybe you should stay behind."

Barinski muttered under his breath, but he wasted no time gathering up his rat cage and following Hector.

Alone, Sully focused on Melita. "How are you really feeling?"

"I feel good. Oh, and Nigel did what you told him to. He cleaned the wound, and I have a new bandage." She hesitated, then added, "You saved my life. Thank you."

Sully eyed the oversized shirt she was wearing. There was no doubt it was Hector's. "I brought a little first aid." He reached into his pocket and pulled out the roll of packing tape and a bottle of painkillers. He popped the top off the pills and shook out two.

"I'm not sick, Sully."

"If I could fly you out of here, I would. But you're going to have to walk, and belly crawl. You're going to be sore for a while. The pills will help you after we're out of here."

She took the pills, chased them down with the water.

"Get rid of the shirt."

She lowered the bottle of water. Capped it. "The shirt? Why?" She shook her head. "I just said, Nigel—"

"Scares me," Sully admitted. "Come on. Take it off. That kind of wound is prone to infection."

"But I—"

"I just stole you a boat. Humor me."

"But I'm fine."

"You won't be if that wound turns septic. It might be already."

"What's the tape for?"

"It's going to keep you alive."

"Was it the boat? Is that what took you so long to catch up? I thought…"

"That I was dead, or that I took off and left you?"

"Dead."

"You sure that's what you thought?"

She avoided his eyes.

"Quit stalling. We're not leaving here until I play doctor."

She pointed to the gun hanging on his shoulder. "Where did you get that?"

"From Krizova's office." Sully gestured to the shirt. "Come on. Open up."

She swore. Another Greek nasty. Then she unbuttoned the shirt. Sully stepped forward, and it forced her back against the rock wall. She wrapped her fingers around the edges of the shirt and opened them slowly.

Blue bra.

More cleavage than he expected.

Smooth flawless skin.

Tiny waist.

Blue lace panties.

Sully glanced up at her. She'd closed her eyes. He dropped

to his knees, pulled a five inch blade from inside his boot and sliced through the wrap Barinski had used to keep the wound clean—it looked like the bottom three inches of Hector's shirt. He told himself to concentrate on the wound.

Yeah, right. He laid his hand on her belly and leaned in to examine the wound.

"What do you think?" she asked.

"About what?" Sully looked up. Her eyes were open now and she was looking down at him with a pretty little pout, drawing his eyes to those sexy lips of hers. He remembered kissing those lips. Remembered how it made him feel. All of him.

"What do you think...about the wound?" The inflection in her voice let him know she was on to him.

"No infection. Barinski just got a free pass to live another day." Sully dug in his pack, ripped open a sterile dressing from the first-aid kit he'd found on the *Artemis* and placed it over the wound. "Hold that." Then he slid his arms around her with the roll of tape in his hand and started to wrap her waist, securing the bandage in place. Around and around he went with the tape, sealing the wound off, trying to be gentle, and at the same time, doing what needed to be done.

"It's going to feel tight, but it has to be. We want it waterproof. The tape will also keep you honest."

"What does that mean?"

"It means you're not going to be able to move as easily, and that's good for the wound. No wrong moves to start it bleeding again."

"I have a pair of jeans drying out on that rock over there. They got wet in my bag crawling in here."

Sully reached for the jeans. "I'll help you get your sweet ass—" He grinned. "I'll be the maid and help you get them on."

"You're in a good mood."

"Freedom does feel good."

"Freedom, or copping a feel?"

Sully liked how she brought it straight back at him. She was nobody's fool. That was good. He didn't want her to be.

Grinning, he admitted, "They both feel good. Come on now, put your hands on my shoulders and let's get you in these jeans before Hector doubles back, decides I'm taking advantage of the situation and snaps my neck."

"Hector wouldn't hurt you. He likes you."

Sully had never given a damn if anyone liked him. "How about you?"

"How about me, what?"

She was going to make him say it. "You like me, Melita?"

"I guess I have to now. You stole me a boat."

She reached for her jeans. Sully didn't lose the grin, or the jeans. "No point in stressing your side when I'm already down here. I'll do the work, you just wiggle."

"You're enjoying this."

"I'm human, honey."

"I'm not so sure. I read your file, remember?"

"It was a good thing, too, or you'd still be at Minare."

"And you'd be able to join a choir singing falsetto."

"That, too."

"With all your experience, I was wondering if you could give me some advice?"

The gleam in her eyes spelled trouble. Sully waded in. "Whatever you need."

"Do you think it would be smart for me to trust a man valued for having no conscience, with the nickname Mad Dog?"

Sully winced. "Read every word in that file, did you?"

"Every word."

Sully scratched his head. "That was the old Sully. I've changed some since then."

She put her hands on his shoulders and she stepped into the jeans. Sully started working them up her pretty legs. He wasn't going to go into detail with regard to his current position on life, or what it meant to him to be sucking clean air. The truth was he had changed, but Merrick and the boys back home wouldn't care one way or the other. He hadn't been recruited to work at Onyxx because he had a conscience. In fact, he'd been singled out because he didn't, and because for as long as Sully could remember he'd dealt with trouble two ways—with his fists or a gun.

The demon side of bad, Merrick always used to say. But he'd said it with a smile.

You make Sly and Pierce look like pussycats, Paxton.

"Sully? I asked you how you've changed?"

Oh, hell, just say it. "I'm happier."

"You weren't happy before?"

"No. Ornery as a wild banshee every day of my life."

"What makes you happy these days?"

"Nothing too earth-shaking."

"Tell me."

She changed her voice again, only this time it went all soft and coaxing. She was learning how to work him, and he was letting it happen. "Breathing fresh air, and taking a piss and being able to walk away from it. Like I said, nothing earth-shaking."

His hands slid over her hips, around her butt. He would have liked to let them linger, but he didn't. He'd put her through enough.

Her hands left his shoulders and she buttoned up Hector's shirt. Sully spotted a pair of tennis shoes, set them in front of her and helped her slide her feet into them, then he stood up.

"If that wound starts aching, or it starts to feel different in any way, tell me. I don't want you dying on me before I get you back to loverboy."

She set her jaw. "Don't call Nemo that."

She was touchy where her boyfriend was concerned. She was about to be reunited with the lucky bastard, she should be happy about that. He wasn't, but she should be.

"I get it." Sully suddenly figured it out. "You're afraid loverboy has found another sweetheart?"

"I told you not to call him that. And, no, that would never happen."

"Then cheer up. I promised I'd take you wherever you want to go. So where do we find loverboy? Ah, Nemo?"

She hesitated, then said, "I want to go to Delos. It's north of here about—"

"I know where it is."

She bent over to retrieve her bag, but Sully snatched it up first, and slung it on his shoulder with his. "I got it. Be careful on the rocks. They're slippery. Here, take my hand."

It had taken all of Melita's strength to make it through the grotto without having a claustrophobic meltdown. She'd almost hyperventilated going in, and she'd had the same reaction going out.

But she was breathing easy now that she stood on the deck of the *Artemis*. She recognized the boat. She'd seen her in the harbor at the village. She'd even approached the owner to help her get off the island, as she'd done with every fisherman who lived there.

She heard Sully turn over the engine and start to negotiate

the boat through the channel. She had no idea how he had gotten the launch in the narrows, but he was proving his navigational skills this minute. If she wasn't seeing it with her own eyes she would never have believed it.

By now the guards from Minare would be combing the island and the coast. Maybe they even knew about the stolen boat. She prayed that somehow Sully would be able to elude them.

His file said he was an expert seaman. No, it said he was a gut-and-go gunrunner. The best in Ireland. Maybe anywhere. She watched him as he slid the big boat between the rocks, so close she could reach out and touch them.

Once they were out to sea, she stood at the railing and watched the island of Despotiko grow smaller and smaller as Sully asked the boat for more speed. She laid her hand on her stomach, acknowledging that the strange flutter she'd felt in the cave was back. It was probably nerves mixed with the excitement of Sully coming back for her.

She had waited so long to escape the island, and now it was happening.

She glanced at the man responsible. He stood with his back straight and his sea legs spread, cemented in the boat as if his shoes had been nailed to the deck. Their partnership was ironic at best. She was traveling with her father's prisoner, and if Sully knew she was his enemy's daughter he would probably throw her overboard.

She looked out to sea. Escaping the island was one thing, but escaping her father was another. He had the manpower and the money to make the impossible possible. She'd seen it many times, and that's what frightened her the most. That, and the fact that Sully had no idea of the lengths to which her father would go to get her back.

She knew it was wrong to keep that vital piece of information from him, and yet she was feeling a little bit happy, too, and she didn't want anything to spoil it—like Sully forcing her to walk the plank in the middle on the Aegean Sea.

No, it was better to keep her secret, and pray that they reached Delos before hell rained down on them. After that, Sully would be free to go back to the U.S. and she would travel on to Mykonos.

Hector and Nigel were no longer on deck. Nigel was complaining about nausea, and Hector had gone down to raid the galley.

She smiled when she recalled Kit curled up sleeping in Hector's big arms. He'd urged Melita to go below with him. He told her she needed to eat something, but she wanted to stay on deck with Sully. She would keep watch, warn him if she saw something threatening.

Sully glanced at her, then motioned for her to come to him in the pilothouse. She moved across the deck and into the tight space. The sun was just coming up now, and in the daylight she could see that he was tired. In the infirmary he'd been clean shaven, and now he had a shadow outlining his rugged jaw. He was dangerously good-looking, and she couldn't deny that she liked his green eyes and how they could speak without him saying a word.

"You all right?"

She blinked out of her musing. "Yes. Your file said you were an expert 'boatman.' Where did you learn about boats?"

"If you read every word in my file, it didn't say boatman. And you already know where I'm from. Still don't trust me?"

"I want to. How does an Irish gunrunner become an American spy?"

"I made a name for myself with some bad boys. It got the

attention of some good guys, and instead of hanging me, they railroaded me into coming to work for them."

"Meaning you got caught."

"No. It didn't go down that way."

"How did it go down?"

"A friend of mine got himself into a bit of trouble. Paddy would never have survived prison. I learned his trouble was actually a setup. Onyxx wasn't interested in making an example of Paddy Paxton."

"They wanted something from you."

"Yeah. Onyxx was looking for some specialized talent. As it turns out what they wanted was me. Paddy was my bullet between the eyes. Merrick knew I wouldn't flush him."

"Was Paddy your father?"

"Nope. Just a friend."

"But you share the same name."

"O'Neill. That's my name. Sullivan O'Neill."

"Why did you change it?"

"It held some bad memories."

She could see he didn't want to talk about it. She switched it up, falling back on his current job. "So now you're a good guy working for Onyxx."

"Is that what you want me to be, Melita?"

"Maybe. Does that offend you?"

"I've never put a value on labels. Black and white..." He shrugged. "I guess I live somewhere in between. What about you? You know who I am and I only know your first name."

"I'm nobody. I like animals, sunshine and someday I'd like a house on a quiet island with a hidden beach and wild lavender growing everywhere. But for now, I just want to go to Delos."

"Are you so sure that's where I'm taking you?"

Melita glanced at the instrument panel. "You said you would take me wherever I wanted to go."

"I did, didn't I?"

She looked at him. "Sully, you promised."

"But Delos is out of my way."

"Are we headed south?"

He nodded.

"But I need to go north. It's only a one-day trip out of your way."

"Delos is two days out of my way. I'm going to be tucking the *Artemis* into a busy harbor by noon to stay out of sight until nightfall."

"Then drop me at the first island we come to."

"I suppose I could do that. Or you could persuade me to head north."

"And how would I do that?" Melita planted her hands on her hips. "Let me guess."

His grin turned rouge. "That hug in the cave was nice. A little more of the same might soften me up."

"Or it might do the opposite."

He laughed. "No doubt. Maybe you could imagine kissing your boyfriend again. A little practice for the homecoming."

"You want me to kiss you?"

"It wouldn't be the first time."

"I never kissed you. You tricked me."

"This time I don't have any tricks up my sleeves."

Melita narrowed her eyes.

He shrugged. "What's one kiss? A little show of gratitude for all I've done for you. You are grateful, right?"

"We made a deal."

"That was before I knew you intended to take the hired help along, and the farm, too. That required a bigger boat, a stocked galley, and—" he reached for the open bottle of whiskey in the cup holder "—more patience."

He raised the bottle to his lips, and when he lowered it, he winked at her. "That's good stuff. Want some?"

"What I want is to go to Delos."

He set the bottle down, reached out and pulled her into the tight space between him and the steering wheel. "Then let's work on getting this tub headed north."

"One kiss."

"One. A small thank-you for coming back for you. I didn't have to."

"Then why did you?"

He brushed a strand of her hair off her shoulder, his rogue grin softening. "I missed my lucky charm." He studied her face, locked eyes with her. "You've got bad-girl eyes, did you know that? Sexy and full of fire. Yeah, I missed those eyes, and the smell of you. You're a breath of fresh air."

"I'm not a bad girl."

"I think you could be just about anything you set your mind to." He rubbed one finger slowly over her lower lip.

"Why did you call me your lucky charm?"

"Luck's been shining down on me lately. There has to be a reason, right?"

His voice, and the way he looked at her—talked to her… That strange flutter attacked her stomach again.

"One kiss, Sully."

"That's all it'll take to head north."

"You promise?"

He flashed her his wicked grin again, kept moving his finger over her lower lip. "On my Irish honor."

"How many times do you intend to renegotiate our deal?"

"That depends on how much trouble you and your friends turn out to be. A man needs energy and motivation to keep going."

The longer they talked, the greater the chance that she would say something suspect. That he would sense she was hiding something. That's why she decided now was the perfect time to convince him that she was willing to do whatever it took to get to Delos.

"Because I'm grateful, and because we need to head north." She leaned forward, raised her arms to settle her hands on his shoulders.

Melita realized a second too late that Sully had spotted the scar on one of her wrists. His smile faded and then he turned his head and searched out the second scar—there was always a second one, that's the way it worked.

The scars weren't overly visible. Her father had hired the best surgeon available to minimize the damage she'd done to herself. But the faint scars would never be dismissed as anything but what they were—a futile attempt to kill herself.

When he focused on her face again, the question was in his eyes before he asked. "Explain those?"

Melita tried to pull away, but she was still between the wheel and his very warm, hard chest. "No."

"Who saved you? Was it Krizova? Is that why he thinks he owns you?"

"I wasn't saved. Death would have saved me. Instead, I was brought to Minare."

He stepped back, and she thought he was going to let her go. And she would go below deck this time. She didn't want to see the disgust that would soon fill Sully's eyes. That was the only way he would view what she'd done. He had endured hell to survive, while she had chosen escape through death.

He said, "Someday you'll tell me why." Then he lowered his head and brushed a single kiss on one scarred wrist, then the other. When he looked up, he said, "I'll take you to Delos."

Chapter 8

Since he was age six, living on the streets of Dublin, Sully's life had been all about survival. Not once in Krizova's prison had he wanted to die. Not once on the streets of Dublin. Not once in his entire life working at Onyxx.

Maybe he hadn't valued happiness, but he had valued breathing. That's why it was hard to accept that Melita had purposely taken a knife to herself and slashed her wrists with the sole intent of killing herself.

He was angry with her for that, or maybe he was just damn confused. But not for long. He was determined to find out what had driven her down that hopeless black road.

She had a boyfriend, a life to go back to. What would have made her want to give up on that? What had caused her to lose hope?

"Are you hungry?"

Sully turned to see Hector standing behind him eating a sandwich.

"I made extra. I can bring you some if you like. Barinski can't eat anything." Hector grinned. "He's too busy heaving his guts up and complaining he's going to die."

Sully offered a half smile over Barinski's misery. "Do you trust him?"

"If you're asking will he make trouble for us, the answer is no. Before Krizova got his claws into Barinski, he was a decent man. Krizova knows how to capitalize on human weakness. I suspect Barinski was in the wrong place at the wrong time like me."

"How did you end up in Krizova's camp?"

"I met Cyrus on the island of Santorini. I was a wrestler in a gambling establishment. The kind where rich people go to be entertained. There was an accident, and I killed the man in the ring with me. I didn't mean to. I thought this is it, I'll go to prison now. Instead, Cyrus paid off the owner of the gambling den, and the next thing I knew, I was on his yacht."

"And what about Melita?"

"I'm not sure I know what you're asking?"

"Who is she, Hector? I saw the scars on her wrists."

Hector avoided Sully's eyes. "I can't discuss her with you. She wouldn't like it."

"You seem to care a lot about what happens to her."

"I do."

"Then why didn't you try to stop her from slitting her wrists?"

"I didn't know her very well then. I had just gotten on the yacht."

"So it happened on Krizova's yacht?"

"Yes."

"And you know what drove her to it?"

"We shouldn't be discussing this. Even though..."

"Even though what?"

"She's the one good thing that has come out of my service to Krizova. I worry about what will happen to her, but I can't betray her confidence."

"Even to keep her alive?"

"She's not in danger of dying."

"How do you know that? She slit her wrists once. She could do it again."

"She won't. She's stronger now."

"What about Krizova? He's not going to be happy that she escaped with me. He's killed people for less. I can't protect her if I don't know the extent of Krizova's obsession with her."

"I believe you care what happens to her. You've proven that by coming back for her. And I believe there's more. I've seen the way you look at her, but I won't betray her to anyone for any reason."

Sully pulled two of Cyrus's expensive cigars from his pocket and offered one to Hector, then cornered the other one between his lips. They shared a match. He took a hard pull off the Cuban and blew smoke out to sea. "Let's just stick to the facts, Hector."

"The fact is she is a beautiful woman, and every man's fantasy," Hector admitted.

"Yours, too?"

"I love Melita like a sister."

"Then as her brother your duty is to protect her, whatever it takes. It might take breaking that code of loyalty you're sitting on. You don't know me too well, but I think you know I'm her best shot."

"Because you're a better killer than most?"

"If that's what it takes. I know she's in love with Nemo. What I want for her is to be safe wherever she ends up."

"She told you about Nemo?"

"Yes."

"It was a sad day for her. Cyrus made her watch."

Watch what? Sully wanted to ask. But he wouldn't. Hector wasn't ready to fold. Not yet.

"Are you an honorable man, Sully Paxton?"

"If you're asking if I intend to do what I promised, I told Melita I'll take her to Delos."

Hector frowned. "Delos? She wants to go to Delos?"

"Is that a problem? What's wrong with taking her to Nemo in Delos?"

"I thought you said she told you about Nemo?"

"She did."

"Then you know Nemo isn't in Delos. He's at the bottom of the sea."

Sully sucked hard on the cigar, blew more smoke. Nemo was dead. Okay, the boyfriend was no longer in the picture. Then why was she pretending he was?

"Delos…" Hector frowned, then whispered, "Mykonos."

"What was that?"

"The first place Cyrus will look for her is Mykonos."

"But she wants to go to Delos," Sully reminded.

"She'll be walking into a trap at Lesvago."

"Is Lesvago in Delos, or Mykonos?"

"Mykonos."

"So you don't think she's going to Delos."

"Delos is a ferry ride away from Mykonos."

From the confused expression on Hector's face he was working through her plan in his head, and he wasn't liking what it added up to.

Like Hector, Sully worked through the information. She'd been on Krizova's yacht with Nemo, and Cyrus had killed her boyfriend in front of her.

Sully said, "She watched Cyrus kill Nemo, and then slit her wrists on the yacht."

"Simon killed him, not Cyrus."

Now who was that? Sully thought.

"Cyrus ordered Simon to whip Nemo to death. I had a hard time watching it, and still Cyrus made Melita watch. Nemo didn't deserve to die, but he wasn't worthy of Melita's love."

"Why do you say that?"

"He told her what she wanted to hear. Men do that. You know, to get what they want."

"So Nemo wasn't in love with her?"

"Every man loves Melita. But few men only want one woman. Nemo knew they couldn't be together. He was nothing more than a guard at Lesvago. Cyrus was livid when he found out that Nemo had touched her." Hector came out of his reticence as if someone had snapped their fingers. "I've said too much."

Not nearly enough, Sully thought, then tossed the cigar overboard and got in Hector's face. "You mentioned Simon. How does he fit in? Come on, Hector. Give up the rest of it."

"Simon is Melita's brother. He lives at Lesvago."

Sully was scrambling to make sense of what Hector was saying. Melita had a brother, and he had killed Nemo on Cyrus's yacht. If she was headed to Mykonos, the question was why? Revenge? Against who? Simon?

"So this is about revenge. She wants to kill her brother?"

"Melita couldn't kill a fly. Besides, she loves Simon even now. She is nothing like him."

"Him? You mean Simon?"

"No, her father."

Father. First she's got a brother, and now a father. Tired of chasing his tail, Sully pulled the SIG from the waistband of his pants and aimed it at Hector's chest. "If you care about Melita, this is your chance to prove it. Put it together for me. Come on, Hector."

"I can't. I swore to her that I would keep her secret."

"I hope you can swim, Hector. Because in less than a minute you're going over the side."

Hector grimaced. "I admit I don't swim too good. But I would rather drown than see the look on Melita's face once she learned I had betrayed her."

"She'll forgive you. I'll tell her I held a gun to your head."

Hector considered that, then nodded. "I do this not to save myself, but to save Melita. Perhaps you are the only man alive who can."

"Not unless I know what's out there waiting for her."

"What if you don't like what you hear?"

"In my line of work I rarely like the facts. I'll deal with them."

"Promise me you won't hurt her."

"I won't hurt her. Who is she, Hector?"

Hector let go of a heavy sigh. "Her name is...Melita Parish Krizova. She is your enemy's daughter. And Cyrus will come for her with a vengeance, my friend. To get her back he will destroy anything and anyone in his path. That will be you. Are you prepared to die for her?"

Sully pushed the *Artemis* hard for the next three hours to get as far away from Despotiko as possible. He shot straight north—it was more important than ever to put some hard miles between them and Krizova's henchmen.

They would be gunning for blood. There was no doubt.

Hector had come up on deck a few minutes ago and told him that both Nigel and Melita were sleeping. She was exhausted, he'd said, and her side was giving her some pain.

They had exchanged a look, Hector had nodded, then returned below deck, telling Sully without words that the deed was done.

He saw the southeast coast of Syros and headed toward it. Using the map he'd stolen from Cyrus's office, he'd charted a route to go along with his plan. He cut the engine and the *Artemis* glided into the busy harbor at Vari. Minutes later Hector was on deck with Kit tucked under his arm and a wide-eyed Barinski at his side. The doc still looked green, and to add to his discomfort, completely confused as to why he'd been forced awake and told to bring his rats and join Sully on deck.

"You still have the gun I gave you?" Sully asked Hector.

"I do."

Barinski shielded his eyes against the sun. "Are you going to kill me, Paxton?"

Sully didn't answer, let the little man sweat. He sure as hell had been sweating after he'd been told he was going to be turned into a eunuch. He crouched down and unzipped the duffel bag at his feet, angled it to allow Hector to see the money stacks inside. One stack had a piece of white paper wrapped around it. Sully said, "There are detailed instructions inside." He zipped the bag, stood and handed it to Hector. "I trust you'll do as I ask and be there when I need you."

Hector accepted the money. "I'll do everything you ask."

"Go quickly."

"Go where?" Barinski backed up. "What's going on?"

Hector ignored the little man. "Where did you get the cash?"

"Cyrus's office." Sully grinned. "It seemed appropriate."

Smiling, Hector slung the bag on his shoulder. "Tell Melita... Tell her..."

Sully nodded. "I know. I'll tell her I held a gun to your head."

"Take care of her."

"What have you done, Hector?" Barinski was livid. "You idiot!"

Sully turned his attention to Nigel. "If you want to live you'll go with Hector. Considering what you were about to do to me back at Minare I'm being more than generous. That's not my nature. A few years ago I would have put a gun in your mouth, pulled the trigger, then kicked your carcass in a ditch."

Barinski glanced at Hector. "Have you lost your mind? You're leaving Melita with this killer?"

Sully pulled his SIG from his waistband for the second time that morning. "It's time to go. Take a walk, or a swim."

Barinski set down his cage. "Hector, we can't just desert Melita. What kind of man are you? I was there when you promised her that you—"

Hector reached out and picked Barinski up by the collar of his shirt. "Don't ever question my loyalty to Melita." That said, he let go of Barinski, nodded to Sully, then left the boat saying, "Pick up those damn rats and shag you ass, stubby. We have things to do."

Minutes later Sully steered the launch back out to sea. It was noon and the sun was hot. He stripped off his T-shirt as he sailed up the coast hugging the shoreline.

Thirty minutes later he slipped into a crowded harbor and docked the *Artemis* in Ermoupoli, the capital of Syros, just twenty miles west of Mykonos.

He pulled the watch from his pocket and checked the time, then went ashore.

The silence is what woke Melita from a sound sleep the first time. The engine's constant purr had lulled her to sleep hours ago, and it was that absence that had alerted her that something was amiss.

She had gotten out of bed and hurried to the cabin door, only to find it locked. Minutes later the engine had started up and the *Artemis* was moving again. But the launch now stopped for a second time. She had mentally clocked the time. Thirty minutes, maybe.

Thirty minutes of rising panic, of calling out, first to Hector, then Nigel. But no one had answered. Not even Sully. They had to hear her—she'd screamed until her throat was raw.

Something was terribly wrong.

Melita wrapped her arms around herself as the panic set in. She didn't want to give in to it, but she was having a hard time breathing now, and she knew what that meant. She was going to be gasping for air soon. It was only a matter of time.

The cabin had no windows to open, no way to see where the *Artemis* was. Had the launch slipped into a cove, or a harbor? Or had they been hijacked at sea while she slept?

The reality of her last thought had Melita in full meltdown mode. Her lungs shut down and she suddenly couldn't breathe.

She tore off Hector's shirt and ripped at the tape that suddenly felt too tight. She needed air. She had to have air. Clawing at the tape like an animal, she jerked it loose from her body, but it didn't help. She still couldn't breathe.

Please, she thought, someone open the door.

She chewed her lip. Paced. Beat on the door.

No air. No damn air.

Melita huddled on the berth and began to rock as her imagination ran wild with all sorts of crazy scenarios. The one that stuck, and had her biting her nails—now that her lip was shredded—was the very real possibility that her father had outrun them and had taken over the boat.

It all fit. Why no one was answering her cries for help. Why Kit was gone from the room. Why she'd been locked inside.

She closed her eyes, knowing that if her father was on board, the others were dead. That's why they weren't answering.

I've told you before when you disobey me, your actions have consequences.

Her throat started to close off, the final sign that her claustrophobia would soon land her on the floor, retching and clawing at the door.

When you disobey me, your actions have consequences.

We both know how much you hate being the catalyst to a disaster.

Consequences.

Melita rocked faster. She should have told Sully the truth. She should have told him who she was, prepared him. No, she should never have left Minare.

It was all her fault this was happening.

Your actions have consequences.

Remember, you have the power. You don't need another death on you conscience to send you off the balcony, or slitting your wrists.

I missed you, lucky charm.

Melita squeezed her eyes shut, remembering how Nemo had died. There had been so much blood it had covered the deck on her father's yacht.

She envisioned the *Artemis's* deck soaked in blood. She could see it in her mind's eye. Sully. Hector. Nigel. Kit. They were all dead.

Remember, you have the power.

We both know how much you hate being the catalyst to a disaster.

No air to scream.

No air at all.

Bile rose up in Melita's throat, and it forced her off the bed. She raced into the small bathroom and dropped to her knees. Gripping the toilet, she retched until she was white as a sheet and too weak to get off the floor. Retched so hard that she was unaware she had torn open the wound on her side.

She tried to stand, but a wave of dizziness sent her off balance. She was there now, in deep claustrophobic meltdown. She'd been there before, knew how it would end.

Eyes wide, gasping, Melita grabbed her throat and collapsed on the floor.

Cyrus Krizova tossed a live rat into the fish tank and watched as six hungry piranhas devoured it in seconds, leaving the water stained red.

Forced to cut his visit short with Callia, he'd arrived at Lesvago in the middle of the night.

Holic hadn't found Paxton and Melita in Cyrus's timeline, and he'd been tempted to kill the bastard for failing him. But they were in the middle of an arms deal worth billions, and the explosion that had taken out the lab at Minare had cost him millions of dollars. He couldn't afford to surrender the deal, not financially. But more importantly it would cast doubt in the eyes of his business associates.

He needed Holic right now, and as much as that enraged him, he couldn't kill him.

He spent the morning analyzing the facts surrounding Paxton's escape, and what he came up with was that Paxton, as good as he was, had needed help escaping Minare. That likely meant Melita had been his accomplice.

He'd run the idea by Holic an hour ago. Holic had supplied an interesting theory of his own into the mix. He had called the fiasco at Minare a mutiny. He said it was Hector who had reported the fire to him. Holic believed that Melita had convinced Hector to torch the yacht. That seemed a bit out of character for her, but he'd listened. Holic's assumption was that Barinski must have aided his daughter in Paxton's release from the infirmary. Barinski hadn't been found under the rubble in the lab, and Hector was nowhere to be found either.

He could believe Hector was part of the mutiny, but he wasn't convinced that Barinski had the balls to spring Paxton—not unless he was outnumbered, or someone was holding a gun to his head. Then again, he couldn't dismiss Melita's talent for attracting men to her cause. She had a history of collecting admirers. They seemed to flock to her side as easily as flies to a dead corpse.

He wondered if Paxton was one of the flies.

Hector worshipped Melita, and to Barinski, she was an angel. He'd used that word more than once.

Angel, my ass. The little bitch was as cunning as a fox. But the fox was loyal to her brother. So not all was lost. If she was running with Paxton it wouldn't be long before she got the itch to see Simon. That would bring her here to Lesvago.

For months she had been begging to see her brother. Her loyalty to Simon was touching. Too bad her loyalty to her father wasn't just as strong.

No matter. She would come.

Cyrus smiled. "Come then, my little fox. Simon is waiting for you, and so am I."

He heard a yacht pulling into Lesvago's harbor. He walked to the wall of glass, looked out and saw Holic was already striding toward the stone steps cut deep into the cliff. He looked past Holic, his line of vision far-reaching. There was no way to penetrate Lesvago without being seen. The house had been built into the rocky cliff and unless you were a mountain goat, the only way in was the visible cove.

He scanned the periphery. He had doubled the number of guards on duty. He really hoped that Paxton was feeling up to the game.

He stepped out onto the terrace. The gardens were blooming and the scent of lavender reminded him of Melita's passion for flowers. She didn't believe that he loved her, but it was true. There were few things in this world he loved, but she was one of them. That's why he would never let her go.

As Holic drew near, Cyrus could see his bruised and battered face. He looked as if he'd been chewed up by an angry dog.

"Have you heard anything?" Holic asked the minute he reached the terrace, winded from all the steps. "Have your men located the *Artemis*?"

"Not yet. The men are still searching, but I'm not expecting to find them with the *Artemis*. Paxton will dump the launch, and he won't need to steal another, will he? He'll use the money he stole from my office."

"What if Melita is no longer with him? What if they separated?"

"Paxton wouldn't pass up an opportunity to use her to get to me. He's too smart. And he has more than one reason to come after me. I've given him dozens."

"The way you talk about Paxton, it's almost as if—"

"I like him?" Cyrus laughed. "I do. Paxton is perhaps the deadliest of Merrick's elite force. But I made him even better. I had a pit dug for him at Vouno. He lived there for months in conditions that would have made a rat vomit. But not Paxton. He's a breed unto himself. A tougher breed than even Merrick knows. He's mine now. And as much as I want to kill him, I'm not sure what I'll do with him when I get him back."

"I don't like this. Too many things could go wrong. He's already proven to be a liability."

Cyrus arched an eyebrow. "Too many things have already gone wrong, Holic, and they happened on your watch."

"I explained that. If Paxton is as dangerous as you say, we need him dead. I want him dead."

"That's your bruised ego talking." Cyrus eyed Holic's battered face. "Of course you want him dead, but it's what I want you need to concern yourself with. You could still be rotting in a cell at Clume. You could be again. Now then, update me on the arms deal. Have you heard from your associate in Austria? Is he ready?"

"He's ready, and has agreed to purchase as many Skorpions as you can deliver."

"Excellent. How are your hands feeling these days?"

"If I'm fixed on my target, he's dead."

Cyrus considered the flaw. An assassin didn't always have that kind of time.

His phone rang. He slid his hand in his pocket and pulled out his cell. "Yes, what is it?"

"We located the *Artemis*. She's docked on Syros."

Cyrus glanced at Holic. "Abandoned?"

"Unconfirmed."

"Confirm. If not, I want them captured alive. My daughter unharmed. Paxton… Shoot him, but don't kill him. Keep me informed." With a smile on his face, Cyrus slipped the phone back in his pocket.

"Perhaps our wait has come to an end. My men have located the *Artemis* on Syros."

Chapter 9

When Melita woke up she was in bed. She blinked awake and immediately saw Sully. He was leaning against the wall watching her, his arms crossed over his chest. He was wearing a black muscle tee and jeans with a gun tucked into the waistband.

She struggled to sit up, glanced at the open door. She remembered feeling sick. Remembered running to the bathroom. Remembered why. But now it seemed as though she'd been wrong. Her father hadn't come for her. Not yet.

She tossed back the sheet to get up, then quickly sat back and pulled it to her neck as she realized she was only wearing her bra, panties and a fresh bandage with tape circling her waist.

"You want to tell me what happened in here?" he asked.

"Do you want to tell me why you locked the door?"

He shoved away from the wall and sauntered toward the berth. "I wanted you safe when I left the launch to run an errand."

"Where's Hector?"

"He took the goat to get her something to eat."

"And Nigel?"

"Barinski went along. He was only too happy to set his feet on solid ground."

"When will they be back?"

"They won't be coming back. I dropped them off six miles down the coast."

"What?" Melita was halfway out of the berth when she remembered she wasn't dressed. She sat back. "Why?"

"By now Cyrus knows Hector and Barinski aided in our escape. I thought you'd want your friends safe. I decided there was no sense putting it off."

"Hector wouldn't leave me. What did you say to him?"

"I told him you'd feel like hell if anything happened to him, and that I'd take care of you."

"And he agreed just like that?"

"He likes me, remember?"

"Where are we?"

"Syros. Ermoupoli."

"So you sent Hector away with Kit and Nigel, locked me up and went out to run an errand?"

"That's almost right." He grinned. "Except I didn't lock you in. Hector did before I dropped him off in Vari. Oh, and Nigel took his rats. Now it's your turn. What happened in here? I opened the door and there you are on the floor in the bathroom, blood everywhere. You scared the hell out of me. I thought—"

"I had slit my wrists again."

"It crossed my mind."

"Don't ever lock me up again."

He sat down next to her on the bed. "So you don't like locked doors."

She shook her head, hating the weakness. That's why no one knew about her claustrophobia except her father, who had loved using it to control her. If she told Sully, would he use it against her, too?

Melita looked away, but he reached out and curled his fingers around her chin and turned her slowly back. "Come on, honey. Give it to me straight. We all have rules we live by. If I don't know yours, you're not going to like how I play the game. You're claustrophobic, right?"

She nodded, unable to say the word.

"I should have realized. You were having trouble on our way out of the grotto."

"I hate it," she blurted out.

"Locked doors?"

"I hate not being able to control the phobia."

"We all have things that make us go a little crazy sometimes."

Melita gave him a droll look. "Name one of yours."

He rubbed his jaw. "Let's see…"

"You can't, can you?"

"I got one. When I saw you on the floor in there." He gestured to the bathroom. "You shortened my life by about a year."

He was dissecting her as if she were a new breed of bug. Hours ago everything had been settled. He'd agreed to take her to Delos. But now Hector and Nigel were gone with the animals, and they were docked on Syros.

What had happened while she was sleeping? She was about to ask when she heard voices on deck. Suddenly Sully was on his feet, pulling his gun and heading for the open door.

"Sully?"

"Come here."

"But I'm not dressed."

"Now, Melita."

The urgency in his voice had her climbing from the berth. She hurried across the room in her blue bra and panties. "What is it?"

He motion to the upper deck, held up three fingers, then crept down the hall, and started up the companionway. Melita followed close behind, wishing she'd had time to put some clothes on.

Four steps from the top, he glanced back. "Stay put."

Melita nodded, then watched Sully disappear into the sunlight. He hadn't been gone more than a couple of seconds when the sound of a gunshot made her jump nearly out of her panties. Two shots later, she headed up the steps needing to make sure Sully was all right. That's when she saw him dive to the deck and roll once. Then like an eel on a downward slope, he belly-crawled to the pilothouse.

Another gunshot ripped through the air, and she saw wood splinter in the doorway of the pilothouse above Sully's head. He was in a crouch now, and she saw him grab a large duffel bag. Staying low, he started back out of the pilothouse. Suddenly he locked eyes with her, then stood up.

What was he doing?

She had her answer a second later. He raised the gun, aimed it at her, then swung the weapon two feet to her left and fired.

It was automatic. No hesitation. All reflexes and instinct.

She peered around the doorway, saw a man lying on the deck. He had a bullet hole in his forehead. She was still staring down at the man when Sully grabbed her hand. "Let's go."

She came out of her daze. "Go? I can't go anywhere without clothes."

"Where we're going you won't need them." His grip tightened on her hand and he pulled her along with him to the back of the boat. She suddenly understood why she didn't need clothes when he wrapped his arm around her and carried her with him as he leapt to the narrow ledge at the stern.

Then he was in the air, jumping off the launch with her fused to his side.

She heard shots behind them as they dropped over the side. The second they hit the water the weight of the duffel bag dragged them under.

Melita's last thought was that whatever Sully had in the bag was as heavy as cement.

Melita was running out of air. Sully kicked himself for not reminding her to take a deep breath before they plunged into the water. Cursing himself for his error, he knew they had to surface. He only hoped that when they did, they wouldn't be spotted.

He started back up, kicking hard to get them to the surface. They broke through the water seconds later. Melita came up coughing. Sully pulled her against him, hoping to shield her from any more flying bullets.

He looked around to see where they were. He scanned the boats in the slips, looked back at the *Artemis*. Six men stood on deck, their serious hardware—Skorpions—aimed at the water as they searched for movement.

"Take a breath," he said, "we're going back down."

"Sully, I can't. Oh, God, you've been shot."

He glanced at his arm. "It's nothing. Take a breath, then hold on to the bag."

"Over there!" Cyrus's men had spotted them.

Sully swore, then ducked back under the water, dragging Melita with him, hoping she'd had enough time to suck in a breath of air. He let the weight of the bag carry them down into the depths. This time he swam hard, moving quickly through the water, pulling the bag and Melita with him. He glanced back and saw she was doing better, aiding their escape by kicking her legs as she hung on to the bag.

He mentally counted the hulls overhead as they swam beneath each one. Four more to go.

Melita was just starting to run out of air when he motioned to her that they were going back up. They surfaced together, and he pulled her toward the fifty-foot cruiser christened *Korinna*. The cruiser was a sleek speed-demon. She had reminded Sully of the *Duvessa*, the badass smoker he'd used in Ireland in his gunrunning days. The minute he'd seen her, he knew she was just what they would need to stay out front of Cyrus and his men.

"Wait. What are you doing? We can't steal a boat like this. Are you crazy?"

Sully winked. "I'm not stealing her. She's ours. My errand, remember?" He hoisted Melita onto the dock, then swung the bag up beside her. "Board her. We're getting out of here now."

She got to her feet. Sully had to kick himself to keep from staring at Melita's little curvy body, and the way her panties were plastered to her sexy ass. There was no time for sightseeing, he reminded himself. They weren't out of danger yet.

He saw her cradling her side. He was damn glad that he'd rewrapped the wound back on the *Artemis*, at least it had stayed dry.

He pulled himself up on the dock and heaved the duffel bag over the side of the cruiser while Melita climbed in.

"How did you pay for this boat?"

"A gift from Krizova."

"You stole the money from my…from Minare?"

"I figured it was better than letting it burn in the explosion."

As he leapt onto the deck to join her, she asked, "What else is in the bag? It weighs a ton."

"Ammunition."

"You came prepared."

He wasn't prepared at all. Not for what Hector had told him. Prepared meant you knew all there was to know about the quicksand before you dove in. Nothing had prepared him for the secrets Melita had been keeping. And even after Hector had spilled his guts, he got the feeling he was in for a few more surprises before this was over.

He should be pissed as hell, and suspicious of every move she made, every word that came out of her sweet mouth. But if he put himself in her shoes, he knew he probably would have done the same thing. The one thing he didn't understand was the lie about Nemo.

She reached out and touched his arm. "You're bleeding."

"I'll tape it up later." Sully stepped into the enclosed cockpit and turned over the engine. It roared to life, and he backed the *Korinna* out of the slip, spun her around and shot out of the harbor.

He felt Melita come up behind him. She stood close, and he saw she was hugging herself. At sixty miles an hour the air had turned chilly. He reached back and pulled her to his side, kept his arm around her. After a few seconds, she wrapped her arms around his waist and leaned into him. Sully glanced over his shoulder, saw that Cyrus's men had taken chase. He pushed the cruiser for more speed. Pulled away.

"Are we headed for Delos?" Melita asked.

"I think that would be a mistake right now. We'll hold off a while. Let things cool down. We'll hide out somewhere close by." He looked down at her. "Don't worry. We'll outrun them."

He'd decided not to tell her that he knew she was Krizova's daughter, or that he knew Nemo was dead. She had enough to worry about without wondering what he was going to do with the information.

He couldn't stop looking at her. She was a beauty all right, those brown eyes and sexy lips. All that long black hair flying in the breeze. He lowered his gaze to her full breasts, the blue lace sucked tight to her nipples.

He said, "You cold?"

It was a dead giveaway what had prompted the question. He should have kept his mouth shut.

She looked up at him, one eyebrow raised. "What was your first clue?"

The minute Melita opened the door to the stateroom she saw that Sully had shopped for more than a fast boat. He had bought her clothes.

They had outrun her father's men, and once Sully had cut their speed, he had suggested she go below deck.

Melita stood in the middle of the small luxury room and stared at the clothes that looked like they had been dumped out of a bag on the bed. For a year she'd survived with a minimal wardrobe and a no-frills bedroom at Minare. She had been raised in luxury, but the lack hadn't been a hardship. She'd never been a woman who needed plush amenities to be happy, unlike her brother, Simon.

She liked pretty things, every woman did, but what she coveted more was the freedom of choice. She had always wondered what she would have been, and what she could be if she wasn't Cyrus Krizova's daughter.

She appreciated the clothes—after all, she had nothing to wear. But what meant more to her was that Sully had actually shopped for each piece, from lingerie to shoes. Even a wide-brimmed white hat.

He didn't look like the type of man who would ever set foot inside a woman's boutique. But since she'd met him, he hadn't been intimidated or deterred by anything.

She found a towel in the bathroom and wrapped it around herself as she snooped around the stateroom. There were clothes in the closet—men's clothes for Sully, jeans, a few shirts, and a half dozen muscle tees.

It seemed as though he had thought of everything. Even about how to keep Hector, Nigel and Kit out of harm's way. She hoped that was true. Hoped one day she would see them again, but she would keep her distance if it meant they would remain safe.

She moved back to the bed and took a pair of black panties and a matching bra off the pile. Sully had good taste in underwear. She checked the size, then arched her eyebrows.

She heard him above deck, wondered how long it would be before he came down. Did she have time to take a shower? She headed into the bathroom of gold and mirrors, slid open the glass on the shower stall and turned on the water. She stripped off her underwear, tossed her panties and bra in the garbage then stepped into the shower. The warm spray felt wonderful on her skin, and she closed her eyes as the tension of the day slipped away.

She was still enjoying the water when she heard Sully call out to her. She had left the door ajar. She glanced toward it, saw it drift open. Saw Sully in the doorway.

Melita froze with her hands tangled in her hair.

"You all right?"

"I'm in the shower, Sully."

"I see that." He pulled his eyes off her and glanced around.

Opened the cupboard above the sink. Then he crouched down and opened the one below it. "Don't mind me, I'm getting the first-aid kit. I'll be out of here in a second."

Don't mind him? Was he crazy? She was naked.

"There it is." He stood, the first-aid kit in his hand. He glanced at her a second time.

She still hadn't moved. She saw him smile as he glanced at the underwear he'd bought her draped on the hook next to the door. "You need someone to wash your back, give me a holler." Then he turned around and walked out, closing the door.

Melita came out of her frozen stupor quickly. "Sully!"

The door swung open and he stuck his head back in. "You need something?"

"Don't close the door."

"Sorry. I forgot." Then he slung the door wide open and left.

She finished washing her hair, scrubbed her own back and shut off the shower. When she opened the glass door, she grabbed a towel and stepped out. She saw Sully sitting on the floor in the stateroom. He'd bandaged his arm, and now had his foot curled into his lap. The first-aid kit was open beside him, half emptied out on the carpet.

She dried off, then wrapped the towel around herself and tucked the end into her cleavage. She stepped into the black bikinis and grabbed a comb from the cupboard. Working the comb slowly through her hair, she stepped back in the stateroom, the towel still tucked around her breasts.

"What are you doing with that knife?"

He looked up. "I drove a sliver in my hand docking the boat." He held up the tweezers from the first-aid kit. "These damn things are useless."

She eyed the knife. The blade looked like it was capable

of taking his entire hand off in one swipe. "Don't you think that knife is a little big, or do you intend to amputate?"

He chuckled. "Not unless it's the only way I can get some relief." He glanced at the towel wrapped around her, lingered a few extra seconds on her legs. "Feel better?"

"Yes. Where are we?"

"Tinos. Fifteen miles north of Delos."

She sat on the floor in front of him with her legs crossed and tucked the towel between them. "Let me see."

"You don't need to bother."

She picked up the tweezers. "Are you one of those guys who can't let a woman do anything for him?"

"Now that's a question we could spend a few hours on."

She blushed, even though she was getting used to Sully saying whatever came to mind. She was becoming more relaxed around him. She wasn't afraid of him at all which was crazy. She had witnessed him in action on the *Artamis,* and every move he'd made had been calculated and dead right. She would hate to be his enemy, she thought.

Then she realized that by birthright, that's exactly what she was.

She set her comb down, reached out and took hold of his hand. "By the way, thank you for the clothes."

"Did you find anything you like?"

"I like them all."

"Easy to please, are you?"

She didn't know how to answer that, so she got busy with the tweezers. "This sliver is deep, and huge."

"I can just cut it out. It would be easier."

She glanced at him. "Give me a minute."

It took ten, but she finally held up the inch-long sliver that looked more like a stick. "I'm sorry if I hurt you."

"What's a little pain when the trade-off is holding hands with you, honey?"

She released his hand. "All done. Is there anything else I can do for you?" she asked, not really thinking about what she was saying too much, or how he would take it.

"Now that you mention it, there is one thing." Suddenly he was on his knees leaning toward her. To keep her balance she had to drop her hands behind her and brace herself from falling backward. She felt that strange flutter in her stomach again.

"You can have dinner with me tonight. There must be a decent waterfront restaurant close by. It's been a while since I had a choice of what I want to eat. You game?"

"All right."

She let her guard down then, and she realized a second too late what was coming next.

He rocked forward and kissed her. It was a careful kiss, a kiss that didn't trespass too far. "Thanks for administering first aid to my hand. You need any first aid?"

When she didn't answer, he said, "I should probably look at your side and change that tape."

"It's fine, for now. It stayed dry."

"Later then. I guess I'll take a shower." He lingered a moment, his face still close. He looked at her lips as if he was considering kissing her again, then locked eyes with her once more. "Ah…yeah. That shower sounds like a good idea. I think I'll take it cold."

He got to his feet, and that's when she remembered she had left her bra on the hook behind the door. She stood quickly and went past him to snatch it. When she turned, he was standing in the doorway blocking her exit.

"Thought for a second you were going to join me." He glanced at the bra. "Did I guess the right size?"

"Yes. Was it a guess?"

He grinned. "The numbers just fell into place. Does that bother you?"

Nothing he said or did lately bothered her. And that was the problem. He was like that sliver. He was working his way slowly under her skin.

We both know how much you hate being the catalyst to a disaster. You don't need another death on your conscience.

They had avoided a disaster today, but what about tomorrow? No matter how much she wanted Sully to take her to Delos, she realized now that the best thing she could do was to get as far away from him as possible. Like Hector and Nigel, he was in danger of losing his life if her father caught up to her.

"What's wrong?"

"Nothing. Take your shower." She snapped out the words with more force than she meant to, then tried to move past him.

He slipped his hand around her arm and stopped her. "Are you mad at me?"

"No."

"You look mad. You sound mad, too."

"I'm not mad, Sully. What I am is tired of owing you."

"I'm not asking you for anything."

"Aren't you anxious to get back to your job? They must be anxious to have you back."

"A day or two more won't make much difference."

He was searching her face and she avoided his eyes.

"What is it?"

"I just need to get to Delos, and you need to stop making me…"

"Making you what?"

Feel things I shouldn't, she wanted to say. She jerked free and stepped back into the stateroom. "I need to get dressed."

She heard the shower turn on and glanced back to see Sully stripping off his jeans, flashing her his amazing backside.

He hadn't bothered to shut the door.

Melita touched her lips and remembered Sully's kiss. She didn't want to feel anything more for him than gratitude, but it was too late. And because she cared about him, she couldn't let him end up like Nemo. That's why he couldn't take her to Delos.

He would be stubborn about it, so she wouldn't tell him that this was where they would part company. She'd just find a way to leave when he wasn't looking.

She glanced at him behind the glass shower door. Her emotions in a knot, she walked back intending to shut the door, but her hand stalled as she watched him guide the soap bar over his chest, then lower.

She tucked herself against the wall and peered at him like a naughty little sneak. He angled his head back, and she watched the water beads dance across his chest, washing the soap away. She liked his wild black hair, liked how hard his body was. Loved how confident he was. Respected him for what he'd survived.

His legs were spread apart, his back arched. Suddenly she was imagining it was her hands moving over his body, a lover's hands caressing him, loving him, taking the same kind of liberties as the water was cascading down his chest and hips, over his naked butt.

He washed himself *there,* and she watched that, too.

The longer she looked, the more Melita realized the magnitude of her mistake. Her heart was beating fast, and she felt a heavy ache between her legs.

She slid her hand inside her towel between her legs and pushed down on her pubic bone as if that would stop the longing from spreading.

Eyes closed, flattened against the wall, she pressed her hand harder against herself. She didn't hear the shower turn off, didn't hear anything as the moment held her suspended and needy.

She licked her lips, moved her hand slowly over her slit. Her lungs expanded. Suddenly she felt something warm surround her and she blinked open her eyes to find Sully standing in front of her, his eyes locked on her hand. Slowly he lifted his head and met her eyes.

Oh, God, let me die, Melita thought, as she felt her cheeks flame hot with embarrassment.

"Need some help?"

Melita dropped her hand away from her body. His wardrobe was the same as hers, one towel—his wrapped low around his lean hips, showing off his deep navel and hard belly. He'd towel-dried his hair, and it hung around his face wild and untamed.

She had to say something. "Proposing another deal, Sully?"

The muscle in his cheek tightened. He raised his hands and flattened them against the wall on either side of her and leaned in. His hip pinned her to the wall and he slid one leg between hers forcing her to spread them open.

Against her ear, he said, "A deal with two instant winners." He moved his leg slightly upward and brushed over her sex.

Melita nearly jumped out of her skin.

"Relax."

She raised her hands to push him way, but it never happened. The feel of his hard chest beneath her fingers only added more heat.

"That's it. Touch me." He raised his knee and caught her vulnerable soft spot. Rubbed slowly.

"Sully…"

"I'll stop if that's what you want. I don't think it is. Am I wrong?"

His voice had turned husky and dark with his own need. He offered her the slightest kiss—a questioning kiss that let her know it was still her choice.

All she had to do was say no. To tell him to stop, but that's not what she wanted. She wanted Sully, all of him.

His damp hair teased the side of her face, and his warm breath skated across her cheek. "Melita, you need to say something. What are the rules?"

She turned her head, looked into his eyes, then raised her hand and touched his cheek. "There are no rules."

"You want me?"

She closed her eyes, kept them closed. "I want you."

With those three little words the deal was sealed.

"Open your eyes."

She blinked them open.

"Who am I?"

She knew why he'd asked the question. "You're Sully Paxton." She smiled. "Don't you remember your name?"

He smiled back at her, then pressed another light kiss to her lips. It was the prelude to the second, an all-consuming hot explosion of hunger that set the tone for the game.

They were going to play it out to the end. No rules. Two instant winners.

He lowered his leg and pressed his body into her. She felt his hard shaft settle between her thighs and she moaned softly and arched her hips. She slid her hands upward to his shoulders. So hard, so warm…

She was the water in the shower now, and her fingers danced over his hard muscles with the same freedom, exploring every inch of him.

When he broke the kiss, he was breathing heavy. She leaned forward and kissed his chest, sent her tongue over his male nipples. A guttural groan ripped through him and his response set off a rush of excitement. She liked turning him on, liked the small power it gave her, even though she was the one powerless in his arms.

She began brushing his chest with light feathery kisses. At the same time, she tortured him by moving her hips and rubbing against him.

She kissed her way up his neck, then along his jaw. He captured her mouth, and when her lips parted, he sent his tongue inside.

Melita's sweet body was the fuse, her ripe mouth the match. Sully's training had taught him that in an explosive situation, you turned and hauled ass out of there, but he wasn't going anywhere.

Hell, no.

He jerked the towel loose from his hips, then tugged hers away from her and let it fall slowly to the floor, sending his eyes to her pretty breasts. For a slight woman, they were full and heavy, with ripe dark nipples. He brushed his hands over each one, cupped them. Then he lowered his head and sent his tongue over each nipple.

She whimpered and arched her back. Her sweet nipples flagged him on, and he pulled one rosy tip into his mouth, stroked it with his tongue. Moved on to the next, as his hands slid down her ribs and settled on her waist.

He felt the tape and it reminded him that Melita didn't need more exercise. That he was being a selfish bastard, and—

"Don't stop, Sully. I'm fine. *Parakalo*. Please don't stop."

He slid his hands over her hips and cupped her sweet ass. He let out a pent up rush of air from his lungs and brought her flush against him. Her breasts moved into his chest, and the contact—skin to skin—had him gritting his teeth. His groin was throbbing, and he rotated his hips against her.

Again he needed confirmation. "You know who's with you, right?"

His question was muffled against her neck, and for a second he didn't think she'd heard him. Or maybe she had, and she didn't want to be caught in a lie.

He felt a surge of possessiveness. He knew Nemo was dead. Knew she still carried him with her, but he'd be damned if this was going to be a three-way.

"Melita, who's making love to you?"

She went still, and he looked at her. He saw she had a pretty little scowl going, her dark eyes searching his face. "I know who, Sully."

He grinned. "Just checking, honey." He leaned in, feeling like he'd just been liberated. Kissing her, he pulled her panties off her hips. When she stepped out of them, he lifted her up. "I need to be inside you. Wrap your legs around my waist."

The minute she did, he was pushing his way into her, staking his claim. He heard her whimper again. This time it wasn't in pleasure, and he realized that he should have gone slower.

She must have seen the regret on his face when he tore his mouth away from hers. She kissed him quick. "I'm okay." Another kiss. "There's just more— You're… Never mind. I'm okay…Sully, and I'm still with you. You. Only you."

He never moved a muscle, his body pulsing in her tight sheath. To prove to him she was *okay*, she pushed downward, seating herself on his shaft and driving him deeper.

He braced one hand against the wall then, never taking his eyes off her face, he started to move inside her in a slow, easy rhythm. He kept moving, picking up the pace until he was thrusting hard and fast.

The knowledge that she wanted him as much as he wanted her sent Sully on the ride of his life, carrying her with him. He knew he wasn't going to last long when she started rocking her hips and milking the rhythm—and him. Every muscle in his body went taut, and he started to go off.

With a harsh groan, Sully pulled out quickly. She let out a moan of regret, and he took his hand off the wall and slid it between their bodies, sending two fingers inside her. His body let go in that moment, and he felt his warm seed slide down his leg.

He had her strung out again within seconds. She arched her hips, begged for him to come back to her. He wanted to, but he couldn't do that to her. He wouldn't be that damn selfish.

He continued to caress her until he felt her start to convulse around his fingers. He slid his thumb upward, catching her sensitive flesh. Her climax shattered her, and she came hard and fast in his arms.

She was still clinging to him when Sully turned his back to the wall and flattened himself against it, closed his eyes.

He was working on slowing his breathing when she shifted in his arms, and he felt her hands touch his face, then her lips slowly brushed over his.

"Are you all right?" she asked.

Sully opened his eyes, then slid his fingers out of her. "More than all right, lucky charm. But I think I need another shower. Want to join me this time?"

"I think if you put me down I'm going to melt on the floor."

Sully grinned, tightened his hold on her. "I've got you, honey, and I'll take any excuse you give me to keep my hands on you."

Then he carried her to the shower, leaving the bathroom door open.

Chapter 10

A long two hours later Melita dressed for dinner. She picked a chiffon skirt and matching top in a soft shade of pink with muted swirls of gray and black shot through it. The skirt had a naughty side-slit that went clean to her thigh, and the matching blouse exposed her upper arms and tied dangerously at the shoulders, leaving the sleeves open to her wrists.

She slipped her feet into a pair of white sandals, then stepped into the bathroom in search of a brush. She opened a drawer and saw a tube of lipstick and a gold hair clip.

Melita felt tears sting her eyes. She had never known anyone like Sully, and never would again. She was sure of that. She couldn't imagine leaving, and yet it was too dangerous for him if her father found him with her.

Her thoughts turned to Nemo. She didn't want to dismiss what they had shared, and the guilt of his death would never go away, but she knew now that she had never been in love with him. Had she been so starved for affection that she'd confused loneliness for love? Nemo had been within reach, and he'd kept her mind off her pitiful life.

She glanced at the shower, remembering Sully, and how he made her feel. Nemo had never made her feel like that. He hadn't made her burn inside with an all-consuming passion that had threatened to stop her heart. And she had never felt protective, or worried about his safety. All the things she felt for Sully.

She didn't understand it. It had happened so quickly. Perhaps too quickly.

She took the shiny gold clip from the drawer and twisted her hair off her neck. She hadn't worn lipstick in over a year, but she remembered how it had made her lips look like wet rose petals. They looked that way now.

Minutes later she stepped on deck and she glanced around the busy harbor. The sun had set and the harbor lights were casting a golden glow over the water, as well as the seafront shops. She was anxious for an evening out with Sully. She would pretend they were on a date—their first and last—in a romantic haven meant for lovers.

She found Sully leaning into the boat railing smoking a cigarette. He was dressed in jeans and a white shirt, the sleeves rolled up to expose his forearms. One arm rested on the rail, one knee was bent. The warm breeze was blowing his hair around.

She liked his hair. It was thick, and there was a slight wave to it. Not much, just enough to soften his square jaw and make him even more handsome.

He must have sensed she was there—she swore he had eyes in the back of his head. He turned around, gave her a head-to-toe glance then tossed the cigarette overboard. A second later a wicked grin told her he approved of what she'd chosen to wear to dinner.

She spun around in a circle, and the breeze caught the uneven hem, flashing him a slender length of her leg. Then she moved toward him, a bit shy even after all they had been to each other below deck—the things he'd done to her surfacing in a flurry, making her feel warm all over again.

"If you want dinner on time you better be careful. I just might throw you over my shoulder, and—"

"Bully me into playing another game in the shower?"

"It wasn't me who started that game. I was just washing your back."

She would love him to be there to wash her back every day for the rest of her life. The sudden thought surprised her and she looked out to sea.

He took her chin in his hand, curled his fingers around her jaw and turned her face back to him. "Is that the look of regret?"

No, it was the look of a woman trapped between a dream and reality. She didn't want to lie to him anymore, and still she couldn't bear to see the warmth in his eyes turn cold once he knew who she was.

And that was the reality. So she went with the old lie and added a little twist to it. By tomorrow he would be free of her and more importantly, safe from her father.

"Of course not. You and I had a moment. Nemo doesn't have to know. In fact, he'll never know what I've had to do to get back to him. The important thing is that I found a way back."

She knew the words didn't sit well by the look on his face. He dropped his hand. "So what happened below deck was insurance. A little payment to make sure I came through with our deal?"

It couldn't be further from the truth, but by agreeing it would give Sully a way out, guilt-free.

She looked past him to the seafront, her silence supporting her motives to secure his promise.

He swore. "I told you you didn't owe me anything."

She faced him again. "It wasn't just for you. I haven't been with a man in over a year. I'm sure that was obvious. It was clear to me it's been long overdue for you, too. I rewarded you for sticking to our deal, and I got the best of two worlds. An enjoyable ride home."

She couldn't believe she had said that. It made her sound like a heartless, manipulative bitch. If she was worried about him following her, she didn't have to now. In fact, he'd probably have the *Korinna* skimming the top of the water full throttle headed for freedom's gate five minutes after he realized she was gone.

"I'm hungry. Can we go to dinner now?" She looked up at him and smiled.

He didn't smile back. Instead he lit another cigarette, angled his head and blew smoke. "Dinner it is. So what will it be, a bottle of retsina with a chopped liver sandwich, or are you hungry for something with more of a bite to it? Shark, with a blood chaser?"

He was angry, the pulse that jerked his cheek told her so. He strolled off ahead of her, puffing hard on his cigarette. He was off the boat, waiting for her on the dock before she could tell him that she was a vegetarian, and that she was going to order a Greek salad.

Cyrus was in the garden setting fire to the lavender. He'd just gotten a call from his man in Syros. Paxton had killed four of his men, and escaped with Melita. If that news wasn't bad enough, he'd been told that Melita had been missing most of her clothes at the time they had boarded the *Artemis*.

His phone rang again, and he was almost afraid to answer it. On the third ring, he put the phone to his ear. "Yes? Argo, how are things at Vouno?"

There was a moment of dead air, then Argo said, "Vouno was invaded this morning. The attack came out of nowhere. We were outnumbered ten to one."

"Attacked by who?" Cyrus listened as Argo explained.

"I wasn't sure until I saw Adolf Merrick come ashore."

"Merrick?" Cyrus considered the news. Paxton. Somehow he'd learned the location of Vouno and contacted Merrick.

"We lost everything. The prisoners and the gun shipment. Pedro and I are the only two who avoided capture."

Cyrus stared out over the cove. The guns were gone, Merrick had scored a win, and by the sound of it, Paxton had violated his daughter. He didn't know what enraged him more, or who he wanted to kill first. Yes, he did. Paxton. He should have left that son of a bitch in that pit to rot.

He took a deep breath and let it out slowly. "I'm at Lesvago, Argo. You and Pedro get here as quickly as you can."

You and I had a moment. Nemo doesn't have to know.

Sully watched her walk toward him, remembering how much they had shared in such a short time. Not for one minute did he believe that what had happened below deck had been part of any plan. She could maybe sell that to a fool, but not him.

They'd had a *moment* all right. More like four.

The one thing she hadn't lied about was that Nemo would never know.

He swallowed his sour mood and promised himself that before the evening was over he'd know what she was up to. He didn't want his instincts to be right this time, but he couldn't deny his Irish gut. And his gut was telling him that Melita was going to run.

"Where should we eat?"

"We'll walk a while," he said, "and see what we find."

They started off the pier, walking side by side. She looked beautiful tonight, Sully thought. Not that she didn't always—from the moment he'd laid eyes on her she'd commanded his full attention. She'd pulled her hair away from her face with the clip he'd bought her, and her lips were soft pink. He supposed that meant she'd found the lipstick. He didn't know squat about those things, but he knew he wanted to see her with her hair up, and he really liked those pretty lips of hers.

"About what I said earlier..."

"Don't worry about it." Sully glanced down at her, kept the game alive. "We were overdue, both of us. The important thing is not losing sight of why we're here. Nemo's a lucky guy."

She avoided his eyes, muttered something he couldn't hear.

"What was that?"

"I said I'm the lucky one."

The lie was getting old. Sully wanted to blow Nemo's head off, but that was an asinine thought. The man was dead. He should feel sorry for the bastard, instead of jealous.

He still didn't understand what was motivating her. Hector said she was going to Mykonos, not Delos. That the reason had to do with her brother. He also said that Cyrus would be at Lesvago waiting for her, and that she probably knew that. Then why the hell go? If Hector was right, what was so important that she'd risk her freedom?

He'd called Merrick on the cell phone he'd bought in Syros, to tell him that Cyrus was likely at Lesvago, but his boss hadn't picked up. He didn't leave a message. Not yet. What worried him was that something had gone wrong at

Vouno. Or maybe Merrick hadn't been able to find the island. He hoped that wasn't the case. Those men in the dungeon were running out of time—if they hadn't already.

They walked along the busy seafront street lined with fish markets, restaurants, gift shops and street vendors. Sully took hold of her hand and pulled her toward one of the vendors.

"Let's have a look."

"No." She tried to pull him back. "He'll harass you to buy something."

"Come on. There might be something we can't live without."

She relented and they began looking at the variety of souvenirs and trinkets spread out on the tables. There were sponges, baskets, handmade pottery, colorful scarves and silver jewelry.

"Kalispera."

"Good evening," Melita said to the vendor.

Sully nodded. *"Kherete."*

"See anything you like, *Dhespinis?*" The vendor smiled at Melita.

Melita shook her head, glared at Sully. "See," she whispered. "He thinks we're tourists with money to spend."

Sully picked up a woven basket and tossed in a couple of sponges, and a marble statue of a goddess with long flowing hair to her waist. Hair like Melita's.

"What are you doing?"

"Shopping."

"Why?"

Sully looked at the vendor. The man couldn't afford shoes for his feet. "He looks like he could use a sale today."

She frowned at him. "Why do you have to make this so much harder?"

Before he could ask her what she meant by that, she'd

walked off. Sully tossed a couple more items in the basket, then handed it to the vendor. *"Poso?"*

The vendor looked into the basket, then Sully. *"Ekato."*

Sully pulled a hundred-dollar bill out of his pocket to pay the vendor, then added an extra hundred, before handing it to him. "Double or nothing," he said, then took the basket and tucked it under his arm. *"Efharisto."*

"*Ne*, Americano. *Efharisto*. Thank you. Thank you."

When Sully caught up with Melita, he asked, "What did you mean back there? What am I making harder?"

She glanced at him, then the basket. "I thought we were going to eat?"

Sully saw she was curious as to what he'd bought, but she didn't ask. He said. "Worked up an appetite this afternoon, did you? Me, too. I could eat the ass off a—" He saw her turn her head away. "I knew I could get you smiling again."

She looked back at him, and she was smiling. "How come I can't stay mad at you for very long?"

"Must be my Irish charm." He took hold of her hand again, spotted a *taverna* on the corner. "*Fevgatos*. How about it? Sound like a winner?"

She glanced at the small bar. "*Fevgatos*, it is."

Sully led her through the door, looked around, quickly checking the place out. The bar wasn't too rowdy, but there was a dance floor. The crowd that had gathered were laughing and having a good time.

It looked safe enough, he decided.

They found a table along the back wall. Sully pulled out a chair for her, then tucked the basket under the table. When he sat, he asked, "Would you like something to drink?"

"Whatever you're having."

"I'm having a beer."

"In that case, ouzo for me."

Sully flagged a waiter and ordered their drinks, then he picked up one of the menus the man had left with them and opened it. It took him less than a minute to decide what to eat. When he closed the menu and laid it on the table she glanced up.

"You know what you want already?"

"I want two hamburgers and some fried potatoes. You? I didn't see liver or shark on the menu."

She gave him a dirty look, then went back to reading the menu. "A salad and a piece of sole."

"Now that I know your secret, I—"

Her head jerked up from the menu. "What secret do you think you know?"

Her question, and how quickly the color had drained from her face, told Sully where her thoughts had gone—straight to her little deception. He said, "How you manage to keep all those curves so perfect."

She relaxed. "I'm not perfect. I'm a vegetarian."

Sully thought about the goats on Despotiko. He asked, "How did that work out at Minare?"

"It didn't. But I don't want to talk about what I had to eat there."

He knew what she didn't want to talk about. Cyrus had made her eat goat.

The waiter brought the drinks, then took their order. Before long Sully had talked her into tasting his beer, and she decided to order one of her own. Then a second one.

It was obvious she didn't drink much. Number two went straight to her head.

"I think we should have one more," she said.

Sully shook his head. "I've had enough, and I think you have, too."

"But it's early."

"One more and I'll have to carry you back to the *Korinna*."

"I used to go to a place like this when I was... Before Minare. I used to dance all night long. I want another drink, and then I want to dance."

"No more beer."

She narrowed her eyes, then looked at the dancers enjoying the rowdy music. "Then I want to dance."

"I don't dance."

She got to her feet. "I wasn't asking you."

She left him at the table and headed to the bar. Sully watched as she slipped between two men, and soon she was on her way to the dance floor with a smiling Greek good old boy who looked as if he'd been handed a fortune in gold.

Sully didn't move. Like a bodyguard confident in his job, he sat back and let her have a little harmless fun. He told himself he wasn't going to interfere. If she wanted to dance, let her.

She looked like an exotic butterfly out there, and she certainly had some sexy moves. She was putting on quite a show.

He intended to keep his ass nailed down, and he would have if she hadn't gone back to the bar after the dance with her partner. A moment later, she turned around and raised a glass of beer at him in a mock salute.

Sully swore, then flagged the waiter. He paid their bill, then got to his feet. He should walk out now. But that's not what she wanted him to do so he decided to enter the game, reminding himself he'd been playing by her rules perhaps too long.

He sauntered toward the bar. Melita had her back pressed against it, and he saw her dance partner had decided to get friendly—his hand had found a home on her sweet little ass.

He stopped three feet from her. "It's time to go."

"But I'm not ready to go yet."

"I am."

"She isn't going anywhere, *file*."

Sully lowered his gaze to where the man's palm cupped Melita's backside, and when he looked up, he said, "I'm not your friend. Now get your hand off her before I break it." He glanced at Melita. "Do you doubt it? Do you care?"

She was no longer smiling. She slid the beer glass onto the bar, then pushed the guy away. He didn't take her decision well and he grabbed her arm.

Like a cobra, Sully struck. He seized the man by the throat, then grabbed his offending hand and twisted it behind his back. "I've broken a few necks before. Tore a man's arm clean out of his socket. Take your pick."

"Sully, stop it! Please, let him go."

He glanced at her, but he didn't let go.

"Sully, please. *Parakalo*."

He leaned forward and spoke in a low tone to the frightened man. "Killing you would be easy, but life is a gift. So I give yours back to you. Take better care, the next guy you piss off might not see things the way I do. Who knows, maybe the next time, I won't, either."

The minute Sully let him go, the man started speaking in his native language. *So sorry. Thank you for my life. She is very beautiful, but she is yours. Take her. Take her.*

Sully dug in his pocket and tossed some money on the bar to pay for Melita's beer, then returned to the table and retrieved the basket. When he headed for the door he glanced at her. She was standing in the same spot like a Greek statue. A very beautiful statue.

"Are you coming?"

She didn't answer, but when he reached the street she was there beside him. They headed back to the boat. He didn't speak and neither did she—not until they were standing on the deck of the *Korinna*.

Sully asked, "Did you find out what you wanted to know?"

She was headed for the companionway. She stopped and looked over her shoulder. "Yes, I did. You're a good man, Sully Paxton. Thank you."

"For what?"

"Dinner."

When she was out of sight, Sully stepped into the cockpit, set the basket down and pulled a key from his pocket. Unlocking a storage cupboard, he reached for the cell phone. No messages. He tried calling Merrick again. Still no answer.

He slid the phone back into its hiding place, reached into the basket and pulled out the marble goddess statue. She had reminded him of Melita, so much that he couldn't leave her there on the street. He had never been sentimental. In fact, for most of his life he'd been a selfish, arrogant bastard.

The boys at Onyxx had agreed that Mad Dog fit his ornery attitude. He was the cranky one in the outfit, the one who let you know it. But something had changed. He didn't have that rage inside him anymore. He could fire it up, like tonight, but even then he had handled the situation differently than Mad Dog would have—the Dog would have snapped that Greek's neck, then kicked him on the way out the door.

He set the goddess on the dash in the cup holder, then reached into his pocket for a cigarette. The harbor was quiet tonight, the water calm. The sky was clear, sporting a million stars.

He inhaled the fresh air. He still couldn't get enough fresh air. Maybe he'd sleep on deck tonight, try calling Merrick again after midnight.

He unbuttoned his shirt, kept his eyes open and his ears tuned in to his surroundings. He'd chosen this harbor with a fast getaway in mind. If it was necessary, he'd be gone in five seconds after he turned over the engine.

He didn't think Cyrus's men would find them yet, but if they stayed here another day, it was a possibility.

He bedded down with the basket beside him. Sprawled out on the deck, his back against one of the plush seats, he glanced at the basket, remembering himself as a twelve-year-old on the streets in Dublin. He had a basket like the one he'd bought tonight. It wasn't as nice, and he'd stolen that one. All he owned had fit easily in that basket, and he'd kept it under the O'Connell Bridge when he had to work—work as in picking pockets and rolling drunks.

He remembered the night he'd shagged his tired ass back to the bridge after a long day on the street. He'd been looking forward to reading that book Paddy had been teaching him to read. When he got to the bridge someone had stolen his basket. The thief's loot had been snagged by another thief. He hadn't cried, but he'd felt like it. Damn, he'd been looking forward to reading that book.

"Sully?"

He looked up to see Melita standing on deck looking down at him. "Forget something?"

"I came up to apologize for tonight."

"You just wanted to have some fun. A year's a long time to be living by someone else's rules."

"Can I sit down?"

"You can sit wherever you want."

She had removed her shoes and the gold clip from her hair. She sat down and leaned her back into the other seat next to him. She glanced at the basket between them. Sully didn't say anything.

Two more side glances, and she focused on the stars

overhead. "Have you ever heard the saying, 'If it's too good to be true, it probably is'?"

"Yeah."

"Well that's what tonight was about. A test, I guess. The truth is I've never met anyone like you. You came back for me when you promised me you would. Dug glass out of me, and saved my life. You found us a boat."

"Two boats."

"Two boats," she corrected. "Saved me again. Bought me clothes."

"Fed you dinner," he added.

"Yes, that, too."

"Bought that gold thing for your hair."

She scowled at him. "It's called a hair clip, and who's telling this?"

Sully laughed. "I was just trying to help out with your list."

"I guess I wanted you to screw up tonight. I mean, I really didn't. But it would have…"

"Would have what?"

She shrugged. "Forget it. I was wrong, and I apologize. I didn't want anyone to get hurt."

Whatever was bothering her had her chewing her lip. He reached up and saved her lower lip, brushed his finger over it slowly. "I could have killed that guy tonight, but I never intended to. I just wanted to get you out of there." And get that bastard's hand off your ass, Sully thought.

"I heard what you said to him. That life is a gift. I'm going to remember that." She leaned over and kissed him. "Thanks for listening. Good night, Sully."

She started to get up, but Sully reached out and put his hand on her arm. "Wait a minute. You haven't seen what's in the basket yet."

She looked like she wasn't going to stay.

"I bought some things for you," he coaxed.

"Why?"

Sully shrugged, then pulled the blue scarf out of the basket, sat up and slipped it around her neck.

She glanced down at it, ran her hands over the blue woven threads. "It's the color of the sea." She looked up at him. "It's beautiful. Thank you."

Then she kissed him again.

Sully slipped his arm around her shoulder when she started to pull back and kissed her like he'd been wanting to all night. She moaned softly and clung to the kiss. It was the surrender he was hoping for, and he scooped her up and set her in his lap.

One more *moment* with him, she thought. Just one more *moment*.

When the kiss ended, Melita reached up and touched Sully's cheek. Wanting to lock him in her memory, she closed her eyes, then sent her fingers slowly over his face. She went over each feature twice, then traced his lips.

Suddenly Sully opened his mouth and drew her finger inside. Her eyes opened, watched as he sucked on her finger, bit down on it gently. His eyes were talking to her, and what they were saying echoed her own thoughts.

And then it was happening again. They were having another moment right there under the stars, and Melita thought it was the perfect way to say goodbye. But like before, he withdrew before he went off and guided her through a solo climax.

When it was over, he rolled away from her and went below deck. He wasn't gone long, but when he returned he was wearing jeans low on his hips. He laid down beside her and pulled her to him once more. She snuggled against him.

He never spoke. Melita wished he would, she loved the low roughness of his voice. She ran her hand over his warm chest, traced a circle around his navel. She sat up and looked down at him. His eyes were closed, and his breathing much slower now.

"Sully?"

"Hmm..."

Melita wondered how to ask the question. "Why don't you stay with me...you know, to the end? You leave me before..."

He opened his eyes, studied her face. He said the word she couldn't seem to get out of her mouth. "Climax."

Melita nodded.

He sat up, slid his hand around her neck and kissed her lips gently. "If I stayed with you, honey, that would make you mine. You're not mine, Melita. This way is better." He touched her temple. "This way you can feed off the images as you like, and remember what you choose to remember."

He reached into the basket and pulled out a silver necklace. As he held it up she saw that the pendant was a blue stone with streaks of white moving through it. He handed it to her, then dug into the basket again. This time he came up with a charm. She couldn't tell what it was. He took back the necklace, opened the clasp and slid the charm down the chain to join the blue stone. Then he leaned forward and put it around her neck.

When Melita looked down she saw that the charm was of a falcon in flight, and the blue stone behind it made it look as if the bird was flying high in the sky, or maybe over the sea.

"A good luck charm for your journey," he said. "You've been my lucky charm. I thought you should have one, too. The stone is sodalite. Some people call it the stone of trust. Trust is a two-headed devil. The devil take me first."

She frowned. "I don't understand."

"A friend of mine used to say that. I never knew what

Paddy meant, either, until I was running guns on the Irish Sea, and let me tell you those boys were some bad seeds. I learned real quick about two-headed devils. But I also understood what Paddy meant. He was telling me to trust yourself first. You can't trust someone else until you learn to trust your own instincts. When you can do that, you pretty much figure out the rest."

"The rest?"

"Your instincts will tell you who else you can trust." He pointed to the bird. "The falcon is for courage. Your life hasn't been yours for a long time, but it can be yours again, Melita. Trust your instincts, then have the courage to choose." He pulled two sponges from the basket, stood, then held out his hand to her. "And these—" he smiled "—I bought them for the shower. I was hoping we'd have an excuse to use it again. Join me?"

Hours later, Melita sat at the table in the galley wearing Sully's shirt watching him raid the cupboards. She studied the scars on his back, knew what they were from, and who had put them there. She'd seen a man whipped to death, and Sully had survived what Nemo hadn't.

She understood why, even though her mind still had a hard time accepting how one man could give in to death, and another would fight for life.

Somehow Sully had learned how to eat the pain as easily as he ate his food. She wouldn't go so far as to say he enjoyed it as much—he was really into that can of sardines at the moment—but as far as digesting it... Like the nourishment he took from food, the pain had made him stronger.

She recalled the picture of him at the prison. It was a picture of a man who defied death.

"Melita?"

She blinked. "What?"

"Where are you?"

He'd turned to lean against the counter. She thought sardines were disgusting but he was eating them like chocolate. He was on his third can. He'd gone through a pound of hard cheese, and he was scraping the bottom of a box of crackers.

"I'm right here."

"Not thirty seconds ago. We haven't talked about Nemo. Want to?"

"No."

"Does that mean you're rethinking Delos?"

"No. What's been happening with us is…"

"Exercise." He grinned and winked at her. "I wasn't suggesting you forget him and take up with me. I'm not a guy who puts down roots. Hell, I don't want to. What I was asking was, are you sure he's in Delos? It's been a year. Maybe he's moved. Or—"

Melita should have been listening, but all she could concentrate on was Sully's admission that he was not the kind of guy who could put down roots.

"Well, hell, who asked you to?" she muttered under her breath, mimicking his words.

"What was that?"

"I think we should leave in the morning," she said, knowing she would already be gone by then. "I wouldn't want to be the cause of you getting root-bound."

"Getting what?"

She stood. "It's late. I'm going to bed."

"Can I come?"

Melita frowned. "Why don't you have another can of sardines?"

She tried to walk past him, but he set down the sardines and snagged her around the waist. "You mad about something?"

"I'm tired." And, yes, she was mad. Mad that she was going to have to give him up. But he'd just let her know that he wasn't hers, anyway. It should make it easier, but…

"There you go drifting again. Thinking about Nemo?"

She looked into his eyes and lied for the last time. "Yes. Nemo keeps me grounded."

"And he's always with you, right?"

"Always. Good night, Sully."

He didn't let her go. Instead, he slid his hands under his shirt she was wearing and cupped her bare butt. "That bed is big enough for two. You didn't answer me. Can I come?"

"You can come."

Chapter 11

Melita stood on the ferry boat that had docked in Mykonos City minutes ago. Waiting her turn to walk down the ramp, she continued to visit with the two elderly women she'd befriended that morning in Tinos while waiting for the ferry to arrive.

Knowing her father as well as she did, by now he'd have guards combing Mykonos Island looking for her. For sure they would be stationed at the harbor at Mykonos Town.

Confident in her disguise, she guided the two gray-haired women in their sixties off the boat. The first one, Ella, had a limp, and Melita offered her arm to the woman as they started down the ramp.

"Which hotel are you staying at?" Melita asked.

Helen checked her itinerary. "Apollon?"

"Really? So am I. Should we share a taxi?"

"That would be lovely, dear. There's our luggage, Ella. Do you see yours, Melita?"

"I'm traveling light," she said, "My husband is already at the hotel. I'm meeting him, but I'll help you with your bags."

"No, you just stay here with Ella," Helen insisted. "I'll retrieve the bags and get us transportation."

While Helen went to find them a taxi, Melita chatted with Ella, and kept her eyes on the lookout for her father's men. It wasn't long before the three women were safely on their way to Apollon seated in the taxi.

Melita removed her white hat and stared out the window at the sandy beach that stretched along the road into town. She had lived in Mykonos Town with Simon for several years. Everything was familiar, and she suddenly felt a little melancholy. She was home, and yet she would never be able to stay.

If her luck held, by tomorrow she would be gone. If not, her father would have won again, and she would end up wherever he chose to lock her away.

She reached up and touched the necklace Sully had given her, rubbed the stone. "Trust your instincts," she whispered.

"That's a beautiful necklace, dear."

Melita blinked out of her musing and smiled at Ella. "Yes, it is."

"A gift from your husband?"

"Ah…yes."

"Will he be at the hotel?" Ella asked. "I'd love to meet him."

"This is sort of a business vacation. I don't know if he'll be at the hotel when I arrive."

"That's too bad. Perhaps we can get together later this evening for dinner."

Melita stroked the blue scarf that hung around her neck. "I'll have to check. He's very busy."

They arrived at Apollon, and Melita put on her hat the minute she exited the taxi. At the check-in desk, she waited until Ella and Helen had gotten their room, then asked the desk clerk, "I believe my husband is staying here. Could you tell me what room—" she scrambled for a name "—Owen Spaneas is in?"

The clerk checked his registry. "I'm sorry, *Kyria* Spaneas, but there is no Owen registered."

"Are you sure?"

"*Ne*, I'm sure."

Melita turned away, settled her hand on her stomach as if she was going to be ill.

"What is it, dear?" Ella asked.

"He's not here. Owen's not registered."

The two women glanced at each other. Then Ella slipped her arm around Melita. "Don't worry, dear. I'm sure there's an explanation. Come with us. You look tired. We'll go up to the room and figure this out. There must be a number you can call."

"I just have to think." Melita closed her eyes, as if she was contemplating her error. "Maybe I made a mistake on which hotel he booked for us."

"You can think in our room while you put your feet up," Helen insisted. "Now come along."

Melita kept her worried look in place, then nodded. "It's so kind of you to help me. I'm sure there's just been some kind of mix-up. And it would be my fault for not listening. Owen never makes mistakes."

"We'll figure it out, dear. Don't worry. It's not good for you to get upset."

And with that, Melita was in. She had a place to stay, and the disguise that would keep her father's men at bay.

It was all going to work out. Now all she had to do was wait until three o'clock, and she could see Simon.

Melita followed Ella and Helen into their hotel room,

removed her hat and excused herself immediately to use the bathroom. Inside she leaned against the door and let out a long sigh. She had a newfound respect for pregnant women, she decided, as she rested her hands on her belly.

Glancing in the mirror she realized her little bundle of joy had shifted. She hiked up her dress and repositioned the pillowcase stuffed with the clothes Sully had bought her. She glanced at herself in the mirror, turned sideways to make sure the round ball was back in place.

She eyed her underwear. There had been no shops open in Tinos before the ferry had left to buy a travel bag. She couldn't carry her clothes in a pillowcase on the ferry; that would have attracted too much attention. She'd come up with the idea for her disguise when she'd seen the panties on a clothesline. She'd felt terrible about taking them, so she had left the woman some of the money she'd swiped from Sully's pants' pocket before leaving the *Korinna* before dawn.

"Are you all right, dear?"

"Yes, Helen. I'll be right out." Melita dropped her dress back into place and flushed the toilet. Opening the door, she stepped out and smiled. "I can't go anywhere these days without a bathroom close by," she said, stroking her belly that looked ready to pop any minute.

"Melita," Ella said, "we have a surprise for you."

"A surprise?"

"Yes. Look who's here."

Melita turned and locked eyes with a man wearing a white linen jacket seated in the chair by the window. She nearly delivered her bundle on the floor seconds later.

"You were right, dear," Ella said. "It was all a simple mistake. Owen explained everything."

* * *

Sully stood and moved toward his *pregnant wife*. "I'm sorry I worried you, honey." He hugged her, then stepped back and put his hand on Melita's swollen stomach. "How's he doing?" he asked. "Did you two make the trip all right?" He turned to the two elderly women. "Did she tell you it's going to be a boy?"

Ella clapped her hands. "Did you hear that, Helen? I thought she was carrying it all out front. You know what they say. It's a boy if they're here—" Ella put her hands on her stomach "—and if it's a girl you get wide in the behind. That's not you, dear."

Sully felt Melita shift a few steps back from him. He gave her the space—she probably needed a few minutes to alter her script. So far she'd been flawless.

He gave her a minute, then asked, "You all right, honey?" He looked over his shoulder at the women. "We haven't seen each other for a while." He winked at the woman named Ella, then turned back and pulled Melita into his arms. "I haven't changed that much, have I, honey?" Then he kissed her in front of the women like a husband who adored his wife, and couldn't wait to get her alone.

Her hands moved to his chest and she pushed back. He released her, saw that her cheeks were flushed, and that she was still struggling for something to say.

Finally, she said, "I can explain Sul…ah, Owen."

"I'm the one who needs to explain, honey. The room mix-up is all my fault, not yours. Ella told me you said I never make mistakes, but this one was mine. I'll explain when we get to our room. These two nice ladies have been inconvenienced long enough."

"We have a room?"

"Of course."

She stepped around him and said, "I appreciate everything you've done for me. I hope you enjoy the town. If you like art galleries visit Little Venice."

Sully wrapped his arm around her shoulder, smiled like a proud papa and said, "I'm in your debt. I'd like to pay you for your trouble, and for taking such good care of my wife."

"Nonsense. It was no trouble at all. She's a delight, and we're just happy everything worked out," Helen said.

Ella put in her two cents. "Such a lovely couple." She winked at Melita, then whispered in her ear, "You're a lucky woman. He's gorgeous."

Moments later, Sully steered Melita toward the door. As he passed the bed, he snatched up her hat and plopped it on her head. "Thanks again, ladies."

They reached the hall, and the door barely shut behind them when Melita wrenched herself away from him and spun around. "What the hell are you doing here?"

"Calm down, honey." Sully smiled at two men who walked past. "You'll upset the baby." Then he took hold of her arm and began marching her toward the stairs.

Sully wasn't surprised Melita had left before dawn. The way the evening had gone he was expecting her to run, and she hadn't disappointed him. She'd been right on schedule.

What had surprised him was Melita's cunning disguise. She'd really knocked herself out. Hell, if she hadn't been wearing the blue scarf he'd given her, he wouldn't have recognized her when she boarded the ferry.

"I want you gone," she said. "Right now."

She tried to pull away again, but he held on. "We're on the second floor," he said, "behave yourself. You don't want to make a scene, do you? A pregnant woman riding her husband's shoulder will draw attention."

"You wouldn't dare."

"You think?"

She didn't challenge him. She stopped fighting and walked beside him until they reached the room.

Sully pulled a key from his pocket, opened the door and pushed her inside. The minute he closed the door, she pulled off her hat and slung it at him.

"I think you had better explain why you followed me. How did you know where I was going?"

"You know you're really very good at this. That con you pulled on those two old ladies… I heard the entire conversation in the lobby. I was impressed."

"I'm not the only one who can pick the right disguise. I never saw you in the lobby."

"You weren't looking for me."

"You faked it, didn't you? You weren't sleeping when I left the *Korinna?*"

"I'm a light sleeper. I also see pretty good in the dark. Did I mention I lived in a pit in the ground for seven or eight months? I'm not really sure. No calendar. No sunlight. No toilet. No clean air. I ate rats and bugs. Drank water that the guards pissed in for a joke. Never did get used to the taste of rat, but—"

"I don't want to talk about Vouno."

Sully arched an eyebrow. "You know the place?"

"No, I've never been there. It was in the file, along with…"

"Along with what?"

"I said, I don't want to talk about it. I really don't want to talk to you at all. Our deal was that you would take me to Delos. You weren't delivering on your promise so I decided to go on my own. So why are you here? Or do I already know? The truth, Sully."

"I will, if you will. Ladies first. Or have you been lying so long you don't know what the truth is?"

She said nothing.

"Have I given you a reason not to trust me?"

"No."

"Remember what I told you about instincts. Last night the signs were all there. You were silently saying goodbye."

"Okay, so now you know I lied about where I was going. That I'm a liar, I can run a good con and I can't be trusted. Now you know who I really am."

"Do I?" Sully shrugged out of the suit jacket and tossed it on the chair. He smiled, then said, "You sure look pretty like that. Would it be in bad taste if I told you it turns me on?"

"Aren't you forgetting something? I'm here to see Nemo."

"Dressed like that? Hell, if I hadn't seen my sweetheart for a year and she showed up ready to pop…I don't know." He pulled his white shirt from his jeans and unbuttoned it. "No, if he was here, you wouldn't be dressed like that. In fact, I don't think you were too worried he would see you at all. How am I doing so far?"

"You're wrong about everything."

He walked toward her. "Let's see what you have in there?"

She backed away, then dashed around the bed. "Don't come near me."

He ignored the warning, forcing her to make a decision. He knew what she'd decided when she hiked up her dress, reached into her little bundle and pulled out the gun.

"There's my snub-nosed .38." Sully rounded the bed and planted himself three feet in front of her. "Use it, honey, or put it down. You might be a liar, but I don't think you're a killer. Am I wrong?"

Melita tossed the gun on the bed, turned away and walked to the window, all the fight draining out of her.

She couldn't look at him. His eyes were talking again, and what they were telling her was that he already knew what he wanted her to confess.

She said, "How long have you known?"

"Does it matter?"

Melita closed her eyes. No, it really didn't. The truth was, he'd played her. While she had been falling for him, he'd been waiting for his opportunity for revenge. He had every right to want to take down her father. The minute he'd learned who she was, he'd probably thought the perfect weapon to use had just landed in his lap. *Use*… That was an ugly word, but it fit. She'd definitely been his lucky charm in more ways than one.

She thought back to when he could have found out her secret, and she knew when it had happened. "Hector told you on the *Artemis,* didn't he?"

"He didn't want to. I held a gun to his head."

She spun around. "You didn't hurt him, did you?"

"What do you think?"

"I don't know you anymore. I thought I did, but I was wrong. Tell me they're all safe."

"Goat, rats, even Barinski, still breathing when I saw them last."

"And Hector?"

"As loyal to you as ever." He continued to stare, and she could no longer hold his gaze. She wanted to hate him for forcing Hector into a confession, and for using her, but she'd known from the beginning Sully's M.O. He was the ultimate survivor. When she'd let the gorilla out of his cage, she had known what he was capable of. She wasn't going to stand there now and whine about it. So she had paid for her freedom by letting him have her body. So what. She wouldn't apologize for keeping the truth from him. She had been only trying to survive, herself. He should respect that.

Still avoiding his eyes, she said, "Yes, I'm Cyrus Krizova's daughter. I'm your enemy. So what's the plan? Are you going to use me to draw him out into the open so you can kill him, or do you plan on killing me and sending my body to Lesvago special delivery?"

"If you think that I would do either, then you shouldn't have tossed away the gun. You should have pulled the trigger on me, honey. Look at me."

"I don't want to. I'll take what's coming, but I won't watch. You deserve your revenge. I just—"

"Just what?"

"I just don't want to see you die for it. That's why I left. I know my father put you through hell. I saw what he did to you, and—"

"Saw? What did you see?"

"A picture of you." Melita looked up then. Even now, knowing that he had no feeling for her but contempt, tears spilled onto her cheeks. "It was in your file."

He walked away from her, rubbing the back of his neck. Suddenly, he stopped and looked at her. "Tell me you didn't let me climb all over you…in you, to protect your secret, or out of some damn guilt for what your father did to me."

Melita frowned. Those weren't the words of a man set on revenge at all cost; still, she didn't trust herself right now. Nothing she was thinking or feeling made sense. "What do you care what my reasons were?"

"You conned those old ladies real good. Did you con me, too? Was anything about the last four days real?"

She wanted to scream yes, instead she said, "There was a lot at stake. It was my fault Nemo died. And it was my fault that Hector will be scarred for the rest of his life. He was beaten because I got caught sneaking off to the village to escape Minare when he was supposed to be guarding me. Being Cyrus Krizova's daughter isn't only my curse, it's a curse to everyone I love. I understand your need for revenge, even using me to get it, but the truth is, I left Tinos without you because I didn't want you to die for helping me escape Despotiko. Last night you told that guy in the bar life was a gift. Maybe you should take your own advice. Leave Greece, Sully. You survived hell. Can't you just walk away and be glad you're still alive?"

"And where does that leave you?"

"I don't understand the question."

"Do you think that Cyrus is going to stop hunting for you? That he's not already here waiting for you?"

"No. But that's my problem, not yours. Unless you plan to use me to get to him, what do you care?"

"That's why you think I'm here? Revenge against Cyrus?"

"I told you, I don't blame you. As awful as it sounds coming from me, my father is an evil man. You either jail evil, or you kill it. I get that. Yes, he knows I'll come. He's here. And that's why you're here…isn't it?" When he said nothing, she confessed, "I'm here to see my brother Simon. I haven't seen him—"

"Since he killed Nemo."

Melita's chin jerked up. "On my father's orders. Simon begged him not to make him do it."

"And that exonerates him?"

"Don't judge Simon. It's not easy being Cyrus Krizova's children. I'm not making excuses, I'm just saying he looks for a person's weakness, and when he finds it, you become whatever he wants you to become. 'I choose for my children.' Do you know how many times I've heard him tell me that?"

"Your weakness is Simon."

"We all have weaknesses, Sully. Except you. If my brother is mine, then I'll live with the consequences."

"So you escaped Minare knowing it wouldn't last."

"What I know is that whatever happens, I don't want you in the cross fire."

"Because you don't want me to die. Why?"

Melita couldn't keep doing this. She turned away, looked out the window. "Because I let you touch me for my own reasons, Sully. Not out of guilt, and not for safe passage."

"Keep going. Trust your instincts, Melita."

She heard him come up behind her, was surprised when he slipped his arms around her and rested his hands on her bundle. "Do you remember what I told you when you asked me why I wouldn't stay with you to the end?"

Melita squeezed her eyes shut. "You said if you stayed with me it would make me yours. And now I understand why you never wanted me that way. I get it."

He turned her in his arms. "Open your eyes, Melita, and tell me what you see."

She blinked open her eyes. Trust your instincts, he'd said. She looked deeply in his eyes, shook her head. "You can't, Sully. You can't…"

"Care what happens to you?"

"People get hurt when they do."

"So you left the *Korinna* to protect me."

"Yes."

"Because?" He wanted her to say.

"You know why. Because I love you."

"I didn't survive the pit to die in Greece." He smiled down at her. "Especially now that I know what I'm fighting for."

"So what's next?"

"I get you out off this dress and make you mine."

Naked, Sully stretched out beside Melita on the bed and pulled her into his arms. There was no need for more words, they had talked enough. She let out a sigh when he kissed her lips, and then the world fell away. Hands caressing, skin against skin, there was nothing between them anymore but love and a carnal need to claim it.

When he entered her and felt her close around him, Sully gave her his body. This time they climaxed together, and he groaned with the satiated pleasure of staying with her to the end. In that moment Melita was no longer the daughter of his enemy—she became Sully Paxton's woman.

The one person he would surrender his life for to keep safe.

Chapter 12

The takeover was fast and furious once Merrick and his men locked on the target. They rescued eighteen men alive at Vouno, carried out five that weren't as lucky, and apprehended over a dozen of Krizova's loyal fighters.

The victory was worth celebrating—the coup de grace was the discovery and recovery of a cache of Czech Skorpions worth billions.

Merrick was riding the biggest high in years. He'd hit Cyrus Krizova were it hurts, and he had Sully to thank for that. As the survivors were airlifted to a medical facility, his thoughts turned to his agent. Paxton had been given up for dead well over a year ago. If this is where he was all that time, in this unbelievable hell, he had a newfound respect for the Irishman.

Merrick headed out of the dungeon, climbed the stairs to the outside. He spotted Sly McEwen on the dock—the last of their cache being loaded.

"Sly, almost ready to get out of here? I want to find Sully. Where's Ash and Pierce?"

"I sent Pierce with the medics. Ash is—" Sly pointed behind Merrick "—over there."

Merrick turned around to see Ash Kelly standing by a hole in the ground with a grate over it. Merrick walked over.

"Ash, you all right?"

"He was in there," Ash Kelly said. "I feel it in my gut."

Merrick looked down into the black pit. "He's alive, Ash. I talked to him. He survived."

"Then where the hell is he now?"

"I'd like to know that myself. But you know Sully. He's not one to sit around and wait for the cavalry to show up. He said he had something he needed to do. You sure you're all right?"

Ash turned around. "I will be when we find him."

Merrick heard his phone beep, telling him he had a voice mail. He'd been so caught up in the raid he hadn't paid any attention to his phone in his pocket. They hadn't been able to move the men until they'd been stabilized, and that had taken two days.

He dug for the phone deep in his pocket, saw two messages listed. He hit voice mail, and when he heard Sully's voice, he said to Ash, "He left us a message."

Merrick was smiling when he finished listening to the messages. He slapped Ash on the back, and said, "Sully knows where Krizova is. Let's go."

As Merrick jogged to the landing, Ash behind him, he listened to the second message.

When he stuffed the phone back in his pocket, he said, "We have one more stop to make. Sully wants us to pick up a man named Hector on Amorgos, then we head for Mykonos."

* * *

"You want to fill me in on these sexy undies?"

Melita was curled against Sully with her eyes closed. She opened them to see the white panties dangling from one of Sully's fingers. She snatched them away and dropped them off the side of the bed.

He was grinning down at her, and she smiled back.

"When I left the *Korinna* it was dark. There were no shops open to buy a travel bag. I couldn't carry my clothes in a pillowcase all the way here, so I improvised. The panties you bought me…"

"Fit," he supplied with a grin.

"Who's telling this story?"

"Sorry. Go ahead."

"I needed a disguise, and then I saw those panties on a clothesline. I paid the woman for them, and the rest you know."

"She didn't think you were crazy for wanting to buy a pair of undies three sizes too big off her clothesline?"

"I didn't exactly pay her. I left the money clipped to the line. And I was generous."

He laughed out loud.

She loved it when he let go. Loved him. His smile and his laugh. His amazing green eyes. She wanted to sail away with him and leave the ugliness behind. But first, she needed to put the past to rest. She turned serious. "Sully, I need to see Simon."

"I suppose you do."

That wasn't what she expected to hear. She had expected him to argue and remind her how dangerous it was to be in Mykonos Town. Even foolish. Hopeful, she sat up and looked at him, ignoring the sheet as it fell away from her breasts. "I knew you would understand. Thank you."

"I don't really understand, but I'll take you to your brother. Tell me about Lesvago."

"You can't go there, Sully." She sat back and tucked the sheet around her breasts. "The house is built into a cliff surrounded by a private cove. It's heavily guarded, and even if you did make it in, you would never make it back out. To reach the house there are a hundred stone steps leading up from the waterfront, and under the water there is a gate that seals off the cove."

"A security gate constructed underwater?"

"Yes. If you sailed the *Korinna* into the cove, she would never get out."

"Then it looks like you're not going to see Simon."

Melita tossed the sheet off her and climbed out of bed. Naked, she jammed her hands on her hips and narrowed her eyes. "Just like that?"

"Just like that."

"You don't get all the say, Sully. You don't own me."

He raised an eyebrow. "That's a matter of opinion. I told you that if I stayed with you to the end, that it would make you mine. I meant every word, honey."

"So I traded one jailer for another."

His jaw jerked, but he didn't fire back. But then, that wasn't Sully. He didn't lose control. Maybe it was the way he'd always been, but she believed it was learned behavior. Something he'd perfected while in the pit because his file suggested otherwise.

"Come back to bed."

Melita glanced at the clock. The morning was almost gone. She bent and turned over the clothes pile on the floor. Her bare butt in the air, she said as she rummaged through the clothes, "If you think I'm going to be a puppet and do everything you say, you're dreaming. I've come this far, and I won't—"

He smacked her ass, and when she jackknifed upward, his arm snaked out and lifted her off her feet. In a blink of an eye, she was back in bed staring up at him. It was obvious by the dark scowl on his face that he was angry with her.

She gave him the same scowl back. "Now what, Sully? Are you going to threaten me if I don't follow your rules? Lock me in the bathroom? I don't need another father."

"It's not the same, and you know it."

"I know that I'm on my back, and you're the one who put me here. You didn't ask, you just—"

He rolled off the bed and stood. Naked and beautiful, he went to the bureau and pulled out a pair of jeans and underwear. While he slipped them on, Melita climbed beneath the sheet and scooted back against the wooden headboard, pulling the sheet up to cover herself once more.

She thought he was going to leave, but she should have known better. He sat down in a chair opposite the bed and lit a cigarette.

Calm as can be, blowing smoke, he said, "I don't know everything about your life with your father. Someday I hope to. But right now I have to go with my gut, and my own experience with your father. Don't use it against me, Melita. I won't be manipulated so you can get your way anytime you feel like it. I've never beaten you, and I never will. But I won't stand back and watch you be hurt, either…by anyone. That includes your brother."

He was right. She should never have compared him to her father. "I didn't mean that. I don't feel like you're my jailer. I've never felt freer than when I'm with you. I just want—"

"To see Simon. I know. Let's talk about Minare. Tell me about the time you spent there. Does your brother know where you've been for the past year?"

She glanced at the clock. "I think so, but I'm not sure. My father sent me there to punish me for my involvement with Nemo. He called it reckless behavior. He doesn't tolerate flaws in the men who work for him, or in his children. If you break the rules your actions have consequences. Nemo's death was a consequence, my captivity at Minare was a consequence. Of course, he claimed he did what he did out of love and concern for my safety. He always talks as if he's doing the fatherly thing, but his children are his property, nothing more."

"Do you think he would ever consider killing you? Your latest betrayal has cost him a lot."

"I've never feared for my life…yet. But every time I disobey him, the punishment gets more violent. The first month that I lived at Minare, I refused to talk to him after Nemo's death. My father warned me that I would pay for my continued rebellion, but I didn't know what he meant until weeks later when the third man died."

"I don't follow."

"Once a week, I was taken out on the balcony and forced to watch a man die tied to a whipping post. My father never told me why the man was being beaten until the third week. He said over dinner that night, 'Are you going to start talking soon, or are more men going to die senselessly for your stubborn rebellion?' That's when I knew I hadn't only sentenced Nemo to death, but three other men I didn't even know. That was the day I realized the extent of my father's evil. I found the cells in the tunnel by accident, and from then on I knew the men in those cells never left Minare alive. I don't know who they were, or why they were there. And I didn't want to know."

"And then I showed up."

"I saw you get off the boat in shackles. I don't know why

I went down there that next day. I had no reason. Then Holic and Nigel showed up and after they left you asked me to help you escape. The morning before, I had slipped away early before dawn to go to the village. I had been doing that for about a month, trying to find someone to help me get off the island. No one would help me because they knew I was Cyrus Krizova's daughter, but I didn't give up. One fisherman told me what I needed wasn't a boat to get off the island, but a gorilla with brass balls and a death wish. You told me to read your file and I did. I saw the picture of you. What my father did to you. How he tortured and starved you. It was horrible, but at the same time seeing that picture verified what I had read in the file. You had survived what no man could, and I knew then that you were my only hope off the island. I knew I'd found my…gorilla."

"You saw an opportunity and you took it."

"Yes. The problem was, by rights, I was the enemy. My father had done those terrible things to you, and I was sure you wouldn't want anything to do with me if you knew. Would you have taken me with you if I had confessed I was Cyrus Krizova's daughter?"

"I don't know. Probably not."

Melita glanced at the clock. 12:30. "That's what I thought. In the grotto I told Hector and Nigel that you couldn't know who I was. I made them promise, if you came back for us, that they would never tell."

"After I saw the scars on your wrists, I forced Hector into a confession. He cares about you a lot." He shook his head. "No, *care* isn't a strong enough word. He loves you. Like a sister. I made him clarify that."

Melita smiled. "Were you jealous?"

"I don't think I knew what I was at that point." He puffed

hard on his cigarette. "All I knew was that I couldn't stop thinking about you, and once I saw those scars, I had to know why they were there."

"Life is a gift." Melita repeated the words he'd said to her last night.

"In Dublin I saw a lot of death. It started with my mother. She was a prostitute, and I watched her die one night entertaining a john. I was hiding under the bed. She always made me hide when they came. I was three, maybe four. The next day I was on the street with nowhere to go."

"You were four years old, living on the street?"

"I hooked up with a guy named Patrick Paxton. My mother's murder set off a search for her young son, Sullivan O'Neill. I would have been tossed in an orphanage. I became Sully Paxton, and Paddy the father I never had. He was a street thief, and he taught me what he knew. I was a quick study, and we made a good team. I turned into one helluva pickpocket. I was a badass little bastard, but I knew what dead meant. It meant if you don't find a way to survive you end up being shoveled out with the garbage like my mother was. Death is no game. When it's over, it's over."

"I felt like I had killed Nemo. I felt like I didn't deserve to live after what I'd done…my reckless behavior."

"Did you love him?"

"I thought I did." Melita lowered her head. "But I never felt for him what I feel for you." She looked up. "And there's guilt and pain in that, too. I don't think it will ever go away."

"What is pain, if not the reality that you are alive?"

Melita felt a chill slide down her spine. "Did you read that somewhere? It sounds like poetry."

"It's a mantra I repeated to myself in the pit. The one thing Cyrus taught me, when I was in the ground, is the art of patience. It's the only game in town when your back's against the wall, or in my case, living in a hole in the earth. The pain," he said, shrugging, "it was my friend in the pit. It reminded me every day that I was alive."

Melita glanced down at her wrists, at the white lines that would never go away. "Knowing what you survived makes me feel weak and selfish."

"Not weak, just a little too hasty."

She looked up and saw that he was smiling.

"And I caution you to never be too hasty again. I can live with physical pain served any way, but the one thing I don't want to have to survive is a life without you in it. Maybe that makes me selfish, but I figure I've earned it."

Melita felt tears sting her eyes. "You love me."

"Did I forget to mention that?"

Melita thought about how he'd made love to her, and how he'd touched her, every part of her, with his mouth and with his hands. His body. Remembered how much of himself he'd given her at *the end*. "No, you were clear about how you felt. You said it in a very wonderful way."

"Which brings us back to where we are now."

"It's true Simon killed Nemo, but my brother isn't evil like my father. At least I don't want to believe that. My brother was born an albino, and he suffers from a rare blood disease. He can't tolerate the sun, and everything around him has to be sterilized because he has extreme allergies. My father hates his weakness, and Simon has had to live with that along with his illness. That's why he tries so hard to please my father. That day Nemo died, my father learned that Simon had been keeping things from him. We had both betrayed him." Melita closed her eyes, suddenly back on the yacht facing her father's wrath. "He told Simon the price for his betrayal, and mine would be Nemo's life."

"And Simon agreed?"

"No. He fell at our father's feet and pleaded with him." Melita bit her lip, remembered how many times she'd pleaded with her father not to lock her in her room. "It never works. Begging is another form of weakness. The rules are, if you betray my father you had better be prepared to accept the consequences. When it was over and Nemo was dead, I was escorted below deck and locked in my stateroom. I hate locked doors, and I was hysterical over what had happened to Nemo. I just wanted the pain and guilt to stop, and the fear of being locked up again took me over the edge."

"Again?"

"Over the years my father has used my claustrophobia to punish me."

"Which has only made the problem worse."

"If a room is small, or a door is locked, I can't breathe. I slit my wrists, only I didn't realize that the room had hidden cameras in it. My father saw me do it."

"He saw you, and didn't try to stop you?"

"I don't know if he could have stopped me in time. I guess I'll never know that. What I do remember is Simon with Nemo's blood all over his clothes begging my father not to let me die. The day after that I was escorted to Minare, and that's the last time I saw my brother. I came here to see Simon because he needs to know I don't blame him for Nemo's death, and that I will always love him no matter what."

He put out his cigarette. "Write him a letter."

"Write him a letter? That's all you have to say?"

"I sympathize, but it's not enough for me to gamble with your life."

"It's my life." She glanced at the clock again.

"What are you leaving out? When you came here you had

to have a plan. And it's obvious there's a timeline. You've been watching the clock for the past thirty minutes."

"You're right, I do have a plan. Simon visits the *Paraportiani* every Thursday at three o'clock. Today is Thursday. Unless he's too ill to leave the house, or out of town, he never misses going to the chapel." Melita climbed out from under the sheet and found her white sundress on the floor. She laid it out on the bed.

"What are you doing?"

"I only have an hour to get ready." She looked up at him. "Please, Sully. It's a good plan. I can see him at the chapel. My father will never even know I'm there."

"Why does Simon go to the *Paraportiani?*"

"To pray." When Sully snorted and raised his eyebrows, she said, "When Simon was younger he wanted to be a priest. He goes to the chapel to pray for forgiveness. I'll dress up like before, and—"

"What if he doesn't show?"

She started stuffing the pillowcase with the extra clothes. "Then I'll go back next Thursday. He'll go to the chapel. If not today, then next week. Or the next." She looked up and smiled at him. "Patience, remember?"

"It could work."

Melita tossed the pillowcase on the bed, and went searching for her underwear. "It will work, Sully. I know it will."

"Does your father know about Simon's Thursday ritual?"

"No. That's the beauty of it."

"So you never intended to go to Lesvago?"

"No." He looked as if he was going to agree. "You see, I do have a plan."

"I'm going with you."

"No. My father's guards are everywhere. I can fool them with my disguise, but you are too easily spotted."

"I go, or you don't."

The set of his jaw told her that this was the only concession he was going to make. "All right. But wear the white suit jacket, and we stop off in one of the shops downstairs and buy you a hat."

"I don't wear hats."

"You will today."

He stood. "There's something I need to tell you. I think this is a good time." He shrugged. "Maybe *good* isn't the right word. It's time."

"Is it about my father?"

"Some history and what he's become since."

Melita listened to what Sully had to say. He told her a story about her father working for Onyxx more than twenty years ago with a man named Adolf Merrick, who was now Sully's boss.

"There was a mission in Prague. I guess his team walked into a minefield. He was critically wounded, and he claims Merrick left him for dead. Obviously he survived, only his face was destroyed in the explosion."

"That's not true. His face is flawless," Melita pointed out.

"But not as you remember, I'll bet."

"I don't remember him at all. I was a baby when he went away. I was three when Mother remarried. Charles was very good to us. I was five and Simon eight, when my father came back for us after Mother and Charles died in an accident." Melita studied Sully's eyes, and she suddenly felt sick to her stomach. "It wasn't an accident, was it?"

"I don't know. But we both know that Cyrus doesn't like to lose anything he thinks he owns."

She watched Sully walk to the hotel window and look out. "There's one more thing he told me. He said he needed a face and so he cloned another Onyxx agent's face." Sully turned and looked at her. "Cyrus Krizova is your father, but he's wearing another man's face."

"Plastic surgery?"

"Extensive surgery."

Melita was suddenly back on the balcony at Minare. Her father was lighting his cigar using a lighter with a silver finish tarnished with age.

"He carries a lighter with him with the initials P.C. on it. I asked him about it. He told me it was an old friend's lighter. He said Paavo Creon shared everything he owned with me before he died. He cloned Paavo Creon's face, didn't he?"

"That's what he claims."

"It just keeps getting worse, doesn't it? When I think I know what he's capable of, I learn something even more despicable that he's done. Well, I'm not going to live by his rules any longer. I'll see Simon, and then I'm leaving and never coming back."

Melita reached for the pillowcase on the bed, and tossed it to Sully. She stepped into the large panties and pulled the elastic away from her waist. "We have to hurry or we'll be late. Stuff me," she said, "then get ready. We still need to buy you a hat."

On Melita's insistence Sully bought a hat in the gift shop. Wearing the white suit jacket and matching fedora, he guided his pregnant wife up the stone path to *Paraportiani*. A tourist crowd had gathered out front, and a guide was discussing the architecture.

Sully looked at the mass of people two ways—the crowd could be used as good cover for them to slip in and out without being noticed, or it could work against them if Cyrus's men were posing as tourists.

He pulled the brim of his hat low over his eyes, and urged Melita to walk a little faster toward the whitewashed chapel on the western seafront. As they stepped through the front doors, the sunshine vanished. The interior was dim, the golden icon glistening in the candlelight.

Melita was about to choose the third row, but Sully directed her into the last pew, and slid in beside her. He wanted to know who all was there, and he didn't much like sitting with his back to the door, but there was no other way. Still, they could be trapped easily inside the chapel if something went wrong.

They weren't early, in fact they were ten minutes late. He really didn't think it mattered—finding Simon here today was more than a long shot. If his routine had changed they wouldn't be lucky enough to see him today.

Melita told him Simon was an albino, his skin as white as his hair. Small-framed, not six feet tall, his body thin from poor health. The chapel was sparse. Sully counted thirty people, and he dissected each one of them, but no one fit the description.

He wished he had been able to make contact with Merrick. He'd left a message on his cell telling him where he was, where Cyrus might be found. It wasn't a sure thing, and knowing Krizova, he could toss a surprise into the mix at any time.

It bothered him that he hadn't heard back from Merrick. He had called three times. Had the raid at Vouno been successful? Or was Merrick still searching for the elusive island, and the men still dying in the dungeon?

He didn't want to believe that. Instead he would believe that Merrick was in the middle of a mop-up and just hadn't checked his phone.

They had been there twenty minutes when Melita's hand clamped around his leg and squeezed. Sully glanced at her, then followed her gaze as she stared at a frail-bodied man who came through a side door wearing a flat-brimmed straw hat, his pale hair barely visible beneath it.

"He never goes out in the sun without that hat," she whispered.

Showtime, Sully thought, then slid his hand inside his jacket and wrapped his hand around the Glock, his eyes missing nothing.

Melita did all she could do not to jump to her feet and run up the aisle when she saw Simon. His hat was the first thing she had noticed as he came through the side entrance—that hat was as familiar to her as her brother himself.

She watched him take a seat in a pew four rows from the front. He sat only a moment, his head bowed, then leaned forward and knelt.

She realized at that moment that this was the last time she would ever see her brother again, and tears surfaced quickly. She brushed them away, knowing Sully was watching her. She wasn't going to fall apart. Saying goodbye was part of the reason she'd come.

She nodded slightly to let Sully know there was no mistake, it was Simon, then stood and slowly made her way to the outside aisle. She and Sully had gone over how they would play this out. He wasn't crazy about being left behind, but she had convinced him that she needed to see Simon alone.

She glanced around as she walked up the aisle, passing the pews one by one. It was a long walk, and it seemed even longer. Simon never moved when she sat down next to him. He knelt with his elbows on the pew ahead of him and his hands clasped, resting his forehead on them.

She knew he was aware that someone had joined him, but he didn't look up. She waited a long minute, then finally she whispered, "Simon, it's me. Melita."

He raised his head slowly, but he didn't turn. He lowered his elbows, and using one hand, he lifted himself and pushed back to join her on the pew. She stared at his hand, as pale as snow, but something wasn't right.

In that second, Melita knew she'd made a terrible mistake—his hand was missing two fingers. She started up from the seat, knocking her hat off as a signal to Sully that something was wrong, then she turned and locked eyes with him before screaming, "It's a trap! Get out!"

She was on her feet now, determined to run, but Holic Reznik reached out and gave her a shove that knocked her off balance and she went sprawling in the aisle. The clothes bundle beneath her sundress made it hard to get up quickly, and she was still struggling when Holic pulled a gun out from under his shirt, turned in the pew and aimed it at Sully.

"No!" Melita saw Holic rest the gun on the back of the pew, then fire two shots. Her head swung to the back of the chapel. Sully was already on his feet, and that made him a perfect target—she should never have called to him.

She saw Sully's body twist left, saw a red stain quickly spread low on the right side of his white jacket. She screamed again, and cried out his name as the people were now all screaming and running for the exit. Before she took a step, someone grabbed her from behind and dragged her backward. She fought the hands that restrained her, but she couldn't break free. She was dragged out the side entrance.

Her captor's free hand covered her mouth and she fought harder. Something sour-smelling went up her nose and fear made her breathe in, sucking the odor deeper into her nostrils. She was immediately nauseous, then too dizzy to think.

And then she stopped struggling.

Chapter 13

Melita woke up in her brother's bed at Lesvago. She'd been in this room hundreds of times, tending to Simon when he was ill. Now she was the one who felt sick—so weak and nauseous she could hardly lift her head off the pillow.

Her thoughts turned to the chapel, and quickly to Sully. *Your actions have consequences. You wouldn't want another death on your conscience.*

She moaned and rolled to her side and drew up her legs. That's when she noticed she was wearing a white satin nightgown. She reached up and quickly felt her neck, clasped her fingers around the necklace Sully had given her. Please, don't let him be dead, she thought. Not Sully.

She heard the door open and close.

"Will you never learn that there is no escape, Melita?"

She raised her head and stared at her father.

"The necklace seems important. A gift from your most recent admirer?"

"No," she lied, not wanting him to take it from her. "More cameras?"

He smiled. "If you remember the cameras were installed in this room to keep your brother's health monitored. But it's true, I've been watching you. You really do look sweet and innocent when you're sleeping, but we both know different, don't we?"

She forced herself to sit up. Her head spun wildly, and she wondered what had knocked her out so quickly at the chapel.

"Quite an ingenious disguise. I must commend you on your creative talent, but then I've always known that you and I share many traits."

She clutched the pale gold sheet to her breasts, stared at his face—another man's face. What did he look like before? she wondered. "Where's Simon?"

"We'll get to him in a minute." He walked to the bed, and without warning backhanded her across the face. Her head snapped back and she tasted blood. "That's the first I've ever hit you. Take note of it. You deserve far worse. You're a foolish little bitch, Melita. But you're my bitch, and so I will deal with it as a father must." His rage suddenly settled. "You've cost me two islands, good men and billions of dollars in lost revenue. And I thought the escapade with Nemo was a travesty. That was simply a blemish, but this you will pay a lifetime for if you willingly left Minare with my enemy."

Melita wiped the blood from her mouth. "Go ahead, beat me. Do your worst."

"Careful. I don't think you understand what I'm capable of."

"Yes, I do. I know what you did to Sully at Vouno. No one could do that and be human. But you're not human, are you?

You have no soul. You're a monster with a handsome face. Someone else's face."

"I see Paxton has let you in on my secret. Well, it really wasn't a secret, or I wouldn't have shared it with him. The information should serve you well. Now you know that I always find a way to get what I want. And my worst, Melita…you can't even imagine."

"Why did you bring Sully to Minare?"

"Ah, yes, back to Paxton. The man who can survive anything. And let me tell you I did give him a taste of my worst. I admit when you were brought to me with your swollen belly it sparked an idea. I actually hope you are carrying his child. I would love to have a grandson with Paxton's zest for survival. And wouldn't it be poetic justice for him to know before he dies that his child would be mine."

Melita instinctively touched her belly. As much as she would love Sully's child, she prayed it wasn't true. Another child for her father to torment and abuse would be sacrilege.

"Of course, Paxton must die. You do realize that, regardless."

Did that mean Sully was still alive? Was he here?

"The only way you can save yourself this time, Melita, is to convince me that he abducted you, and took you from Minare by force. Is that what happened?"

Melita wasn't about to lie. "No. The truth is, I abducted him."

"You expect me to believe that?"

"I don't care what you believe. I needed help off the island. I read his file. As you said, he is a man who knows how to survive. He supplied a boat, and I supplied—"

"Your body as payment."

"If that's what you want to believe, but it wasn't part of our deal."

"Let me guess. You set him free, and he agreed to take

you to Mykonos Town to Simon. You don't have to answer. I know you, Melita. Simon is one of your weaknesses. He always has been. And that brings us full circle. I admit you've tested my patience these past days. I even considered ending your life. But now…if you are carrying Paxton's child—"

"I'm not."

"Time will tell. Now, are you ready to visit Simon?"

"You're going to let me see him?"

"I don't want you to have made the trip for nothing. Can you walk?"

She wasn't sure, but she would crawl if she had to. The room spun as she climbed out of bed. She flattened her hand against the wall to keep her balance. Her legs held her up and she let go of the wall.

"Holic assures me that the drug will wear off shortly."

The idea of Holic's drug in her system made her sick, and angry. Melita glared at her father. "You're making a mistake where Holic Reznik is concerned. He is no friend."

"I'm aware of Holic's shortcomings, but he is useful to me at the moment. When his services are no longer needed, I will deal with him. Come. Simon is in the garden."

Wearing only the white nightgown, Melita forced one foot in front of the other, and trailed after her father. They left the bedroom and walked down a wide hallway into the spacious living room. It was bright and airy, due to all the windows that offered a clear view to the cove. She glanced down at the water, wondering where Sully was at that moment. How badly he'd been hit. She'd seen the blood, but from what her father had said, he must have managed to get away.

She rounded the white leather couch, focused on the open

glass doors that led into the garden. Her father stepped to the side and she entered the garden—a wonderland of beautiful flowers and fountains.

Simon shared her passion for lavender, and she breathed in the fresh scent, hoping it would clear her head. She needed to regain her wits, and be ready if an opportunity to escape presented itself.

She noticed that there had been a new addition to the garden. A life-size statue stood in the center, and its likeness to Simon was uncanny—even his hat had been recreated in stone. She glanced around, expecting to see her brother sitting on the bench in the shade under the large cypresses, but he wasn't there.

She turned to her father. "I thought you said he was here?"

"He is here. Don't you see him? Can't you feel his spirit?"

When she looked around again, then back at her father, he pointed to the statute. "He's right there, Melita. I had it commissioned. It looks just like him, don't you think?"

Can't you feel his spirit?

Melita shook her head, already rejecting what she knew was coming. "No!"

"I'm afraid so. Your brother has been dead over a year. He died a few days after you were taken to Despotiko."

"You're lying. This is just another one of your cruel games."

"I never joke about death, especially when it has taken one of my own. Onyxx blew up the *Pearl.* Somehow explosives were planted without my knowledge. I managed to escape, but your brother never made it out alive."

"No!"

"Simon no longer suffers, that's the only peace in this tragedy. But those who have taken him from us will pay, I assure you of that. My son was a weak man, but I loved him anyway, as I love all my children. Even though you refuse to believe that a monster with another man's face could possess such an emotion."

Melita's knees buckled and she collapsed at the foot of the statue. She cried out, the truth of her father's words stripping her defenses and taking all her strength. Her cries dissolved into moaning, then pathetic whimpering that sounded much like a dying animal.

"Onyxx killed your brother, Melita. Paxton's comrades. You've been sleeping with the enemy. Your brother's killer. Do you think Simon will ever forgive you for that?"

She raised her head, tears streaming down her face. "Onyxx didn't kill him. You did. You killed your son! You killed my brother!"

He snapped his fingers, and suddenly footsteps sounded on the stone path that led into the garden from the front terrace. Seconds later a bulky guard with a scar on his chin and angry eyes appeared.

"Take her back to the bedroom, Argo. My daughter's visit with Simon is over."

A pair of thick arms lifted her up and carried her back inside Simon's room. In shock, she didn't realize what was coming next until he opened a narrow closet that ran the length of one wall. She glanced inside. Simon's clothes were gone, and what she saw bolted into the wall made her blood run cold—iron handcuffs.

"No!" In a panic, Melita tried to fight the arms that held her, and beat on the guard's chest. He took the blows without flinching and stepped into the closet, setting her on her feet. She tried to surge past him, but he pushed her back in between the handcuffs and quickly manacled her wrists to the wall while her father watched.

"I know you're mourning Simon and I sympathize, but you know the rules, Melita. Betrayal always results in punishment."

In seconds the door would close, and soon she would be suffocating on her own fear. She moaned in misery, wept for Simon and for herself.

The guard stepped back and she felt her father's hand lift her chin. "Feel free to scream. The closet is soundproof, and it won't be a disturbance to anyone. No one will hear you disgrace yourself."

"Please, no," Melita begged. "Please don't lock me in here."

"I'm expecting Paxton soon. When I've dealt with him, I'll be back." He leaned forward, kissed her forehead, then reached up and curled his fingers around the stone pendant that Sully had given her. He jerked it free, breaking the chain, then stepped back. "Close it up, Argo."

The closet doors slid shut, and when Melita heard the lock slide into place, the darkness settled around her and she started to scream.

The bullet had ripped through the strap muscle along his hip and gone straight through. An inch to the left and he would have been gut shot, and his breathing days over.

Sully tossed the suit jacket to the floor in the bathroom on the *Korinna*, and opened a bottle of whiskey. He jerked his jeans past his hips and poured the liquor on the open wound. "Son of a bitch!" he swore, as a lightning bolt of pain ripped through him.

Gritting his teeth, he checked the watch in his pocket. It had been an hour since Melita had been abducted from the chapel. He'd had a devil of a time fighting his way out of there, and more trouble on the outside to reach the *Korinna*. But once he'd gotten to the cruiser he'd had no trouble shaking Cyrus's men.

He couldn't get the look on Melita's face out of his head.

Not when she realized that she'd been tricked, and not when she'd witnessed him being shot.

Holic Reznik had been the perfect stand-in for Simon. He was small and thin, and with a wig and Simon's hat, he'd sold the con completely.

Sully drank the rest of the whiskey in the bottle, then grabbed the roll of tape and wrapped his hip, fusing the torn muscle to his body, pulling the tape tight to seal the wound and stop the bleeding. The pain intensified, but that was all right, it would keep his edge up.

He sliced the tape off the roll with his knife, slipped the weapon and tape into the duffel bag, along with his arsenal of guns, then headed for the cockpit on deck. He had the cruiser skipping over the water headed northwest up the coast seconds later.

He asked the boat for everything she had, the needle on the speedometer dancing on seventy miles an hour as he searched the coast. The problem was, Melita had never given him the exact location of Lesvago. He heard his cell phone go off, and he put it to his ear.

"Sully? I got your message, and—"

"Merrick. Damn, I'm glad to hear your voice."

"We rescued the men. Found the cache of guns, too. It was one helluva—"

"Where are you now?"

"Forty miles from Tinos. We'll be there in—"

"I'm not there any longer. I'm headed up the coast of Mykonos to Lesvago. Got any ideas where that might be?"

"What's happened? Your message said—"

"Change of plans."

"I'll put Sly on. He's been to Lesvago."

With Sly's typography of the island coast, and specific

landmarks, Sully realized he'd passed the bay. He doubled back. Found the entrance.

"Sully, are you still on the line?" Sly asked.

"I'm here," he said. "Lesvago is up ahead."

"Merrick says stay put and wait for us," Sly instructed. "Sully… Paxton… Damn it!"

Sully put the phone in his pocket. He remembered what Melita had said about getting trapped in the cove if he went too far in. He turned the cruiser into a maze of craggy outcrops close to shore, well out of sight, then pulled a pair of binoculars out of the utility cupboard and scanned the cove. Lesvago had been built into a cliff that rose up from the water.

It was the perfect bird's nest for a criminal, Sully mused. Damn near impregnable. Again he thought back to what Melita had told him, and he scanned the cove, spotted a number of guards, as well as the many steps that terraced the rocky landscape.

Sully's phone rang again. He answered it. "Yeah."

"Merrick says don't do something stupid. Can you see the house?"

"I see it. One yacht out front. There should be two," Sully said, thinking out loud, wondering if Cyrus had already fled with Melita. "How long before you get here?"

"Another thirty minutes."

Too long, Sully thought. "Did you pick up Hector on Amorgos?"

"We did. Is something wrong? Your breathing is—"

"I took a bullet in town."

"How bad?"

"I've lived through worse. I'm going to leave my cruiser moored left of the first rocky crag. I'm going in. You pick up the trouble when you get here."

"Merrick's orders are you wait, Sully. We'll figure this out together. We've waited too long to get Krizova for something to go wrong. He could run."

"He might have already. I need to know that sooner than later. If he hasn't then there's someone inside who needs my help."

"Who's inside?"

"Krizova's daughter."

"Melita's there?"

"You know her?"

"We've met. My future wife is a friend of hers."

"Wife? I guess I've been out of the loop awhile."

"Cyrus won't hurt his daughter. Stay put."

"Melita's the one who helped me escape Despotiko. She was abducted a little over an hour ago when she tried to contact her brother."

"Simon?"

"Yeah."

"Sully, Simon is dead. He died a year ago. We've got him in the agency morgue back in Washington."

Sully swore, knowing what the news was going to do to Melita.

"Sully, listen. Krizova is using Melita to draw you in. Don't fall for it. Sit tight."

"It's more complicated than that."

He could hear Merrick in the background telling Sly to keep him talking. To hold his ass down until they got there. There was no reason to wait. The party had started already, and everyone who knew Dog Paxton knew he was the life of the party.

He disconnected, set the timer on his phone and stuck it in his pocket. Stripping off his shirt, his boots and socks, Sully said a silent prayer that he was strong enough to swim the channel, then jumped over the side of the *Korinna*.

* * *

"He hung up," Sly said.

Merrick swore. "That means he's going in. Damn it! Ash, get this boat airborne. When I get there I don't want to find Sully dead and Krizova gone. We've waited too long for this."

He caught Sly glancing at him out of the corner of his eye. "Sully said Cyrus might already be gone."

"What else did he say?"

"That he was shot earlier. I don't think he's in good shape. And there's something else. He was damn concerned about Krizova's daughter."

Merrick turned to look at the man they had picked up in Amorgos. "What do you know that you haven't told me, Hector? Why is Sully so worried about Melita Krizova?"

Hector had been staring out to sea. He turned to look at Merrick. When his answer came it was the most ridiculous thing Merrick had ever heard.

"Because he loves her."

Merrick snorted. "Loves her? Obviously you don't know Sully Paxton. He's a block of ice when it comes to women."

"I know him," Hector said, "and I know Melita. She is fire and you are right, Paxton is ice. But when fire touches ice it melts. He loves her. It is why he has never left her from the moment he learned who she was. It is why he will give his life for her if he has to."

That gave Merrick something to think about for the next half hour, and the more he thought about it, the more worried he became. A man in love was thinking with his heart instead of his head. If what Hector said was true, it would be a first for Sully, and the last if he made a mistake. And he'd already made it by thinking he could take Krizova on alone.

When they found Sully's cruiser in the cove, Ash whistled as he pulled up alongside it. "Where the hell did Sully get that wicked little bitch?"

Again Hector enlightened them. "With the money he stole from Krizova at Minare."

Chapter 14

The one thing that didn't fit when Melita was telling him about Lesvago was the hidden iron gate. The channel was narrow enough that a few guards on the cliffs would be able to stop anyone going in or out. So why did Cyrus need an invisible gate underwater?

Sully soon had his answer when he located the gate, and it put a smile on his face. The gate was state-of-the-art, but more importantly it sealed off the entrance to an underwater cave.

He came up for air, careful not to be spotted by the guards, took a deep breath, then went back down. He swam deep this time, checked out the gate and found a narrow gap next to a rock and squeezed through—if he was thirty pounds heavier he wouldn't have made it.

He moved swiftly through the water, trying to conserve his air, and when he was sure he'd gone far enough, he surfaced and found himself in a grotto that housed a small submarine.

He tried to get inside, but it had an electronic hatch, and so he left the sub and pulled himself up on the dock. Catching his breath, he got to his feet and followed a footpath to a narrow passageway. From there he found a stairway and climbed up to a landing, then two more sections of stairs, which put him in a doorway to a lit corridor.

He was inside the house, and he could hear voices. He recognized one of the men, his voice bringing back months of pain—Pedro was at Lesvago. Obviously he'd avoided capture at Vouno.

He waited a few minutes longer, and when he heard one set of footsteps coming down the corridor, he stepped back and hugged the wall. The minute the guard walked by, Sully reached out and wrapped his forearm around the man's neck, dragging him through the doorway. A second later he snapped the man's neck and let him fall to the floor.

It wasn't Pedro, that's what Sully noticed first. Then he saw the Skorpion. He took the weapon, then pulled the guard to the edge of the stairs and sent him on a dumpy ride to the bottom.

The noise brought Pedro on the run. "Basil? Basil, what happened?"

The minute Pedro turned into the doorway, Sully raised the butt of the gun and smashed it into Pedro's chest, stealing his breath and his balance. The guard crumbled on the floor. Dazed momentarily, he looked up at his assailant, wanting to speak, but unable to draw air to get the words out.

Sully loomed over the guard, the gun aimed at his chest. "Remember me?"

Pedro's eyes went wide, and he struggled to find his voice. "I was only doing my job."

Sully picked up Pedro's weapon, shouldered it and aimed the other Skorpion at Pedro's chest. "Talk or die."

"If I talk I'll still die. Cyrus will kill me."

Sully shrugged. "Now or later."

"What do you want to know?"

"Is he here?"

"Yes."

"And Melita? Where is she?"

"I don't know."

"Wrong answer."

"Argo might know. He's seen her. I haven't."

"Get up." Sully backed off, and when Pedro got to his feet, he nudged him with the gun. "Get me inside."

They went through a series of corridors. "What part of the house is this?" he asked.

"The bedrooms." When they heard voices, Pedro stopped, and pointed to a closed door. "Inside or you'll be spotted."

"If that happens you'll be dead," Sully reminded.

They moved quickly through a door into a large bedroom. Sully glanced around, surprised when he spotted Melita's dress and the pillowcase stuffed with her clothes on the floor.

She'd been in this room. His eyes went back to the bed. The sheet was rumpled and he knew she had been lying there. He almost missed the necklace, half-hidden in the sheet. He glanced around. The room had a long wall closet, a nightstand and an adjoining bathroom.

Sully took the room apart in more detail, spotted the camera. He'd told Pedro he wanted inside, so here he was, and there was Cyrus watching his every move.

He nodded at the camera. "I hope the party hasn't started without me."

A second later Cyrus's voice sounded over an intercom system. "You made good time for a man with a bullet in him, Paxton, but then I knew nothing would keep you away."

"You know me, I like to play."

Cyrus laughed. "Yes, you never disappointed me. Not like so many of the others. You're a tough son of a bitch, Paxton. But I made you tougher on my island. I made you the man you are today. Pedro, disarm our guest, and escort him to the living room."

Pedro turned and smiled. "The guns, pretty boy, put them on the bed. Then the Glock you have in your pants."

Sully walked to the bed and laid the guns down. Then he pulled the Glock from his waistband and placed it next to the necklace he'd given Melita, his fingers curling around it. While Pedro was busy retrieving his Skorpion, Sully pocketed the necklace, keeping his back to the camera.

"You heard the boss. *Greegorah!* Let's go."

Sully turned as Pedro opened the door and motioned for him to move down the corridor. He felt the Skorpion nudge his back as they walked down the hall.

"Now who is going to die, *file?* It is not me."

Sully stepped into the living room. Cyrus was sitting on a white leather couch smoking a cigar. He was dressed in a white suit, and Argo was standing behind him with his arms crossed, hugging a Skorpion to his chest.

The guard from Vouno smiled, and Sully smiled back. "Glad you could join us. I know how much you enjoy a good game."

"You're a freak, Paxton. I've never known anyone who can eat pain the way you do. Your wound must be on fire from swimming the channel, and still you're on your feet."

Sully glanced around hoping to see Melita. She wasn't anywhere in sight.

"If you're looking for my daughter, she's not feeling well at the moment. It was a shock for her to learn that her brother is no longer with us."

"An accident?" Sully asked, pretending he didn't know Simon was dead.

"No. Merrick and your comrades killed my son while trying to capture me months ago."

"Care if I sit down?" Sully motioned to the leather chair ten feet from Cyrus.

"Sit. I'd prefer you well-rested for our games. Where are Hector and Barinski?"

Sully pulled his cell phone from his pocket and sat down on the chair. "I don't know. They ran like the devil was chasing them once we left Minare." Sully saw that piece of news caused Cyrus a bit of distress.

"Pedro, bring me the phone."

Sully tossed it at the guard, and he took it to his boss.

"Is this what you used to contact Merrick? He hit Vouno, and stole my guns."

Sully had wiped out all the messages. There was nothing on the phone to give Cyrus an edge. "His number's in there in case you want to give him a call. Maybe if you ask nice, he'll give them back. He's probably on his way back to Washington."

"Leave you behind? I don't think so."

"I told him I needed some time."

"With my daughter?"

Sully grinned. "She is beautiful. But I'm not the only one who thinks so. Reznik around?"

Cyrus laid the phone on the coffee table in front of him. "Somewhere."

"I'm surprised he's still alive."

"Why do you say that?"

"Did you ask him what he was doing the night the yacht at Minare was set on fire? Did he lie, or did he tell you the truth about his plans for Melita?" Sully knew if Reznik was alive then Cyrus had bought his lies about that night. He intended to cast some doubt, and buy a little more time.

"You seem to think you know something that will interest me. Why don't you tell me?"

"Why not ask Reznik?"

Cyrus looked at Pedro, motioned for him to find Reznik. Sully watched as the guard disappeared down a hall. Not long after, Holic Reznik walked into the room with his shirt open, and his eyes dilated, Pedro behind him.

"You wanted to see me, Cyrus?" He glanced at Sully. "Paxton, how's the wound? I hope it hurts like hell."

"A minor scratch," Sully lied. "You almost missed."

That didn't sit well. Reznik's face contorted, and it emphasized the old bruises from their previous encounter at Minare. "I would have enjoyed killing you in that church, but I was instructed to only wound you."

Sully sat back in the chair and crossed his leg over his knee, the motion fluid. He saw Reznik frown, questioning himself on his aim and the shot.

"Grazed my hip," Sully said as if he'd read Holic's mind, and answered the embarrassing question an assassin would never ask. "I was telling Cyrus about your dinner plans with Melita at Minare." He glanced back at Cyrus, angled his head as if a thought had just occurred to him. "Or maybe she was part of your deal with him. A little fun in the sack to keep him loyal."

Cyrus looked at Holic. "What's he talking about?"

Holic leaned against the bar in the corner of the room. "I don't have any idea."

"Too high to remember? Then and now?" Sully asked. "I remember. I remember seeing her dress all full of blood. She said something felt like it was cutting her in two. When I dug that piece of glass out of her side, I knew why."

Holic glanced at Cyrus. "He lies. If she was injured somehow, it was escaping Minare with him."

"Why don't you ask Melita," Sully suggested, anxious to see her and make sure she was all right.

No longer as calm as he was minutes ago, Cyrus said, "As I told you, Melita is spending the afternoon alone to grieve for her—"

An explosion outside cut Cyrus off, and shattered two windows that faced the cove. Krizova leapt to his feet, and Sully watched Argo run to the window. "Holic's yacht is in pieces."

The second Argo delivered the message, Sully's phone alarm went off. He threw his weight into the side of the chair and rolled onto the floor, taking the chair with him as a shield. Another second later the small charge of Astrolite that he'd put inside the phone exploded on the coffee table. Krizova let out a agonizing howl, and Sully tossed the chair aside and scrambled to his feet, taking notice that Krizova's white suit was spattered with blood.

He rushed Pedro and tackled him to the floor. They wrestled, and Sully came up with the gun. He didn't think twice when he pulled the trigger and Pedro slumped to the floor. Then he was running for the hall as another explosion shook Lesvago's foundation.

The well-timed explosions told Sully that Ash had found the rest of the Astrolite in his duffel on the *Korinna* and the rapid gunfire that followed promised that Merrick and Sly were on the move taking down the guards out front. He hurried back into the bedroom he and Pedro had entered earlier and fired a shot into the camera.

He had to find Melita. Maybe Cyrus had her by now and was escaping to the sub. He couldn't let that happen. He had to think. Cyrus said Melita was spending the afternoon alone grieving. *Alone.* No, he wouldn't leave her alone unless she was locked up somewhere.

He glanced at the pillowcase on the floor, then to the white dress she'd worn to the chapel. This was the room she was in. His eyes locked on the closet, then to the dead bolt. Why would anyone put a dead bolt on a closet?

He heard Cyrus shouting at his men as he ran past the door and down the hall. Heard him tell Argo to get Melita. The door swung open and Sully spun around and fired his gun. Argo's eyes went wide and he grabbed his chest, dropped to his knees and fell over.

Get Melita. She was in the closet.

Sully raced to it and turned the dead bolt. He almost hoped she wasn't there knowing what being locked up would do to her. He swung the door open and there she was, her face pale and her eyes wide with fear.

"Sully. Oh, God, Sully."

"I'm here," he said, his voice hollow with regret that he hadn't been able to prevent Cyrus from hurting her one more time. "I'm getting you out of here. Hold on." He shoved the door wider to let more air inside the tight space, then looked at the locked cuffs around her wrists.

Get Melita.

He spun around and hurried back to Argo, rolled him over and started searching his pockets.

"Sully!"

"I'm here, honey. Hold on." He found the key in Argo's pants' pocket, then hurried back and opened the irons that had rubbed Melita's wrists raw. It was obvious she'd been fighting the manacles as her panic attack had escalated.

She would have collapsed if he hadn't pulled her to him the minute she was free. He held her tight, felt her body tremble, whispered, "You're safe, Melita. No more locked door. I promise."

"I saw Holic shoot you. I thought—"

"Shh… It's all right now."

"No. Simon's dead."

"I know. I'm sorry."

He heard footsteps in the hall, and he raised his gun once more. This time it was Ash Kelly who appeared in the doorway.

"Dog Paxton, damn it's good to see you." Ash grinned. "I told Merrick you were playing decoy for us. It was just like old times. He was pissed you ignored an order to wait for us, but he'll get over it. Where's Krizova?"

"He headed for the sub. I couldn't sabotage it. It was locked down. If Cyrus makes it, he'll be gone. Go out the door and turn right. Take the stairs. How many guards left outside?"

"None."

As soon as Ash left, Sully grabbed the pillowcase and ushered Melita out the door. In the hall, he met Merrick and Hector. He told Merrick where he thought Cyrus had gone, and that Ash was in pursuit. When Merrick took off on the run, Sully turned to Hector. The big guy's attention was focused on Melita.

"Are you all right?" he asked.

"I am now."

Sully pushed Melita toward Hector, then handed him the pillowcase. "Get her out of here."

"Sully, no!" She turned to him. "I'm not leaving you."

Sully pulled her to the side, touched her tear-stained cheek. "Melita, listen. I need you safe right now. Go with Hector."

"And will you come?"

There was gunfire in the stairwell. Sully jerked his head up, then shoved Melita at Hector. "What are you waiting for? Take her home."

"Sully, wait!"

He had turned his back, and was moving toward the stairs when he said, "Hector, shag your ass."

At the bottom of the stairs he found Merrick with Ash. Ash was down, and for a moment Sully thought he was dead. He knelt beside his friend, saw he'd taken a bullet in his thigh and one in his shoulder.

"Holic tagged me," he explained. "I hate that bastard."

"I had Cyrus," Merrick said. "I had the son of a bitch and he got away."

Sully got to his feet, saw that the sub was gone. "Did you hit him?"

"Yes, I hit him, but he didn't go down."

"He's probably wearing a vest," Sully reasoned, remembering the Astrolite in his phone. Krizova had been hit, but the damage had been minor. It should have torn him in half.

Merrick let out an angry cry like he was screaming at the gods. Then another, and another.

When it was quiet again, Merrick's phone set off. He pulled it from his pocket and flipped it open. After looking at the number, he glanced at Sully. "It's him." He pressed the phone to his ear. "What do you want, Cyrus?"

"How does it feel to know that you've lost the game one more time? That you almost had me, and I slipped through your fingers?"

"It feels like a victory coming my way soon," Merrick answered. "I'm closing in. You know it. You're running like a coward. I'll see you soon."

"Have you learned who the traitor is among you yet? You must have considered it. Think, Merrick. Who hates you as much as I do?"

"Another puzzle piece?"

"If you want to call it that. Tell Paxton I applaud his genius, and to take care of my daughter for me. I will come for her and him when the time is right. Until next time, Merrick, enjoy your small triumph."

"Merrick, we have to get Ash to a hospital. He's slipping into unconsciousness," Sully said. "Where's Sly?"

"I'm here, Sully."

Winded, Sly jogged toward them on the footpath, holding his side, his shirt covered in blood.

"What the hell happened to you?" Merrick demanded.

"We missed a guard. He took me by surprise. Hector shot him." He glanced at Sully. "Don't worry, Melita's safe."

Sully stepped forward and ripped open Sly's shirt. "Shit! I'll get the cruiser." Then he dove into the water and swam like hell.

Chapter 15

"Damn it's good to see you, Paxton." Pierce walked toward Sully, grinning in the corridor at Onyxx headquarters in Washington. He reached out and hauled Sully forward, thumping him on the back as he gave him a bear hug.

That wasn't Pierce's style, and when they parted, Sully said, "Who is she? Who turned the gator boy into a lover boy?"

Pierce laughed. "There's been some changes around here, that's for sure. But your ugly face hasn't changed. Did you hear Sly's getting married, and Bjorn's got two kids?"

"Sly told me he's getting hitched. Bjorn's got kids? I haven't been gone long enough for that."

"It's a long story. I'll fill you in later. Beers at Chadwicks later?"

"I'll be there."

"Ash and Sly are coming. Merrick told me they both got out of the hospital today, so I gave them a call."

"I hung out with Ash earlier today. I know he blamed himself for Castle Rock. Shit happens, you know. It's the nature of the business we're in. We're big boys, and it's not like we don't know the risks."

Pierce was frowning.

"What's wrong?"

"Sly said you were different. Not as ornery. I know you had it rough. I saw that pit."

Sully smiled. "What doesn't kill you makes you—"

"Horny," Pierce said, finishing the saying. A joke the team carried between them.

"Did I hear right?" Sully asked. "You got yourself a lady?"

"I do. I'm not marrying her yet." Pierce grinned. "She's playing hard to get."

They shared a laugh.

"Merrick said you hooked up with Krizova's daughter?"

Sully put his hand out in front of him, pride shining in his eyes. "She stands about so high, weighs a hundred pounds, maybe, and can shake the ground I walk on."

"You admit it? Hell, you have changed. Mad Dog would never have admitted a woman makes his knees weak."

Sully laughed. "Merrick in his office?"

"He's there. He told me you've got her stashed. You think she's safe from Cyrus?"

"I wouldn't be here if she wasn't. I'll see you tonight."

Sully knocked on Merrick's door, then stepped inside. "You got a minute?"

Merrick looked up. "Have a seat. I was just going over this request of yours. It could take some time."

Sully took the chair in front of Merrick's desk. "How much time?"

"A few weeks, maybe longer. Still want me to pursue it?"

"I do. About Krizova. I filed my report. I hope there's something in there that helps. I should have tried harder to disable the sub."

"The blame isn't yours. You had other things on your mind. The decoy idea was risky, but it worked. If it hadn't I would be reminding you that you disobeyed my orders to stay put. The truth is, I had Cyrus in my iron sights. I had an opportunity to take him out, and I didn't make good on it. We captured some of his men on Vouno. Maybe one of them will talk."

"I still wish—"

"It wasn't meant to be this time, Sully. I have to believe that. We had some successes, we hurt him and we got you back. I'd say we had a pretty good week." Merrick opened a file. "Your physical checked out. Wound's healing. You're good to go."

Merrick grinned, and Sully knew what his boss was thinking. "You sure she's all right?"

Sully was more than sure. "I'm keeping tabs on her. Hector tells me she's doing fine. About the prisoners at Vouno. Hear any news about how they're doing?"

"I've checked on them. Two didn't make it. The others will be in hospitals for a while." Merrick handed Sully a list of the survivors. "Don't know if that's important to you, but I figured you might want it. They're listed, and the hospitals where they're at."

Sully took the paper and stood. As he headed for the door he turned back. "I appreciate what you did to save those men. And me. If you hear anything about—"

"I'll let you know the minute something comes through."

An hour later, the list of survivors in his pocket, Sully stepped into the hospital elevator and rode it to the sixth floor.

As he headed down the corridor, he saw a uniformed guard sitting outside the door at the end of the hall.

"The name's Paxton. NSA Onyxx."

The guard nodded. "He's been asking about you. Go on in."

Sully opened the door and stepped inside. The room was brightly lit, almost too bright, he thought. But then there had been so much darkness at Vouno, he understood the need for sunshine and clean air.

He focused on the man in the bed. Roth Erwin had a feeding tube in his arms, and he was plugged into a half-dozen machines.

As if the man sensed he was there, Roth opened his eyes. "I was hoping I would see you again."

The smile he offered Sully was too big for his gaunt face, and his eyes were still sunken into his skull. They were glazed with a kind of pain only another man living in the same hell would understand.

Sully pulled a chair close to the bed and sat down. He didn't know what to say, but he wasn't in a hurry to leave.

"I told them, Paxton. I told the others you'd come back for us. I saw it in your eyes, you know. I told them to hold on, and to believe in you. I believed."

"You held on real good, Roth. You did good."

"You doing all right?"

"I'm fine."

"You look a helluva lot better than the last time I saw you. If I take a nap, will you be here when I wake up?"

Sully had time to kill. He didn't have to meet the boys until later. He nodded, then he smiled and said. "Take a nap. I'll be here when you wake up."

Melita's home on Amorgos overlooked the sea and a secluded lagoon below. The island was a mix of mountainous cliffs and hidden beaches. In fact, she had her own hidden beach.

It was a paradise, and Hector had said it was Sully's gift to her.

Sully…

Every day she took Kit for a walk down the rocky spine of the mountain. With Sully's basket curled under her arm, she picked fresh lavender and wild thyme and oregano that covered the coastal ledges. She loved the flowers and the fresh herbs, but mostly it was an excuse to scan the sea in hopes of seeing a fast boat speeding toward the lagoon.

It had been three weeks since she'd seen Sully at Lesvago. She knew he was all right, Hector had told her that much. Sully had phoned him to make sure they had gotten to Amorgos safely. Hector was good company, and the guards were friendly, but she missed Sully.

He would come, or at least that's what she prayed for every day. So far it hadn't happened, but she would be patient, and feed off the memories of the short time they'd spent together.

She had mourned Simon over the weeks and although the pain of his passing would be forever with her, she was learning to live with the loss.

Her basket half-full, Melita found a rock and sat down. She looked back at the whitewashed Byzantine house built on a rocky knoll. Hector told her that Sully had instructed him to buy the prettiest house on the island of Amorgos. It had to have a view of the sea, plenty of room so she never felt claustrophobic and enough land to feed a herd of goats.

"Melita, *greegorah!* Come quickly, you have a phone call."

Sully…

Melita jumped up from the rock, forgetting the basket, and

ran up the rocky path. She entered the house with hope in her eyes, and immediately knew it wasn't Sully on the phone. Hector was talking, and she knew it was Nigel.

She took the phone. "Nigel, where are you?"

"I'm in Washington, Melita. Sully's agency has given me a job. I just wanted you to know."

"That's wonderful. Have you seen him? Have you seen Sully?"

"Yes. Just once. He's been away a long time and he's busy catching up."

"Yes, busy." Melita closed her eyes. "I'm glad you called."

"You don't have to worry about this call. It's a protected line and I've been assured that you're safe there. I'll check in again when I can."

"All right. Thank you for the call." She hung up and glanced at Hector. "He sounds happy. I'm glad for him. I forgot my basket. I think I'll go get it, and take a walk along the beach." She turned to head back out the door.

"When he has time, I'm sure Sully will call you."

She glanced over her shoulder. "You're right, when he has time, he'll call."

Three days later, while Melita was on the hillside with her arm hugging the basket, and Kit running ahead of her on the path, she heard the sound of a boat in the distance. She looked up as she did every time she heard the familiar sound, only this time the boat was headed straight for the lagoon.

A fast cruiser that was skipping along the water at a dangerous speed. The driver was either a seasoned boatman or a…gorilla with brass balls and a death wish.

Melita dropped the basket and started to run. She was only halfway down the hill when the cruiser docked.

* * *

Sully saw her on the hillside. When she'd spotted the boat she'd started to run. He leapt out of the boat, forgot the flowers he'd brought her, and headed up the dock. His heart had been pounding hard in his chest. Hell, it had been pounding since he'd got off the airplane in Syros, and had headed for the harbor where he'd picked up the *Korinna*. He was nervous. It had been three weeks, the longest three weeks of his life. His love affair with Melita had been born out of fours days on the run. What if she had come to her senses and realized that he wasn't what she wanted?

Hell, she sure looked good. She was wearing a blue skirt and one of those blouses that showed off her shoulders. Her black hair was flying around her.

He stopped at the end of the dock. She hadn't slowed down. She was moving like her skirt was on fire. At that moment he knew there was a God in heaven. He didn't deserve this, but he was ready to take it, and promise to be thankful for the gift of life, and the gift of Melita, every day from now on.

That is if she hadn't changed her mind. It didn't appear so. She was still coming.

Then all of a sudden, ten feet from him, she put on the brakes and came to a dead stop. Those beautiful brown eyes of hers were wide, and her lips were parted as she tried to catch her breath.

She never moved, stood there staring at him.

He said, "I didn't come all this way just to look, although you are a sweet sight for my eyes, lucky charm."

Her face broke into a big smile. "A sweet sight. Yes, you are, Sully Paxton."

Then she was running again. She was in flight the last two

feet, and he scooped her up in his arms, pulled her close and buried his face against the side of her neck.

The moment undid him. He squeezed her hard and groaned. "God, it's good to hold you again, honey. I've been dreaming about you for weeks."

She raised her head, sent her hands into his hair and kissed him. "I've been dreaming about you, too. Every night. I knew you would come. You promised."

"I don't remember making that promise."

"You did. It was in your eyes when you told me to go with Hector."

"I've got something for you." Sully let her go and pulled the blue stone necklace with the falcon charm in flight out of his pocket. "I bought a new chain," he said, then slipped it around her neck and hooked the clasp.

She touched the stone. "You found it at Lesvago?"

"I meant to give it to you then, but there wasn't time."

Sully bent and kissed her, and at that moment he heard yelling coming from the house. He looked up and saw Hector standing on the terrace waving his arms in the air.

"Welcome home, *file mou*. We celebrate tonight, *ne?*"

"We celebrate," Sully called back. "Then you will go to bed early, my friend."

Hector's laughter rolled down the hillside, but the lovers didn't hear it. Melita had slipped out of Sully's arms, lifted her skirt to flash him her slender thighs, then challenged him to a race to the hidden beach.

Melita won, but Sully owned the day and claimed the prize. He clasped Melita's hand, pulled her down to the white sand, and there he made love to his lucky charm.

Epilogue

At sunrise Sully took Melita for a boat ride in the *Korinna*. He turned the cruiser up the coast, past the windmills that flagged the city of Hora. Thirty minutes later he cut the engine in a quiet cove just below Panagia Chozoviotissa, acclaimed as the most beautiful monastery in all of Greece.

He pulled Melita into his arms and kissed her. She was wearing a pale blue sundress, and the blue stone pendant dangled from the silver chain between her breasts. "I wanted to be here sooner," he said, "but there was something I had to do and it took longer than I expected."

"Nigel called. He said he saw you and that you were busy."

"Too busy to call you. Is that what you thought?"

"It crossed my mind." She glanced away, then looked back at him. "I missed you. Your face. Voice. The way you look at me. Touch me."

"I missed you, too. I called every day and talked to Hector

to make sure you were all right, but I didn't know when I was going to get here, so I didn't know what to tell you. I thought if I hedged, you'd read me wrong."

"So what did you have to do that took so long?"

Sully kissed her again, then took her hand and squeezed it. "Wait here."

He left her and went below deck. When he returned he was carrying an urn. When she saw it, her smile slid.

"I don't mean to cause you more pain, but I thought this was important, and that you needed—"

"Simon home." She held out her arms and Sully placed the urn in her hands. She pulled it close and closed her eyes.

"There was a lot of red tape to go through to get him released to me. I thought cremation was appropriate."

She opened her eyes. "I don't blame Onyxx for Simon's death, Sully. My father drove him into his grave, not your agency. My brother was never free to choose who he really wanted to be. I didn't like who Simon was all the time, but I loved him for who he could have been. Not the man my father forced him to be."

"If you don't like this place—"

"It's beautiful here, Sully. Simon loved the sea, and now he's home." She looked up at the monastery clinging to the cliff. She said a prayer, then Sully stepped back into the cockpit, turned over the engine and moved the cruiser slowly out to sea while Melita opened the urn and set Simon free.

When Sully looked over his shoulder, she was holding on to the necklace he'd given her, and he heard her say, "Courage, my brother. Spread your wings and move with the current. You're free now."

When she came to him in the cockpit, she slid her arm

around his waist. Sully wrapped his around her shoulder and kissed the top of her head, then he turned the cruiser for home.

"I love you, Sully. Now and forever."

"I love you, too." When she looked up at him and smiled, Sully spoke what was in his eyes. "Now and forever, Melita. I promise. On my Irish honor."

* * * * *

Mills & Boon® Intrigue
brings you a sneak preview of…

Karen Whiddon's Bulletproof Marriage.

After two years of thinking her Lazlo Group spy husband Sean McGregor is dead, SIS agent Natalie Major is stunned when she calls for help from a mission gone bad – she's trapped by enemy fire – and out of the smoking ruins her husband strides towards her, back from the dead…to avenge his own "murder" and to win back the woman he loves!

Don't miss this thrilling new story in the MISSION: IMPASSIONED *series, available next month in Mills & Boon® Intrigue!*

Bulletproof Marriage

by

Karen Whiddon

If reinforcements didn't show up soon, Natalie Major thought grimly, she might as well paint a target on her chest and leap into the open. The unknown assassin—or assassins—were that close. The decaying concrete warehouse she'd holed up in only had two ways out—and one of them had been blown to rubble.

She needed help. Corbett Lazlo, her father's oldest friend and owner of one of the top private investigative agencies in the world, had promised to send someone. She'd asked for the best.

Now she wished she'd asked for the most prompt.

Gallows humor. She'd never been particularly good at it before, though she'd grown more proficient.

Her husband wouldn't even recognize her now if he were still alive. Once, he'd been Lazlo's top agent. She'd married a Lazlo Group spook, just like her own father had been. Retired now, and in a wheelchair, her father lived in relative seclusion. Her beloved husband, Sean, hadn't been so lucky. He'd been killed two years ago this week. Lazlo's group seemed to be the ruin of everyone she loved, so in honor of her dead husband and disabled father, and in defiance of the Lazlo legacy she could easily have embraced, she'd worked her way to the top of SIS, the British Secret Intelligence Service. There was no job too difficult, no task too dangerous for Sean McGregor's widow.

Until now.

She scouted the area. Trapped inside the abandoned warehouse, she was fast running out of options. The concrete walls made a good shield against bullets, but she needed to see her enemies. Right now, she could only hear them. And it was hard to fight when you had no idea who the enemy might be. Or where they were hiding.

Plus, cement was cold and hard and reminded her too damn much of a tomb.

The shooters fired off another round of shots. AK-47s. Random bullets ricocheted crazily and dangerously off the cement walls and floors. She couldn't even dodge them, having no idea where they'd go.

She'd found the abandoned warehouse two days

ago. A concrete bunker in a run-down area of Glasgow had seemed relatively safe. Not wanting to endanger others by staying at a B and B or hotel, she'd used the concrete warehouse as her base, returning to sleep and regroup while attempting to gather information on whoever had sold out her team. Since Millaflora—a low-down, no-good mole operating as a double agent inside the SIS—had already been caught, she had no idea who she was looking for.

Officially, she was on administrative leave, supposedly holed up, incognito in an unknown luxury hotel on the French Riviera. No one in her office knew she'd come to Glasgow, not even her supervisor.

And though she'd tried to take extraordinary precautions similar to those she used when deep undercover, her enemy had found her.

Whoever "they" were.

She supposed the whys and the hows didn't matter. Not now. All that mattered was that if help didn't arrive soon, she was dead.

Her ammo nearly gone, no backup, and no alternative plan—pretty shoddy situation for an undercover agent who'd recently been promoted to team leader.

It had to have something to do with the code. Natalie was sure of it. She'd been so close to cracking it. She and her team.

Now they all were dead and she was on the run.

And she had only herself to rely on. In seven years of service, she'd never had a single casualty. Until now. Now she'd lost her entire team. They'd been eliminated, killed in a way that left no doubt she was next. All the codes they'd been working on had disappeared, at least as far as anyone knew. She'd told no one that she'd made her own private copy.

Not knowing who was on her side, she hadn't dared to contact SIS. She'd called her father, knowing he'd contact Corbett, knowing Lazlo would help.

"Come on, reinforcements," she muttered. Her father'd told her Corbett had promised to send help. The head of the Lazlo Group never went back on his word.

A movement across the alley caught her attention. Finally! Someone had arrived to help her out of this hellhole.

She took another look and blinked, wondering if the stress had finally claimed her mind.

Out of the mist and smoke, a dead man strode toward her, keeping close to the wall, staying in the shadows, but coming. For her.

Natalie began to shake.

Shots rang out. Crouching, the man began to run. More shots. So far, he hadn't been hit. He'd always been lucky that way.

At least, until the day he'd died.

Dead. He was dead and buried.

Rocking back onto her heels, she rubbed her eyes and took another look.

She hadn't been wrong. The man she'd loved more than any other, her soul mate, her husband, the man she'd mourned, the man she'd never thought to see again, kept moving toward her.

Frozen, she watched as he continued, his low crouch purposeful and unafraid. Or maybe he didn't care. After all, a man couldn't die twice, right?

Her heart drummed in her ears. Sean. Her husband, Sean. This couldn't be real, couldn't be happening.

She wasn't the type to faint—not anymore. Too many hard lessons learned. Instead, she'd taught herself to push back, to fight.

But how did one battle a ghost?

From the smoke and the grave, against the periodic bursts of gunfire, he continued to come toward her. He moved exactly the way she remembered—purposeful and bold, dodging bullets as though he were untouchable. She'd often thought that very arrogance had been what had gotten him killed.

Killed.

Yet here he was, ducking under the concrete overhang into her shadowed hiding place, solid and real and alive.

When he reached her, he stopped, his dark gaze intense. She couldn't move. He was still beautiful, even in the dust and the dirt and the danger. She caught her breath, unable to speak.

"I'm here," he said, his voice husky, as though too long unused, a hint of wariness in his gaze.

"I..." She moved toward him, inspecting him, still unable to believe what the fates had just returned to her.

"Get down," he snarled, yanking her behind the concrete wall with him as the shooters let loose with several rounds of shots.

"What the—" he cursed, letting her go. "They've got AK-47s. You must have royally pissed someone off. Why are they trying to kill you?"

She still couldn't find her voice. Unable to help herself, she let her gaze roam hungrily over his muscular body—the way her hands used to.

"Either I'm dead, dying or you're not dead," she said, feeling like an idiot, still not sure what to think.

"No." His dark gaze locked with hers, daring her wrath. "I'm not dead."